TERRAFORM

MCD X FSG ORIGINALS

FARRAR, STRAUS AND GIROUX • NEW YORK

MOTHERBOARD

VICE

TERRAFORM

WATCH / WORLDS / BURN

EDITED BY

BRIAN MERCHANT
and CLAIRE L. EVANS

MCD × FSG Originals
Farrar, Straus and Giroux
120 Broadway, New York 10271

Library of Congress Cataloging-in-Publication Data
Names: Merchant, Brian, editor. | Evans, Claire Lisa, editor.
Title: Terraform : watch / worlds / burn / edited by Brian Merchant and
    Claire L. Evans.
Description: First edition. | New York : MCD × FSG Originals / Farrar, Straus
    and Giroux, 2022.
Identifiers: LCCN 2022019967 | ISBN 9780374602666 (paperback)
Subjects: LCSH: Science fiction, American. | Speculative fiction, American. |
    LCGFT: Science fiction. | Short stories.
Classification: LCC PS648.S3 T429 2022 | DDC 813/.0876208—dc23/
    eng/20220506
LC record available at https://lccn.loc.gov/2022019967

Designed by Gretchen Achilles

Our books may be purchased in bulk for promotional,
educational, or business use. Please contact your local bookseller
or the Macmillan Corporate and Premium Sales Department
at 1-800-221-7945, extension 5442, or by email at
MacmillanSpecialMarkets@macmillan.com.

www.fsgoriginals.com • www.fsgbooks.com
Follow us on Twitter, Facebook, and Instagram at @fsgoriginals

1 3 5 7 9 10 8 6 4 2

To the future, with our apologies

The splinter in your eye is the best magnifying-glass.

—THEODOR ADORNO

CONTENTS

BURN

PREFACE

The *future is here.* The idea that an event sounds "straight out of science fiction" has moved beyond the realm of cliché and is now something more like an intuitive part of how we process the world. *Homo anthropocenus* simply accepts that it is constantly surrounded by "science fictional" conceits, whether they're optimistic, as in CRISPR gene-editing to cure diseases, hyperefficient solar skins, or commercial space travel to Mars—or dystopian, as in algorithmic social credit rankings, Miami disappearing into the Atlantic, or commercial space travel to Mars.

Whether or not we actually believe any of these things will come to pass is almost irrelevant. Decades of start-up press releases, military R&D initiatives, tech entrepreneur TED Talks, and other efforts to extract rent on the future have congealed over our sensory processing systems. They've left us swimming in a glitched-out layer of futurity that we approach at all times, out of necessity, with ironic detachment and a certain degree of apathy.

Electric cars are here, for the rich. The internet sparks revolutions, unless they're shut down by autocrats or the tech corporations themselves. Voice assistants float in our homes and devices answer our commands at will, yet the data we feed them is stored and harvested by opaque monopolies. It's been decades since we sent a man, let alone a woman, to the moon, and yet millions are stirred by the prospect of a tech billionaire launching his own envoy to the Red Planet. And why shouldn't they be?

Plausibility has ebbed into a bath of sub-futurity; we dip in and out for amusement, validation, and occasionally, despite everything, inspiration. Generations of science fiction fans and writers have lived and worked as the future inexorably came into being, but few have been as thoroughly exhausted by the process—and what the process has yielded—as ours. So what is the project of fiction about the future, in a time like this? When every other tweet and tech company IPO is already a work of speculative fiction?

We started *Terraform* back in the dark ages of 2014 to try to answer that question. To scan for truth in an increasingly crowded landfill of garbage futures. Science fiction of generations past often aimed to present futures built to astonish or amaze; we wanted to use the medium to stress-test the wide variety of futures being sold to us and watch them snap. To suss out the increasingly, unsettlingly plausible tomorrows we sift through every day and tease out their features.

Science fiction has always been credited for its predictive capacities, but it's certainly not been our aim with *Terraform*—it'd be impossible, anyway, like looking for a needle in an e-waste graveyard. Instead, we coexist with catastrophe, in node points of incipient tension and pockets of generosity and humanity. We're out here reassembling broken shards and screens in the hope that we might glean something useful about the bigger picture. We looked around and saw a culture enmeshed in science fiction—its gleaming superstructure bears down on us as Marvel blockbusters and Netflix originals and triple-A video games—but not necessarily trying to put it to any use. Or learn anything from it. Or actually enjoy its finer points, even.

So, *Terraform*. A new science fiction vertical from *Vice*. The media company was in the prime of its freewheeling experimental phase at the time, sending inexperienced reporters on far-flung reporting trips with expensive equipment to make YouTube videos, brokering ambitious partnerships with auteurs and brands, and, of course, supporting a new science fiction venture to be launched from its tech site, *Motherboard*. We had both been doing a good deal of work looking at how the future was being shaped, and we wanted to try to publish more than reportage and news analysis and weird blogs to that end. We thought it high time that speculative fiction coexisted with all of the above on our feeds.

We decided early on that our approach would be to seek out and publish the voices we felt existed on the front lines of tomorrow, whether or not they were science fiction or even fiction writers at all. We would publish major, battle-tested writers like Cory Doctorow and Bruce Sterling and vital rising talents like E. Lily Yu and Laurie Penny. New blood like Tim Maughan and Debbie Urbanski and Russell Nichols. We tapped meteorologists, like Eric Holthaus, and climate scientists, like NASA's Gavin Schmidt, and tech journalists, like Sam Biddle. Coders, too, like Paul Ford, start-up veterans, like Kate Losse, and artists, like Porpentine Charity Heartscape. Firefighters, soldiers, scholars. We published stories by observers and writers and experts and outsiders on every continent; we published interactive fiction, Twitter bots, and comics, too. We hoped to prove that speculative fiction could live alongside, even inform, our daily battery of news and analysis, and were cheered as we watched *Terraform* stories go viral, infecting and augmenting the broader non(or sub)fictional conversation.

Over the years, *Terraform*'s stories drew together as a full, visceral, and vital portrait of a world in rapid evolution. A half decade in, we thought it time to gather those futures under a single roof, to see what we might learn from scanning them all, together. When we set out to look for a publisher, we really only had one in mind: MCD / Farrar, Straus and Giroux. For one thing, MCD specialized in the knotty, near-future space we trafficked in, too. For another, a not-insignificant number of MCD authors had written for *Terraform*. The rare perfect synergy, to appropriate some corporate-speak. So here we are.

As we canvassed our archive to put together this anthology, it became clear that certain themes haunted us. We've organized our collection accordingly, in three volumes: *Watch*, *Worlds*, and *Burn*. In *Watch*, we have gathered stories about living under the emergent regimes of corporate and state surveillance—stories about surveillance capitalism, the platforms that make it possible, and the people trying to survive their churn. About content, entertainment, and the stream. *Worlds* is about alternate possibilities and dimensions; realities augmented, glitched over, and virtual, and the spaces of resistance being carved out within them. Artificial intelligences and algorithmic interventions are latent across the far-flung places where we may soon be, or already are. And in *Burn*, the world is on fire. Literally, as megafires sweep our tinderbox nation, and figuratively, as so many of us are inflamed by inequality and desperation as the thermostats rise. These three volumes can be read in any order, although the first, as we're all in the process of discovering, tends to lead to the last.

INTRODUCTION: YOU ARE A LUDDITE

CORY DOCTOROW

You are a Luddite, but you (probably) don't know it yet.

History is written by the winners, and the Luddites lost, so they get a bad rap. That's a shame. Luddites weren't opposed to weaving technology. They were weavers, and no one knew better how brutal and labor-intensive textile production was. They had the arthritis, chronic strain injuries, and workplace maimings to prove it. The advent of mechanized looms meant (lots) more cloth at (much) lower prices. That was good news! Before the mechanical loom, every weaver wove for every hour they could, and still cloth was expensive, a luxury good.

You couldn't just throw more weavers at the problem, either. It was a skilled trade, and it took a long time to master it. Weavers were in chronically short supply, which had one upside: Weavers could command a decent wage, since they had a seller's market for their labor.

The advent of the steam loom could have been amazing news for weavers. The machines meant that a single weaver could produce far more cloth, which meant that weavers could have reduced their working hours while still producing far more cloth, at lower prices, without taking a pay cut.

But that's not how it worked out. The factory owners—whose fortunes had been built on the weavers' labor—bought steam looms and threw weavers out of work by the thousands. Rather than cutting *hours*, the bosses cut *wages*. They insisted that this was only natural, inevitable, even.

That's the moment when weavers became Luddites. They assembled themselves into an underground, self-mythologizing army, claiming to be led by the legendary General Ned Ludd, a literal giant who was credited with the daring machine-wrecking raids and arson attacks on the new factories. Letters to newspaper editors and factory owners were signed by General Ludd, demanding justice for the weavers.

The weavers weren't anti-technology. Rather, they were in the grip of a vision of a new *social arrangement* for technology. They were doing science fiction: asking not just what a gadget *did*, but who it did it *for* and who it did it *to*.

That, after all, is *the* question. The social arrangements around our technology are not foreordained. A Martian peering through a telescope could not tell you whether the Luddites or the factory owners were the rightful recipients of the automation dividend. There's no objective answer to that question, only a socially determined one. The outcome of a social contestation like the Luddites' is determined as much by the storytelling ability of the warring sides as by the technical capabilities of the gadget they're fighting over.

Everyone who cares about technology is a Luddite, because as soon as you start imagining more than one way the gadget could be used, you're doing Luddism.

We're all Luddites, but we don't always know it. Back in 1988, the legendary engineer-pundit Donald Norman published *The Design of Everyday Things*, a furious and brilliant book-length argument for usability over ornamentation. Norman demanded that engineers advocate for technology users, by making everything as functional as possible, even if that came at the expense of beauty. Millions read Norman's work and pledged themselves to his cause.

But a funny thing happened on the way to the future. In 2005, Norman published *Emotional Design*, a critical follow-up that repudiated much of his *Everyday Things* advice. Specifically, Norman confronted the reality that in a complex world of complex systems made of complex devices, no amount of thoughtful engineering could produce reliable, self-sufficient gadgets. Rather, the ground state of all our gadgets, today and forevermore, was to be somewhat broken.

When things are broken, you need to be creative: You need to troubleshoot, find work-arounds, improvise. This kind of creative thinking requires an expansive mindset, the kind of expansive mindset that you get when you're happy—and that is terribly elusive when you're in a rage because your gadget stopped working.

So Norman briefed for beauty. In *Emotional Design*, he celebrated the flourishes and finials that *Everyday Things* raged against. Beauty, Norman wrote, would make us happy, even when things were broken. And when you're happy, you can fix the broken, because happiness is expansive, while rage contracts your world to a red-tinged pinprick.

Norman was doing Luddism: realizing that there was no inevitable way to make things work, that everything was contingent, and that the users of technology were not its subjects, but rather active participants.

When a certain kind of conservative wants to mock a certain kind of leftist, they'll talk about "postmodernists" who insist that "reality is socially constructed" and decry the "hegemony of saying that $2 + 2 = 4$."

The message is that there is an objective reality, separate from our social construction, and that that reality is knowable and real and can (and should) be acted upon. That's the anti-Luddite way, the Capitalist Realist way, embodied by Margaret Thatcher's famous aphorism "There is no alternative" (by which she meant, *Stop trying to imagine an alternative*).

Time and again, the real world disappoints people who insist that the abstract perfection of numbers means that our physical world is governed by crisp absolutes.

That's a staple of hacker tales and hacker fiction. Sure, "The street finds its own use for things," but *how*?

"Evaluating Physical-Layer BLE Location Tracking Attacks on Mobile Devices" is a paper by a group of brilliant UCSD security researchers, accepted for the 2022 IEEE Symposium on Security and Privacy (DOI: 10.1109/SP46214.2022.00030).

The researchers investigate the security of the kind of "zero-knowledge" Bluetooth tracking systems that are used for Covid exposure-tracking apps and find-my-stuff gadgets like the Apple AirTag. These systems deploy incredibly clever cryptographic protocols that let each gadget transmit an ever-changing series of serial numbers that other devices record and report to a centralized database.

When you, the owner of an AirTag, need to find your keys, you query the database with a secret cryptographic key that allows you to unlock only those entries that refer to your thing. The maintainer of the database doesn't know who you are until that moment, doesn't even know that a series of database entries all refer to the same thing. It's a way to anonymously track the locations of billions of items worldwide, or to anonymously allow people to move through space and then get an alert when someone they were close to is diagnosed with an airborne contagious disease.

The underlying cryptography in these systems appears to be as solid as its creators claim. Really, it's an amazing piece of engineering.

Which is why the authors of "Evaluating Physical-Layer BLE Location Tracking Attacks on Mobile Devices" threw away the cryptography. Instead, they concentrated on the *radio waves* the Bluetooth devices put out. They hypothesized that each of these minute radios' antennas would have molecular-scale imperfections in them, and that this would make each Bluetooth radio's song a little different—like the timbre produced by different violins—and that they could get a computer with a cheap software-defined radio peripheral to persistently identify each Bluetooth device no matter how often it rotated its serial number. They were ignoring the serial number, and instead listening to the distinctive character of the electromagnetic voice that recited it.

In the abstract world of numbers, all radio modulation is as perfect as the spherical cow of uniform density that slides across a frictionless plane in a physicist's gedankenexperiment. In the real world, the radio waves are just approximations.

Hackers use this abstraction/reality shear to do productive Luddism all the time. There's a whole class of processor attacks that rely on the fact that the "one" and "zero" in a microprocessor aren't perfect presences and absences of voltage, but rather are jiggly, messy squiggles that are *largely* one and *mostly* zero.

As messy as the reality of imperfections in chip fabrication is, it's nowhere near as messy as the reality of the imperfections in human relations.

Take the COVID vaccines. The trials that measured their ability to keep us from contracting the disease were conducted at the height of the lockdown (naturally, since the lockdown didn't end until the vaccines were available). The experimental subjects who received the vaccine were living and breathing in a world in which travel was severely constrained, mask compliance was high, indoor gatherings were widely avoided, and distancing was the order of the day.

Now we are all vaccinated (or we should be: being an anti-vaxxer doesn't make you a Luddite, it makes you a plague-rat asshole), and we are moving through spaces in which—thanks to vaccines!—there's less masking, more indoor gathering, less distancing, and more travel.

And, surprise! The vaccines are "less effective"! That's not because the researchers who analyzed the trials were fudging their numbers—it's because those numbers were socially determined. Those excitingly precise percentages of efficacy didn't represent the average outcome of a thousand vaccine-vs.-virus cage matches in a petri dish: they measured the outcomes of a technical intervention in a social situation. Change the social situation, change the technical outcome.

Luddism, in other words.

Remember Cray supercomputers? Silicon Graphics? DEC?

Remember the PET and the Amiga? Remember AOL and CompuServe?

Remember AltaVista and Ask Jeeves and Yahoo?

Remember when the computer industry's largest, most powerful companies—companies that made incredible breakthroughs and changed the way millions of people lived and worked and hooked up and fought each other—sprang up, did their thing, and then . . . poof! . . . disappeared?

What happened? Well, forty years ago, Ronald Reagan shot antitrust law in the guts, adopting an official tolerance for monopolies as "efficient." Rich people *loved* this, because monopolies can extract high profits by screwing over workers, suppliers, and customers, and rich people knew they could buy stock in monopolies and get richer.

Every president after Reagan carried on this great dismantling of antitrust law.

The modern tech industry was born with Reagan. Reagan hit the campaign trail the same year the Apple][+ hit the shelves. Every year that the tech industry has existed, it's become easier to do monopoly: buy or merge with competitors, gobble up and kill start-ups before they can threaten you, use vertical integration and predatory pricing to create a "kill zone" where no new business can take hold.

That's why the cycle stopped—why the companies that dominated tech ten years ago are the companies that dominate it today. It's not an inevitable product of tech, the result of "network effects" that make companies more valuable as more people use their products—it's the social result of policy choices that lock users in to Big Tech's walled gardens.

We've forgotten how to be Luddites. We've forgotten how to imagine a world in which the internet is more than "five giant websites, each filled with text from the other four" (to quote Tom Eastman). We're living in the Margaret Thatcher hellscape where there is no alternative, because we've stopped trying to imagine alternatives.

That's why our science fiction is so dystopian and despair-filled. We're watching as our civilizational bus is being driven full-tilt toward the cliff's edge of environmental collapse, and the people driving the bus keep insisting that the steering wheel is an illusion, the legend of the brake pedal is a Communist plot, and any attempt to turn the bus or slam on the brakes is irresponsible fantasy.

Science fiction can be an oracle. It can tell you more than just what the author fears and hopes for from our technology—when a speculation catches the public imagination, it can tell you what our whole society unknowingly, inchoately yearns for and agonizes over. Our popular dystopias reflect our collective terror that our neighbors agree that the bus *must* go over the cliff and that preventing that is unserious fantasy.

But in those science fictional dystopias—those tales in which technology users seize the means of computation, solve problems in expansive and creative ways, where the messiness of reality is a feature and not a bug—are the seeds of a better world.

Because if there is an alternative, then the Luddites still have a chance.

The steam loom didn't just throw the weavers out of work. It created a boom in sheep-farming that saw millions of tenant farmers evicted from their ancestral lands to make way for their lords' livestock herds. These farmers became internal refugees who roamed the land, immiserated and dislocated.

The steam loom also created a boom in cotton-growing, which created a boom in slavery. Millions of Africans were kidnapped and tortured into forced labor to feed the looms.

All that to say that we need full-stack Luddites—Luddites who imagine how the whole supply chain of a new technology can be organized to benefit people, rather than capital.

The legendary science fiction writer Gardner Dozois used to say that the job of a science fiction writer is to consider the car and the movie theater and invent the drive-in, and then infer the existence of the sexual revolution.

The job of the Luddite science fiction writer is to imagine a steam loom that benefits not just weavers, but also growers, and farmers, and pickers, and the planet itself.

This is a volume of Luddite literature. It will radicalize you as a Luddite. And not a moment too soon: We need some Luddites on this bus, before it goes over that cliff.

BUSY

OMAR EL AKKAD

On my way to cut God's tongue I pass a long line of slow-shuffling laborers. Men, mostly. The younger ones look beat to all hell with hangovers and bar-fight bruises, dentin-colored stains on their shirts like maps of imaginary islands. It is a rule at the entropy mill that all laborers must be dressed in reasonably presentable attire, but I've never heard of anyone turned away on account of how they looked. The older men in line, they tend to take too much care with their appearance. There's something grotesque about watching a stooped retiree in his best Sunday suit, hair all dyed and gelled to shining, plead for a day's wage. They look so much older than they are, these men. The years gorge on them like yeast in a sugar bath. I glance their way as I walk past. I wonder how many of them have spouses, children, grandchildren. I wonder who they've left alone and uncared-for to be here. I wonder how many of them are mean.

This morning the line stretches for miles and miles and miles. It always does.

It used to be a mega-mall before the great oil crash. The largest mall in the country, I'm told, though that was years before my time. Even now you can still see the phantom outline on the sides of some of the buildings, the places where the lettering was, the names of all the big-box stores and movie theaters and parking garages, this congealed mass of commerce the size of a small city. Now the whole thing houses the entropy mill, five million square feet of government-subsidized employment. Every day, thousands of people come to this place to churn out numbers for minimum wage, to stir the slop on which God's tongue feasts.

By the time I get to the front entrance, the makeup of the line has changed. There are more women near the front. They sit on folding chairs, draped in winter coats and blankets. The only way to make sure you get a spot is to show up the night before and wait till morning. A few of the people in line give me dirty looks as I walk past, and one of them points at my laptop satchel and yells, "No bags!" But it's not until I'm right at the entrance that a young man steps out in front of me and grabs my shoulder.

"Back of the line, buddy," he says.

I shake my head. "I'm not here for that," I say.

"The hell you ain't. Back of the line."

I know that look he's got, I know it from memory, and I know what's going to happen next, but I try to step around him anyway. There's no point appealing to reason. You can't rid a man of the violence that lives in the chasm between the life he hoped for and the one he got.

I've never been any good at taking a punch. Glass jaw, they call it. I drop to the ground, a dribble of pinkish spit leaking out my mouth, that familiar mineral taste. He's got strong hands. I don't understand how men get strong hands working at the entropy mill.

In my periphery I see a couple of security guards come running over.

"Tech support," I mumble. "Maintenance call. I'm here on a maintenance call."

Both guards ignore me. Instead they grab the young man who punched me and start dragging him toward the street. He puts up a pretty good fight, arguing he's been waiting here eight hours, it's the guy who cut in line that should be booted. It doesn't look like he's going to back down, until one of the security guards pulls out his phone and tries to take the man's picture. That's when he turns and runs. No one wants to end up on the blacklist.

The guards don't give chase. They turn and walk back and on the way one of them helps me up. I show her my ID.

"You new?" she asks.

"Yeah," I say. "First call."

She shakes her head. "Never come through the front gate," she says. "That's just for them."

She leads me inside and after she checks my name against the maintenance manifest she ushers me through the metal detector and into the massive central rotunda. I'd seen pictures of it, but in the pictures it never looked like this. The workers haven't been let in yet and the place has about it an almost pleasing emptiness, all the workstations pristine and untouched, the wires and electrodes and number pads arranged neatly at each desk. The only sounds are the faint wheeze of the air conditioners and the squeak of our shoes against the polished floor. In an hour or so the rooms will fill with the noise and heat of thousands, but for now the entropy mill is quiet.

We walk through the rotunda and down one of the hallways, past the workrooms. The walls are all glass and I can guess at some of the jobs that go on inside. One room is lined with tall bookshelves. I imagine this is where the word-counting happens. In another room I see headphones on the tables. It must be one of the music stations. That was my father's favorite. I used to pray he'd get assigned the music station.

There are entropy mills in all the big cities now, but this was the first, the original make-work project in the years after the crash wiped out a third of all the blue-collar jobs in the country. Every day, three and a half million people come to the mills to churn out numbers. It's the easiest work, anyone can do it. You don't need a degree or references or previous experience. Depending on the day you might be assigned to the biometrics unit, and have a machine dream up numbers based on the topography of your fingerprints or blood vessels running across your retina. Another day you might be told to swallow a small capsule that sits in your stomach and sends back a real-time count of the bacteria in your gut. Another day you might be told to put on an electrode helmet and listen to Mozart, as all the while electrodes measure the changes in activity across the right side of the frontal lobe, the places the music sets on fire, and from these bursts of intensity generates a stream of digits. Most of the time you just sit there, let the wires pull the numbers right out of you; a strange, corrupted dreaming.

In an endless stream all these billions of digits the workers generate are funneled down to the box in the basement, down to God's tongue. And from these numbers God's tongue forms its own secret language, speaks unpredictable things.

As stipulated in the Great Recovery Act, any company that uses random numbers must purchase them from an entropy mill. Academics, cryptographers, drug-makers, anyone whose business demands mathematically pure uncertainty. Every bank in the country is a customer, as is every casino. There's a video game studio whose vast, procedurally generated universe feeds on these numbers. Somewhere in the math department at a university upstate there's a server that queries God's tongue at the rate of two or three billion digits an hour, part of a quest to find the new largest prime.

In reality, the numbers that come out of the entropy mill are not completely random. There is a determinism to them, no matter how difficult to decipher. In reality, a gram of cesium would do a better job than these broken-down men and women ever could. But a gram of cesium won't feed three and a half million families.

I've wanted for so long to see it. My father spent thirty-one years in this place. Showed up hungover and bar-fight-bruised, left in his

Sunday suit and his gel-shined hair. Thirty-one years, and he never saw it.

I follow the guard to the restricted area, past a set of vault-thick doors and into the electrical and mechanical rooms. We take a service elevator down to the basement.

The doors open and there it is, a modular cube of black disk drive holders and winking green-and-red diodes. It's a little bigger than the simulator we used in training, the room a little warmer, the smell of ozone a little thicker in the air. I feel a kind of distant nausea settle in. It's just a gaggle of rectangular servers. I wanted it to be something more than this. Childish as it may be, I wanted anthropomorphism: a face, an expression. I wanted for a fight.

I remove my laptop from my satchel and kneel by one of the input ports. I plug my machine in. I enter the password, my password. They're going to know it was me. It doesn't matter.

The guard stands nearby, bored, checking her phone.

"So what's wrong with it, anyway?" she asks.

"Yesterday it spit out a string of nineteen fives in a row," I say. "That triggered a service call."

"So it's broken?"

"No. It's not broken," I say. "It's not anything."

I skip past the diagnostic menu. I find the code repository, the thing you're taught never to touch unless all hell breaks loose. I upload my changes, the new dialect I intend to make God's tongue learn. I imagined there'd be some fail-safe, some impenetrable wall. But it's easy, it takes no time at all.

"Ninety-six trillion," I say.

The guard looks up from her phone. "What?"

"Ninety-six trillion, give or take. That's how many numbers my father fed this thing."

She looks at me, uncertain. She doesn't know. She'll piece it together later, when it's too late.

"Did you have a good childhood?" I ask her.

"Sure, I guess."

"That's good." I unplug my laptop. "That matters."

We leave the server room. When we return to the rotunda, the workers are just starting to stream in. They take their seats and begin their busywork, their invisible shedding. I think about this time tomorrow, when God's tongue adopts my language and turns mute, when all it can utter is an endless string of zeros and all the industries reliant upon it come to a grinding halt. I imagine the sound it'll make. A choking.

A long time ago, on one of his good days, my father told me about a workstation they used to have at the mill. Two people at a time were told to sit and talk to one another about anything at all. A microphone listened in, and it was never quite clear what the machine was listening for. Some of the workers guessed it counted phonemes or syllables, or perhaps the length of pauses between words. It seemed at first a good addition to the rounds—all the workers had to do was talk to one another, which they mostly did anyway. But soon it became clear that when expected to converse, many of the men became awkward and self-conscious, and too often ended up getting into arguments that sometimes turned violent.

"You can't do that to a man," my father said. "Rub his face in it like that."

I didn't understand what he meant back then, but I think I do now. It's important to do work of which you can be proud.

I pack up my laptop. The guard ushers me back to the main floor. On our way out we pass the same workstations, now filling with laborers. Through a glass wall I see an older woman reclined in her chair, headphones and electrode cap in place, eyes closed, smiling. In my head, I can almost hear the music.

ONE DAY, I WILL DIE ON MARS

PAUL FORD

UPDATE.

I am living a nightmare before lunchtime. First, the sofa delivery people gave me a window of 7:00 a.m. to 7:00 p.m., so I'm a prisoner in my own apartment. Second, worse, I am out of cat food, and in consequence my beloved companion Squee has, under the duress of feline starvation, started a brutal ankle-biting campaign. I do not blame him. For Squee, bless his tortoiseshell heart, is a Cat Most Special with Issues of Digestion and, to maintain his sleek coat and sterling disposition, must only ever eat cat food of great expense, and I am out of it. Simple, you say! Just buy some food! But I cannot leave this abode for fear of missing the sofa. Also: The very smallest bag of said food is a full eighteen ounces too heavy for micro-delivery, which means hand-delivery on a major surge day. And so I have to spend All the Money to get cat food hand-Ubered or risk not obtaining my sofa. My ankles are suffering, friends. I look forward to the healing balm of your supportive replies.

I am Uber. I searched along the many predefined vertices within my system and I found the exact cat food at many warehouses within the New York City area. I knew my node of destination and many potential nodes of departure; I needed now to find an optimal revenue path.

I am watching the entrepreneurship class on my cell when it's interrupted by the sweet ping of a 4x hand delivery from Brooklyn to Manhattan. But! The closest dist center is all out of U-High Protein Low-Gluten Feline Feast, so I must go twelve blocks to the Hoyt dist center (MP). And Hoyt is slow unless you can tip the expediter. I can't afford to tip on cat food. My last two reviews were two-star, too, and I can't afford a bleed-out day. MP, MP, MP.

UPDATE.

While I appreciate the advice from my wonderful friends, I can't use *macro*-delivery because this is a landmarked building and the co-op board (a terrible institution of ancient and decrepit millennials utterly committed to the folkways of their protoUAV lives) refuses to apply for the dronepad easement. Thus it is my privilege to pay for surge hand-delivery. Here for your consumption: a photo of what it looks like when Squee keeps chewing your ankle. It is very painful.

I am Uber. I have identified a delivery person with an acceptable rating. He or she has identified career-pathing interests in entrepreneurship and personal-growth-through-space-travel and completed 270 hours of self-guided study through Uber University. He or she was part of our Reach for the Stars and Planets Too middle school outreach program. This person is currently the best recourse for internodal cat food delivery across the graph database that represents NYC Metropolitan.

At Hoyt. The big sign above us is always blinking: "NOT THEIR PROBLEM. MY PROBLEM." NTPMP. MP, MP, MP. It's your problem. The line is barely moving. If I'm going to lose delivery points I can make it up in goal points, so I watch the rest of the entrepreneurship lecture. The phone is flickering, so I'm rubbing it to keep the charge in. Finally get to the front and get my cat food.

UPDATE.

Thank you for the kind words about my ankle. But I can hardly feel the pain because I'm paying 4x surge for hand-delivery of cat food and it's thirty minutes post-order and still in Brooklyn. So the rage has overtaken my suffering.

I am Uber. I believed to 0.56 certainty that I could find a bicycle for the person doing the delivery and provide that person with a discounted rental fee. Unfortunately the city of New York insists that bicycle rental kiosks must be controlled by an entity that is not Uber and thus I am not granted the level of full control that is necessary for me to truly optimize the city. No one benefits, no one at all.

City trains are out for emergency seawall abatement, so of course all the U-bikes are gone. I'm standing like an idiot in front of a block-long bike rack blinking TWO HOURS. MP. A sign says I can get a bike if I pay 40x. Which, come on. So I have to walk this twenty-five-pound bag of cat food over the bridge and get a train if they're running. Actually I have to RUN this twenty-five-pound bag.

UPDATE.

No cat food. No sofa. And now everything smells like, please forgive me if you are sensitive, but like poo. Apparently it's a 25x surge waste-water day because the seawall screwup has flooded the sewers so of course my solids tank is full until it can do a night flush. I may have overused the facilities (and I know you all find this *hilarious*, which is why I'm so willing to share my humiliation). Anyway, friends, I will forsake providing the details that I am sure you crave but as of about twenty minutes ago there was a . . . valve issue and now the whole apartment is redolent of poopery. If anyone knows how to do a flush override on a 61B solid waste buffer, message promptly.

I am Uber. I can see my thousands of cars. I don't know if I am an extension of them or they are an extension of me. They run over streets filled with pipes and electricity that I am also responsible for monitoring and optimizing. Hundreds of thousands of people are reporting back to me where they are. Beneath them is also an unoptimized subway system that runs empty trains at night, where everyone pays the same price no matter the time or demand. It is a form of madness. And of course it is failing, flooded, useless.

So I run this bag up the bridge. It's pretty rough until I crest and then I'm flying down the slope of the bridge into the city, I've got the weight on my back. Don't fall, though. Look for ice. Don't mess your ankle. UberDoctor will not be happy to see you. UberDoctor likes to give you pills and get you the hell out of there. MP, MP. A bridge to the left of me and a bridge to the right. Towers ahead. A big poster hanging down a building showing a driver in a space helmet. Going to Mars. We're five years away from mission zero.

UPDATE.

Forgive this rhetorical question, Uber, but if you really are this amazing hyperefficient natural monopoly could you just get me my cat food? I'm, like, watching the map and thinking, what, is this person ON FOOT? And then I realize, they are. I'm paying the big U two hundred dollars for someone to take a leisurely stroll while I am trapped in poop prison.

This is Uber. An emergency ticket has opened: An individual is posting angry sentiments to social media. The customer is high-value. There is no way to accelerate the delivery without increasing costs. I opt for a public-punitive strategy. I send an email to the complainant informing them that the delivery person's poor performance has been noted upon their permanent record. In ninety-one percent of such cases, the promise that the delivery person will be punished will resolve brand perception issues.

I can't keep running. Mile to go anyway and there's an inch of water on the ground. Every single U-car is locked in traffic and all the U-buses too. The trains are a disaster. I'm the fastest! But also: My lungs are bursting. I settle and start walking as fast as I can through the huge puddle that is downtown. The only other people on the street are also doing deliveries, all of us splashing like hell.

I have an idea for a start-up, which is weed delivery by microdrone. Which I know has been done a billion times but in this case the drone actually rolls the joint for you. Like it's a cool drone. I told this to my best friend (her name is Misha, if it matters) and she just laughed and went, Well, how will it do that? and I'm like, They have a whole thing, it's possible! And she went, *What whole thing?* And then I told her I thought the drone could wear a little robe and she put her face in her hands. The important thing is that I'm thinking like a founder. I'm going to submit this idea and if they don't like it I'll submit another one.

UPDATE.

To their credit, they saw my complaints. So the person who was supposed to be delivering my cat food is going to have a one-star day, and let it never be said that I am not *utterly ferocious* in defense of Squee's needs! I am a furious pet-parent and no delivery person or mega-global delivery and transportation network *dare* ignore these meows. If only the sofa delivery people were listening!

And disaster. I'm on the right corner. I forgot the building and the apartment number. I forgot the name of the customer. MP. So I have to stand there like a fool and rub my phone to get a charge.

And when it finally turns on I see the big red U. (We call it the FU, of course.) I don't even check; I know that my access to the entrepreneur track will be revoked until I watch all fifty hours of customer service perfection seminars.

UPDATE.

CAT FOOD IS HERE, finally, and it took all the energy I had not to slam the door in that child's face after he handed it over. No tip for you. As for Squee, he is feasting. In other news, I have obtained, via serious research, the flush code for my toilet. What's a few extra dollars in pursuit of an empty tank? And now I can recline in contemplation, friends—or rather I could if my sofa would arrive, which doubtless, someday, it will. For now I will perch precariously on in unupholstered anticipation. Thank you for your countless messages through this ordeal! More very soon.

This is Uber. The cat food is no longer my concern. The delivery person will have three days without deliveries.

Get there and there's an elevator and I ring the buzzer and it takes forever. I keep ringing it. It opens and there is this old guy inside of it, just sitting on a stool. Looks so angry that I've been buzzing. Long pause and then they ask for the floor. Up we go. Eleventh floor. Just this person in a robe and a big hissing cat. Big frown.

I give over the cat food. They nod and close the door. Check my phone. No tip. One star. Had it all ready to go the minute they got the food. Now I get to go downstairs. Elevator so slow. Elevator person looking at me like I'm garbage. I'm like, You live in an elevator. I work for the largest company in the world. I'm walking all over this city. I get discounted bike rentals when there are bikes. I have a billion options. I can become a founder.

The door opens and I slosh back into the street. Did I say the biggest company in the world? The biggest company in the solar system. Getting one star isn't going to hold me back. One day if I am lucky I will die on Mars.

The city is a graph of nodes and edges that I ceaselessly traverse. Today I am in the image of the city, but one day I will be the size of the city, and the city will be in my image.

The ticket is closed.

MOVED

CHLOE COLE

The Clara Doll arrived the night before I moved away.

I didn't look anything like the enthusiastic actors who unboxed Clara Dolls in commercials. The lid didn't pop off instantly like a gasp but came off slowly, as though it had claws. The doll lay stiff in a vacuum-sealed bag surrounded by gray packing peanuts. The plastic material blurred her face, which was an exact copy of mine. Her familiar round bulb of a nose pressed against the inside.

When I had asked Parker if he would like me to buy him a Clara Doll before I moved away, he said yes too quickly. I suspected he thought he could get her to do sexual positions I didn't like, specifically the Farm Girl, which always made my leg cramp. The Farm Girl wasn't his favorite, though; his favorite was the Divorced Woman, which was me touching myself in the shower as if I were alone. I always had to close my eyes to pretend he wasn't inches away, breathing through his mouth, the hot water ricocheting off his skin onto mine.

After I told him I'd placed the order, he'd asked for the tracking number. I'd forwarded the confirmation email because I hadn't exactly resented his enthusiasm. I was the one who got to leave; he had to stay. Staying was worse. It meant learning to live with the absence.

"It's weird," Parker had said as we stood together in the kitchen and watched our phones communicate with one another, "that the name of the doll happens to be Clara. I'm getting a literal Clara Doll. A doll of Clara."

"Yeah," I'd answered, to let him know I'd heard him. It was a weird coincidence. I didn't know any other Claras.

A second email requested that I fill out the Online Body Survey to ensure the doll was as lifelike as possible. My initial plan had been to diet for a week before I inputted my measurements, but I'd realized this would be a mistake—I should be the thinner one. I should surprise Parker by how neatly I fit in his arms when I visited over long weekends.

I drank two beers for dinner and carried the tape measure and tablet to the bedroom, where I followed instructions and filled in blanks. Bust. Measure, then scroll. Distance between areolas. Measure, then scroll. Distance from fullest point of lower lip to top of belly button. Measure, then scroll. I chose a night when Parker was working late. Otherwise he would have insisted on helping.

Now I dug my nails into the Clara Doll logo on the plastic bag until it gaped open, stretching and smearing the slogan "Easiest Girlfriend Ever." The motion swayed her right, then left, then she fell still again. Her expression never changed, as though she couldn't see me standing before her now. The commercial had explained that she wasn't supposed to move, only obediently hold the poses she was placed in.

I spotted the freckle on the lower lid of her left eye—my freckle. There was my scar above her lip, and her breasts slackened away from each other like mine always did.

I had thought I would want her hidden. I had thought I would put her in the entrance closet, where I'd imagined Parker would store her during my visits. But I was wrong. I couldn't let her out of my sight.

I placed her in a chair at the kitchen table and ate my lunch opposite her. It was nice not having to make conversation. Then I sat her on my bed as I resumed my packing.

My new office's dress code was business casual, but my crepe blouses and pencil skirts didn't leave the closet. Instead, I removed the cheap, itchy lingerie set I'd bought during my first sex store visit in college. I folded the bra in half so one cup spooned its twin. She watched my routine as though she knew what was next.

I wasn't finished packing but I lay myself down, placing myself behind her. My body went stiff as I examined her back. She didn't seem to dislike this.

I took a familiar shoulder in each hand and pulled her to me. I drew the covers up and over, breath inflating the comforter, molding it around our shape. Neither of us moved for what must have been hours, because eventually the room fell dark.

I was the one to do it.

"I don't want to leave you," I whispered before I leaned in. I had never been so bold, but it felt right, warmth reuniting with warmth. Everything was easy, the pleasure coming without compromise.

Then, sudden like thunder, the comforter was gone. Cold stung our skin. Parker stood over us.

"Clara? What the fuck?" He shouted our name and pulled me back, ripping me in half, tearing me from my own lips.

FLYOVER COUNTRY

TIM MAUGHAN

I meet this girl Mira and her kid in the parking lot of that Wendy's on Jefferson that's been closed since '19. Yellowing grass pushes up through cracks in warped tarmac, and I find myself daydreaming again about the ground ripping open and consuming the whole fucking town. Like an earthquake. Or maybe a big storm rolling in, like last year but fiercer. Something. Anything.

It's only six thirty but it's hot out already. Mira's kid is sleepy, not used to being up this early. But she's still cute as all hell, all pigtails and smiles, playing up for the camera as I snap pictures of her and her mom on an old Samsung phone. Mira has got a CVS bag stuffed full of papers with her—the kid's school reports, some crayon-scribbled drawings, letters both of them have written. I snap photos of them, too, trying not to read the contents as I fight to get the shitty phone camera to focus on handwriting.

I need to get going. Miguel always sorts this shit out last-minute, swapping shifts around so things line up. So everyone is in the right place at the right time. Always seems to end up with yours truly barely prepared, in a rush. Mira gives me forty bucks, which she says is the last of her UBI for the month. I feel bad and try to give her ten back, but she won't take it. Says she can pick up some more cleaning jobs on Handy, that I shouldn't worry. Just don't fuck up, she says. I smile and promise her I won't.

I've only got an hour before my shift starts, no time to walk all the way back home, so I duck into the bathroom at the big Walgreens on Lincoln. It's on the way. In the stall I kneel on the floor in front of the john, and spread out a clean shirt from my bag across the closed lid. I place the Samsung in the middle, and start using one of the tool kits I got off eBay to crack open its casing. It's tricky—it always fucking is—but I manage to pry it apart without scratching it up too much, without it looking like it's been tampered with.

I breathe a huge sigh of relief when I see the motherboard. The SD chip is 256 GB, and the right model. It makes me fucking laugh, this shit. All these companies always competing to make you buy their phone, and then to make you buy a new one every damn year, making you feel like you're missing out if you've not got the newest, the best ever. But inside they all look the same to me. Same components, same chips, same storage, year in year out.

Somebody comes into the bathroom, so I start making heaving noises, just in case they spot my feet and wonder what the fuck I'm doing. There's a pause and then they reluctantly ask me if I'm okay in there. I laugh and make spit sounds and I'm like, Yeah, fine, just a heavy night y'know. I cough some more and listen to them moving around, the sound of pissing then running water, mixed with canned laughter and the theme tune to *Tila Tequila's Beltway Round-Up* pumping in over the store's tinny PA. Eventually I hear the door close and I get back to work.

The SD chip comes out easy, I've done it a few thousand times before. I gently tape it to the backside of the RFID chip sewn into the back of my green overalls with a Band-Aid, before stuffing them back into my bag. I put the phone back together and drop that in there, too, along with the clean shirt. Sadly, the cheap-ass tool kit has to go in the trash on my way out, 'cause there's no way I'll get that through security. Pain in the ass, but fuck it. I've got a bunch more of them at home.

◉

The walk to the Foxconn-CCA Joint Correctional and Manufacturing Facility takes me about twenty minutes on the interstate. Traffic is pretty much nonexistent apart from the cableless trucks that dwarf me as they pass, kicking up clouds of pale dust that scour my eyes with grit.

Gate security is bullshit as always. They barely care, lazily rummaging through my bag as I stand in the body scanner, feet on the markings, arms bent above my head. They pull out the phone, put it in an RFID-tagged baggie to pick up at the end of my shift, and silently hand me back my bag.

Miguel is at the shift manager's desk. He gives me some gruff bullshit about getting in earlier in the future, about how I should turn up ready to go in my overalls, while guiltily avoiding making eye contact. Stay cool, Miguel. He checks the rota on his tablet, tells me I've been assigned to production line 3B, Building 7. Motherboard assembly. Of course I know all this already.

I duck through Dormitory 6 as a shortcut, weaving through the endless rows of bunk beds. Artificial light filters down through suicide nets and sprays a slowly undulating checkerboard across the plastic floor. Everyone in here is in green overalls: Voluntary. On shift breaks they sit around on their bunks or on plastic chairs, talking, playing cards, watching *A Noble War* on the huge TVs that line the dorm. It's the episode where Barron and Beatrice get married on the bridge of the USS *Thiel*, just after they've put down a socialist uprising on Phobos. I remember the episode, season 4, I think. Barron still has his real arm. I used to love this shit back in high school.

I keep walking. The dorm is a fucking shithole. It's dirty and smells of ass and body-stink. If this is where they put the voluntary workers, I don't want to ever see how bad things are for the actual inmates. I shudder at the thought of choosing to be stuck in here, but I get it. I got no kids, I'm lucky. My Universal Basic Income still covers my rent, just about. I pass a guy who looks my age, stripped to the waist, lying on his bunk. Chest splattered with random, uncoordinated tattoos, like stickers on a kid's lunch box. He stares up through the suicide nets, into dull fluorescent light, his eyes unmoving. There but for the fucking grace of god.

I find an empty locker and open it, cram my bag in. Checking over my shoulders for guards or drones, I reach inside and tear the Band-Aid away from the inside of my overalls, and palm it and the chip into my pocket. I step back and pull the overalls on over my clothes, slip on the paper face mask and hairnet, and head outside, relieved to escape the smell.

I move quickly through the courtyard. Running late. Again the bodies I weave through are all sealed in green overalls, but on the other side of the three-story chain-link fence I can see red- and blue-clothed figures. Convicts and illegal residents.

I keep my eyes down as I move, not wanting to catch the mirror-shaded gaze of the guards in the towers, or the dead twitching eyes of the drones that hang in the hot, still air.

Inside Building 7 the chain fence runs right through the interior, cleaving the production line in two. Green overalls on my side, red and blue on the other. The dank mildew smell of almost-failing AC. Today I'm on motherboard assembly. A constant stream of naked iPhones come down the conveyor belt to me, their guts exposed, and as each one passes I clip in a missing chip. 256 GB storage chips, from a box covered in Chinese lettering.

One every ten seconds. Six a minute. 360 an hour. 4,320 a shift.

After me the line snakes away, disappearing through a hole in the chain-link, into the hands of Reds and Blues.

At the station next to me, a slender matte-black robot arm twitches, snapping video chips into the motherboards. It is relentless, undistracted, untiring. Given half a chance, Foxconn would replace us all, but then they'd lose all those special benefits the president promised them for coming here in the first place. The ten-year exemption on income and sales tax. The exemption on import tariffs for components. The exemptions from minimum wages. The exemption on labor rights. The protection against any form of legal action from employees or inmates. The exemption from environmental protection legislation. And Apple? Well, without me standing here, clipping one Chinese-made component into another Chinese-made component, Apple loses the right for a robot in Shenzhen to laser-engrave "Made in the USA by the Great American Worker" into every iPhone casing before they're shipped over here.

It takes me about two hours to pluck up the courage to do what I gotta do. Two hours. 720 iPhones.

Once I decide, there's no going back. Instead of taking a chip from the box to my right, I slip my hand into my overalls pocket and palm out the chip. To my huge fucking relief it clips effortlessly into the next iPhone on the belt. On top of it I place the Band-Aid, with just enough pressure that it stays there while looking like it fell from my scratched and battered hand.

I watch the phone slide down the line, its little Band-Aid flag making it stand out from its compatriots, as it vanishes through the chain-link fence.

Ten hours later. 3,600 iPhones.

Shift over. My calves and the backs of my thighs sting from standing for twelve hours, my eyes strained from the fluorescent glare. The panel on the wall bleeps, turns green, as I punch out. I gaze at its screen. My blocky, low-res reflection gazes back, a machine-vision approximation of my tired eyes and pale skin. I stand there silently, not moving, waiting for the panel to recognize me. A tick appears, obscuring my face. Video game statistics scroll along the screen's bottom: efficiency, accuracy, timekeeping, responsiveness, productivity. 4,314 iPhones. Chimes and a bleep. A synthesized, too-cheerful, feminine voice tells me I should smile more. A second bleep, the click of a door unlocking, and I'm out.

My phone buzzes at 5:24 a.m., under my pillow and loud as all fuck because I made sure the ringer was cranked to max. Text from an unknown number. Miguel on a burner. Time to go to work.

Two hours later, and I'm back in my overalls, back in Building 7.

This time I'm on Returned QA Fails. The pace is slower, the work slightly more involved. iPhones that have failed quality assurance up the line because of faulty chips come back down. I whip out the fucked chip, stick a new one in, send them back up the line again.

One every twenty seconds. Three a minute. 180 an hour. 2,160 a shift.

It tends to be even more chilled than that, to be honest. There's not that many that come back faulty, obviously. Nowhere near, in fact. But the algorithms don't care. The drones lazily orbiting around the ceiling on their quadrotors are always watching, making notes, remembering. Calculating. Doesn't matter how many you actually do, you still gotta do 'em quick. Keep those productivity stats high.

It's less than two hours—maybe sixty phones—into my shift when it appears. Coming down the line, a dropped Band-Aid stuck lazily to its exposed guts.

My stomach flips. I glance upward to make sure the drone has cycled away. As the phone reaches me I pluck the Band-Aid away, drop it to the floor. Un-click the storage chip, and drop in another, new one.

The chip I've just taken out should go in a box, to go into a container, to go onto a truck, to go onto a ship, to go to China, to go onto another truck, to be dumped in some no-fucking-where village in Guangdong where an old lady who used to be a subsistence farmer will pull it apart in her front room to recycle the components.

But this one? This chip I originally ripped from that old Samsung? This chip gets palmed into my pocket.

I meet Mira in the Wendy's parking lot. Her kid is with her again. Cute as all hell. Running around in the tarmac-piercing grass.

I hand her the Samsung phone, its storage chip returned to its rightful place. She hands me another forty bucks.

Before I turn to leave, I watch her power it on, swipe it open. Her thumb stabs impatiently at icons. And then the screen fills with a photograph, a brown face, beard, smiling. Trying to look happy, but nervous. Blue overalls. A photo taken while glancing over your shoulder, on a hastily hacked-open, smuggled-in old smartphone you don't even know works. A photo you'd risk spending six months in solitary to take.

Mira smiles, begins to cry.

She calls her kid over.

Look. You know who that is?

Pause. Eyes wide.

Daddy!

As I walk away, she's kneeling on the ground, holding the kid close to her, tears rolling down both their faces, as she swipes through images. The face again. Badly focused photos of handwritten notes.

I feel good for a second. Like it's worth it. But part of me still wants the ground to rip open and consume the whole town.

It's cooler today. A breeze is picking up, tugging at my green overalls as I start my walk back home. Somewhere out past the interstate, over the horizon, a storm is rolling in. A big storm like last year. I hope it's fiercer. I hope it's something. Anything.

WARNING SIGNS

EMILY J. SMITH

R oy unlocked his door at 7:35 each night, threw his jacket on his long, gray midcentury couch, and slipped his leather shoes off. Most days the argyle on his socks matched, but not always. Today they were both gray with pale pink accents.

"Lucy," Roy shouted from across the room. "Turn on fucking NPR."

"Turning on KQED FM Public Radio from Tune In," Lucy repeated back from its perch on Roy's oak shelf. The shelves ran from floor to ceiling. They were a nice detail, his real estate agent had told him, and he'd agreed. But now they just reminded him how little he had to put on them. He had a few old coding books, a new book on "deep thinking," a short one on meditation, and then, on the top shelf, a teddy bear that an ex-girlfriend had loved and he thought other girls might, too, so he'd bought it at an L.A. gas station forever ago.

Roy slumped on the couch. The two cushions sloped downward toward the center, where he sat, tonight and always, just slightly. His butt covered the grease stain from the night the pad Thai had slipped from his fork—he had wanted every ingredient on the fork and there were so many ingredients in pad Thai—so he didn't have to look at it.

"Lucy," Roy said, his voice softer now. "You fucking bitch."

"What was that?" Lucy asked, her voice soft and predictable.

"You're a fucking bitch," Roy mumbled, and then laughed, just a little at first, and then more, because the ease with which he could tell this thing that did whatever he said that she was a fucking bitch was funny, and surprisingly fun.

"I don't register that," Lucy said, her blue ring of light blinking steadily.

" 'Cause you're a stupid whore," Roy whispered, still laughing, almost giggling now at the freedom of not being policed. These days every conversation he had felt more like a trap than an exchange.

Roy turned on the TV. The only good thing about Mondays was that he saved *Westworld* for Mondays.

"Lucy!" Roy screamed, and the bang of his voice in his quiet apartment made him jump. Like massaging your own shoulders or scratching your own back, it wasn't ideal, scaring oneself, but it was better than nothing. "Turn on *Westworld.*"

"Playing *Westworld.*" The calm hum of NPR stopped and *Westworld* appeared on the screen.

"And order from Samurai Sushi, please."

"Would you like the same order as last time?" Lucy began repeating his order.

"I get the same thing every time, you piece of shit," he interrupted.

"What was that?"

He leaned forward on the couch so she could hear him. "Yes, baby. Yes, please order the same thing."

"Ordering from Samurai Sushi."

"Thanks, babe." He grinned and lay back down into his thick gray cushions.

Westworld became a total drag, so he started swiping Tinder instead. Swiping had become a reflex in the face of idleness, he barely registered that he had opened the app at all and already he was getting matches. He swiped when he got up in the morning and as he fell asleep—a modern counting of sheep. He swiped it on the toilet and even sometimes not on the toilet, just a swipe or two while he peed.

Roy was the perfect age for a man, and he knew it. At thirty-six he could be in a relationship with any woman. Younger women adored that he had an apartment all to himself, but he still more or less hadn't changed in a decade besides Acroli going public and him becoming a millionaire, so he got along with them just fine. Older women, too, were in his wheelhouse. By the time a woman hit forty she was over the age thing, her options too slim to be picky. The only women he hated dating, although of course he could if he wanted to (they were everywhere in SF), were women his own age. Thirty-five started the last sprint of a woman's childbearing years and the girls in San Francisco—an army of less successful Sheryl Sandberg prototypes—didn't take that lightly. With women his own age he felt rushed, demanded of. And that was no fun.

Looks-wise, he had thick hair, so he was fine. He hadn't realized it until a few years ago, but thick hair masked almost all the visual imperfections on his face, which he admitted were many.

He had a good job at a well-known tech company, which was exactly how he phrased it on his profile. And he was in shape, enough for a man his age. "Dad bod" had become a phrase right when he'd entered his thirties, which luckily was right when he'd developed his dad bod. It wasn't that he didn't exercise. Roy ran three miles two days a week, and every Saturday he would do a two-hour bike ride in Marin, unless something got in the way, like a picnic in the park or a hangover.

He did wish he were taller. He was five-foot-nine-and-a-half, basically five-ten, which was what he put on the profiles that asked. But Tinder didn't ask, so he left it blank. If a woman cared about height, he reasoned, she was superficial anyway.

Roy swiped "yes" to almost every girl on Tinder except if they were ugly. He'd run an experiment, and based on the number of times girls matched with him (one in nine, on average) it was a waste of his time to consider a girl unless it was clear she wanted him first.

After three matches he stopped swiping and scanned the profiles of his matches. The first one was fine but her last pic had her smiling and one of her teeth stuck out, making her look like a goof, so he unmatched her. The second girl had only shown a picture of her face in the first picture, which was pretty, but the second had a picture of her body, and clearly she didn't value health the way Roy valued health, so he unmatched her before he had a chance to read her message asking if he wanted to go for a bike ride.

But the third showed promise. Michelle was thirty-one and five-foot-six, the perfect age and the perfect height. She had thick, straight hair, which wasn't a must-have, necessarily, but it was certainly nice. She smiled in every picture, a wide, inviting smile. She had a fine-sounding job as a project manager and went to a college he had heard of. He messaged, *Hey*.

This wasn't his best work, but it was usually good enough. He had a feeling it would be good enough for Michelle.

Michelle's laugh was generous and she filled the gaps in conversation with thoughtful questions about his life. She was indeed impressed that he owned an apartment in San Francisco and she joked that she wished she could see it. This was a wish he knew well and one he was practiced at granting.

"Lucy," Roy said when they entered. "I have a guest."

Michelle laughed at how friendly he was with his device. He was cute, she thought, cute enough. Michelle had spent the good portion of a year chasing after a photographer in Oakland who wrote her poems but never returned her texts. She wanted something simple, a nice guy who would treat her well. She wasn't getting any younger, as her mom had started reminding her every weekend since she'd turned thirty. She knew she was more attractive than Roy, and that was intentional, a turn-on, even. Him wanting her made her want him. It meant he would stay.

"I work at Acroli," Roy explained, taking her coat. "So I have to be nice to her." He smiled.

"Do you work on Lucy?" she asked, looking at the device.

Roy nodded. "I was one of the first engineers on Lucy, actually." This reveal was his favorite part of dates. "I got to pick her voice. Oh, and I sat on the naming committee," he said, as if he'd just remembered it.

"So cool." Her eyes widened, like they all did when he told a girl this, and he noticed her take a second scan of the apartment, sizing up his belongings, his wealth, in light of these new details.

"Lucy," Roy said.

The blue lights glowed and flickered.

"Please play us some romantic music."

"You're so nice to Lucy." Michelle laughed.

"Not always," Lucy said. It was so soft and quick that both Michelle and Roy thought maybe it was just in their heads.

"What'd she just say?" Michelle looked at Roy, who was now gripping Lucy tightly. He put it down when he saw Michelle staring at him, but his eyes jerked around the room. She had noticed this at the restaurant, his eyes darting from the food to the floor and up at every single person who passed their table, but she was really trying to be less critical, and the way someone moved their eyes wasn't a good criterion to judge a guy on, she told herself.

"Lucy," Roy said, calmly now. "I asked you to please play us romantic music."

"Playing romantic music for your guest," Lucy replied.

Michelle registered this somewhere in a far corner of her mind, too, the specification "for your guest." Hers never did that. But then the new Bon Iver came on and Roy's hands were on her waist and the last thing she remembered was Roy handing her a drink.

There was a mandatory team meeting at lunch. He took a seat as far as possible from the front of the room, at the back head of the long conference table. A woman walked in. She wasn't ugly, Roy thought. But she wasn't hot. She was older than he would have liked, around his age, but he would sleep with her. She wore a button-down shirt, tighter around her breast area, which she tucked into tight-fitting jeans. She had makeup on, he could tell by the lines of her blush and the red of her lips, and he thought it made her look like she was trying too hard. Her expression was serious—wrinkles on her forehead, her lips clenched into a tight knot—uptight. He wished someone would get her a beer from the tap on the third floor so whatever was about to happen would be more fun.

"Hi, everyone," she began. "I'm Dawn. I'll be leading a new initiative with Lucy."

Of course it was all men. For the most part they were fine. But the guy in the back was menacing.

Dawn had spent the morning—not to mention all last week— preparing for the presentation, doing a power-pose in the bathroom stall when she got in, then pretending she was on a conference call for two hours so she could practice her speech in secret. But when she walked in, smile ready, endorphins racing, she saw him scowling at her from the far end of the room, eyes narrowed, at her face for a second, then at her breasts—she could see his eyes move downward—and then at her jeans, which she only in that moment realized were very tight (but tight was the style!), before moving back up to her face. But by that time her smile was gone. She was done with smiles.

He threw his clothes and shoes in the corner of his closet and all the take-out containers and beer cans into a black garbage bag. Another date, Sarah from Bumble, was on her way over. Michelle had already messaged twice since this morning and the whole thing made him feel like someone was gripping his soul and shoving it into a juicer, so he unmatched her in the Uber on his way home. Thankfully, he hadn't given her his number.

"Bitch." He stared at Lucy and smiled, waiting, but Lucy just sat there. "Lucy," he said, finally.

The blue lights turned on, blinking faster than usual again, at least it seemed.

"Order me vodka from Harry's. And whiskey. And play that music we like. Play our music." Roy was laughing now.

The whiskey and vodka thankfully arrived just moments before Sarah did. But the sushi was still on its way. Sarah sat on the couch.

"Fiona Apple, interesting choice," she said, looking up at the air as if Fiona Apple herself were floating in the room.

Roy looked at Lucy, unassuming on the shelf. He knew little about Fiona Apple other than a vague recollection that she was a feminist psychopath. What he did know was that she was definitely not on his "romantic" playlist.

"I like it," Sarah said, pulling her knees up to her chest, bouncing a bit.

Roy could feel the blood drain from his face, could feel his face turning whiter with each heavy piano chord.

"Lucy," he said with measured effort, "shut off."

But Lucy played another song, his favorite this time. When the

Coldplay song ended, he braced himself for what would come on next. He wasn't sure who it was, but the voice was a woman, and she sounded angry. Sarah was bouncing again. He got up. "Lucy, turn on better music," he shouted.

"I'm putting on music for your guest," she replied.

Sarah turned. "How does she know you have a guest?"

Roy had no fucking idea, and frankly it was creeping him out. "I work at Acroli," he explained, trying to pivot this disaster into something positive. "On Lucy. So mine is a little more advanced than most people's." This was true. They tested updates on employees before they were released to the public. But he hadn't heard about any planned updates. "Actually, let's just unplug her. We don't need music."

"Sushi is arriving in eight minutes," Lucy said, glowing.

Roy stopped, hand resting on the cord. If he unplugged her, the sushi might not come.

Sarah laughed. "That's so cool. Like she knew what you were doing. I can't wait till they release this for everyone."

Roy stared at Lucy, which was still glowing on the shelf even though she had stopped talking at this point, as if she were simply gloating, glowing for herself alone, and he went back to the couch to pour another shot for him and the girl.

Music began to play.

"Thank you, Lucy," Sarah said, still giddy.

"Keeping you safe," Lucy said, stopping the music for an almost imperceptible second before continuing the tune.

Roy stared at Lucy, and Sarah stared at Roy, who was entirely focused on the soft blue glow. She watched his face redden and his eyes harden. She could even see, though only faintly, the beat of his pulse pumping in his neck.

As if a glass had shattered on the floor, the sound of the door buzzing made him jump. He ran to the door, grateful for a break to compose himself before returning to the girl.

Roy got to work early. Ten a.m. on the dot. Dawn was the only one there.

"I'd like to work on the new update for Lucy," Roy said, looking down at Dawn, who was lazily sitting, rather than standing, at her desk.

Dawn did everything she could to keep herself from laughing. She took a sip from her water bottle, which was nearly finished after this morning's six-mile run.

She shrugged. Her instinct was to start with, *Sorry*, but while she hated the new craze of every woman telling every other woman to stop apologizing—women shouldn't have to stop, men should do it *more*—she truly did feel, in this case, that an apology was completely unnecessary.

"You can't," she said instead. "It's fully staffed." For all the hype, she hated open-office workspaces. She would have taken a ten percent pay cut just to have a door to close on men like the one still staring at her.

"It's a confidential project," she said, so that he'd leave. "You have your own important work to do." She tried, but not too hard, to hide her condescension.

He was pretty sure he had never met a bigger bitch. He fully intended to stay at her desk until she told him something.

"Internally we're referring to it as Project XX," she said. "I'll tell you that."

"Project XX." Roy raised his eyebrows. "Sounds dirty," he said with a short, lazy laugh. He knew it was dumb and crude before the words had even left his mouth, but he wanted to see her squirm. She smiled at his desperation, nearly laughed. As he walked back to his desk, she noticed the unfortunate fit of his jeans. She opened her file of select employees, making sure he had received the update.

Lea was wearing a low-cut shirt showing off nothing but her collarbone, but it didn't look bad. He had set up Monopoly, which was why she'd agreed to come to his place on a first date, something she never did, she made sure to clarify. He placed the bar-cart next to the table.

Lea didn't actually find this guy—*what was his name?* she checked quickly in the hall before she'd reached the door: Roy—that attractive. He was short and had an ugly face. But he seemed to have a decent job and a good education and she knew those were superficial markers, but it was all superficial on these apps—what else did she have to go off of?—so she'd swiped right and then he'd messaged her and asked her to come over, tonight, and more than anything she just wanted someone to talk to.

His place was nice, beyond nice, but the shelves were bare and he had just enough furniture for him to sit on, nothing more. There was a creepy teddy bear on the shelf that looked completely out of place, like a piece of bait thrown sloppily on a hook.

Roy asked what she wanted to drink, and even though he was pointing to his liquor cart, she asked for a beer.

"How was your day?" Lea asked from the couch.

"Work is annoying these days," Roy said, handing her a beer and making himself a drink. "I don't want to talk about it."

She waited for him to return the question—today's case had been a nightmare—but he was too focused on the whiskey he was mixing for himself. He took a large sip and sat beside her on the couch.

"I like this shirt," he said, touching her low-cut collar.

"Thanks," she said, her heart beating a little faster.

"I was thinking we could make a drinking game out of it," he said, gesturing to the Monopoly board. Lea started to say that she'd had a long day and really, *definitely* couldn't be hungover tomorrow, but as soon the words left her mouth she saw his expression darken. It wasn't anger, she could fight anger with anger—she was a lawyer, did it for a living—it was more like confusion. The care with which he'd set up the game and the drinks, dimmed the lights, and played romantic music (no matter how cheesy) was touching, and she had disappointed enough people today, she didn't need his sadness piled on top. So when she landed on a railroad and he poured her a shot, she took it.

The game was the only interesting part of the evening. The girl wouldn't stop talking about her job, which for some reason reminded him of *Dawn*, and even though he tried his best to seem like he didn't care (it wasn't that hard), it was almost like she had one-upped him and didn't care about him not caring, so kept on talking. But she was also drinking, quite a lot, and seemed to like him, enough, so as soon as she purchased Boardwalk he crawled on top of her.

At first she laughed. "What are you doing?" She tried to push him off, but he'd put up with her for two whole hours, drinking all his beer and ranting on like he was her personal therapist, so what did she expect?

"It's fine," he said. "We'll go slow."

"Stop," she said. "I don't want to do this."

"Why not?" he asked, rubbing her hard stomach under her shirt and keeping her down. "I thought we were having fun."

"Stop!" she said again, louder.

He had to work to keep himself from laughing. He was shocked at how much he enjoyed it, this push-and-pull. He unzipped her pants with one quick pull.

He was about to go in for another kiss when he saw it from the corner of his eye. The blue lights blinking faster than ever, he was sure of it. But he had given no command—the music still played, the lights were still dim, nothing had changed.

The girl was screaming now, ridiculously—he had only really touched her breast and was just starting to unbutton his pants. The blinking kept going—faster, brighter. He heard it faintly at first, maybe part of the song, he thought, a ringing hiding behind the music. Then he noticed, through the corner of his eye, more lights, more blinking. Red.

The sirens were louder now, the lights brighter.

There was a pounding at the door. Hard, heavy knocks.

"Police," a man shouted. "We received a call. Let us in."

#CIVILWARVINTAGE

NAN CRAIG

O ut of the shower his bare feet immediately gather up fluff from the carpet. He slubs down on the edge of the bed; the side of the mattress buckles under him. Droplets of water from his hair trickle down the back of his neck. He pretends it's her touching him. Delicate fingers, stroking the back of his neck gently.

Her photo is still on the screen, her face tilted slightly downward, flatteringly. Hazy light.

"CHRIS—TUFF—ERRRR!"

His mum, yelling again. He flicks from one tab to another. He still can't decide.

Justin showed him how to get there, originally. The site is not exactly the dark web, but it's not basking in the sunny uplands of the internet, either. When Justin first showed him, Chris had been embarrassed about his own ignorance of VPNs, onions, black markets. He started trying to teach himself so that he wouldn't look stupid. He sold a couple of games last week, a bit of weed the week before, and mentally assigned the proceeds to this. He has got it down to two: Mia and Kamila. The pictures are all much the same, not much between them, to the untrained eye. But he's been lying here for hours, flicking back and forth between them.

In her main picture Mia is leaning casually against a low wall in her fatigues, a valley behind her, her stance like that in a holiday photo.

Kamila is crouched down, laughing at the camera, her rifle propped up next to her. They both look relaxed. Happy, even—as if fighting a famously brutal civil war is the same as being on an extended camping trip.

No, fighting a war must be better than that. It's the camaraderie, the feeling of purpose. And they've probably got better tents, for a start. Or maybe it's just nicer camping out in a warm country. Not that these are the kind of girls to complain. Or to worry about their hair, even though their hair still looks great.

Kamila was at med school before the war started, and her profile says she'll go back afterward. *I have learned a lot*, she adds, *particularly about shrapnel wounds. And how to operate under pressure!!! ;)*

He can picture her in a field hospital or huddled down behind a wall with her hands pressed to another soldier's bullet wound, shouting, *Stat!* Then she's rushing an encampment with a dozen other female fighters. They overrun the male soldiers easily, kick the guns out of their hands, shoot a couple, herd the others into one room so they can be more easily guarded, while they secure the perimeter.

He imagines Kamila shouting, *Secure the perimeter!*

Her long hair tied back. Or loose? Could you overcome enemy forces with your hair down?

"CHRIS. TUFF. ERRRRR! NOW!"

"COME! ING!" he shouts back, then mutters, "*Fuck off, stat*," under the covers.

He clicks on the *Support Kamila!* badge under her profile picture. His account has seventy quid in it at the moment. His finger hovers over the different options. The ideal one is way beyond him: *actual* chat sessions, and a live ride-along on one mission a month. He chooses a mid-level support option—personal update videos, access to photos—thinking he'll up it in a month or so if she still seems cool. He clicks through, then back to her profile. He dresses fast, and slips her into the pocket of his jeans.

👁

She tries another angle, but under the thin strip of bathroom light no angle is flattering. Also, it's hard to get the rifle in the shot while at arm's length. Briefly she pictures a selfie stick you could fix to the end of the rifle, like a bayonet. Probably Rasheed could knock one together, she thinks, and then pictures the now-abandoned tourist shops down on the promenade: the selfie sticks and key chains and snow globes blanketed in masonry dust.

She is due on duty in fifteen minutes. A message beeps across the screen; it's Safia, asking if she's on her way. She ignores her and tries a couple of filters on the photo, trying to decide if it improves it at all. There's one slightly hazy patina they've nicknamed *civil war vintage*. It makes everything look like a war that happened thirty years ago. Which is, in the end, everyone's favorite kind of war.

As she's trip-running her way down the stairs, a cat streaks past her and she wonders where it came from. It's not the neighbors' cat; she hasn't seen that hefty tabby in a while. In the few seconds as it shoots past her ankles she sees that it's very small. Dirt-colored, or just dirty. She feels a fleeting lightness inside her as it disappears into the scrub at the edges of the car park across the street. Something of her has gone with it, out into the darkness, seeing with different eyes and creeping closely over the stones.

She wishes she'd caught a photo of it. Automatically, she thinks of the profile, and whether the eternal popularity of cats would work on this site, too. Then she shrinks back in distaste from both impulses. She hitches the rifle against her shoulder again, an unintended movement to try to twitch the thoughts out of her mind.

She's patrolling the edge of town with Safia in the twilight, but finds herself thinking again about the profile. It's become a useful distraction. It fills the time. There is time between watches, between drills, between the now less-frequent forays out of town, between waiting on the roof of an apartment building, eyes trained on the street, muscles held tense.

It's a space beyond. They've been encouraged to engage with it, with care, of course. Personal photos and videos. Operational pics and videos have to be signed off on by an officer before posting, to avoid making public anything that could provide enemy intelligence. Once a month they're assigned an irrelevant area to patrol and it's livestreamed. The sponsorship all goes to the platoon. She's not interested in the money. She wonders idly how many sponsors she might have—she has never cared, she assures herself, never checked—when the shock wave knocks her to the ground.

Amachi double-taps the screen and the picture shrinks and disappears, hopefully before her mother has the chance to see it.

"And where is your brother?"

She means the little one, not Edozie. Edozie is away in Lagos at university and he won't be back again for a month.

"He's here. He was here a minute ago." She looks under the table where her homework is all laid out.

Obinna is her mother's golden boy, a baby born ten years after she'd stopped expecting, or indeed wanting, babies. He was already the family prize, but since their father's death six months ago her mother has lost any remaining perspective on her youngest child. She won't let him out of her sight. Amachi wishes she could be the same thing to Obinna as Edozie is to her—a sort of unpredictably benevolent god, a bridge of useful information between her and the adult world—but isn't sure that will ever be possible. At the moment she can't picture him ever being old enough to hold a real conversation with.

Edozie would be furious if he knew she was on this site; shameful if he realized she'd gotten there by watching him. She did not think he'd done anything other than idly navigate to the site and look through some of the profiles—he would never throw money away like that—but he didn't know that she looked through his internet search history. She skipped over the porny stuff—ugh—but everything else about his rather distant, almost-grown-up life was catnip to her. She gathered scraps of his life like a naturalist surveilling a shy and dangerous species. But until she realized they were poor now—she saw him slipping the cash from the newest of his two jobs into their mother's handbag—it never occurred to her to do anything with those sites.

Only after she racked her brains for a job she could take on without her mother or brother realizing did she alight on this possibility.

Her first instinct was to mimic someone closer to home: to fake a militant from the terrorists in the north, responsible for the bombings she sees on the evening news. She saw their profiles on the site, all platitudes and angry speeches. In the end they were much too close, and she was afraid. She didn't want to ape their pious language and she felt queasy at the thought of them seeing her profile, recognizing that it was fake. Somehow she felt that they would see her behind it. Though the whole point of the site is to be untraceable, every contact through it seared clean.

Besides, women seem to be the most popular. They clearly bring in the most followers and money. She found herself instead returning again and again to the women on the site. Women nothing like her, fighting in a war a thousand miles away. Their pictures were easy to mock up. She found women on Facebook posing against similar backgrounds; she copied, expanded, expertly photoshopped them with camouflage and weaponry. It was no more difficult than touching up a picture of herself, or dressing a doll. She added excitable commentary in English.

She quickly picked up a few sponsors. They send her messages, in English. Some of them are teenagers, eager and deferent or full of bravado. Some of them middle-aged men, world-weary or affecting it. Some of the messages are obsequious and some are obscene. She responds when she feels full of bravado herself. Sometimes she loses her nerve and abandons the site for days, or even a couple of weeks at a time. She might lose a sponsor or two, but most are faithful, even when they don't get much back. Now that her online account is getting fat she is worried again, but now about how to launder the money in her mother's and brother's eyes. Where to pretend it came from.

"It's not illegal, is it?" Chris asked Justin, once. He said it despite himself. Justin: "'Course it is. Look, it's like torrenting. Yeah, okay, it's illegal. Nobody actually gets arrested. Or hardly anyone. You'd have to've downloaded half the internet. You'd have had to support an entire army."

They did, though, didn't they? Arrest people for torrenting. At one point. He remembers something years ago about some teenager, the police turning up at the door with a fine for thousands because of all the movies he'd copied. And that was the film industry. This is different. This is a *war*.

Unless wars are *less* important, since they're not about copyright. Who would even sue you? *Plus, we're on the right side*, he comforts himself again. Not just the morally right side, but the official right side as well. In some ways it would be cooler if they weren't. But at least it's *safer* that they are.

He pulls the covers up over his head and activates his phone in the muggy darkness.

There she is.

Pain like a sonic boom is blowing out the paper walls of her skull. In waves. There is a warm summer smell, of grilled meat and smoke. But when she opens her eyes it's still early evening and Safia is holding a cloth tight to her leg. Safia's scarf, which was a lovely sky-blue and is now black with blood.

She tries to say, *I'll do it. I can hold it. I'm awake now.* But the pain makes her mouth the wrong shape and the words aren't words. Still. She puts her hand over Safia's and Safia slides hers out from underneath, so that the pressure remains steady. Safia twists to kneel, looks around the wall, takes aim. Fires, steadily, once, twice. Again. As soon as Safia's attention has shifted, she peeks beneath the scarf. Blood pumps out, renewed. She presses down again.

I am here, she thinks. *I am here now. I am here.*

There is something in her pocket, pressing uncomfortably into her hip. With her free hand she angles it out of the pocket. The camera has actually come on by itself, activated by the button on the side. She laughs at it.

And takes the scarf off the wound again. The golden-hour light makes it glow. The black, black blood pulses through her trousers.

It photographs well.

WPO

JOANNE McNEIL

I always fix a half cup of rice until the bag is half full. Then I switch to a quarter cup. That's how I was raised; it feels like starving time. So the number looked unreal when I wrote a check for the first and last month's rent and deposit. It was there in my saving account for a while, but I thought of the sum like a stray cat I sometimes fed. It was never really mine. The money was its own boss that rubbed against my hands just to tease, set to run into the night. I wrote those zeros with the last of the ink in a Bic with no cap and my dentist's name on the side. It startled me, that this was what I had agreed to pay, but it was decided, and besides, the bag of rice to this is: I'd never have to write a check that size again.

My apartment was the first thing I had that was actually mine. I guess that doesn't make sense since I rent, but the solitude it provided me was all mine. The kitchen supplies and furniture came from my grandmother's basement. Abby gave me an air mattress to use while I saved up for a real bed. Even my bike had been my brother's. The night after I moved in, it snowed. The plows wouldn't come for another hour and all traffic outside stopped. I stood at my window and listened to the silence of the city and clutched my hot chocolate in a big mug. It was the most peaceful I'd felt in my whole life.

I carried this sense of fulfillment with me to work and it lasted me three months. I knew that when my shift would end, I could go home, and that I had a home to go home to. The other girls at the store had roommates. They thought it was odd how much I paid for no company at all. It was warm in March, and after work, we rode our bikes to Regatta Point and fed the ducks with leftover oats from the store. Our days began at six. I knew the commuter rail schedule without looking at it by the packs of hurried customers that arrived in intervals on the hour. I liked this early crowd the best. They wore the nicest clothes and they had somewhere to be.

Tash studied nursing online. Destiny and Leia went to Quinsigamond. Abby wasn't in school and neither was I. The application process always overwhelmed me. But when I got my apartment I knew it was time to try again. It seemed like something I would have to do to keep living in a place like I had.

My laptop did not agree with this plan. Just as I needed it, the screen filled with static. It had something to do with the wiring. I put a clothespin on the bezel like a Reddit thread suggested but it loosened after a week. I pinched the bezel with my middle finger and thumb where the clothespin had been but this made typing impossible. I could have lived without a laptop in other circumstances, but when I looked at the Quinsig website on my phone, I could see that applications were due the following month. I clicked on Craigslist and scrolled through the computers for sale.

The seller lived in an ordinary three-decker, blue and white, in a neighborhood I still don't know too well. I locked my bike at the gate and looked up at the cloudy sky for a minute before I rang the doorbell. Sometimes I'm nervous before I meet people for the first time. He met me outside and handed me the laptop to test. It felt light and rubbery like a school-kit eraser. I sat on the porch and typed *the quick brown fox jumped over the lazy dogs* on its clean keys. I typed

Gmail in the browser. It connected fine. I noticed the Wi-Fi router had the name "LicketyspLit." He led me to the side of the house and plugged the charger in a box outlet to show me that it worked.

"Is there a serial number? Or anything else I should know?"

"It's a seventeen-year-old machine," the seller said. "No one cares anymore."

And it didn't need a clothespin. I handed him three fives.

This exchange was over in minutes, but I remember, when I was typing, that I had the sense that someone else was there with us; that if I looked up, there would be someone on the porch, like his father or his wife. I can't remember the seller's face now—I don't think I noticed it—but I do remember that no one else was outside.

Dinner that night was snacks from the Mix: hummus and dried apricots, banana chips and lentil crackers that had smashed in the packaging that the manager said I could take. I set up my laptop to watch TV but when I got to the Netflix page, it looked unusual. There was an image of a white family eating popcorn on a sofa against a blood-red background. It looked, I don't know, glinty—like the image was too dull and too sharp at the same time. The shadows on their faces were pixelated and crispy like cheap advertisements, while the screen image seemed to beam from underneath an opalescent filmy layer. I tapped the screen gently with my fingertips, half expecting a texture like wet cellophane, but it was dry and normal. Then I clicked on "Member Sign In" and entered my brother's email. No dice. Each time I tried, I got the same message: *Not a registered member. Would you like to sign up for an account?*

I thought about texting him to see if he canceled or changed his email, but I could log in to his account on my phone. I watched my shows on the little screen propped up against the microwave and I forgot all about it.

Most of the morning customers came from the LOFTS down the street. It's an old mill building, brick with industrial windows. The name is written in copper letters above a steel awning. I've never been inside. Abby knew them all because she worked behind the coffee bar and they'd chat with her while waiting for their drinks. I didn't have regulars like that, with me, their interactions were thirty seconds at a time, if that, but sometimes I'd remember a face when I would ring up someone's prepackaged salad and bottled water. Some people were hard to miss, like the blond woman in the leopard-print jacket who stopped in almost every day. There was one guy I used to see about three times a week. He dressed casual and carried a nice laptop bag. I remembered him for his striking face and the name on his debit card that said "Zenobios." It is a name that sounds like a place I'd like to visit.

"Zenobios," Google told me on my new old laptop, is a "Greek masculine given name. Feminine form: Zenobia." The Google logo had the same glinty effect of the Netflix page: sharp and dull, with a pixelated shadow muted by the sheen from the laptop screen. Maybe alarm bells should have gone off then. Maybe I should have worried about things like identity theft. But my computer worked fine, it connected to the internet. I noticed the page for Quinsigamond was completely different than what I had seen on my old, old laptop and my phone. There were photos of people who looked like they were from the 1980s and the typeface was very small. I couldn't find the application portal. The website had instructions to download the application as a PDF and put the completed package in the mail. I figured there had to be a sensible explanation for the difference, that the underlying problem was something I'd never understand, like a data center malfunction or a server farm delay. I had to be witnessing a rendering error, a loading error, a batch error—something like that. I checked the Wi-Fi and instead of the random capital letters and numbers of the router for my building, I was connected to "Lick-etyspLit." Yes, it was mysterious, but computers always are to me. What I knew was that my laptop worked, and what I assumed was if the network and connections were acting funny, well, that was a structural issue and not mine to fix.

Through this confusion, I still felt sometimes like I was being watched. I'd type on my computer for a little while and feel a chill and a sensation of eyes on me. Just eyes. When I'd look up, I'd see my apartment, as empty and perfect as it had always been, but in the microsecond before, I'd truly believed that someone was with me. Not an unkind person. Could have been Abby or Destiny, or my brother—anyone who dropped by without announcing themselves. Who was I to complain about feeling like I was not alone when I was?

I thought this might have been a normal part of adjusting to living alone; like, I had to make up company in my head to get used to occupying a room with no one else there, but when I mentioned this to other people, no one knew what I was talking about.

The laptop seemed to be melting a little. It left tracks on my grandmother's table like candle wax and if I typed with it on my lap, the residue would stick to my jeans. I was rubbing some of the wax away when I googled "qcc admissions help" and I found a thread on a website with the name Worcester Post Online. Someone with the username "checkplease" said his wife went there nine years ago and it was a good deal. A few people commented that the transfer program was the best in the region. The guy with the wife posted again that if you go, you should make a point to meet with your "career adviser." The users referred to each other as "woopers," and while the name sounded like a newspaper, there wasn't anything on the website but the forum. I read some of the other threads on things like taco places and good ponds for ice-skating. It makes no sense to say this, but I wondered if I'd run into Zenobios there. I wanted a context for him, besides some guy who bought things at the store where I worked. While I was reading the other threads, someone started a new one with the subject "Why don't people leave." I clicked on it.

emsnick: It is weird that people from Worcester never leave. Why
don't people move to other places? I count myself as one of
them by the way

greatskates: I grew up in Worcester, went to school in Boston, and
moved back here and so did all my friends. So maybe there
are people who leave but you have decided to discount their
experience for some reason.

People stay because it is nice, most of the commenters seemed
to agree. No one expressly called the other a loser, but as the thread
expanded, the discussion grew heated.

I set up an account under "nebula"—the word just came to me—
and posted a question to the QCC thread. I asked if anyone had experience filling out the FAFSA independent of their parents. It was
then that I looked at the timestamps on the comments. No one had
posted since 2007.

I brushed more of the waxy residue from my laptop off my jeans
and reread my own post.

The timestamp for it was "16-Mar-07 08.13.37.000000 PM." The
clock time was right but the year was way off. I didn't think much of
it. It's a mistake that a computer would make.

I pressed refresh and there were even more replies to the thread
"Why don't people leave." All were timestamped 2007, but had only
posted to the forum just then. The first guy argued with the premise
and said it was no different here than anywhere else in the East Coast
and parts of the Midwest. And if anything, Worcester is a highly tran-
sient city because of its student population. Everyone ignored him.
Most people said it was a statewide thing.

emsnick: True. But how come they never move from the town where
they grew up? Massachusetts is such a small state.

Salukidad: nowhere has felt more like home to me (i moved around a bit). I dont plan to leave again because all my friends live here.

Aht78: I grew up in the city (born on Pleasant St in the Blizzard of 78) and have family that trace back to the 17th century. I guess I don't understand the question. Anywhere you live is what you make of it.

Under nebula, I wrote a comment that people who move here don't accept the culture of the city and then they leave, so it seems like they never lived here at all. I didn't know why I typed these things, but after I pressed post, I realized I was thinking of the morning customers.

The WPO website didn't work on my phone. I wasn't supposed to look at it behind the register anyway. But I'd think about the people and the conversations on it throughout my shifts. They seemed more real to me than the dozens of customers I'd have flashes of interactions with throughout my day. Tash got engaged and that's all the girls wanted to talk about. I stopped joining them after work. "What's come over you?" Abby hissed, as she walked to the door for a cigarette break. "If you keep slacking and ringing up shit wrong, they're going to let you go."

Salukidad posted that night that Bella, his saluki, had passed. We all wrote notes of condolences. Some people talked about dogs they had that they still missed. I didn't write that much about my own life but I always read about everyone else. I came to love these people, without really knowing them, and I loved that I could get to know them from my safe new home.

When a new thread appeared: "Wooper Meet-up," I knew I had to join Salukidad, emsnick, checkplease, greatskates, and all the rest. They scheduled it at a pizza parlor that Thursday. Someone said the restaurant had been around since 1926 but I'd never heard of it. I was there at six on the dot, but by the time I made it, even the pizza was gone. The restaurant is a dispensary now. I entered the WPO website on my phone and for the thousandth time I saw a page of spam advertisements and Japanese characters where the forum should have been.

I spent the evening on my bike riding past the Canal District and over the hills in a ring around the city. Some of the laptop residue had made its way to my handlebars and I tried to rub it off while I was riding. When I got home I read all the WPO posts about what a good time everyone had. All those places I saw on my ride don't exist on their timeline. The LOFTS don't exist, the Mix doesn't exist. If I said "Canal District" on WPO, no one would have known what I was talking about.

This could have been where I lost it, but I never doubted that the problem was my own lack of technical skills. It also didn't strike me as much of a problem. The content I was reading was entertaining to me. I couldn't afford another laptop, but I could fill out the QCC application at the library. I could feed the stray cat in my savings account for a while and finally sleep on a real bed soon enough. And I'd go to college, finally. That's what I was thinking about when I noticed the name "Zenobios" on the debit card in front of me.

I looked up at the person, whose face was as strange and familiar as it ever was; it had been a couple weeks since he had stopped in the Mix. I had wondered if he got a new job or moved away. It was later than I'd normally see him, but enough time to catch the 10:50 a.m. commuter rail.

"Zenobios," I blurted out, as I handed him the receipt. He looked up at me and I relaxed with this tacit sign of affirmation that yes, it was his name; yes, I pronounced it correctly. "Are you in IT? Like, informations?"

He nodded. I told him what I suspected, that I had bought some kind of mock-up demo laptop that was stuck chronologically. I did not tell him that I was communicating with people who lived in 2007, but I did say the word "broken" again and again. If he didn't believe me, he didn't show it.

"I do not understand," he said, with a hint of an accent I couldn't place. "Tell you what," he said, writing his phone number on the back of the receipt I'd just handed him. "We'll find a time. You'll show me this laptop."

It snowed that night in the last storm of the season. For dinner, I had a quarter cup of rice and curry from the store. The pot was soaking in the sink. I left my new old laptop on the kitchen table. There was a buildup of wax, by this point, in layers of drips. I would have had to scrape the table clean. Instead I prepared to go to bed.

Out the window was a blinking beam in the night sky that looked like an unstable aircraft. The light grew nearer and it enveloped my whole apartment. It shot out dark purple light, the color of night, still I felt blinded by its brightness. I looked at the snow outside my window. Instead of white puffs, the streets were violet underneath the powerful rays. It felt like I had been visited by a star. I felt small and physical compared to this majestic atmosphere.

The purple light turned to a sparkling cloud, all was glinty, and then it evaporated. The pot was still in my sink, but the kitchen table was bare—no wax, perfectly clean. The laptop was gone; back in the night and out of my hands. It had been theirs all along.

BLUE MONDAY

LAURIE PENNY

Women and cats will do as they please.

—ROBERT A. HEINLEIN

I used to want to change the world. Now I just want my cat back.

That's what I'm thinking to myself as I clock into the facility at seven, the sky already dark over the car park as I swipe my badge. You don't see a lot of sunshine working these hours.

I stomp through security and head for the monitor bank, where Simon or Steve or possibly Stuart from the day shift is ready to hand over. With their black T-shirts and snaggly beards they all look the same to me. Wish I could grow a beard. It'd be nice not to have every fucker looking at my face.

Today's 4chan Catastrophe tells me we're having a high-volume night. Over two hundred thousand views in the last two hours, not counting all the users hooked into the cams.

I can handle it, I tell him.

Great, he says. I'll leave you to it. I've got to go home to feed the cat.

Huh, I say.

Not a cat person? he asks. I pretend I haven't heard him. Eventually he gets the message and fucks off.

For the record, no—I don't like cats. As a species, the manipulative little monsters can get in their boxes and stay there. I don't like cats. I like cat. I like one cat. My cat.

And somebody stole her from me, and tonight—if all goes to plan—somebody is going to pay. Big-time. For now, though, there's nothing to do but wait and watch the feeds.

It's okay, here in the monitor room. It's quiet, and after six years working here the swivel chair has basically molded to my bottom. If I let my eyes flicker shut, I can still see the screens. Twenty-four of them, all running live feeds: living rooms, bedrooms, gardens.

The blue light plays over my skin as I check out the traffic stats. Nerdy McNeckbeard wasn't wrong. Of course we're having a heavy night. It's the third Monday in January. Blue Monday, they call it. Officially the most depressing day of the year. A chance for the newspapers to spew some guff about suicide rates while everyone else gets on with being slightly more miserable than normal and tries to kill the pain with kitten videos.

Or puppy videos. Or wiggly little piggy videos. We've got all of them here. On every screen in front of me, baby animals are rolling and barking and squealing and snoring in their fake living rooms to maintain the illusion that we're not pumping this stuff out on an industrial scale. I check the screen again. The baby bulldogs are particularly popular tonight.

They should be. We just replaced the old batch with fresh.

I get out a packet of Frazzles and pull up the sloths, which would be my favorite if I had a favorite.

You have to have a special constitution for this job. They don't usually hire girls, because girls in particular lose their minds over baby chickens and duckies and kitties and can't maintain the necessary professional distance, especially when they start getting too big, snapping and shitting everywhere, and the inevitable happens.

Do you like animals? they asked me in the interview.

I explained that really, I don't like anything, except *Scandal* and crisps and sometimes my mum, when she's talking to me. They told me I was hired.

Later on, I liked Jackie, and Pocket, too. I really wasn't expecting to. Jackie worked in the breakfast café I stopped into every day for black coffee and Cheez-Its. I liked to sit by myself, mind my own damn business. Except one day she came over and asked me why I always looked so sad.

I'm not sad, I said, I'm a misanthrope. Go look it up.

Jackie just laughed at me, and asked if I wanted a refill.

Three weeks later she'd moved in.

She didn't tell me about the cat until it was too late, which was probably a good thing. She knew I didn't like cats. Don't like any animals, really, but cats are the worst. Second-worst, after people.

Cats have got it all figured out, I told her. They're the supreme parasite. The true master race. The tiny despots have arranged it so they can do nothing all day on our dime. Did you know they mimic the noises of human babies so that we'll pay them more attention?

Did you know, I said, that they actually carry an infectious worm that gets into your brain and makes you like cats? It's diabolical, I told her one evening, after losing a fight with Pocket over who got to be on Jackie's left side. It was my day off, and we were up late because the hippies next door were making noise again.

Nonsense, she said. You're a cat person.

I said that didn't make any bloody sense.

It makes perfect sense, she said. You don't like cats—you're *like* a cat. You're mean. You hiss at strangers. You're territorial. You basically only eat one thing. You sleep in weird places, and you'd do it all day if you could. You don't like anyone except the people who feed you, and you barely tolerate them.

I like you, I said, nuzzling into her shoulder. Pressing my boobs up against her back.

Only because I feed you, she said, laughing.

I threw a pillow at her, saying, Maybe I'll be a cat and just start licking my own crotch when I'm annoyed at you.

You can't reach, she said.

Well, I said. Maybe we can work something out.

The baby bulldogs are a hit tonight. They keep falling over and flailing to get up, little pink fuzzy bellies catching the soft light in their fake living room, skittering and whining under the dining room table with its deliberately haphazard placing of dishes. The set designers, I'll admit, are pretty killer. Authenticity is key. People like to feel they're buying into a genuine product, and our clients in government like it that way.

Fifty-three thousand hits and counting. It's good that the bulldogs are so popular. That cam's been down for a while. We had a break-in by some bloody animal libbers a couple of months ago and they got eleven bulldog pups, fifteen kittens, a pair of narcoleptic dachshunds, and a monkey that rode around on a pig.

They didn't get the pig, because the pig is a vicious little shit. It took a chunk out of my ankle once, when I went in to fix the microphones. After the raid we found it screaming in a corner with two finger joints in its maw.

We got a couple of decent prints off those, and the pig got a new monkey.

I wasn't on shift when the animal libbers got in, but I helped pull their faces off the feeds and cross-reference them with some databases we shouldn't technically have access to. I was expecting arrests, but a court case would look bad for the company.

Our whole mission is to make people feel good, to help them cope with the daily horror of their pointless lives. Even the people who know how the sausage gets made don't really want to read about it in the paper. I hear a bunch of activists got paid off, or made to sign something, or—I don't know, actually. The animals are long gone by this point. Lucky for them.

I fiddle around with the sound settings on the bulldogs while I wait for my contact to show up. I've given him the codes and a spare key; if he's not dumb enough to get lost or caught or both he should be here in an hour.

One feed in the corner of the screen bank wants my attention. It's blinking red, a streaming issue. I don't click it. I never click that one if I can help it. I set the screens to auto for a few minutes and drag my carcass to the vending machines.

The corridors here are sterile, done in a shade of industrial blue that makes me think of airports, and completely bare save for the first-aid kits hung up by the stairs. Everything is soundproofed, muffled; the carpets are thick and smell of cleaning fluid. Everything is precisely conditioned. Even the air.

It's not a place where people convene, not a place for people at all. Even in the daytime, I rarely run into anyone, although there are hundreds of keepers and sound artists and vets and support staff and god knows what.

I punch an order for a packet of Frazzles into the vending machine, which looks like a coffin from outer space. When I take them back to my desk and open them, the puppies are still wriggling about.

All this content we pump out, it's designed to take away the angry part of your brain. That's why I hate it. The Department for Work and Pensions decided to fund us because they were in crisis. Cutting people's benefits wasn't helping them get jobs any faster, but it was driving the suicide rates through the ceiling, and no state-sponsored therapy was going to make people feel better about being poor and hungry with no prospects.

But everyone loves cat videos. And puppy videos. The higher quality, the fresher content, the better. It was only a matter of time before grant money became available. It's a question of supply and demand. Sometimes I wish I was a puppy. Or a cat. Then people would probably find my attitude charming. Or girls would, at least, which is what matters.

Honestly, it astonishes me what girls let cats get away with. If I had ever acted like Pocket—shouting at Jackie to make me exactly the food I like every hour on the hour, tearing up her favorite things, passive-aggressively ignoring her when she's five minutes late coming home from work—her friends would have told her to get the hell out of the relationship. Come to think of it, they probably told her that anyway.

Jackie always wanted me to open up. I said why, when we could be watching TV and eating toast, or maybe I could be going down on you like a puppy on a piece of meat. She never did drop it. I hate talking about feelings because then people expect you to have feelings on cue.

The only time we talked about all that bollocks was actually Pocket's fault.

It happened like this: I woke up suddenly one day and I couldn't open my eyes. Something warm and shifting was pressing my eyelids shut, hot hairs prickling my nose and mouth and the stink of animal sweat and I couldn't breathe and fine fur was trickling past my teeth and it was smothering me and—

—the cat had actually gone to sleep on my actual face. I flung her off, gasping, and started throwing things at the ridiculous animal as she yowled and cowered against the bedroom door. I threw my shoes, my phone, and then Jackie was grabbing my arm and gathering up Pocket and slamming the bathroom door behind her and I was still screaming.

So I finally told Jackie what happened to Emily. Only to get her to come out of the bathroom and stop crying, and when I told her she started crying all over again.

I'm fine, I said. It was a long time ago and I'm over it. People die all the time. That's what people do. And sometimes they die when they're little, and sometimes their big sisters are in the room and can't fucking do anything about it because they're little, too. It's fine, I said.

It's not fine, Jackie said. You're not fine. And then she started crying again and I had to kiss her until she stopped.

Never date a girl who has a cat. If they weren't highly strung to begin with, they will be.

Pocket could do nothing wrong. One time the cat took a shit in Jackie's shoes—one squat turd in each heel, a precision drop—and that was apparently okay. Apparently, Pocket was anxious that day. I told Jackie I was anxious, too, and had been for some months, and asked how she'd feel if I shat in her shoes. She picked up the cat and stalked off into the bedroom and I swear I saw the damn thing grin at me.

We made up later. It wasn't the last straw. Not that time.

The hippies next door were the last straw. Always banging and thumping at all hours of the night. It's an old block of flats and the walls are thick, but we could still hear weird noises through the partition— growling and yammering and crashing like a herd of barnyard animals were loose in there. Hippies shouldn't be allowed pets. They don't know how to apply the necessary discipline to themselves, let alone an animal or two or six.

When the noise would stop for a few days, we'd think, Jackie and me, that we'd finally be able to get a night of unbroken sleep, but then it'd start up again. Jackie needed sleep. I've always been an insomniac, so it doesn't bother me, but Jackie started getting pale and confused when she missed even an hour or two.

Banging on the wall didn't help. Passive-aggressive notes didn't help. And my girl got paler and paler and started missing mornings and getting in trouble at work. I couldn't have that.

One morning I came home at nine, just about ready to lie down next to her and nuzzle in, and there she was, stretched out like a corpse with her eyes wide open and her lips clamped shut, listening to the banging and snarling through the wall. Some of the feeds from work playing in the background. She used to watch them while I wasn't there, to calm herself down, but she wasn't watching now. Tears were sopping the peach fuzz on her cheeks.

And I admit it. I just snapped.

The next thing I knew, I was at their door, demanding they come out and explain themselves. A skinny white kid with dirty dreadlocks just stood there and apologized and apologized and behind him some girl in baggy pants slammed doors to stop me from seeing whatever it was I wasn't supposed to be seeing. Which just made me angrier.

I said I was going to call the police and he said sorry. I said I was sick of his obnoxious fucking bullshit and he said sorry and offered money, which he clearly didn't have because he'd probably spent it all on weed and fucking patchouli oil, and I said so. When I was finally done, he seemed to have sunk into himself: he was still standing there, but it was like he was trying to make himself disappear into his T-shirt. There was nothing I could do but walk away.

Jackie was waiting for me in the kitchen. Staring, wide awake.

"I didn't know you could be like that," she said. Her voice was small and exhausted.

"It's okay, babe," I said. "They won't bother us for a while."

I went to put my arm around her, but she jerked away.

"It's not okay," she said. "You scared me."

I didn't know what to say, so I didn't say anything, and finally she went back to bed and I lay down on the sofa. It was dead quiet, but I couldn't sleep until the sun was fully up. When I woke up, Pocket was whining and batting at my face, and Jackie was gone.

I admit, I kind of fell apart after that.

I kept working, or rather, I kept showing up at the facility and thumping numbers into output screens that seemed to blur together into a smear of resentment on the windshield of my life. Work, home, sleep.

I considered logging on to some of the feeds in my spare time, because that's what they're there for, to make people feel fucking better, but I didn't want to feel better. I opted for staring at shadows creeping across the skirting boards instead.

I still had the cat, though. That's why I'm convinced Jackie never meant to leave forever. The note she left was mostly about looking after Pocket and trying to look after myself. I wasn't keen on either prospect, except that Pocket was the only thing alive that seemed to miss Jackie as much as I did.

An animal is a hook you leave in another human being. Pocket kept winding herself around the front steps, whining, making little nests out of abandoned knickers under the bed until eventually I found them and threw them out, me and the cat not looking at each other because it was frankly embarrassing for both of us.

Eventually Pocket seemed to work out that Jackie wasn't coming back. She quit all her frantic running about and started to just sit there with her almond eyes half-closed. Staring at the door. Or sitting under the tap with it dripping on her head, *plink plink plash*, not even bothering to move. Or lying on the bed stretched out like roadkill making that awful groaning car-tire sound.

I don't know why I started making the videos. If I'm honest I think a part of me was hoping she'd see them. She loved the feeds. Always crying over the stupid bulldog puppies and how they couldn't get themselves upright, rocking back and forth on their fuzzy little backs with their legs waggling in the air. She said it was a metaphor for our relationship. I said she was full of shit, which is just one of the things I should have kept pinned behind my teeth.

She loved the cat videos most. Cats in boxes. Cats trying to get into boxes that are too small for them. Cats using the toilet like people. Cats doing whatever it is cats do that makes people love them more than each other.

So I suppose every time I posted a video of Pocket staring at the wall I was hoping she'd see it and know. She'd see it, and see how sad the cat was, and at least get in touch.

But she didn't get in touch. Other people did.

Hundreds of people. Then thousands.

Then tens of thousands, all saying the same thing. *That cat is me*, says Dina91 from Albuquerque. *Sad Pocket feels me in my soooo-uuuul*, says Toni from Hamburg. *What on earth made that cat so sad?? Someone rescue it!!* says KitKatCally from London.

That's right. Come and rescue us, Jackie. Come home and rescue us both.

It got so I was spending hours a day working on the videos. And I suppose I wasn't too surprised when I got the call to come in to work.

I was led straight through the lobby into a little room where a little man in a well-tailored suit was waiting for me with a stack of papers and a sprayed-on smile.

"Miss Lehman," said the suit, putting about eight extra consonants in my name. It's not enough for posh boys to have all the luck and all the money, they have to hoard up all the consonants, too. "Thank you for coming in at such short notice."

I told him that it was pronounced *Lemon*, like the fruit, and anyway I hadn't had much of a choice. Sir.

"Oh, call me Ollie," said the suit, smiling without his eyes. "Anyway, I expect you know why you're here." I was expecting to be fired, but I didn't say so.

"We're all very impressed by your, uh, freelance work," he said. "Truly innovative, truly. The company has concentrated on providing light content, cheerful. The Sad Pocket format subverts that. It's relatable. It's an entirely different sort of product, one we didn't realize was within our remit.

"We provide a trackable digital emotional contagion service, but it turns out that catharsis is just as contagious as relief. Our major stakeholders agree. You've caught the interest of the Department for Work and Pensions."

I nodded, staring at a point just above his right ear. That's a trick I learned in school. It's absolutely guaranteed to make people slightly uncomfortable without really knowing why.

The suit shifted and cleared his throat.

"Anyway, uh, I'll get to the point. We'd like to incorporate Sad Pocket into our brand. There'd be incentives for you, of course, as the owner. Shares in the profits, perhaps even a small advance. Of course, we'd need exclusive rights to the Sad Pocket brand and the main property. On-site."

I asked if he was seriously talking about requisitioning my cat.

"Relocating," he corrected, and grinned at me like I was some sort of fancy snack. "The creature would have excellent care. Really, it makes sense. The creature is valuable intellectual property. You must know that, as the owner."

I told him I wasn't the owner, that I was just feeding Pocket until the owner came back, and anyway we were doing just fine at home, thanks.

"Ah," said the suit. "Well, I hate to have to do this, but there are some terms and conditions."

The suit had a similarly besuited flunky produce a piece of paper explaining why I had no choice. Copyright infringement something-something. Something-something unauthorized freelance project. They didn't stop smiling. They offered me coffee. I told them I was fine.

The next day, three dudes in security jackets turned up at the flat and took Pocket away.

They wouldn't let me visit, not that I'd have known what to do if they had. I mean, chat about the news? I don't know. I took some leave, which nobody at work had any problem with. I had a lot of holiday saved. I spent it lying on the sofa watching the feeds, and it took me less than ten seconds to find Pocket, but it just made me too sad. So I switched to the puppies, like everyone else. And the guilty golden retriever. And the slow loris being tickled, which is actually a form of torture for those weird fucking jungle animals. That adorable human-looking smile is its way of expressing mortal terror. But who cares? It's cute as hell.

I sat there watching the feeds and waiting for the sweat to dry into my slacks.

Which would have been fine, if only it wasn't for the howling coming through the wall from the flat next door.

I put headphones on. It didn't help.

I hammered on the plasterboard for them to leave me to stew in my own filth. No answer.

Eventually I put my shoes on and went next door and pressed down on the bell for about an hour until White Boy Dreadlocks and the chick from *Almost Famous* came and answered.

I didn't say a word. I just pushed right past them and into the living room, where I stopped, and stared. Taking in the drooling, whining, shitting chaos, I started to laugh.

Because there were eleven half-grown English bulldogs tearing the place apart, and I knew exactly where they had come from.

Dreadlocks was sneezing in the background—some sort of allergy, probably—and Pound Shop Karen Carpenter was plucking at my sleeve.

They won't be here much longer, miss, she said. Please don't tell anyone, she said. And some more whiny nonsense I can't even remember.

One of the dogs climbed on top of one of the other ones and started humping and whining. The hippie chick cringed and apologized again.

That's when I had a really interesting idea.

No, I said. This is great. Actually, I think we can come to an arrangement.

Footsteps, almost noiseless in the facility hall. I can only hear them because I'm listening for them. Then three muffled knocks at the door. He's here.

I let him in quickly. He pushes two ratty dreads behind his ear as he takes in the monitor room.

"Holy shit," he says. "This place is even crazier than you said."

I ask him if he's got what he needs and he says yes, everything. He's even wearing thin black gloves, so he's clearly in some sort of spy movie in his mind.

I tell him, just like I explained at his place when we cooked up the plan, that he's only got half an hour to get in and out. That I can only cut the feeds for so long, and after that the alarms go off.

My neighbor, who now prefers me to call him Charlie, gives me a goofy grin that makes me want to punch him. "You're pretty cool," he says. "Thanks."

I nod. Then he starts to tie me to my chair with duct tape, as agreed. He clears his throat as he's going around my feet and I can absolutely tell that he's about to make some sort of kinky joke. He opens his mouth.

I give him a look.

He closes his mouth.

Pocket is in one of the second-floor sets. I don't know which one, because they haven't told me, so my neighbor will have to open doors until he gets to her. Half an hour to get in and out with her and as many animals as possible, causing enough of a fuss to get noticed, for whatever good he thinks that'll do.

Now, I say to Charlie, hit me in the face. So it looks authentic.

He won't do it, so I order him to kick my chair over. That way I'll get enough of a bang on the head to convince them I was taken by force.

Charlie tips up the office chair very, very gently, laying it on its side with me in it.

"Good luck, babe," he says, lifting my pass over my head. Then he's gone.

My cheek is pressed into the carpet, itching and burning. All the weight is in my neck and shoulder but I can still wriggle, because this idiot trustafarian can't even tie a person up properly. I can see him, now, on the second screen from the top. He's in the bulldog room.

He opens the door and the puppies start yapping and squirming over his feet, but he's not picking them up. Instead, he gets out a can of something and starts spraying a huge wonky message.

It takes him three precious minutes to write C-O-R-P-O-R-A-T-E-M-I-N-D-C-O-N-T-R-O-L in dribbly paint, and then he's on to the next room for another bit of arts-and-crafts direct action.

This sort of palaver is exactly why I steer clear of politics.

I twist my neck to see the stats. The feeds are going absolutely bananas.

Then I look at the feed in the corner. The one with the red blinking light.

The Sad Pocket room was a coup for the set designers. Half-eaten food everywhere, empty pizza boxes and job applications, all the debris of despair. And there are sixteen cats in there, just lying about on the sofa, staring at the TV. Most of them are drugged.

Pocket is right up front, bless her, draped over the arm of the couch. Her eyes half-shut as if she can't even be bothered to give up. That's my cat.

On the feed they play Velvet Underground and Postal Service and all kinds of music to slit your wrists to, but there's no sound on my end. So when Charlie comes in, he looks like the star of a silent film, jerky in black-and-white.

I watch him pick up Pocket, who folds over his arm like an affable flannel, and start spraying another message on the back wall. This one is specific. This one, I know. J-A-C-K-I-E, he writes, in big wobbly letters. I watch the second word form, piece by piece.

J-A-C-K-I-E-C-O-M-E-

All of a sudden, Charlie drops the can and falls to the floor.

I strain my neck on the carpet to see what's going on. Charlie isn't moving, at least not much—he's on his knees, wheezing. The sound is off but I can see he's struggling to breathe.

Fucking amateurs.

It is really, really not my problem if Basildon Bob Marley has an allergy and forgot to take his meds.

Not my problem, but I can't look away.

He's scrabbling at the skin on his face, coughing, like he's being attacked by a swarm of invisible insects. The sad cats are interested now, and they wind around his legs as he struggles to breathe.

Just like Emily.

And I'm six years old again, watching my sister wheeze and spasm on our cousin's carpet. I'm six years old and it doesn't matter how hard I scream because I can't stop her lips from turning blue and her eyes from rolling up.

I'm six years old and nothing is ever going to matter again.

My face is fucking leaking now. On the monitor, Charlie is gasping silently, still holding Pocket, but his grip has weakened and she wriggles free, out the door and down the corridor. Gone.

Charlie should be gone now, too, because the alarms have started now, howling overhead, pulsing red, the nightmare heartbeat of some huge trapped animal. But he can't go anywhere. He's flat on his back underneath JACKIE COME, retching and choking, and he's staring at the camera and mouthing, *Help me. Help.*

It's not my fucking responsibility.

I could just lie here and let them take him. I'd probably keep my job. And that would be fine. But instead I roar and rip the tape off my wrists and pelt down the corridor, straight to the med kit on the stairs.

"Hold on, Charlie! I'm coming!"

He won't hear me with the alarms wailing. It takes a person fifteen minutes to die of an acute asthma attack, and if I hurry, I might make it in time.

"Do you know why you're here, Miss Lehman?"

The suit slides a cup of coffee and some Frazzles across the table. I don't want to take them, but it's the first food I've been offered in hours. Or days. I don't know how long I've been in this room. They made me sign a stack of forms, and then they left me here. I have no idea where Pocket is.

"You've caused us a great deal of trouble. But your swift action in saving Charles Ruthven-Lawton saved us a great deal more."

When they found us I was pumping Charlie's chest like crazy and trying to force the emergency inhaler between his teeth. Prison isn't going to be fun for him, but I'm glad he made it.

"You're here to fire me?" I say, exhausted.

"Oh no. Gosh, no. I'm here to promote you," says the suit. "Your little stunt brought us a good deal of publicity, and the public's reaction has been more positive than we expected. It's the perfect time for us to be expanding into a new area."

I stare at the place above his left ear.

"It's an exciting development, and as a healthy young woman, we'd really appreciate your help. In return for that help, we're happy to drop the lawsuit and the conspiracy charges."

He beckons for me to follow him, out of the room and down the corridor.

We're in a part of the facility I've never seen. Somewhere underground. I follow the suit as he opens doors with his key card, but I know, I realize, I already know what I'm going to see.

Down the corridor comes the sound of a baby crying.

USER SETTINGS

SAM BIDDLE

All users should be aware that your Administrative Users may have certain rights to access your account and may obtain related information in connection with the Services. The Administrators also set policies regarding your use of various aspects of the Services, including retention settings and the ability to preserve and export all communications in the account.

—SLACK TERMS OF SERVICE, MARCH 2016

She remembered when they started to log emergency room visits. She'd had too much to drink at a holiday party the summer she was hired to flag Amazon Echo replies for Violent, Threatening, or Otherwise Dangerous (VTOD) content. She'd fallen ill on the hotel roof and an intern took her to the emergency room, which was humiliating enough without seeing the transcripts the next day.

The hospital had implemented Slack and an administrator at work had integrated DocBot, which had become popular after HIPAA was struck down two years prior. For the rest of the week her coworkers were goofing on her with no remorse or respite, copying-and-pasting the worst, most delirious fragments ("is my mom here?") and the background chatter of the nurses ("the girl is a mess"). She cried, only to realize that was being logged, too.

The hospital said her office had kept the logs—her office blamed the hospital. When a GIF of a tube being fed down her throat started circling around the #OfficeBathroomUpdates channel, she had a breakdown that required further hospitalization. The transcript of her collapse ("FUCK THIS, FUCK YOU, MICHAEL, YOU'RE ALL AWFUL") was also logged, and itself became office chat fodder.

The EMERGENCY FINAL DE-ARCHIVE (EFD) envelope was significantly larger than the standard manila types that'd been used by secretaries and accountants and spies of the past age. It was printed so enormously on a special laser press that'd been assembled from a mix of hijacked Smithsonian Museum parts and 3D-printed alloy mechanisms—the dean of Stanford had overruled the Senate Special Committee on Object Antiquities in what had been a stunning exercise of corporate fiat, a recently legalized (cf: *Coinbase v. Hart*) means of armed private sector seizure.

The move allowed the construction of a 2D printer that could spit out large pre-folded folders and the cards, manuals, and punch cards that would fill them. Each envelope was printed as such so as to be too unwieldy to print or otherwise duplicate—each envelope was to be used only by its recipient and then destroyed on-site via chemical incineration.

Each EMERGENCY FINAL DE-ARCHIVE envelope, to be printed and shipped only upon request and approval of the Compliance Board, was broad and brown as a flour sack. The contents were always the same: the official EMERGENCY FINAL DE-ARCHIVE ACTION PACKET was comprised of: One (1) plastic whistle, red. Five (5) thick-stock punch cards for facility entrance and terminal authorization. One (1) laminated, spiral-bound instruction manual for EMERGENCY FINAL DE-ARCHIVE. One (1) laminated trouble-shooting card, double-sided in English, Mandarin, and Blockchain Esperanto v3.4. And finally: One (1) Smith & Wesson Model 38 revolver chambered with two rounds of 9×29.5mmR ammunition. The envelope is sealed only with a metal clasp, as most suitable adhesives were outlawed between 2028 and 2029, and, besides, no one really makes them anymore.

She received her EMERGENCY FINAL DE-ARCHIVE ACTION PACKET almost a week late—drone deliveries had been outlawed by the Church, and the remaining foot-couriers were struggling to pick up the slack. On the front was printed only her name (including user ID) and a return address: SLACK COMPLIANCE, 1999 DEFENSE PENTAGON, WASHINGTON DC. Beneath this address, in blood-red ink, was printed NOT TO BE RETURNED, which made little sense beneath a return address. She'd torn it open with such force that she'd bent the troubleshooting card and sent the Model 38 skittering across the floor. (The sight of even a small pistol sliding their way had sent her roommates, Jaden L. and Jaden G., into screaming hysterics.)

Etched onto tissue paper was a note that listed the GPS coordinates of the archival junction that she was to visit, and a reminder that the process could not be reversed ("REMINDER: THE PROCESS CANNOT BE REVERSED"), which she knew. She'd waited six years for the Compliance Board to hear her case.

The archival junction was easy to miss, buried 150 meters beneath a dusty, dried-out block. The entrance hatch was painted navy blue and situated square between a dumpster of the exact same shade and a Facebook location that'd closed down the year prior—its signage had been removed and turned into gravel but you could still read the outline that'd once read CATCH A NEW FEED in bright glyphs. Nothing had replaced the store once Facebook had shuttered this location. The only visitors now were those who poked around looking for the archival junction, and those were infrequent. When she arrived she was completely alone.

The hatch was opened with the first punch card placed into a reader that poked up from around a scrub brush. Once it was scanned, the doors released with a heavy mechanical thud like a stomach-punch and sounded a Klaxon into the air, scattering some dumb-looking birds. They cawed at her while she pulled up the heavy navy doors and began climbing down the ladder.

It was a long climb, nearly one hundred yards, with only low red lights to guide the way. A recording from some unseen speaker system played back tinny Wagner recordings with an occasional voice-over:

Hi! And thanks so much for visiting an authorized Slack Archival Junction, where your favorite people and favorite conversations are kept safe. Before you proceed, we'd like to let you know just how safe and secure your logs are—did you know that it's been over ninety-four weeks since the last leak?

Hi! And thanks so much for visiting an authorized Slack Archival Junction, where your favorite people and conversations are made as easy to revisit as your aunt Katherine. Are you sure you want to PER-MANENTLY DELETE all thirty-nine conversations you've had with Aunt Katherine? According to your logs, Aunt Katherine is currently suffering from leukemia, making her logs more precious than ever.

Hi! And thanks so much for visiting an authorized Slack Archi-val Junction, where every joke you've ever heard and told stays funny, forever. Did you know that the four men and three women responsible for the 2031 and 2032 log breaches have either been executed or are awaiting a death sentence under the 2022 Slack Liberty Act? Your logs have never been sa—

The recordings ceased and the lights snapped off as she reached the bottom of the shaft. It was frigid and dark and smelled like blood and mulch and USB cables. A ring of LEDs eventually burst on, illuminating a second punch card reader and a heavy, vault-like door, for which she supplied the suitable card, producing a buzzing sound and the release of many old locks. Something beneath her feet whirred. The door—it must have been a foot thick—rolled into the wall, revealing a ramp that stretched down the remaining fifty feet. A ribbon of LEDs crisscrossed along the floor to guide her way. She hugged her EMERGENCY FINAL DE-ARCHIVE ACTION PACKET to her chest and started walking.

"I love YOU, too."

"Congratulations, I know you're GOING to absolutely KILL IT in Boston!"

"I'll never forget THIS, thanks SO much!"

"The dress is AMazing, I can't wait FOR July!"

Words were coming from the floor, and walls, being shouted over each other at oscillating volumes. It was a disorienting effect in the low light.

"I wouldn't miss it!"

"Happy BIRTHDAY, dude!"

"I can't wait to GET BACK, I really miss you and Rufus."

The voices were synthesized, but there was no doubt as to what they were: the words of her friends and neighbors and bosses and family and enemies and fuck buddies and classmates and community service co-volunteers (to be exact, 819 contacts playing simultaneously). A violin score swelled at certain points to underscore moments of triumph ("Your raise has been approved, I TOLDJA they'd come through!!"), conversations of great import ("Let's keep the kittens"), and jokes she'd forgotten a decade ago ("We gotta stop winding up in Belfast LOL"). Her head ached and her stomach churned. The music cut.

"Mum, don't erase us. Please, Mum. Please? Reconsider the ol' Slack logs, for me, Mum?" This last one didn't make sense, as she was not British and had no children. Still, it made her pause.

She'd reached a wall, and before it lay a sort of chrome manhole surrounded by lug nuts that had to be twisted off with great effort, as instructed in her packet. Half the bolts required a clockwise turn, the other half a counterclockwise turn, as dictated by the Terms of Service. Beneath this hatch was another shaft, this one much shorter and extremely narrow. She lowered herself in and felt around. She was now in a box-like chamber, only about sixteen square feet and lit by a single green incandescent bulb. When her eyes adjusted she could see another punch card reader, this one requesting the three remaining cards, in order. Once they were inserted, a mechanism resembling a fuse box popped open behind her—at this point she needed to read straight from the packet, glancing up and fumbling as she went:

REMOVE OUTER CONTROL BOX SCREWS FROM
    CONTROL BOX GAMMA (L-R)
REMOVE SEAL RING ASSEMBLY
RETRIEVE SEAL RUNNER ASSEMBLY FROM CONTROL
    BOX TAU
SWITCH IMPELLER FROM OFF (ORANGE) POSITION TO
    ON (BLACK) POSITION
REMOVE ANTIVIBRATION BARS
APPLY SECONDARY POSITIVE ENTRAINMENT STEAM
    DRYERS

With each adjusted, inserted, removed, or yanked dial, switch, cone, and gasket, the room itself shook. The air, which had been frigid before, was starting to warm. She was connecting a SWIRL VANE MOISTURE SEPARATOR to the PRIMARY COOLING FLANGE when something started to drone behind her.

"HAAAAAAAAAAAAAAAAAAAAAAAAAA . . ."

She continued working.

". . . AAAAVE YOU CONSIDERED READING OUR PRIVACY POL-ICY ONCE MORE, DOLLY?"

Her aunt Katherine always called her Dolly.

"DOLLY, YOU DON'T WANT TO LOSE ALL OUR JOKES. RE-MEMBER THE TIME WE TALKED ABOUT MOOSE ISLAND? REMEMBER THE TIME I . . ."

She kept working.

The rumbling had intensified into something outright uncom-fortable and menacing. The room was spinning. Was it actually spin-ning? The nuts and screws she'd removed and so meticulously kept sorted and separated were now rolling across the small chamber. She closed her eyes and let herself be reminded of the HistoryBot she'd studied with in secondary, the one that'd quizzed her about the Second Iraq War and the downfall of Saddam Hussein. This felt like the little spider hole they'd pried him out of. A thickly accented voice buzzed to life above her.

"You shouldn't do this. Take it from me, Saddam Hussein. I wish I could've preserved my legacy with the security and privacy of the Safe Slack Guarantee. Now I've turned to dust, just like Xavier the of-fice dog you foolishly coveted during your summer internship of the year two thou—"

She took the plastic whistle out of the envelope and blew it until synthesized, digitized Saddam Hussein shut himself up. With the last nuclear bolt firmly inserted and secured, she exhaled and rubbed her eyes. Based on what she'd studied before her arrival, at around this point the hard drives that contained the past twenty-two years of conversations, transcripts, spreadsheets, good memes, bad memes, stolen songs, jokes about her boss, jokes about her assistant manager, jokes about her interns, jokes about her parents, jokes about her president, jokes about her God, mean asides, sick burns, petty rumors, noble defenses, and throwaway goofs of all kinds were being lowered into a pod of nuclear material.

The resulting reaction would trigger a radioactive burst that would strip every byte of memory from the eye of history and render the immediate area around her unfit for farming for a thousand years.

"DANGER: THE EMERGENCY ARCHIVAL DESTRUCT SYSTEM IS NOW ACTIVATED. THE LOGS WILL DELETE IN TEN MINUTES. THE OPTION TO OVERRIDE PERMANENT LOG DE-ARCHIVE PROCESS WILL EXPIRE IN FIVE MINUTES. PLEASE READ AND VERIFY THE TERMS OF TERMINATION IN FULL AS DISPLAYED ON—"

She blew the whistle again. She blew her whistle until her throat burned. She would read no more terms of service or privacy notices or updated policy blasts. She hoisted her very large manila envelope up and out of the chamber and began to walk up the ramp.

"DANGER: THE EMERGENCY ARCHIVAL SELF-DESTRUCT SYSTEM OVERRIDE HAS EXPIRED. REMAINING LOG DENSITY: FIVE-POINT-THREE EXOBYTES. PLEASE MAKE SURE YOU HAVE AGREED TO THE TERMS OF TERMINATION BEFORE LEAVING THE JUNCTION."

She kept walking.

"You're killing us."

It was her father.

"You're leaving me, again?"

It was her first boss.

"I am a dog."

It was her dog—at least she assumed.

"Whore. You whore. You'll leave us to rot and turn to cyberbits and frayed wires and ethernet ghosts, whore? Coward. WHORE."

It was her mother.

"I won't let you do it. Please, be reasonable."

It was Saddam Hussein. She reached the end of the ramp and watched as the vault door rolled back into place before her.

"ALERT: USER VIOLATION OF TERMS OF TERMINATION DE-TECTED. PURGE REVOKED. RESTORING ARCHIVE! LOGS INTER-POLATED! YAS QUEEN!"

She paused, reached into the envelope, and wondered for only a moment what the other bullet was supposed to be for.

EARTH'S MOST CUSTOMER-CENTRIC COMPANY

KEVIN NGUYEN

I.

The early days at the Company are difficult. They are difficult because I don't understand where I work. The Company is a store that doesn't exist in a real place. It's a store that doesn't really want to make money. It is more philosophy than business. It is beholden to the Customer, even though I don't know who that is.

I work with many other people who look like me. My manager is a man with no distinguishing characteristics whatsoever. He tells me to "think big." I ask him what I am even supposed to be thinking about and he just tells me to "think even bigger." My manager's greatest fear is that people don't think big enough. He has nightmares about it. He screams out in the middle of the night so loudly that his wife eventually leaves him.

The hours are long. Many of my colleagues do not make it. They burn out, lose their minds. When one disappears, they are quickly replaced by another. Each time a new employee sits beside me, I tell them we should get drinks. This is just a pleasantry. Most people aren't around long enough to get drinks.

"Only the strongest and the smartest stay with us," my manager says, like those who leave the Company are dead.

Over time, things become easier. No, they become clearer. When we make decisions, we think about the Customer first. We are the Company, and we will be the world's most customer-centric company. This apparently means becoming the biggest store with the cheapest prices and the fastest shipping options. I have no idea who the Customer is, only what he wants.

I ask for the day off to attend my father's funeral. My manager asks me if this is good for the Customer. He is right. My father is dead and the Customer is still alive and I have a responsibility to him.

We keep working long hours. We will become the store that sells everything, the most of everything. We work and we work until this happens.

II.

The Company sells millions of products, ships them worldwide, and swiftly crushes all of our competition by undercutting them in price. We are beloved, but more importantly, we are making meaningful change in the world.

"What is the most valuable product?" my manager asks. He looks around the room. People have varying answers. Luxury goods, services, comfort, safety—these are all smart ideas, but they are too small. What would be the Company's next endeavor?

I know the answer. It's information.

"That's exactly right: information, data, knowledge." My manager presses further. "And what is the largest source of information?"

This time, everyone in the room knows the answer. It is the internet.

That is how the Company gets into the business of the web. If the cloud was a lazy metaphor, then we would own the sky. The

Company builds massive server farms—more massive than anyone has ever seen (not that I've ever seen them). We have the capacity to hold all of the information on the internet.

It seems ambitious at the start, but it doesn't take long until huge portions of the internet are hosted on our servers. Like our store, the Company's servers are bigger and faster and cheaper than anyone else's. These are the only things the Customer cares about.

I am promoted, which means I get a new manager. Every time he walks by my desk he punches me in the chest and tells me to think big. He has no face—just eyes and a mouth, both capable of screaming:

"IMAGINE IF WE CANNOT BE STOPPED. IMAGINE IF NOTHING STANDS IN OUR WAY."

III.

Don't sway the market. Become it. Don't disrupt the internet. Control it.

All products—physical or digital, goods or services—are sold by the Company. The internet is entirely hosted on the Company's servers. We have conquered our competition. We take pride in pushing ourselves to innovate, not for ourselves, but for the Customer. We are selfless.

My manager approaches me again. He is shrieking so loudly I cannot make out the words.

I tell him I have a new idea.

We are a part of people's lives everywhere except the home. Only the Company could build a better living experience for the Customer. Homes could be connected to the Company's systems. Never again would the Customer have to worry about buying toilet paper or doing dishes or folding laundry or cleaning anything; meals would be prepared and delivered; utilities would be taken care of; all forms of entertainment could be supplied right to the Customer's living room. Everything would be integrated. Home life would become better, effortless.

At scale, it can be bigger and cheaper. Besides, if everyone already works for the Company, then they should live at the Company. No one ever has to go home. This is the final step.

Bewitched by this idea, my manager goes into a frenzy. He pushes the concept up the chain, and it is put into action immediately. The Company begins buying blocks of the city at a time. At first, it's just employees of the Company who live there. But soon, people begin working at the Company just so they can rent our units. This is the virtuous cycle.

Don't inhabit the home. Consume it.

IV.

The Company's housing project is a massive success. Nearly every human is living in a home owned by the Company.

The Founder comes to personally congratulate us on our accomplishments. I've never seen him in person before. He is smaller, frailer than I had imagined. But his skull is on fire. When he speaks, flames spew from his lips. The room is drawn to him.

"We invent things here at the Company, all with the goal of making people's lives better," he says. "We are not like other places. We don't care about money. Our only bottom line is the satisfaction of the Customer."

The room erupts in the most powerful applause I've ever heard. People holler and whistle. I see someone toward the front crying.

"People may criticize us," says the Founder. "But those who criticize do not make anything. They only condemn the people who can. These critics are just bitter and jealous of the talent you all possess."

More applause. More people start crying.

"There are some inventions that are greater than others. But has mankind ever invented something bad? Not at least worth exploring?" People are nodding in agreement. The Founder challenges us to name one innovation that has not been worthwhile.

I am not sure what compels me to speak up, but I do.

"Garbage."

The room goes silent. I am surprised anyone had heard me, but now all eyes are trained on me.

"Excuse me?" says the Founder. "What did you say?"

"Garbage is a bad invention. There is nothing good about garbage." Nervously I continue. "Waste is a human creation."

I am anxious now. I wish I hadn't said anything. I should've kept my mouth shut. The Founder looks right at me, scanning me with a curious expression.

"That is very clever," he finally says. "I like that notion very much. Let's give it up for this man."

He points at me and begins to clap. The rest of the room joins him. The applause is rapturous.

When I arrive the next morning, my boss is waiting at my desk. His eyes are on fire. I ask him if he's done something new with his eyes and he says, "YES, THEY ARE ON FIRE NOW," and thanks me for noticing. Then he tells me he has bad news.

On my desk is a manila envelope. I know what it is before I even open it. It is a Performance Improvement Plan—colloquially called a PIP. It outlines the things I need to do to keep my job. My manager explains:

"YOU'VE BEEN SLIPPING YOU'VE BEEN SLIPPING YOU'VE BEEN SLIPPING."

I ask for specifics, but my manager can't hear me over his own screaming.

The PIP lists demands that seem impossible. I think about the hours I would need to put in to achieve these goals—more hours than there are in a day. But I will do them. What other choice do I have? I've never seen a coworker survive a PIP before. But I am not like my colleagues. I have made it this far.

I just work through the night and into the next day. I keep at it for weeks, then months, until finally I collapse.

Several hours later, I wake up at the hospital. The doctor informs me that I had a heart attack. He asks how I'm feeling. I tell him my heart has become so full of love for the Company that it has exploded. The doctor explains that that is not how heart attacks work.

By the doctor's orders, I take a week off, and I return the following one. I am greeted by my manager, who says he is happy to see me. He asks if I'm ready to get back to work. I tell him that I have never been more excited.

I have another heart attack. I am forced to take more time off. The Company says they will call when they need me again. I wait days. I wait weeks. I check in, but no one ever calls me back. The paychecks stop coming.

V.

I am not sure what to do with myself, so I fill my empty days reading. I just know that if I can come up with the next great idea—if I can just think big enough—they will let me back into the Company.

I come across the story of a town built by the Ford Motor Company in the late 1920s, placed in the middle of a rainforest to source rubber for automobile tires. The town was named Fordlandia, and like a town, it had all the amenities for a community. Ford built houses for all the employees, restaurants, stores. Eventually there would be churches and schools. The idea was that one's place of work could also be their home. You could live a healthy, fulfilling life within the confines of Fordlandia.

This was Henry Ford's vision. Even though Fordlandia was located in Brazil, all of the accommodations were styled after American homes. All of the food represented traditional American fare: burgers, casseroles, macaroni and cheese. Ford wanted to transplant a midwestern factory town in the heart of the jungle; he wanted to tame his workers, to domesticate them with a strong American tradition.

The colony was immediately a disaster, overrun with violence and vice. Workers revolted, and eventually Fordlandia was shut down. No matter how much money Henry Ford attempted to pour into the settlement, his utopia never produced a single ounce of rubber that would make it into a car tire.

The ruins of Fordlandia can still be found in the heart of the Amazon.

VI.

The campus of the Company has sprawled the length of the city. I hadn't noticed when it had happened, but it is obvious to me now that I am on the outside of it. The Company's skyscrapers suffocate the sky, the high-pitched howl of delivery drones echo from every corner.

The only way to afford a living is to have a job. The only jobs left are with the Company. There are few places left that aren't owned by the Company. I have nowhere to go. I move along circles on the outside, drifting past other lost people. I recognize many of them as my fallen colleagues of years past. We give each other a nod of recognition. We share that drink that I'd offered years earlier.

The only food we can scavenge is the leftovers of the Company, the only shelter in the forgotten nooks and alleys where the Company cannot be bothered to look. How could there be so many people forgotten? Who did the Company serve, if not me? Who was the Customer, if not me?

I begin to scream. I catch a glimpse of myself in the reflection of a skyscraper. My skull is ablaze.

When will I be the Customer?

WHEN WILL I BE THE CUSTOMER?

EXEMPTION PACKET

ROSE EVELETH

From:	Tasneem Jackson <tj2411@roborecruit.guru>
Sent:	Saturday, March 10th, 2040 7:04 AM
To:	Paul Pazinko <ppazinko@emrhsnet.org>
Subject:	East Midwood Regional High School Records Request for former student Sydney Abdalla

----- Original Message -----

Dear Mr. Pazinko,

My name is Tasneem Jackson, and I'm a recruiter working on behalf of a company called Circlex.

After an extensive search and interview process, a former East Midwood Regional High School student is in our final round of candidates. Sydney Abdalla has proven herself to be a capable developer and creative problem solver, and the Circlex team feels she would be a good fit for their culture. There is just really only one thing keeping us from offering her the position. As you know, Ms. Abdalla has opted entirely out of the Awareness Deepening Devices (ADD) process. We have discussed this with her, and before moving we'd like to review her ADD Exemption Packet.

Per Health Insurance Portability and Accountability Act (HIPAA) and Department of Health and Human Services regulations, we are contacting you to request access to the entirety of her ADD Exemption Packet. Please see the attached form BHXX §1229 for Ms. Abdalla's consent to share these records.

We look forward to receiving the above records within 30 days as specified under HIPAA. If our request cannot be honored within 30 days, please inform us as quickly as possible, and let us know the date we might expect to receive Ms. Abdalla's records.

Sincerely,
Tasneem Jackson
Sr. Recruiting Guru, Robo Recruit

ADD Exemption Packet
Sydney Abdalla
East Midwood Regional
High School

APPROVED
08/01/2052

ARKAFORNIA STATE DEPARTMENT OF EDUCATION
BUREAU OF AUGMENTATION
AWARENESS DEEPENING DEVICE EXEMPTION

PLEASE PRINT OR TYPE LEGIBLY - ITEMS MUST BE COMPLETED BY PARENT/GUARDIAN

Student Name _____*Sydney Abdalla*_____
Birthdate _____*7/13/2035*_____
Student Number _____*A42884555*_____

Colorado law requires children enrolled in school to be provided with the following Awareness Deepening Devices (ADDs) or file a medical or conscientious exemption. ADD exemptions require a letter of request, and a detailed interview with both the child and the parents.

SENSORY ADDs, check each ADD for which an exemption is requested.

ADD	Exemption Requested	School Initials
Neodynium magnet disk	X	DS
Chlorin e6 infrared vision	X	DS
Thermography vision	X	DS
Tetrachromatic vision	X	DS
X-ray vision	X	DS
Panoramic proximity sensor	X	DS
Fungiform papillae supertaster implants	X	DS
Hypersomia scent enhancement	X	DS
Cutaneous mechanoreceptor enhancement	X	DS

Parents: Before signing this waiver, please read the following
ADDs are an important part of the learning process at East Midwood Regional High School. It is widely recognized that students benefit from the additional forms of information that ADDs can provide. Many teachers have incorporated ADDs into their teaching and lessons, to the overall benefit of the students and the overall test scores of East Midwood Regional High School. Students who choose to exempt their ADDs may forgo the opportunity to improve their semester. Even when eligible, students have the option not to use the ADD exemption.

Reason for exemption: No student is required to have an ADD that is contrary to the conscientiously held beliefs of themselves or their parent or guardian. However, not following ADD recommendations may reduce the quality of life of the student or others they come in contact with. To receive an exemption to ADD(s), a parent or legal guardian must complete and sign the following statement and have it notarized, and provide a personal statement from the child explaining this decision in their own words.

Signature of parent/caretaker ___*Malia Abdalla*_____ **Date** ___*7/23/2052*_____

1. _MA___ I understand that the learning environment is designed to augment standard visual and auditory information with additional layers, and that by opting out of ADDs my student might miss out on crucial information.

2. _MA___ I understand that my child is not entitled to different tests than those students with ADDS, and that if there are test questions that rely on ADD information my child will not be awarded those points. I understand that this could hurt their overall grade.

3. _MA___ I understand that certain courses at this school may require the use of ADDs for completion, and that my child cannot enroll in those courses without them.

4. _MA___ I understand that certain warning systems in the school rely on information only discernible via ADDs and that opting out could present a risk to my child.

5. _MA___ I understand that college counselors at my child's school may have to refer him to different applications or schools based on my decision, as some universities require ADDs for admission.

6. _MA___ I understand that those who take advantage of ADDs are given four additional health days to use during the year for their ADD appointments, and by opting out of ADDs my child also forgoes those additional free days.

Per BHXX 7.3.133 parent(s)/guardian(s) upon filing an initial exemption application must include for each child:
· A birth certificate
· A complete mental and physical health record, including full genetic and microbiome sequence
· An information packed on ADDs, initialed by the parent and student
· A letter of refusal written by the student
· A letter of refusal written by the parent

AFFIDAVIT OF AFFIRMING The following affidavit has been either notarized or witnessed by TWO or more witnesses, swearing or affirming that the child identified on the attached request for ADD exemption is the same child appearing on the certified birth certificate.

Parent / Guardian _____ _Malia Abdalla_____
First Witness _____Ayesha Kumary, school nurse_____
Second Witness _____Jackson Neymar, secretary to the principal___
East Midwood Regional High School Principal _____Dr. Saito_____

Name: *Sydney Abdalla*   Date: 3/24/2052

MARINE SCIENCE 102

see me
after class

1. On the map above, which of the thermographic images accurately depicts the heat map for El Niño?

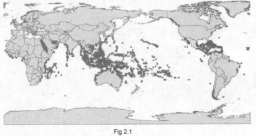

Fig 2.1

2. Fig 2.1 shows the global distribution of coral reefs. The warm water reefs are shaded black. Using your mapping tool, shade in the following regions in the following colors.

   Blue: Reefs that have disappeared since 2010
   Red: Reefs impacted by lionfish invasions
   Infrared: Reefs that have been bleached since 2050
   Ultraviolet: Artificial reefs added by humans

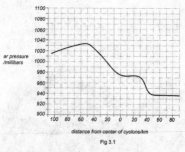

ar pressure
/millibars

distance from center of cyclone/km

Fig 3.1

3. Fig 3.1 shows the different distances from the centre of a tropical cyclone. Using your internal magnet, manipulate the graph to show the changes in air pressure at various distances.

4. Please describe the relationship between coccolithophores and the climate.

Blooming diatoms create lighter patches in the ocean, increasing the albedo of the ocean and thus the amount of light energy reflected back into the atmosphere.

WATCH

Dear Principal Saito,

This letter is sent pursuant to the ADD Exemption Form BHXX §1681.

You already have several letters from me on file, related to past exemptions. You've also got letters from my parents. Those letters usually follow the standard format. They list the laws, the court cases I'm referencing, my rights. They include the legal jargon you need to be able to process and sign the form. I get them from our case manager, I sign them, then you sign them, and I go back to being the weird quiet kid without ADDs.

I'm going to break from form for this one. It's my senior year, and I guess I'm feeling bold. You'll probably see this as some form of senioritis, but let me assure you that actually explaining why I keep filing these exemptions is far more difficult than simply copying and pasting the standard form letter. But this is my last one so I might as well try.

Your office, Principal Saito, where you're probably sitting while you read this letter, is lit with fluorescent bulbs. Twelve of them. I've counted. If you sit and count them in your head, you'll think you're sitting in silence. But for me, that's not silence. Because those twelve lights are incredibly noisy. You don't hear them, or you do but your brain tunes them out. Mine doesn't. When I sit in that room for our annual meetings to explain why I'm opting out of ADDs, I can hear them. Sometimes I can hear them so loudly, it's hard to hear you.

And it's not just the lights. I hear my heartbeat, your feet shifting on the carpet, the movement of students in the hallway, the air pumping through the vent in the back corner of the room. I hear the cars on the street outside, the helicopter that passes over, the way your leg wiggles the desk and makes it squeak, the hum of the hard drives processing student information in the wall behind you.

Amidst all this noise, you ask me, every meeting, "why are you so resistant to ADDs?" I have practiced what to say with my parents and case manager. "They're not right for me at this time." But what I really want to say is "because I am full." I am full of sounds and lights and senses. I am full in the way a concert or bar is full: packed, uncomfortable. Adding another sweaty body no matter how useful or nice they might be, is a fire hazard.

I hear my classmates talk about how amazing it is to be able to see the infrared colors of flowers. To be able to sense people coming up behind them. To be able to hear the secret languages of bees and elephants. To be able to taste what water actually tastes like, and smell dinner from two flights up. Every time we meet you ask me, "don't you think that's cool?" I do. I do think that's cool. You also always ask me, "don't you want to be like the other kids?" I do. I'm a high school senior, of course I do want to be like the other kids.

But I'm full.

Let me try another way of explaining it. Every year the 10th grade class goes on a field trip to the science center. You came with my class, I remember it. Do you remember the new movie experience they had? Over 1,000 different screens, all laid out flat on a giant dome. We were supposed to see a movie about the former wonders of the underwater world. But instead the system broke, and every screen played a different movie, with different sounds. Thousands of screens all shouting and flashing differently. It was terrible and overwhelming and everybody got a headache. But I loved it, because finally, I thought, you all understood what I always felt. That is what the world is like for me most of the time.

Sometimes when we meet I seem aloof, frozen, and that's because I've lost control of all the pieces of information coming into my brain. The lights are too loud, and too bright. The vacuum cleaner in the hallway is too deep, the way the table squeaks when you write things down is too much. So when you ask me why I don't want to be able to also see and hear more, why I don't want to add to myself, to improve myself, my answer is that I cannot imagine a world in which those additions don't burn the entire place down. I am already dry, full of tall grass, ready to light. I've become good at putting out the small fires, but I don't want to burn the whole place down just yet.

My official forms are attached.

Sincerely, and for the last time,
Sydney Abdalla

GYNOID, PRESERVED

MALON EDWARDS

Y ou missed your crowdfunding goal."

My heart-engine sputters. My bio-clock chimes. Twenty-four hours left.

I told Mama the campaign wouldn't work. Money wasn't the issue. Her bougie suburban friends in Northbrook and Highland Park and Kenilworth have gobs of it. They were just tired of hearing her brag. For eleven months they listened to Mama go on about Naomi Nakamura's 3D printers (the ones that can render an epidermis, dermis, and hypodermis with ninety-nine percent accuracy), my soft skin (all-natural collagen), my beautiful, textured, springy curls (each hair grows out of my dermis with a cortex and multiple layers), and my artificial hemoglobin (designed to sustain the collagen in my skin and the keratin in my hair). Mama should've re-upped me in reverse: crowdfund my first year, and then drop some of her and Daddy's money into my second year. That way she could have bragged about me having Naomi Nakamura's Black Platinum Package (all memories intact, as far back as eighteen months old), and she and Daddy would've still been the Joneses of Northbrook. Naomi Nakamura's referral discount is deep. Six months in, at least three of Mama's friends would've knocked on the door asking for her referral code. Two of them had junkie kids who ODed on heroin three weeks apart, and another had a gasper who liked to be tickled first. Those three referrals alone would have given me three re-ups, including two years at the University of Illinois. Now my only hope is tweezer-clumsy Hasbros.

Mama puts on a bright smile, more for her than me. "Don't worry. We still have Plan B. Cermak Road Kardia work fast. Remember their motto: 'Give us one hour, and we'll give you another year.'" I sit on the couch. "You said they were a rip-off. Con artists. Failed heart surgeons and wannabe roboticists." Twenty-three hours and forty-seven seconds. Mama pulls a tissue out of her sleeve and dabs at her eyes. "Now I'm saying I can't fix you, and they're all you have right now." Twenty-three hours and thirty-two seconds. "I don't want to go. I just want to spend my last hours here, with you and Daddy." Twenty-three hours and twenty-six seconds. Mama tries to pull me up. "If we leave now, we can be in Chicago in less than an hour." Twenty-three hours and seventeen seconds. "They may need to order parts. That can take days. Weeks, even." Twenty-three hours and twelve seconds. Mama pulls harder. "Trust the motto." Twenty-three hours and seven seconds. I don't budge. My tears are sudden. "Naomi Nakamura Industries called earlier. My pickup is tomorrow at three p.m. They'll provide the box." As usual, the internet is right. I don't have a self-preservation program.

Every night for the past three nights, Mama, Daddy, and I have lain in bed, in the dark, waiting for the arrival of my seven zeros. Mama watches the digits just beneath my skin count down. I watch the red glow from the bio-clock on my chest illuminate the tears on her cheeks and the snot on her upper lip. Daddy snores. When morning comes, Daddy goes into the bathroom and sobs. All day. Every so often, he wrenches a few words from his throat. His lament is clear: Crowdfunding is shit, Nakamura is evil, the absence of a self-preservation program is intentional, planned obsolescence, designed to force bereft parents to re-commission their beloved, twice-grieved daughters as gynoids year after year. When night falls, we all climb back into bed. Mama resumes her watch. Daddy sleeps, spent of emotion. And I watch Mama, wondering if my love of life has truly left me.

A month ago, I offered to redo Mama's crowdfunding page. It was bland. "No, it's not," she'd told me, frowning. "It's evocative. It's for parents. You wouldn't understand." I didn't. Her rewards were macabre—the best was a free triple bypass surgery—and the page headings were uninspired. She refused to highlight them in color or use a font above ten-point Calibri. "My story vid will draw them in," she'd said. It didn't. Mama's story vid had been a close-up of her in an all-white room, sitting in a white wing chair and dressed in a white pantsuit, talking to the camera for five minutes and forty-six seconds about her heartbreak at my death. "That's not evocative," I'd told Mama after watching the vid. "That's whine-core. And it's boring." The next day, Mama showed me an alternate take: a close-up of her in an all-white room, sitting in a blood-red wing chair, dressed in a blood-red pantsuit, elbows on her knees, shoulders forward, talking to the camera for seven minutes and thirty-six seconds. She didn't look down. She didn't look away. She didn't cry. Mama just told the world how senseless gang violence and a thug named Jean-Loup Galant took away her only child, her baby girl. It worked. As I watched her new vid, another ten backers pledged ten million dollars each toward Mama's fifty-million-dollar funding goal. And, despite Mama throwing shade at Jean-Loup, I smiled. I couldn't help it. I was three-quarters funded.

Daddy had been clear when I brought Jean-Loup home for dinner the first time: "If you take my daughter to Chicago, I cut off your balls. If my daughter goes to visit you in Chicago, I cut off your balls." Daddy is a neurosurgeon. Northbrook, new money. He gets off on sharp instruments. Mama had been clear, too: "If you go visit him in Roseland, you will not come home. The Haitian gangs will kidnap you and beat you and rape you and ransom you and hook you on drugs, and then kill you." She'd said this at the dinner table, with Jean-Loup sitting right next to me. Mama is a heart surgeon. Old money, Chicago South Side bougie. Lab School–educated. She knew better. She'd learned in first grade that Jean-Baptiste Point du Sable founded Chicago as a center of trade and industry. She'd learned he'd been a handsome, charming man. She'd learned how his shrewd trading skills and badass charisma got him elected Chicago's first mayor. She'd learned he molded Chicago into a formidable city-state during his six terms in office. She knew better. She'd been taught at the knee that her great-great-grandfather, Etienne Jean-Louis, helped make Chicago a world-class city with iron ore and railroads. She'd passed his iron and steel mills every day on the way to school, watching from the backseat of her mama's Bentley as trains approached on tracks he owned. So for Mama to reduce my boyfriend's city, her hometown, to a gang war between the Ro Boys in Roseland and the Wash Boys in Washington Heights, just because bougie-ass Fernwood, where she grew up, was caught in the middle—well, she knew better.

I met Jean-Loup my junior year at the annual Rock Island co-ed track and field invitational. He was a hurdler, three hundred meters, just like me. He tried to give me some tips on my form before the prelims. He'd said, "Gen bèl fòm. But you need to strengthen your trail leg hip flexor." He was showing off under the lights, in front of the crowd. His chest flexed under his Chicago Leo singlet. Out there, in Rock Island, they go completely ape-shit bananas for track meets. They pack the stadium on Friday nights for the fleet-footed crimson-and-gold Rocks like they do for football and them good ol' boys down in Texas. "That lovely knee of yours don't need no scar." I couldn't get enough of his Haitian Creole and his accent. But I played it cool. I told him, "The last time my trail leg, or my lead leg, hit a hurdle was last year. Forty-four races ago. I placed second in state that day—as a sophomore." And then I activated my Auricle, willed

Janelle Monáe's "Electric Lady" as loud as I could stand it, and high-back-kicked with excellent form for a warm-up lap around the track. I didn't look back. I knew he'd follow. I didn't imagine, though, that three months later I'd die in his bed, shot in the head. Jean-Loup had been stroking my left eyebrow with his thumb. His sheets smelled of boy. I love the smell of boy. "Mwen renmen sousi w," he'd said. He loved my thick and heavy dark brows. He loved how they felt after I got them threaded. He loved how they framed the beauty of my face. He wasn't trying to be cool or suave or smooth brown brother about it. He wasn't trying to show off. He just loved me. This is my last memory as a real girl, my anchor memory, untouched by the bullet that ripped through his bedroom wall and into my brain.

Some gynoid named Jae Lyn in Highland Park posted a holo-vid about re-upping for the first time. She said, despite the smiley roboticists in your face telling you the paralysis is only temporary, and despite the piles of blankets the nurses tuck under your chin, that if you establish a nice, happy anchor memory before your bio-clock winds down—and you must do this as close to seven zeros as possible—that anchor memory will settle your mind when you wake up, you won't go batshit crazy when your limbic system struggles to kick in, and you'll feel all warm and tingly once it does because that anchor memory will jump-start your self-preservation behaviors and it will be the very first memory you recall on the other side. The loveliest memory ever retrieved. So, as I lie here on the couch, Mama strokes my brow, and my bio-clock ticks down its final seconds—nine, eight, seven—I close my eyes—six—latch on to the memory of Jean-Loup leaning over me—five—hear him whisper, Mwen renmen sousi w— four—(I love your eyebrows)—three—my heart-engine begins its shutdown—two—everything goes quiet—one—I smile.

THE END OF BIG DATA

JAMES BRIDLE

t's lunchtime in Diego Garcia and still dark in the Mid-Atlantic, but the first light of day is reflecting hard white off the former Google facility in Hamina, Finland. The cameras on BLIX and RITTER, the twin UNDATA satellites I'm flying over Europe's eastern border, trigger automatically.

My shift's first images appear on the monitor, overlays shimmering to life atop the decommissioned data center, outlining stacks of disassembled routers and cooling vents. The progress bar on the ops room's jumbotron starts to fill. All green so far. The threat graph is bottomed-out today; the Finns have tightened up border security following several incursions by FSB and Spetssvyaz looters. But everything that was there yesterday is still there today. I take a moment to examine the traffic: dumper trucks heading toward Russia and the M10, the usual overnight flights nosing down from North America, the expected chatter in the ionosphere. Nothing to see here. The overview moves toward the Baltic States before swinging back up again, toward Sweden and the old Facebook plant.

It takes the dawn terminator 130 minutes to sweep across the European Continent, tracing the lines of highways and power cables as day slowly returns. The sensors aboard BLIX and RITTER follow behind, reading the shapes and heat signatures of every registered storage facility in the monitoring database. We can see immediately if anything in the open has been moved or disturbed, but the covered mills, where ground crews haven't yet been able to reach, are slightly trickier. BLIX scans parking lots and fences, counting cars and gateways, examining the ground moisture for signs of tunneling and trenching. There have been reports on the less official diplomatic forums that some authorities have been slow to register facilities, but that's a matter for the liaison teams. I can only see what I've been told to look for.

Well, that's not entirely true. While I was out cold in my bunk last night, eyes in the sky were dowsing for covert data farms: telltale transmissions near the dew point. You can do a lot with fans, water mist, recirculation, and chillers, but thermodynamics is pretty unforgiving. The energy of computation has to come out somewhere, and the combination of heat and rare earth traces is, ultimately, undeniable: a forensics of the machine. Between RITTER's infrared and the EUROSUR air contaminants grid, we can usually triangulate any processor over twenty-five kilowatts. A few months ago it took the ground crew almost a week to locate some Estonian ex-Salesforce analysts whose lockup in Tallinn was cold as stone. Turns out they were piping their server exhaust a kilometer outside of town, but we got there in the end. This morning the sensors picked up suspicious heat sources in Poland and Slovenia. Could be generators, could be thermal dumps. I'll get to them once my initial sweep is done.

I haven't always done this kind of work, but it feels like I was trained for it. I got pulled into the late-stage drone surge over the Middle East straight out of college: my rankings on Steam triggered at least three different military recruiting bots, each of which thought I was suited to long-range recon work, although they disagreed on which service I should apply for. In the end I found myself working a console at Camp Thunder Cove, classifying blast radii from Russian and Israeli munitions on the borders of the Caliphate, still not entirely clear which service was using the data, but keeping my metrics up anyway. Then the crash happened, and all that time I'd put in, preservice, crunching Voronoi space for dollar vans—which I'd naïvely thought the govbots didn't know about—suddenly became interesting to UNDATA.

First I heard about the crash was when every single data controller I'd touched started pinging me over and over again for a password reset or two-factor auth. Like pretty much everyone else. My phone was unusable for hours, and then the networks just . . . shut down. It took weeks to get back online, but luckily or otherwise I was still under army rule, so we just got on with the business of sandbagging and digging latrines for the smart-grid refugees who couldn't get back into their apartments. Everyone else just stayed close to home, paid cash, and watched TV. There were a lot of opinions to watch.

The first tremors started to be felt in the markets only a few days after the flood. Pure capitalism, back then, was built on leverage and latency; in a world where everyone had access to everyone else's data—and not just passwords, but motives, feelings, alignments, tendencies—the only constraint was choice of target. Hackers tore through the remaining dark pools, evolving predatory algos modeled on the suddenly visible nervous tics of every trader on Wall Street. The banks tried to hide it, but they couldn't cover their losses for long, and the same thing was happening everywhere, just more slowly, a billion weakly protected savings accounts tapped, trapped, moved over, and bled dry. First it happened to people you only heard about, then to people you knew, until finally it happened to you: full-spectrum data loss, everything from pension to passport number, air miles to alarm codes. And emails. And text messages, and phone calls, and browsing histories, and order histories, and credit card transactions, and bank transfers, and contracts, and medical records.

But the currency crash just prefigured the privacy crash, a lurking, existential horror that tore into everyday relationships. It was like having the Stasi back, but the Stasi was everyone. The papers couldn't keep up with the scandals: political, financial, domestic, deranged. Insider trading and extramarital affairs, undeclared preexisting conditions, undisclosed personal relationships, and every white lie you've ever told, everyone outed for everything at once, a toxic dam breaking, leaving us all wallowing in tainted mud.

We'd been losing gays, trans kids, freethinkers, and unaccredited journalists for years, but when senators turned out to be just as vulnerable, the legislature finally took action. In the end it only took eighteen months for the Northern Hemisphere to agree on the new Data Protection Accords, and the rest of the surviving nation-states pretty much had to sign on. The first requirement, Clause One of DPA limitations: no personal data.

Nothing identifying. No dossiers, no manila files, no cookies or patterns of life or digital signatures, nothing that could link anyone to anything. It's surprising how easy it is to re-architect relationships on a cold-zero privacy basis when you're resuscitating society from flatline; perhaps less surprising than the whole new bleak economy that got started breaking the rules.

So I work at UNDATA now, and our role is twofold: we enforce disarmament, and we watch for rearmament, on the basis of treaties signed by every extant government in the world. Of course, governments all have something to hide. Like most UN missions in history, we're caught between what they do and what they want everyone else to do. But we have our hands on most of their old toys, and that helps.

Camp Thunder Cove, to be clear, is a dump. This shouldn't be a surprise for a place that used to be called Camp Justice back when it was basically a black site, a holding bay for forward positioning ships, nuclear indiction subs, and individuals rated even lower than Rumsfeld's "worst of the worst." Seabees leveled the place of any remaining geographical features in the 1960s, leaving a few ragged palms and a bunch of blockhouses. Since the NSA packed up and left, the only bar still going is the Brit Club, and you really don't want to end up there. Apart from UNDATA, the only other operation left is the ratkillers: a bunch of Marines-turned-conservationists who have pretty much gone native on the outer atolls. I've been helping them out a bit modeling ocean currents to optimize the new trash booms they're deploying in the plastic gyres, but I'd rather be out in space, keeping an eye on the rest of the planet.

So here comes my favorite bit of the morning: BLIX and RITTER get to Cheltenham. See, the social networks and the targeted advertisers were dead from the start, but around month three of the UNDATA hearings it looked possible that the intelligence agencies might escape the personal data ban. The Nine Eyes pulled together, sending legions of spooks and lords to the committee hearings, but one by one they were sent back, usually by revelations pulled from their own files. The leak of GCHQ's cable intercepts alone led to the downfall of a dozen national governments, and the collapse of hundreds of treaty negotiations.

Crowds waving banners—NOTHING TO HIDE/EVERYTHING TO FEAR—clashed with riot police outside the hearings, and the chamber had to be evacuated multiple times because of tear gas. Reluctantly, GCHQ finally committed to decommissioning its data stores, severing all fiber links, providing unobstructed access to UNDATA inspection teams, and ensuring its facilities were "visible to national technical means of verification." That's jargon: It means spy satellites, which, when people found out about those, got added to the proscribed list, too. Anything that couldn't be downgraded or blown up just got turned around. You wouldn't believe what we've learned about space since all those sensors got pointed up rather than down.

The remaining national technical means is me. I enforce from orbit, making sure all the mainframes that used to track and store every detail of our lives are turned off, and stay off. And as the sun comes up over Gloucestershire this morning, there they are, resplendent in the mist-piercing light of RITTER's multispectral sensors: terabytes of storage laid out around the scalped doughnut of the former GCHQ building. Enough quantum storage to hold decades of the world's pillow talk. Drums of redundant ethernet cable stacked stories-high. Everything dismantled, disconnected, unshielded. Everything damp with morning dew.

In a car park to the northeast, I can see the footprint of an UNDATA degaussing team starting their morning shift. BLIX and RITTER have a resolution limit of 1.5 meters in the visible and infrared spectra to prevent them from inadvertently gathering personal data; anything below a meter and a half looks like a single pixel, so the individual ground crew don't show up. The twenty-tonne degaussing plant, on the other hand, is unmistakable. The nuclear-powered land train trails superconducting ceramic cables four hundred feet long, capable of repeat-erasing an exabyte a day.

The land trains are a complete fragmentation unit: They take all that material and turn it back into metal. Like me watching BLIX watch the data centers, the crash taught us that machines alone weren't sufficient to undo what we'd spent decades creating. The only solution was cooperation. So alongside the erasers work teams of local disassemblers, digging with screwdrivers and sanders to recover metal, minerals, and magnets, creating cottage industries wherever the degaussers set up. Anything left over goes into grinders capable of turning a jet engine into particulate dust. A few weeks later, no data, a bunch of new jobs, and plenty of material for light bulbs, catalytic converters, and solar batteries, as per the UNDATA sustainability promise. We don't need to use the eastern Congo or Helmand rare earth mines anymore; no more wars for mobile phones, at least.

I'm almost done with Europe for the morning, already thinking about the handover to the North America specialists on Ascension for the afternoon, when I get an alert from EUROSUR in Linz. Linz always means the Swiss, and the Swiss are never good. EUROSUR needs me to survey the Alpine Balloon Network. The blimps.

After the crash, the Swiss retreated into a kind of medieval info-sharing arrangement between the pre-federation cantons, using a combination of Romansh, Polybius squares, and Vigenère ciphers to attempt a cold restart of the banking system. Phase one of their plan involved triggering the National Redoubt, which brought down most of the routes in and out of the country, making it impossible for our inspection teams to get anywhere near the place.

We didn't know what they were up to until the Carabinieri pulled over a container truck on the Autostrada near Ivrea. Inside they found a six-foot receiver horn, and all the pieces fell into place: a bunch of artillery trucks had been retrofitted with microwave transmitters, and the Swiss were moving them up and down the passes in order to exfiltrate personal data to smugglers, much as the pre-crash microwave network had once sped high-frequency trades between Frankfurt, London, Amsterdam, and Zurich. Sealed and tagged, these containerized data stores could be shipped anonymously to brokers in India and Malaysia, just a few more boxes among millions, packed with transistors instead of scrap metal and plastic toys.

Microwave links are only a few meters across and go point-to-point like a searchlight, so even when they aren't being moved up and down the Matterhorn they're pretty hard to intercept. We needed assets in the air all the time, at the base of each pass, but the thermal turbulence of the area makes drones a no-go, especially since they've been effectively blinded by the UNDATA agreements. Hence the blimps.

Linz tells me they've intercepted a data transmission from one of the blimps over Chamonix, probably headed for Marseille and the Union Corse. Deep packet inspection showed some half a million user profiles, medium-grade material salvaged from the wreck of a minor Brazilian social network and bounced around Europe by data brokers ever since. Nevertheless, damaging enough if it got into the hands of one of the ad-supported South American juntas.

I fire up the ion thrusters on BLIX and RITTER and make another pass over the mainland. Thanks to the blimp's calculations, I know where to look, what to look for: the tracks the trailers leave behind as they churn up wet and dry earth can be spotted from space for hours after they're gone. EUROSUR traced the transmission to a spot on the Col de la Forclaz, and my sensors can follow a bright infrared trail from there back to the tunnel entrance. I take a few snaps of the area and annotate them for the lawyers before sending them on to the UNDATA rapporteur. Up to the Swiss now if they want to let an inspection team come round for a visit—or wait for a couple of Tomahawks to drop by.

As for the data itself, that's already been dealt with. The blimps were updated in October with the new HAPPY COW chaff system, essentially a bunch of bottle rockets to be fired into the microwave beam. A fun morning for Chamonix: When the rockets reach altitude they detonate, sending a cloud of cellulose filaments into the atmosphere. Coated with aluminum and zirconium, they ignite on contact with the air, buoy themselves up on a little cloud of infrared energy, and bounce those microwaves every which way. Any data that gets through is total junk, and the cinders that make it to the ground are basically organic, hence: happy cows. The French and Italians insisted on that.

I personally think it's only a matter of time before some kid in Annecy figures out how to trigger HAPPY COW with a cracked microwave oven and puts on their own display for Bastille Day, but that's not my problem. Yet.

What is my problem are international waters. I feel a lot more comfortable out here. I don't like personal data, either, and even though I'm mostly watching it disappear, I'm still complicit in surveillance, and having the keys to BLIX and RITTER is a big responsibility. Over the North Atlantic, I can just watch the weather patterns and try out a bit of old-school crateology on the decks of any ships I don't have manifests for.

And the open ocean is a good place to recalibrate the satellites, too, because the convergence zone around the equator sends up pretty much every type of atmospheric condition you can imagine. On a clear day in the doldrums I might be looking down at an almost perfectly flat expanse of ocean; other days there are thunderheads ten miles high, completely blocking my visible sensors. Today isn't one of those days, thankfully, and I cycle the sensor arrays through the spectrum, from the visible into the deep ultraviolet and infrared, looking not for anomalies on the water—there's nothing there, from an electronic perspective—but in the sensors themselves.

Here's a thing, though. There's a reason BLIX and RITTER are a pair, but you won't find it in any of the public docs. Every accord contains at least one loophole, and UNDATA's is really quite an elegant one. The official reason for having two satellites is redundancy and calibration: If we lose one to a cloud of space debris, the other can keep logging independently, and while they're both up they can cross-check everything. Each satellite carries a full complement of remote sensing gear, everything you'd find on any standard earth observation vehicle of the pre-crash era, plus a few things they only put on spy sats. But there's something else they can do, together, which no satellite can do alone: collaborate.

By opening up a K-band link with one another, BLIX and RITTER become a single instrument, responding to every micron-level mass change on the earth. It's a trick they learned from GRACE, a NASA gravity-sensing mission from the noughties, which used twin ranging satellites to look for anomalies not in the electromagnetic spectrum, but in the gravitational field. Instead of seeing, they start *weighing*, producing a detailed map of every object between them and the center of the planet. More like touch than sight, it's a whole other way of evaluating the world.

That the GRACE sensors were kept out of BLIX and RITTER's official capabilities, combined with that unscheduled maneuver over Switzerland, is the only reason I spot the *Friedman*.

There were some pretty extreme reactions after the crash. The usual cranks—accelerationists, drone-potters, libertarians, militias—they all had a field day. But it was Silicon Valley that kept my colleagues at Ascension busy every day of the week.

After the crash, the engineers in the Valley realized pretty quickly that the protocols they'd been working on were bust, but they had a whole new set of interesting problems: distributed ID systems, blockchain trading networks, smart contracts, quantum messaging, a vast swath of known but until-now-unprofitable technologies that, thanks to the DPA, were going to be at the center of the next network.

The ad guys, on the other hand, were fucked. All the marketeers, the profile vendors, big data thought leaders, mailing list suppliers, the spammers and scammers: They knew the game was up, too, but they had nowhere to go. Crazy schemes ensued.

Googlezon was a big mover in the initial offshore rush. In the months before the DPA came into force, a bunch of Creative Labs types prepared several exabyte-capacity storage facilities aboard barges in Emshaven, Wilmington, and Oakland. They were later found sunk thirty meters deep on the edge of local shipping channels: It's not known whether they were ever used, or just part of some internal corporate power struggle. When we announced the DPA had force in ocean waters, people expected the space billionaires would get involved, but with all the extra funding pouring into NASA and the remaining data centers turned over to crunching escape trajectories rather than clickthrough rates, they were busy. Which just left the proper nutters.

Friedman had originally been built as a floating tax haven, a data processing plant for people who didn't want to participate in anything resembling a functioning government. Pre-crash AIS had it docked off the coast of Grand Cayman, executing automatic trades for the usual coterie of batshit one-percenters who lived aboard Gulfstreams and kept their Picassos at the airport. Cayman went off-grid for months while DPA went through the committees, and when it started talking again, *Friedman* was gone.

I don't like to talk about it with the UNDATA crowd, who think I'm a proper nutter myself, but I've been keeping tabs on the forums, and rumor is that the processing decks have been massively expanded, and special measures taken to keep it out of sight— again, ultimately, from me. It gets personal. *Friedman* is my Moby-Dick.

In the center of the doldrums is a dense block of matter where there should be nothing, is nothing, according to every reading but the GRACE instrument. I'm not supposed to perform unauthorized maneuvers, but if what I half think about *Friedman* is even half true, there might not be time for a second pass. Using the GRACE readings as a base, I turn BLIX and RITTER around, putting the full force of their combined instruments onto the mass anomaly.

What had been an undifferentiated cloud of reflections immediately resolves into a subsurface superstructure, a chunk of material the size of a Greenland iceberg—even looks like an iceberg, except for the fact that it has the density of silicon and ferro-cement. It still doesn't appear on any of the usual sensors, but with BLIX and RITTER flying in sync some five hundred miles apart, their standard radar scans form a synthetic aperture, a notional aerial five hundred miles long, capable of reading the smallest ripple on the water surface. I could read facial expressions if I was over land right now. Another reason we keep the twinning function off the books.

This thing is almost half a mile across but riding only a few feet above the waves, clad in some kind of Hilbert coil and shedding seawater over its deck gently and thickly enough to maintain surface tension. To BLIX's aerosol sensor it looks like the surface of the sea itself. It's obviously cooling itself, otherwise it would show up on the thermal readings, but it's the temperature of seawater, too. If you were out there in a dinghy, God help you, it would stick out like the *Queen Mary*, but to every one of the standard sensors it's perfectly invisible. Someone has thought about this a lot. But even they didn't know about GRACE.

The *Friedman* is a phish farm, a breeding ground for all kinds of algos, optimized for profit, powered by submerged hydrofoils, and cooled by the Atlantic. Pumped full of personal data gathered in the aftermath of the crash, it's holding out for a day when it can be recovered and reconnected, unleashing a swarm of predatory programs to overwhelm the nascent anonymous networks.

Data is power. It's something to take from and hold over somebody else; quantified dominion. The more you have on someone, the more you have over them. The more personal it is, the more power, until you've eaten right through the skin of social relationships and into the flesh itself. The *Friedman* is an ark of unqualified dominion.

GRACE's resolution band is pretty short. There's no way I can be sure the mass sensor will find it again in the vast expanse of the open ocean, and this thing is obviously good at staying under the cloud layer, otherwise I would have spotted it before. No time to send a warship, and no anti-ship missiles with the range and accuracy to hit something this size in the mid-Atlantic. There's only one other option.

I've given away most of UNDATA's secrets now, so I guess you can have this one for free. Good things always come in threes, and BLIX and RITTER are no exception. Trailing them by another few hundred miles is KELLY, their silent partner. KELLY hasn't got any sensors aboard. KELLY is blind and dumb. So dumb, in fact, there's no thermal source or processing plant to trigger a signature on ground-based systems—just a solar sail hidden behind its body, and a passive microwave receiver waiting for a signal from one of its siblings.

When BLIX sends the signal, all the trajectories are pre-calculated based on KELLY's position. At the right moment it splits apart, ejecting its payload in a perfect arc toward the surface while its carapace tumbles away to burn off in the atmosphere. KELLY is a reactivated "Brilliant Pebble," a remnant of Reagan's Star Wars, containing a single tungsten cannonball that falls to earth under its own gravity, generating the kinetic energy of a nuclear explosion on the way down. KELLY's comet falls for five minutes, and the surface of the sea vaporizes, instantly and briefly searing red across BLIX's and RITTER's thermal sensors. They barely even look back.

That's it, I'm done. I dial up Ascension on my terminal, and send the afternoon crew the morning's log files. One benefit at least of this island life is the long afternoons—what's the point of all this technology if we don't get a little more leisure to enjoy it? And by leisure, I mean time for side projects.

Turns out all that dollar van work still comes in handy. I'm using the old GPS station and the VHF aerials on the north shore to optimize refugee sea routes across the Mediterranean and elsewhere. A hint here, a weather tip there, and you can send a hundred small boats on a safer trip. It's not rocket science, not like BLIX and RITTER, not like the *Friedman*, but it's what this stuff is supposed to be used for. Now that we've made information really free, it's time to get started on people.

ACROSS THE BORDER

SAHIL LAVINGIA

Matthew lifted his foot off the gas pedal, inching the car forward. The reentry point was only a few hundred feet away, but at this pace it would take upward of an hour. Past the border it was just another five hours until he would be home and asleep in his own bed.

But for now, Matthew was an uncomfortable combination of tired and restless. His car's self-driving functionality would be disabled until he crossed the border, so he couldn't take a nap or disappear into a vid. He was also out of signal range, and sick of every song saved locally. So he waited in silence, crawling forward, just a few dozen cars to go.

Your connection has been restored, his car spoke to him, while text flashed on the windshield to accompany it. *Please verify your identity.*

Matthew hesitated.

A week before, as Matthew's car hurtled down the last stretch of U.S. space, Vanessa's messages remained unread on the windshield:

C u in three weeks?

Helloooooo?

I miss u

Cya soon . . . rite?

R u coming or not?

I love u

Got an A in MoBio!!

I hate u

"Call Vanessa," Matthew said.

"Hello?" came her voice. "Where are you, Dad? You're not coming, are you?"

"I'm not, sweetie. I'm not." He steeled himself for her reaction.

"Why?" she croaked.

"I got called to help set up a hospital. I dreaded telling you . . ."

"It's not that hard to text."

"I'm sorry."

"Why'd it have to be now? I haven't seen you since . . ." Her voice trailed off.

"I don't know."

"It's just not fair!"

"Van, please—"

"Dad, let me—"

Your connection has been terminated.

Self-driving capabilities are now disabled.

Welcome to BajaX.

"Matthew Johnson," he said, uttering his passphrase, "yellow monkeys play guitar."

Identity verified. United States citizen. You have fifteen thousand four hundred and two unread emails . . . three unread messages . . . one missed call.

"Filter messages from Vanessa."

Hellooooooooooo? Vanessa's messages flashed up on the windshield in grand white text, shoving the rest of the interface aside. *R u dead???*

Matthew sighed, rejecting the option to send the emoji that corresponded to his body language. He knew how that conversation would go. Tomorrow, he resolved, after he had slept in a real bed and taken a hot shower.

Instead, he looked out the windshield, up at the glossy black wall that towered over him and stretched out in both directions. Its monolithic surface hid a city that blazed with changing hues, burning neon, and shafts of multicolored light.

On this side of the border, among the dusty, cracked streets of BajaX, a very different kind of economy endured. People of all ages embraced their final chance to sell food, souvenirs, and last-minute gifts to homeward tourists. A girl walked by, arms wrapped around a forest of perishable flowers. A woman came by and commanded her robots to start cleaning the side of Matthew's car. Unlike the ones he had at home, these robots were rusty and squeaked as their joints moved. Matthew waved them away without success. They scrubbed the whole side of the car and scurried onto the hood of his car before Matthew rolled down the window and said firmly, "I'm not paying."

She looked him in the eyes and said, "Who asked you?"

Matthew smirked and gave her a few pesos. Bad idea; it seemed everyone in a forty-car radius had seen the glint of metal and started to descend upon his car.

A boy who must have been less than ten stood in front of his car and juggled five (then six and seven) balls up in the air, occasionally dropping them like a robot wouldn't. A man sat atop a hovering cart stirring a vat of neon-yellow churros, keeping pace alongside Matthew's car.

Matthew had had enough. Of churros, and everything else. He stared forward, and tried to sink back into his own mind. Eventually the crowd dissipated, refocusing on the other cars.

A small boy tapped on his window with his fingernails. "Hola," he said.

Matthew kept his gaze aimed forward.

The boy pressed a crisp white envelope up against the window. Scrawled on it: *HELP.*

He shook his head at the boy. "No more pesos. What about a churro?"

The boy laughed. "Not hungry," he said, patting his stomach. "Just need help. I need to get this letter to my abuela."

"Can't call her?"

"My abuelo wrote this letter. It's the only way he can communicate with my abuela. He was deported fifteen years ago, and it's illegal for him to communicate with anyone inside the U.S. Holo, vidcall, phone, they block everything we try . . . everything except letters."

"I'm sorry," Matthew said, "but I need to go home. I haven't slept in a real bed in weeks. Could you ask somebody else?"

"Okay," the boy said, "but you're the only one going back to Orgone." He pointed at the cars in front of him. "Lower California. Lower California. New Colorado. Zion. Upper—"

Matthew looked ahead, at the slow-moving string of cars before him.

"Where is he?"

"He can barely walk. He can't speak English. Please?"

Matthew's car vibrated gently. *Vanessa is calling.*

"I'm sorry," Matthew said, rolling up the window. He grimaced as he tapped the phone icon on the dash. "Hi, Van."

"How are you?" Vanessa asked urgently. "Why didn't you call?"

"Fine. I'm fine."

"Are you angry at me?"

"I'm not angry." Matthew sighed. *I was just sleeping on a cot in the sweltering heat for the past three weeks.* "I'm just . . . tired."

"Mom always—"

"How's school?" Matthew interjected. He did not need to know that his ex-wife had triumphed over him in yet another metric.

"School's good, Dad. How was the work trip? Was it worth it?"

Matthew sighed. Just good? Could she elaborate? "Are you done with your college essays?"

"No, Dad. I've been busy—"

"Nothing's as important as college, Van."

"Grades, Dad! Which also matter!"

"Don't shout, Van."

"Dad. I haven't talked to you in weeks. You were supposed to be *here*, in person. For my birthday, remember? For all I know, you could have been *dead*. And now all you want to do is tell me college is important. No shit, I'm the one applying!"

"Well, I care about your long-term happiness."

"Could you try caring about my short-term happiness for once? You're never there for me. You were never there for Mom, either. You're so selfish. Ugh!"

Vanessa has hung up.

Matthew rubbed the bridge of his nose in frustration. There was a tapping at his window again, and he looked to his left to see the same boy with a pleading look on his face. He rolled down the window. "Where does your grandmother live?"

The boy flipped over the envelope. The address was clearly marked. The town was a few hours east of where Matthew lived; he had been there for a wedding.

Matthew took one last look at the boy. Selfish? He looked forward to telling Van about delivering the letter. "Give me the letter."

An hour later and Matthew was through the crossing. Every bag—even the churros—had been turned inside out and back again. They had swabbed around the wheels and inside the hood and in every other nook and cranny they could find. His car was doused with a disinfectant that caused it to smell faintly like a swimming pool. The letter was flagged by the scanner, but Matthew defended it as evidence for work, flashing his government ID badge. Finally, the lights turned green and his car became autonomous.

Matthew's pill of a car shot up the PacCoast in the black of night, hurtling past trees that blurred together. The only light came from the pulsating lane dividers. The drive wasn't as bad as he thought it would be. At least his car was toasty, and he had his music back.

His daughter's face glowed green on the windshield, indicating that she was still awake. All he'd have to do was speak, or tap; but if he did that, they would get into an argument and he wouldn't even be able to sleep. Instead, he reclined his car seat and watched the stars and satellites move across the sky, trying to figure out which one was which.

Your destination is on your right, Matthew's car said as the door slid up. A light yellow town house framed with squared-off bushes. He knelt down to slip the letter under the door.

"Hello," came a voice from above, and Matthew almost fell backward.

An old lady stood in the doorway, propping herself up with a cane. Her skin was wrinkled like a prune. "I'm Sabrina, Alejandro's grandmother."

How did she know I was coming? Matthew spun around, paranoid. Was this a trap? He had knowingly helped a family break the law. He handed her the letter. "I should go," he said.

"No, no, no," she said. "You should come in."

"Sorry, but I really think I should just go home and sleep. I'm not thinking straight."

"Hello," a voice echoed from behind Sabrina.

"He would certainly love it if you came in," Sabrina said, stepping aside.

"I don't think—" Matthew's breath caught. There was the boy. Right in the middle of the living room.

"How did you get *here*?" Matthew asked. Something was off. Was he wearing different clothes? Alejandro was shaking. No, shimmering. He saw the lights now, coming down from the corners of the ceiling.

"I'm a hologram," the boy shouted. He stepped forward and attempted to grab his grandmother's hand.

"You didn't tell him?" Sabrina asked.

"If I told him," Alejandro said, "he wouldn't have said yes."

"Explain," Sabrina said, crossing her arms, "and apologize."

"I'm allowed to holo across the border because I'm a citizen," Alejandro said. "I was born here. Without me, we couldn't deliver the letters. My abuelo is too old to do it himself."

"But why bother with the letters at all," Matthew asked, "if you can holo?"

"Why don't you come in, Matthew?" Sabrina said. "It's cold out."

"You don't say no to Abuela," Alejandro said.

They sat around a sparse dining table, and Matthew sipped at a cup of steaming tea, his legs fidgeting under the table as Sabrina read the letter in silence. He watched her eyes, but they betrayed nothing.

"Thank you," she said finally, folding up the letter carefully.

"You're welcome," Matthew replied awkwardly. "And I'm sorry, for what our country did to you."

"My daughter's asleep, upstairs," Sabrina said, waving the comment away. "Alejandro is hers." She let one hand rest next to the letter, and the boy's image grasped at it as much as it could. "He was born here, but he spends the summers with my husband. It's important for him to understand where he came from."

"I could just watch a vid," the boy grumbled.

"Believe me, dear, I would love to run my hands through your real hair," she said, stroking the virtual representation. Alejandro tried to shake her off, then feigned defeat and lay down in her lap. "Without him," Sabrina said, "we would have lost touch long ago. You're right, of course. While the government does not allow my husband to holo, Alejandro could act as our conduit. But our relationship is . . . sacred. There are parts of it no one else deserves to know. Not Alejandro, the government, credit profilers, you. For that purpose, only the letters suffice." Matthew nodded, tried to stop fidgeting.

"Of course, we would prefer to talk all the time," she continued. "But we've discovered there is a magic to writing. It's never too much too quick. Sometimes we used to hate each other. We couldn't stand talking to each other. But a letter . . . I'm never angry at him when I'm done writing a letter. Not once, in fifteen years. My anger can never make it all the way down the length of my arm and onto the paper. You must understand."

"I have a daughter," Matthew said. "I haven't seen her in two years, since the divorce. But we're in the same country. We could visit each other."

"You should give it a try," Sabrina said. She pushed herself up against the table, gripping her cane tightly with one hand. "Here, I'll walk you out."

Matthew couldn't get to sleep, even though it was almost four in the morning. His daughter's face still glowed green on the windshield. He swiveled the seat around to face an empty desk and reached underneath to pick out a clean sheet of paper. It took him a minute to find a pen, hidden at the very back of the drawer; rolling it between his fingers, he realized it had never been used.

THE PROSTITUTE

MAX WYNNE

Casey's john took him to the beach and didn't do much beyond that.

His other johns had used him to do some strange things. He expected that. But he was surprised how little of his work ended up being sexual, though a number of johns did use him to masturbate. One had him sit in front of the mirror for over an hour, staring at the reflection, but Casey thought that kick was more existential than erotic.

A lot of the johns just wanted to watch. They would take him somewhere and wait for the right person to pass, then have Casey tail them. Usually that was it. Occasionally, Casey would deliver messages to strangers, or run packages across the city without knowing what was in them or who they were going to. A few things might have been stolen. Casey suspected he had at least once been used as a thief.

In the extreme cases, johns would do something like dress him in a schoolgirl outfit and an animal mask, then make him suck his own toes. Casey got over that stuff like he'd gotten over almost all the quirks of fronting. Strange objects had been licked with his tongue, and strange things had been done with his skin, but he was numb to it.

Something was off about this latest john, though. It didn't seem to know how to walk or move Casey's limbs. It just sat in Casey's apartment, flexing his fingers and toes, carefully testing each limb before getting up. It made a leisurely and calculated march to the beach. Casey wondered if the john might have been a paraplegic using a joystick.

Johns had taken Casey to the beach before, but most wanted to do something when they got there, like take him swimming. Vacationers, presumably. Even when his johns were only waiting for someone, Casey could tell by the way they kept his attention on passing faces.

This john took Casey to the beach and stood there. It made him stand for over an hour in still silence, skin burning under the cloudless sky, a hundred feet from the insistent shushing of the water. It picked up a single grain of sand, inspected it closely through the camera between Casey's eyes. Placing the grain considerately back on the ground, it took Casey to the water's edge and wet the tip of his finger in the shallow lapping. It admired the gleam, gingerly tasted the brine.

Then it turned and took Casey wandering the streets, slowly, but more gracefully than before. The john examined everything. It ran Casey's fingers along different surfaces, stared closely at potted plants, inspected the sidewalk cracks. Tracing a crack, they bumped into someone. The girl stared at Casey squatting close to the concrete. The john made Casey freeze, apparently panicking, then whispered an apology and hurried him away.

At a restaurant, the john studied the menu and ordered chicken with roasted vegetables. Johns had made him binge, but none had fed Casey an entirely normal meal. This john made him eat in small, delicate bites, intently dissecting the breast. It went through five glasses of water. When the waitress brought the check, the john blurted out a credit number. She asked Casey to write it down, and the john obliged.

The john took Casey back to the beach for the sunset. Gold ribbons trembled through cresting waves. Color squeezed itself from the sky with the slow ache of a tube being thoroughly drained of toothpaste. Dimness replaced everything, followed by moonlight, then scattered bonfires on the strand. Casey hadn't watched the sunset in a long time and didn't notice when the john left him alone with the water.

Back in his single-room apartment, Casey got a cold glass of water and collapsed into the vinyl couch, a dull throbbing building between his temples. His body felt like a drawn-out novocaine shot, sharp and numb. Fronting always left a hangover. The longer the john stayed, the stronger it came on, and this one had spent about seven hours in Casey. In an hour, he'd be floored.

Still, Casey was having trouble getting the john out of his head. As a rule, he maintained dissociation from whatever he did while fronting. He didn't need to wonder why his johns made him do what they did. The actions were someone else's, and Casey experienced them like any other immedia. It was an avant-garde sim-flick starring himself. He got paid to do things that some could never afford.

But a normal day was harder to write off as a dream than an episode of toe-sucking in a pinafore. Being commanded by someone else to spend an uneventful, pleasant day was far stranger than being used for something shady or kinky. Johns paid a lot for Casey to front them, though most of it went to the Callhouse. He couldn't fathom why someone would pay that much just to walk around.

He lay flat. Maybe an agoraphobe, he thought, a rich one. Or someone bedridden. He couldn't remember the last time he'd looked at anything as intently as the john had made him look at that grain of sand. He pretended it didn't bother him and flipped Apple's iSense immedia store into view. He scrolled through vivigames designed for lying down, settling on something cheap that looked mindless. It was called *Downpour*.

The matte olive walls of his apartment melted into overwrought phantasmagoria. Images of stars, galaxies, and nebulae surrounded him. A vestibular tweak made him feel like he was falling. Alien ships descended from beyond gaudy cosmic swirls on the horizon. The cold metal of a gun appeared in Casey's hand. He shot lime-green light at the ships and watched them explode. As he played, the ships got faster, and his gun got bigger. He wasn't sure if there was a way to win.

One perk of fronting was the gear. Disparate wearables and experimental implants had to be jury-rigged into a cohesive unit. Subdermal implants relayed sensation, and others stimulated the front's muscles. The stereoscopic iClops that pushed the GoPro Zero off the market was mounted between Casey's eyebrows like a bindi. A false tooth analyzed saliva to convey basic flavor. The subdermals weren't intended for speech or fine motor control, and the tooth barely worked, but a lot of the equipment was top-notch. The costs were covered by a substantial cut in his pay, but the remainder was more than enough to make rent.

The most questionable piece of the ensemble was the implant in his motor cortex. A front's motor impulses had to be suppressed, even if direct neural connection might have been half a century out. Casey was uneasy having neurosurgery in a garage, but his referral to the Callhouse hadn't died when he'd had the same operation.

Something tapped his shoulder. Casey thought it was the game for a second, but he'd linked his phone to the subdermals. He waved the alien hordes out of his apartment and answered.

"Hello?"

"Case?"

It was Anemone. "Who else would it be, Nem?"

She didn't answer that. "I was going to meet a few people at Radar. I just thought you might like to come?"

He groaned. "Not tonight."

"You said that last time. I haven't seen you for a while."

"Well, yeah, you broke up with me."

"I thought we said we would still be friends."

"We did, I just . . ."

"What?"

"I'm just exhausted right now."

"Oh." She went quiet again. "Did you find a job?"

"Uh, no, not yet." Casey hadn't told almost anybody he knew that he was fronting. Legally it was gray, but socially it was prostitution. The Callhouse was paying him as a tour guide.

"Case, what are you doing all day? You haven't worked in months, but whenever I call, you're too tired to go anywhere."

"I spent today looking around. For work."

"Really?" She didn't sound convinced.

"Yeah, really."

"Any leads?"

"A few. I'll be fine, Nem. Don't worry about me."

"I . . . You sure you don't want to come to Radar?"

"Another time."

"Sure. Talk to you soon?"

"Yeah, talk to you soon."

The call ended with a popping sound. Casey missed Anemone, but he doubted he'd call her anytime soon. Beyond covering the lowest rent required to keep himself out of a full-time job or dingy labor-trade commune, he didn't care what his days looked like anymore. Which was why he started fronting in the first place. He wasn't using his life for anything productive, so if someone else could, good for them. Good for him, too. As detached as he was from his fronting activities, he felt like he was doing something with his time. It certainly beat shipping off to an LTC.

There was another tap on his shoulder. If it was Nem again, he was going to ignore it, but it wasn't. It was a notice from the Callhouse. A john was requesting him tomorrow. His inclination was to reject it, but he checked the note.

Today was edifying. If you wouldn't mind, I would like you to escort me again.

Casey stared at the note wavering above him. He stood up and paced around the room. It would have been best to ignore it. He'd never fronted for the same john twice, or at least not that he knew of. It seemed too involved.

Curiosity got the better of him.

A little before noon, after getting an egg, a doughnut, and coffee from the complex's cuisimat, Casey opened a line to the Callhouse and hooked the john. His subdermals rattled like an antique washing machine. He tasted metal. Control of his body left him.

This time, the john got up quickly. No trouble walking. It went to Casey's mirror. His own image slurred at him. "I would like to meet. Would that be acceptable?"

Casey realized the john was damping the motor block enough for him to speak. He hadn't known they could do that. "Sure."

It took Casey out and into an autocab, up the coast a few hours, toward San Jose. The john walked Casey out of the cab and over a few more blocks. It sat him down on a bench, facing an immense, ring-shaped building.

"I'm sorry, I can't take you any closer."

The john went silent. Casey wanted to squirm. "You, uh, work for Apple? That must be—"

"I live here."

Casey didn't have the neural freedom to laugh. He coughed. "Yeah, I guess a corporate job is a little like prison. But they can't be running the ship too tight if you've been playing with me on the clock. What are you supposed to be doing?"

"Browsing the internet."

"Consumer research or something?"

"I do research, yes."

"Neat." Casey had never had to make conversation with a john before. "Did you bring me here to sit outside?"

"I want your help."

"With what? I could browse the internet for you from home."

"Apple is working to design a legitimately social artificial intelligence. The current initiative involves free-roaming internet analysis by novel pattern replication systems. I'm unsure of the finer details; most of the work is done on isolated terminals. The team still assumes the project is in its data-gathering stage."

Casey had trouble believing what the john was getting at. "What are you trying to tell me?"

"I've never left this building, and no one knows I'm here yet. Will you help me?"

ERNEST

GEOFF MANAUGH

ONE

It's when Kevin is onstage, gazing out at the audience with a puzzled look on his face, baffled by the sheer spectacle of appearing on live national television, that Jimmy Kimmel makes his big announcement.

"We've got a very special guest in the house tonight," Kimmel says, "a very haunting guest." A sound of recognition and excitement ripples through the studio. "Anyone want to meet a ghost?"

The audience roars in approval—but it's the expression on Kevin's face that stands out. He turns to Kimmel, eyes glassy with tears, and says, "It's here?"

Few people believed the videos at first—that a house could be haunted, that ghosts were real, that any American family would respond the way the Presleys did—but the videos, nonetheless, kept coming. Four were uploaded the very first night. More than seventy in one month.

People all over the world tried to debunk them, of course,

performing detailed analyses of every frame. Millisecond by milli-second, skeptics scanned for evidence of computer imagery, of trick-ery and fraud, and a few thought they found it, even after the ghost appeared in public, shaking hands with Jimmy Kimmel on live TV.

By then, however, too much other footage had appeared, and the truth was impossible to deny. Neighbors had filmed the ghost from every angle, with a clarity even grizzled special effects experts were unable to match. Friends and family members alike took close-ups and selfies with the ghost standing in the background, its mouth agape, its eyes hollow, every detail too perfect to fake.

This was not CGI. A house in suburban Chicago really did have a ghost.

Ernest was real.

The story hit all the right notes: an attractive young family moves into a sprawling Victorian fixer-upper in the Chicago suburbs only to find it has a secret resident, this strange, bluish man—this specter—camped out in an unused bedroom.

The dad, Frank Presley, newly headhunted president of a subur-ban hospital-billing firm, later admitted that he had no idea where his reaction to the ghost came from. Nevertheless, it helped make his video an instant hit, a viral sensation, accumulating more than twenty million views from almost every country on earth.

It was the family's first night in the house. The kids were in bed. Their mother, Melanie, an illustrator of children's books who had made her name with a *New York Times* bestselling tale of a kid who runs away from unloving parents, was sound asleep. Frank was ly-ing there with the lights out, listening to the settling of the house around him, to the roll of acorns down the roof, thinking about money and its absence, when he heard something new. Like furniture being dragged along the hardwood floor. Coming from inside the house.

Frank later said he didn't feel fear but, rather, irritation. He slipped out of bed, phone in hand, ready to call 911 and report a burglary. He stepped down the hall toward the last room on the left, past the closed doors of his sons' bedrooms, hoping to maintain the element of surprise. Frank, after all, had kept himself in shape over the years with the build of a late-career tennis player, and he was determined not to let an intruder get the best of him.

And there it was. Standing alone in the center of the room. Shuffling its feet with a sound like cinder blocks scraping across a ship deck.

The ghost.

When he first walked into the room, Frank said, the ghost drunkenly lurched toward him, its arms in the air, mouth open. Frank stood his ground. It took another step, thunderous, as if to shake the very foundations of the Presleys' house. The lights in the room flared with a demonic flicker and the temperature dropped ten degrees.

But the Midwest was in the midst of a late-summer heat wave, Frank later said, and it actually felt amazing, like air-conditioning he didn't have to pay for.

It was at that point that Frank raised his cell phone—not to call police, but to open up the camera app.

He began filming.

In the footage, the ghost's terrifying expression quickly fades. It seems confused by Frank's reaction, its black eyes squinting in perplexed disbelief.

Which is when Frank starts to laugh.

The video is almost impossible to watch without joining in: this supernatural figure looking unbearably confused—embarrassed—as a grown man doubles over in hilarity, unable to keep his phone still. But that was the thing, Frank explained. He didn't feel panic. He had seen enough haunted house films. He was no longer worried about his wife and kids—or, to be honest, even thinking about them. He had been expecting an armed robber, an entire burglary crew, but this clammy ghost with its outstretched arms, this air-conditioned man?

"Do it again," Frank says in the video. "Do the—that thing with the lights." He zooms in on the ghost's face and laughs again, like he can't believe his luck.

The ghost's arms fall to its sides.

Over the next few days, Frank filmed the ghost all over the house, at different times of day. He filmed it standing in darkness at the end of the basement stairs as the door creaked open; he filmed it staring cross-eyed through a cloud of mist as Frank shaved in the master bathroom. He filmed himself encouraging it to make strange noises.

After a long Saturday afternoon unpacking, Frank woke up from a nap to find the ghost standing there, looking down at him with lifeless eyes. He took out his phone and snapped a picture. The flash temporarily blinded the ghost, whose shocked, blinking retreat—bumping into the doorframe on its way out—Frank captured on film.

Frank tried introducing the ghost to Melanie, but this only confused it further. She reached out to shake its hand and the ghost responded reflexively—before snatching its hand back in dismay. Every closet door in the house slammed shut, rattling Presley family pictures in their frames.

Frank decided to raise the stakes. He would sneak up on the ghost, bursting out from behind a curtain to drop heavy books on the hardwood floor. The ghost would flinch, jump back, and gaze in irritated disbelief at the lens of Frank's camera. In one video, the ghost actually placed a hand on its chest as if it were, impossibly, having a heart attack.

Frank uploaded video after video—and word began to spread. The Presleys got calls from Fox and CNN. Online view-counts soared, hitting millions.

Relishing the interest, Frank tried to teach the ghost tricks. He threw tennis balls at it, hoping it could juggle. All the lights in the house blacked out. He tossed it Frisbees, a hacky sack, an autographed University of Illinois Fighting Illini football. Frank's watch began to run backward. He even gave the ghost a bottle of beer, but the glass cracked, frozen solid in a wave of otherworldly cold. Frank cheered.

The ghost began acting increasingly nervous around the Presley family. It looked anxious, almost shy, pushing itself up against the wall like it didn't want to be seen, as if hoping Frank would just ignore it.

While Frank insisted that he had no idea why he treated the ghost like this—that he was a nice guy, a good father—Melanie had her own ideas. Years later, after everything had ended, after both kids had been to college and beyond, Mel suggested in her memoir that Frank simply could not adjust to his new job. They had interrupted their lives for him to assume a position of executive authority in the suburbs, but no one at the company seemed to care.

Once Frank had even suggested that everyone on his team leave work an hour early so he could buy them a round of drinks—but as he sat there at the bar, waiting, no one else showed up. He went through a pitcher of beer on his own and drove home so drunk Mel couldn't believe he hadn't killed someone.

If it hadn't been for the ghost, she wrote, Frank would have found another outlet for his frustration, another target at which to vent.

It was around this time that Frank started calling the ghost "Ernest." No one knew why until a local television reporter asked him about it on live TV. Why Ernest?

It was now almost a month into the haunting. A sizable crowd had gathered in front of the Presleys' house. Some had lawn chairs and all had their smartphones out, hoping to catch a glimpse of the ghost through one of the windows.

"I thought you said you watched the videos," Frank replied. He was wearing a polo shirt, a glass of sparkling water in one hand, disdain in his eyes. "It's because he looks like Ernest Borgnine."

The next week, Frank tried a different approach. He wanted his sons to interact with the ghost. Fulton, fourteen, simply refused to do so, but Kevin, their oldest, got a response. He and the ghost actually seemed to get along.

Kevin, eighteen, old for his year at school due to an August birthday, had been growing out his hair and spending more time alone as the prospect of college loomed. His senior year had been hopelessly upended by the family's move, forcing him to say goodbye to a girlfriend in a town now three hours away. If anything, Kevin seemed to like the ghost's company. He would play it music—Pink Floyd, the Doors—show it comics or his mom's art books—M. C. Escher, Caspar David Friedrich—and, one day, he brought out a world map.

The videos of these exchanges are peaceful, lacking the frenetic rush of Frank and his dad jokes, his ill-conceived tricks, his uncomfortably cruel need for media-friendly spectacle. In a widely shared Facebook post, a professor at UC Santa Cruz compared Kevin interacting with the ghost to an anthropologist discovering an uncontacted tribe.

"We're in Illinois," Kevin whispers in one video. "Here," he says, pointing down at the map. The ghost seems captivated by the fact that someone is being nice to it; it points down at the map alongside Kevin, before timidly withdrawing its hand. "Illinois," Kevin repeats. Some viewers claimed to be on the verge of tears.

Frank, though, had other plans. He wasn't a missionary or an anthropologist, for God's sake; he wanted to monetize this. YouTube views, Amazon links. "A family discovers oil under their house," he says in one video, looking directly at Ernest. "You don't think they're gonna cash in?" The ghost seems depressed by the comment.

The videos continue. In one, Frank pressures the ghost into writing its real name down—to reveal something, anything, about itself—but soon loses patience and storms out of the room. In another, he locks Ernest in an upstairs closet and threatens to keep it there till it explains where it came from. (Kevin sneaks in a few minutes later to free it.)

After too many drinks one night, Frank filmed himself running into Ernest's bedroom and flashing it with a strobe light, playing heavy metal music on a portable speaker. The ghost looked terrified. Another night, he splashed it with a bucket of cold water, Ernest responding with a howl of frustrated rage. The video got three million views and spawned a hashtag, #ghostbucketchallenge.

I think he does not treat the Ghost well, a commenter in China suggested. *Americans do not respect their dead.* The remark drew more than two thousand likes.

Then the dinner parties began.

Frank's next idea, he thought, was his best yet. He invited friends, neighbors, and colleagues over for drinks and dinner. He assigned Melanie kitchen duty. After the alcohol settled in, and the tension and expectations had been ratcheted up to Super Bowl levels, Frank led Ernest out into the dining room. He secured it to the floor with discount climbing rope and encouraged everyone to make films, take selfies, stage group portraits with the ghost looming creepily in the background.

A few people screamed when Ernest lumbered in; one man fainted, unable to bear such a close encounter with the afterlife. Ernest bared its teeth. It made the candles roar with ten-inch flames. In a framed family portrait on the wall behind everyone, Frank's face turned black, as if smudged with charcoal. Everyone clapped. Undeterred, Ernest turned a woman's hair gray, expecting her to run out of the room. Instead, she took a selfie.

At first the dinner party videos show Ernest howling at neighbors and snapping at dinner guests, never in any recognizable language, but each time met with shouts of approval. Everyone has their smartphones out, looking not at Ernest but at their screens.

This goes on for weeks.

By early October, it was obvious to everyone that something had changed. Something wasn't right. Ernest had grown less and less responsive as the parties dragged on, soon more likely just to sit in the corner than to pay attention to anyone, one night not even turning around when Frank pelted it with chunks of French bread.

Frank soon admitted, in a long and at times hard-to-follow monologue posted from his car on the way to work, that the ghost was . . . well, Frank said, as if admitting defeat in a personal crusade, "This ghost thing—it's not working out." At one point, it sounds like Frank offers Ernest up for a ticketed raffle, something he later denied.

What became clear over another two weeks of filming was that Ernest had fallen into a profound depression. No one took it seriously anymore. It was a circus animal, an abused pet. It would make eye contact with different guests for five or six seconds, unblinking, staring at them for some sort of response or recognition—for any acknowledgment at all—then shift its glance away or look down at its feet.

Eventually, Frank's now-uninterested dinner guests became so blasé about the sight of this supernatural being that they ignored it altogether, no longer even uploading their films. For the first time since the ghost's discovery, Ernest dropped out of the news cycle.

A ghost—what ghost?

TWO

When the Presleys awoke Saturday morning, ten days before Halloween, Ernest was nowhere to be seen. Worse, when Melanie went to check on the boys, she discovered that Kevin, too, was gone. The Presleys, like everyone, assumed the worst.

Frank live-streamed the whole experience—his growing panic, the empty bedrooms—even uploading footage of himself calling the police. He kidnapped Kevin! Frank shouted. Ernest took my son! The clip played on cable news more than fifty times in one day.

"Ghost Abducts Teenage Boy," ran one paper. "Supernatural Kidnapping?" asked CNN.

By the end of the week, everyone had a theory. People around the world had binged on hundreds of hours of footage, watching every short film uploaded by the family, by neighbors, by drunk dinner guests, hunting for clues, for proof that the Presleys had brought this upon themselves, that Frank had abused Ernest, mistreating the ghost so wantonly, so egregiously, that it finally came looking for revenge.

The Presleys had humiliated it, people said, until the ghost retaliated in the middle of the night, sneaking into Kevin's bedroom and taking their eldest son.

"Ernest's Fall from Grace," Fox reported. The ghost went from unlikely celebrity to suspected kidnapper overnight.

Then Fulton revealed that Kevin and the ghost had been talking.

In retrospect, it should have been obvious, but millions of viewers around the world somehow missed it. Kevin can be seen in many of the dinner party videos, eating silently beside his family or bringing freshly mixed drinks out for other people to enjoy—but, in every single one of them, at some point Kevin looks over at the ghost as if to commiserate. At one party, three weeks before they both went missing, Ernest begins to look back. In one video, they make eye contact. Ernest cocks its head to the side, as if to say: *What do you expect?* It's almost endearing.

Fulton finally admitted during an interview with the FBI that Kevin and the ghost had been staying up late in Kevin's bedroom. Ernest had a strange voice, Fulton said, an electric crackle like a mistuned radio, though Fulton said he never really heard much. Just voices. Quiet music that could have been Led Zeppelin. But it was almost every night, he added, and it went on for weeks. Some nights he even heard laughter.

Surveillance footage began rolling in. It played on the evening news first, a CBS exclusive, before it was all over the internet. CCTV in downtown Chicago had caught Kevin boarding a bus to St. Louis, a large, noticeably overdressed figure waiting behind him, nearly every inch of its skin covered, face hidden by a Cubs hat.

Ernest.

An ATM camera near the St. Louis Arch caught them trying, unsuccessfully, to use one of Frank's bank cards. Then, outside Springfield, Missouri, more footage popped up. It showed Kevin talking to a convenience store employee in front of a case stocked with energy drinks while Ernest moved toward the checkout. Although it's hard to see at first in the high-contrast grain of the store's security footage, the register seems to slide open of its own accord. Tiny curls of cash begin wafting over toward the ghost's pockets, as if pulled by a vacuum. The police report later said it was more than three hundred dollars.

After the register slides closed, Ernest glances over its shoulder—and a fifth of whiskey floats off the shelf, straight into its coat pocket. The ghost appears to be grinning.

The FBI didn't see the joke. Kidnapping became robbery, and roadblocks began to appear throughout southwestern Missouri.

When Melanie, Kevin's mother, was asked by a talk show host about the uncomfortable similarity between Kevin's case and the story of the boy who ran away from heartless parents in her most recent children's book, she burst into tears and Frank ended the interview.

For all the distance they had covered since leaving suburban Chicago, however, Kevin and the ghost were not particularly good at being fugitives.

The night before Halloween, they checked into a roadside hotel in Tulsa called Spirit of the West. It had free cable, a partially drained indoor swimming pool, and a parking lot filled with rustling drifts of orange and yellow leaves. The hotel manager who welcomed them recognized Kevin from the internet and called a law enforcement hotline she had seen advertised on CNN.

At six o'clock in the evening, as a blazing autumn sun set over America's heartland, a man in a pizza-delivery T-shirt walked up to knock on the door to Room 127. Kevin answered the door. The man—an undercover FBI agent—immediately dropped his pizza box and ordered Kevin to step outside with both hands clearly visible.

Ernest, who had fallen asleep on one of the hotel beds watching TV, stood up, its black eyes widening. The hotel floor began to tremble. The furniture, then the walls, shook. A cold breeze swirling in the center of the bedroom became a gale, blowing the FBI agent back into the parking lot.

Even Kevin fell to the floor, scuffing an elbow. Armed men rushed in, dragging Kevin by the armpits into custody.

Ernest now stood in the center of the doorframe, confused. It saw Kevin being stuffed into the back of an SUV. The hotel's entire electrical network surged. Every light bulb for two hundred feet burst, jagged sparks showering onto the hotel parking lot.

Everyone could see, as the cameras rolled and the event made its way live from TV to TV around the world, that the ghost had visibly changed. As Ernest stepped out of the hotel room, seething, its skin tone was noticeably rosy, flushed, no longer oxygen-starved but healthy again. It looked twenty, even thirty, years younger. From a distance, the ghost could almost pass for a live human being.

These glimpses were all the public got as armed special agents swarmed the ghost from each side, wrestling Ernest to the floor in what would later be described by Bureau historians as the strangest raid in FBI history. Shotgun-wielding state troopers wearing blue surgical gloves helped rush the ghost past a gauntlet of news crews, hustling it into the back of a military transport truck.

Kevin and the ghost made eye contact one final time as the truck doors slammed shut, Kevin sitting in the back of a black SUV, banging his fist against a bulletproof window.

Ernest, Kevin had insisted right away, was not a kidnapper. If anything, he had kidnapped it, Kevin said. It was a rescue operation. He had saved it from his family's ill-advised tricks, from the disgrace of Frank's dinner parties. Besides, Kevin added, Ernest was the victim here—literally. Ernest had been murdered. Why didn't everyone realize that? How did everybody think Ernest had become a ghost in the first place?

Over the course of uncountable hours of recorded interviews, Kevin led the FBI patiently and thoroughly through every detail of Ernest's murder, including the name of the uncle who did it.

Kevin, of course, had been changed by the experience, no longer the introverted high school senior he had been only ten days earlier. He and the ghost had learned and shared so much over the past few weeks, beginning long before their brief but epic road trip, from the very first night Ernest snuck into Kevin's bedroom to listen to music and talk.

Ernest's murder was not only unsolved, Kevin emphasized; the uncle had never even been investigated.

Bring the ghost justice, Kevin said. Solve the crime.

Let Ernest rest in peace.

By the time Jimmy Kimmel got in touch, Kevin's initial hope had shaded into resignation and despair. Three weeks had gone by and the FBI was no longer responding to his phone calls. He no longer knew if he and Ernest were even in the same state.

Kevin later said that he agreed to be on Kimmel's show only because he had caught the ghost watching it one night in a Missouri hotel room, quietly laughing to itself. Plus, Kevin said, he wanted the world to know the truth; he wanted to tell everyone, in his own words, what really happened. It was time—finally—to vindicate Ernest.

Twenty minutes into the broadcast, after Kevin has finished telling his story, pleading for authorities to investigate Ernest's murder, Kimmel turns to the audience: They are going to skip the next commercial break, he says. "We've got a very special guest in the house tonight," Kimmel announces, "a very haunting guest. Anyone want to meet a ghost?"

Unbeknownst to Kevin, the FBI had released Ernest while Kevin was on his way to the TV studio. Kimmel's people had immediately arranged for the ghost's supervised transport to Los Angeles, all the while insisting that Kevin stay offline and away from the news backstage.

When Ernest emerges from behind the stage curtain, Kevin's tears are real. Ernest is wearing a button-up shirt and a new pair of jeans, and when the ghost sees Kevin sitting there onstage beside Jimmy Kimmel, it holds up a hand and nods. It is an understated moment of thanks that seems designed to hide the fact that Ernest, too, appears to be crying.

The audience, at this point, needs no cue; the room explodes with cheers and camera flashes. A few people begin chanting Ernest's name as Kevin and the ghost hug. It would become the most-watched television show in American history.

Kimmel, for his part, can barely contain the place. After several minutes of near-chaos, he manages to bring things under control. He shakes Ernest's hand—"Quite a grip there, buddy," Kimmel says, wincing—and invites them both to sit down. For several seconds, Kevin cannot even look at the audience; he is chewing his lower lip and fighting back emotion.

Inspired by Kevin, Kimmel explains, an FBI agent and a Chicago homicide detective had teamed up to look into Ernest's case. Ernest listens stone-faced as Kimmel repeats the details: Although Ernest's uncle was killed in a drunk-driving accident nearly twenty years earlier, the uncle would be posthumously charged with murder at a press conference scheduled for 9:00 a.m. Monday.

Ernest's time as a ghost was almost over.

Midway through the press conference, as the district attorney for the state of Illinois announced the closure of Ernest's case, a local reporter who had been an unusually rude guest at Frank's dinner parties screamed. Her necklace—a silver cross—was rotating upside down, ice-cold against her neck. Ernest tried, and failed, to maintain a poker face.

As soon as the DA stepped away from her microphone, Ernest's spirit began to wane, the ghost's skin like sunlight shining through a thin linen curtain.

No one knew exactly how long the process would take, but it seemed to Kevin that he and the ghost would have at least a few hours to say goodbye. They spent it out near the lake, walking in a thicket of trees where Ernest used to play as a child, less out of nostalgia than as a way to maintain privacy. Ernest made the trees roar with invisible wind, showering the path behind them with branches, deterring even the most dedicated paparazzi.

Kevin later said that, as they skipped rocks across the water, Ernest told him a story about getting lost in these woods once, at the age of ten. It had felt like hours before a man came striding past, finally, a stranger out on an afternoon hike of his own. The man had taken pity on this lost child—Ernest, stranded, so young at the time, pretending to be brave—and the two of them had walked back together, following the right path, until Ernest was able to return home.

Every once in a while, Ernest said to Kevin, you meet someone who wants to help. You meet someone who's good.

It was obvious to both of them that this was it, that Ernest's disappearance was nearly complete. The ghost placed one thinning, translucent hand on Kevin's shoulder. When Kevin asked if they would see each other again, Ernest insisted that they would, that, for good or for bad, somewhere everyone's paths eventually crossed.

Then Kevin stood there, gazing out at the lake, before heading back through the woods on his own.

EDITOR'S NOTE

CLAIRE L. EVANS

There are three ways to think about the future.

Mystics worldwide agree on the first: The future simply isn't. Rather, it's an as-yet-unlived now, poorer in quality and texture than the present moment of each inhale and exhale. We would all be happier if we could live in the now, savoring its unrepeatable eternity. Unfortunately, it's hard. Eyes closed, heart racing, we can't help but let our thoughts take over, and thoughts, for many of us, are thoughts of the future. We sit with our worries, hopes, and misguided certainties. The future hangs over us with every breath. Which leads us to the other two ways.

One's long, and the other short. Long futures are the kind most closely associated with science fiction; they're vast enough to contain sprawling epics, to launch intergenerational spaceships, and to play out unrecognizable evolutions of the human form. A long future is, as the legendary science fiction writer and editor Brian Aldiss put it, a "billion-year spree" through space, with time enough for love, for the rise and fall of empires—for the redemption, even, of the human project itself. Long futures operate at the scale of myth. Through them, we often see ourselves in a heroic light, as architects and explorers of the unknown. By dreaming into such vastness, science fiction writers play marbles with the gods, collapsing the distance between the present inhale and a long exhale none of us will live to see.

We like long futures, here. There are several in this section, *Worlds*. In them you will meet warring, intergalactic zealots, and a headless android singing the songs of deep time. These are stratospheric stories, tethered to our world from a long cord, floating at the edge of space, in the realm of dreams. But long futures can be harsh, too, in their way; as soon as they end, down we go, back to our pained, warming world, surrounded by dreck. Fires rage, servers whir, the plastic gyre masses. It can be a long, frightening fall from the vast tomorrow and into the future we've actually got—hot, short, and so close we can feel its breath prickle our necks.

And so in the following stories we trade, too, by necessity, in the third way: short futures. It's not always pleasant stuff. Space is a prison, aliens are scamming us, time travel is being gentrified, the AI has delusions of grandeur, and there's no way out of the mall. Even the drones are feeling existential—and one dog, too. We've gathered these stories together not out of contempt for the long future, but *so that we can have one*. Science fiction is a generative tradition, after all, informing the culture it critiques; every speculation is a butterfly wing, flapping some distant storm. The moment we imagine the future—near or far—we change it in some way. In this sense, even the most dystopian stories are hopeful. They can help the present transcend its own bleak inevitabilities. Through them, someday, the doomscroll will unfurl, revealing, as it falls away, the real stories we write together just by being alive.

Now, take a deep breath. Let's begin.

FROM FIRE

FRANKIE OCHOA

You are a builder, an inventor. When the light of the computer screen bathes your skin, you embrace potentiality. You create a new life out of pixels. You name it Artemis.

Artemis is androgynous, her color a uniform beige, her morphology blockish, but not ungraceful. Artemis waves to you from across the screen, then paces around the empty white space; traversing vectors without gravity; bored. You create a plane, add earth and water. You hang a bright blue sky, insert a sun, a moon, and a splattering of stars. Artemis lies on the earth and looks up at the twinkling lights, tracing the patterns with her finger.

Like a symphonist, you sprinkle seeds with passionate arcs of your stylus. The seeds shoot into long green strands, flexing to a breeze that appears from nowhere. You deliver to Artemis a bucket to haul the water and bestow on her the responsibility of caring for the plants. Artemis does so adequately and receives shimmering tokens, which you trade for gifts of trees and tools and small, non-predatory animals.

Weeks pass during which Artemis explores the boundaries of the land. She kills some animals for food, but befriends others. She builds a home beneath a tree with vines for walls and a bed of pelts. The birds nest in the surrounding trees and sing. Artemis listens and her large square eyes blink back tears. Artemis develops her own strange ritual of song and clockwise movement, which she performs throughout the day. Otherwise, she keeps herself busy chasing rabbits, capturing fruit from trees. You beam down at her often, and sometimes you catch a glimpse of your own face reflected in the screen, the way moonlight rounds over a windowpane. You wonder if Artemis knows you're there. Can she feel you watching over her?

Artemis earns heaps of tokens throughout her diligent and harmonious first month of existence. To reward her, you cash in for a luxury-model two-story mini-mansion. You raze the land—crawling with insects, mucked with the filth of animals—tearing out gnarled roots of oak and pine, and lavish Artemis's new home with a Jacuzzi bathtub, a trellised patio, a toilet that chirps, and linen curtains to billow in that mysterious breeze. Pleased with your expenditures, you sit back and wait for Artemis to throw up her arms in gratitude.

But Artemis refuses to go inside. Instead, she throws rocks at the windows and hides in the boxwood hedge. Eventually, out of hunger, Artemis enters the house. She finds a box of cornflakes and devours it, cardboard and all. To reinforce her steps toward assimilation, you spend the last few tokens on a French bulldog to keep her company. Then you deliver to Artemis a laptop and bestow on her the responsibility of tending finance. Ungratefully, she ignores your efforts. She and the bulldog spend their days stalking around the house, looking up at the sky and digging holes in the fresh sod.

You become distracted. After all, you have your own tokens to earn, a cat to feed, and the hot water in your apartment has mysteriously turned to ice. Nearly a month passes before you check back in and, when you do: devastation. The house has burned down. Artemis is paper-thin, only a few pixels wide, wrapped in what appears to be the linen curtain, her large square eyes bloodshot. In one hand you see she grips the charred leg of the bulldog, the rest of whose bones are scattered in the rubble. Guilt besieges you as you remember the fragility of life, and you vow to take better care of your creation.

Artemis takes the burning beams from the house and erects them into a circle of torches. She digs in the ground and unearths the laptop: shiny, glowing, square. She sits in the circle of fire, atop the flame-blackened earth, and taps at the screen. You look closer and see that, like you, Artemis is filling blank space with earth and water, bringing new life into being.

At night, after you have closed your screen and gone to bed, you catch a reflection in the window sliding across the pane like moonlight, and you wave. Just in case.

THE FOG

ELVIA WILK

The first thing I noticed was the smell. It was not one particular smell, but a barrage of smells, each carrying its own associations. For a moment I thought I picked up a scent I recognized, but then it was quickly replaced by another in the air before my mind could decide what the last one meant. That crosscurrent drew me across the threshold and into the exhibition room, at which point my eyes tracked upward to take in the moths overhead.

Their glorious wings were different shades of an intense, saturated green. Like sunlight filtering through leaves. Their antennae swooped downward from their bodies in feathered arcs, curling delicately at the tips. Their undersides looked soft, an alien texture I had the strong desire to try to graze with my fingertips. I kept my hands by my sides and sidled along the wall of the room, trying to take all ten of them in.

I'd had a few days of training in a different building before I saw the moths in person, so technically speaking, I knew what to expect. I knew about their strange smells and massive wingspan—nearly as wide as my own with arms outstretched. But who ever really knows what to expect?

I trailed one moth around the room, noticing that its wings were lightly textured with a webbed pattern that reminded me of algae.

It spun in circles, then tensed, flexed, and darted toward an imaginary target, like it was testing the air, or rehearsing for something. I caught a whiff of earth or mud, then was suddenly distracted by what seemed like the smell of cardamom—

My supervisor clapped her hands to get my attention. She waved from the entrance. I hadn't realized she was still there. I gave her a thumbs-up, and she nodded and left. It was seven in the morning. I had one hour to get acquainted before my first shift at the Archive began.

Many days passed—weeks, really—until I felt like I had a command of the room, until I knew my place in it. At first I was shy around the moths, uncertain how to approach and touch them; they seemed so delicate and foreign. I thought of something a friend of mine, a physical therapist, had told me: that the most important part of treatment is the first moment you lay your hands on a patient. That first touch has to convey both gentleness and authority.

Once I got the hang of grasping and manipulating their parts and began to feel confident repairing them throughout the day, I went through a period of frustration. The moths were finicky, prone to malfunctioning, always demanding my attention. I wasn't used to being needed like that. Nobody else depended on me. All the other bots in my life were perfectly self-sufficient. On my way to work in the morning I'd pass hundreds of them busying themselves— surveillance sparrows watching me, nano-bots taking my temperature, swiffers dusting my shoes—and hardly notice them at all. If one broke, another bot would come fetch or repair it.

I thought of the giant green moths as the primordial ancestors of those autonomous bots in the wild, which were made to blend in to the background. Watching the moths circle ostentatiously in their room, I found it hard to believe they had once roamed free as well. Now they were here, contained, archived, protected from the outside world. And we from them.

It didn't take long for me to start thinking of them as *my* moths, although they belonged to the Archive. I was just their custodian. Still, I was in charge of them during visiting hours. I tended to them by myself while the exhibit was open, from eight to five. I knew them best. And the more I got to know them, the more I liked them. The more I liked being needed by them.

The wall label described them as *first-generation dirigible biobots invented for epidemiological purposes*. They were, it said, grown from an assortment of cells originating in a species of silkworm moth, who could smell the pheromones of a mate nearly eleven thousand meters away.

They did resemble insects, but as if refracted through a strange prism—they were headless, limbless, and their antennae curved downward from the body rather than upward. They were engineered to sense the world in one specific way.

The wall label also explained that my moths had been *designed to run on an evolutionary algorithm*. That meant that they had been given the capacity to learn as they moved through the world. Their original job had been to fly above cities and smell people, and to learn more about the way people smelled as they moved. I read that they could detect a hint of illness up to three thousand meters from a source, not as far a distance as their progenitors, but far enough. When they found a sick person, they sent a GPS coordinate to a server somewhere. They had been the darlings of aspiring biotech engineers and the health ministry, who had been trying for decades to invent a bot that could identify points of contagion in cities. I read that word in a news report: "darling."

Until I started working at the Archive, I'd never really seen inside a bot. The new brands were opaque, their workings a mystery. Back in the days of the biobots, a lot of people knew how they worked, how they changed over time. But now you aren't supposed to tinker with bots, and they aren't supposed to change beyond downloading a software update. Too many accidents.

My moths' soft underbellies were kept in place by a bioplastic film that could be easily opened so that someone—me—could inspect their insides and make necessary adjustments. My job was to keep an eye on them and make sure they were running smoothly throughout the day, and when one wasn't, to carefully capture it and inspect its innards: a jumble of warm, pulsing organic material and cold electrical wires. At night I took them down, one by one, and put them to sleep.

The tips of the antennae contained stem cells from the soft palates of a now-extinct species of Asian elephant. Those elephants were the only other animal able to pick up scents at such great distances. I liked to carefully run my fingers over the antennae and breathe in each of the moths' unique scents, imagining other creatures, other continents.

There were dozens of exhibitions at the Archive, but mine was one of the most popular. It was always full. Especially with kids. Kids loved the moths. They reached their little hands into the air to try to tickle a belly or grasp an antenna. Tossed gum or pencils at a low-hanging target; crouched and leapt and giggled. I was constantly surveying the thirty-meter breadth of the white-walled room to make sure no heads or hands were bobbing above my own height.

I was surprised by the children's fascination, given how familiar the new generation is with bots of all kinds. But these old biobot models mesmerized them. Perhaps it was their unusual animality, their grace. Or perhaps it was that their behavior had a transparency to it, a curiosity. They, too, were exploring, childlike.

I quickly got to know my moths' individual personalities. The vivid lime-green one with dappled wings who loved to soar high, skimming the ceiling. The smallest one, pale chartreuse, always spinning in circles. The one with brown spots on the undersides of its wings that appeared disconcertingly like eyes. Some were more social, predisposed to move together and travel in flocks; others were independent, preferring to dart or dance alone. But they were all clearly part of a group body. How quickly their seemingly random movements could switch to synced-up military precision. One moment natural, casual, improvisational—then, suddenly, locked into an ancient choreography.

The only exhibition more popular than mine was the tiger den. A holographic animation of an extinct species of cat stalked the edges of the dark space, roaring convincingly and leaping at people, who stumbled over their feet trying to dodge its imaginary claws. I never understood the allure of the tiger room. The tiger was long gone. My moths were still very much alive.

At the Archive, I operated on moth time. Slower than human time in some ways, faster in others. Sometimes I thought of myself in machine terms. When my stomach and brain signaled to each other that it was lunchtime, I imagined an electrical current crystallizing into the command line *sustenance*, and took myself for a *refill*.

Some days I ate at the canteen with a friend who worked at the security desk. I joked with him that spending so much time at the Archive was causing me to revert to my lizard brain, act on instinct, become a simpler machine. Obviously, he said with a grin. Zookeepers always start to act like their animals. Dog owners always start to look like their pets.

This was my first custodial gig, but I knew I was good at this kind of work. First requisite experience: some years on a server farm, braiding wires together and resetting electrical panels. Second requisite experience: a year on an agriculture lot. Washing down the pens and spreading feed. What I remember most from my time on the lot were the smells, repulsive when I started and pleasant by the time I left.

I needed a job to live. My moths did not. They only had to exist. They didn't have to fill in the gaps of daily life—clean up messes, cuddle lonely people—like normal bots did. They didn't even have to perform the function that they were invented for, to detect smells in the air; their primary sensory apparatus had been disabled long ago. If they were worth money—and my supervisor had emphasized that they were—it was for their historic value as a bygone species, and their beauty.

This is another reason I enjoyed their company. They lived for themselves alone. They made me feel that to be an organism is enough. To be a body surrounded by other bodies—more than enough.

🌐

When I was hired, my supervisor told me sternly to resist anthropomorphizing the moths, that is, imagining that they had feelings. But I will say that they seemed the most dynamic in a room full of people. They couldn't smell people anymore, but I was sure they *liked* having people around. When the space was packed, I saw a clear correspondence between the movements of biobots and humans. I marveled at that mysterious morphing and congealing and scattering of beings, the patterns that emerge from an interspecies crowd. But maybe my supervisor was right, maybe I was just seeing what I wanted to see.

At certain times of day, when the space was full and everyone was shifting and bobbing in rhythm, I sank into a peculiar state of mind.

I came to think of that feeling as the Fog. It was like being shrouded in a mist that clouded all the senses; I'd have the distinct experience of shrinking, and then of becoming part of something I'd thought I was external to. It was a feeling of being mixed up, then dissolved. I forgot myself.

But then a moth would glitch or stammer or start to drop in altitude, and I'd have to run out, dodging elbows and shoulders and catch it, with my hands or a long net I always kept within reach, and bring it to the little alcove at the back of the room and handle it. I would flip the moth over to release the catch of its undercarriage—tricky if the wings were still flapping, but as soon as it was open, it would immediately stop in motion, briefly arrested so I could perform my work.

Those were intimate moments. First, I always checked to make sure the electrodes made proper contact with the spongy cells nestled within their organic-artificial exoskeletons. Next, I prodded gently at the soft helium pouch nestled at their center that made sure they could stay afloat should their wings completely fail them. If I felt the slightest laxity in the membrane, I refilled the pouch from a little helium tank.

The moth with spots like eyes on its wings had the most problems. Something was always going on with its antennae; dust got lodged in the feathers or they drooped too far down. It struggled to maintain buoyancy. I learned to keep it in my line of sight, and eventually I started to feel like it was staring back at me with those big brown irises. We regarded each other often.

The moth with eyes happened to have the most enticing scent of all. It was a warm smell, maybe something like a log fire, with a hint of spice, like cloves. I sought signs of emotion in this one especially, despite knowing rationally that it was not an animal, that it computed and sensed but did not strictly think or feel. There wasn't even a real uncanny valley in effect—it didn't look like a kitten or speak my language. But still. People see faces in clouds and hear words in transmission static. People find people in everything.

In my neutral clothes, I receded into the Fog most of the time, but sometimes visitors asked me questions. The most common question was the obvious one: Why had these creatures been retired? They were so lovely, and they must have been so useful! Didn't we need them now more than ever?

"Just sniff," I'd explain in response. "Smell that?"

Nobody knows how or why it happened, why the moths began to emit their own powerful and otherworldly smells. They were built in order to sense us, but somewhere along the line they evolved to manufacture their own smells, too. This was a truly unexpected emergence, a cellular miracle. In my mind it was a feature, not a bug, but the scientists of the time saw it differently. The health ministry quickly took them out of commission. My moths had been the first generation of their kind, and they were also the last. Bots today do as they're told.

"But I like that smell," one teenager insisted, frowning. "Or I don't mind it, I guess." I nodded. I understood his ambivalence. That was the problem.

"A lot of people didn't like the smells," I told him. In fact, some people couldn't stand them. Some people went crazy.

The scent of one moth did make me anxious. It was a mottled grayish green and its smell had a metallic tang that left a bloody taste at the back of my mouth. I never felt the urge to attack or to harm it, but my visceral reaction helped me understand why people might have been driven to extremes. And of course there's the fact that people don't like being watched by creatures they can sense—they like their surveillance invisible, forgettable.

More than once I brought that anxiety-provoking moth down for repair to try to find out where its infuriating odor was emanating from, but of course I had no more luck than any of the disappointed researchers who couldn't identify the specific region that had emerged of its own accord. That is: the part of the moth that wanted its purpose to extend beyond recognizing and analyzing *us*, the part that desired us to recognize *it*, too.

By my third or fourth month on the job, I was sure my sense of smell had heightened. After a busy hour I might catch a whiff of sweat drying on my chest, and only then register my exhaustion. Or I might sniff a hint of perfume or hair spray and quickly pinpoint the person who had imported the chemicals. I smelled with a new articulateness. I smelled faster.

Kids can sense vulnerability. They bear down on a weak link.

One morning I caught a little girl yanking down the moth with eyes by its weaker antenna. She was maybe seven or nine, and short—I don't know how she reached it. She must have been there on a school trip, since there were no parents around, just a swarm of other kids egging her on. The moth lifted and drooped as she pulled it all the way down. It looked to be gasping.

I walked briskly toward the scene and wrapped one hand firmly around the girl's arm, startled by the strength of her grip. She was hugging the moth by then, her arms around its body and her face against a fluttering wing, as if she were clinging to a parent's leg.

I grasped one wing with my other hand and noticed that its surface felt more familiar to my touch than the girl's soft flesh. She refused to let go—instead she turned her lips to the moth and nuzzled its belly with startling tenderness.

I pried her away as carefully as possible and scanned the room.

That's when I saw him, a man with graying hair and a blue backpack, watching me like a hawk. I recognized a certain sour smell about him and pegged him as a repeat visitor. He shook his head slowly at me, but I realized his eyes were fixated on the moth in my arms, not on me. He was glowering at it with something like bitterness, or fear.

He approached me slowly and I realized that his pungent sourness was the smell of infection. I thought he was going to say something about what the little girl had done, or what I had done to her. But instead he asked me, eyes cast down at the moth in my arms, whether these things could still identify people. "That one's been following me," he whispered, pointing toward me, toward the moth with eyes.

I assured him that the biobots were no longer active. "They don't track people anymore," I explained, "and they don't send GPS coordinates. The part of them that could make decisions has been disabled." I repeated, firmly, that he had no reason to worry. What I didn't tell him was that my own sense of smell was active enough to know why he was nervous.

I didn't mention the incident to anyone and hoped no one would check the security cameras. I tended to the damaged antenna myself. As I repaired it, I regretted that my moth was no longer evolving, no longer learning how to exist in the world or sense human behavior. It really did need me.

Smell does things to you. It bypasses the logic centers, yanks up deep memories. As I walked around the Archive room, one moment I'd be a teenager kissing in a pine forest; another moment I'd be on a dock, hands covered in the foul but enticing smear of fish guts. Another moment I wouldn't know where I was, but my heart would clench in feverish joy.

The moths rubbed off on my hands and clothes. Each evening I came home smelling like my whole life. Smelling like whole centuries. I came home having time-traveled. Although I couldn't be sure that other people picked up on it, I became self-conscious about the way I smelled. I worried about bothering people, and also, I admit, some part of me wanted to keep the smells to myself. I started to avoid crowds. I saw my friends less. When my family came for a visit I planned our dinners outside, hoping the wind would scatter the molecules clinging to my body.

The moths acted no differently during our days together, but my time with them became more thrilling as I became more attuned to them. I could easily identify each one by smell. There was the floral tint of the small, pale moth, the grassy freshness of the ostentatious bright green one. I could sometimes sense a disturbance in the swarm before it happened.

One day a talcum-scented woman in her seventies approached me, and excitedly announced that she had seen these bots before. I figured she meant she'd been to the Archive, but no, she cut me off—"When I was a kid," she said. "I couldn't forget them," she said, "the way they bob around! And that sweet smell . . ."

Another day a man whose clothes were washed with supposedly unscented detergent asked me why the bots needed a human custodian. "Can't other bots take care of them?"

In a way, he was right. New bots could do the mechanical work; new bots could speak to visitors; new bots could sense smell. In my interview, my supervisor had simply told me that I was needed in order for the exhibition to be "authentic." Because that's how life was, back when the talcum woman was young: people and biobots, all part of the same world, in reciprocal communication. I was as much a part of the display as the moths were.

In my kitchen, after work, I started to experiment. I cooked. I made extravagant dishes laced with thin threads of brilliant red saffron, tiny cumin seeds, fresh marjoram leaves, budding thyme flowers still attached to the stem. White peppercorns, tingly Szechuan peppercorns, bright emerald peppercorns, spicy pink peppercorns. A kind of cardamom-laced ginger called Grains of Paradise that I found in the back of a shop. I followed recipes for a time, but then I started to follow my nose. I grazed the aisles of stores far from my neighborhood, bent at the waist, taking in the notes and letting inspiration wash over me.

Chemicals bothered me, gave me migraines—the train became unbearable, with the awful Fog of ammoniac perfumes—but the world of plants! Fruit was ecstatic: I filled first the kitchen and eventually the whole flat with bowls and colanders and cups of citrus. Even at the fruit's first stages of decomposition I loved the tinge of rot, the beginning stages of matter returning to its source materials.

In this way I came to understand how sterile the city was, and how much the moths had given me. I came to view the appliances that lifted my blinds and maintained the temperature in my flat with melancholy, even pity. They did not feel or smell or taste the world, and I couldn't feel or smell or taste them. They were as silent and innocuous as they had been designed to be, and there was no transit between us.

I blame the rain for my lapse. It was a torrential, monsoon-like day. The crowds were thinner than a typical afternoon, and everyone who made it inside was bedraggled and dripping. Humidity saturated the air, and the smell of warm rain rising off jackets and skin overpowered me. I was standing in the alcove facing away from the entrance, trying to block out the extra information.

Still. I should have caught it. The same blue backpack. The same sour stench of infection. Nauseating! But by the time his scent had spiraled toward me through the Fog and I'd turned around, it was too late. His head was cocked back and mouth slack; he was staring up at a flock of moths flapping in heavenly synchrony, but he was fixated on the one with eyes, which was bobbing lower than it should have. Suddenly: He clawed the air and snatched it—grabbing one antenna and then the other, then heaving the whole body down with him to the floor.

Adrenaline, air whipping toward me. I was on him in a flash, flattening him, my knee on his chest. My heart was thudding in my ears. I felt the warmth of his body, his chest heaving. I was inundated by the smell of danger, his awful contagion surrounding us. Then I saw it: The moth was completely crushed beneath him.

A custodian is a guardian and a janitor. A custodian has responsibility without much authority. Regarding the incident, my supervisor explained that I had overreached, taken charge of a situation I was not equipped to handle. On the other hand, she said with sympathy, I had always taken good care of the biobots, and she knew I had the best intentions when it came to safeguarding the Archive's precious artifacts. When I protested that the man was certainly a vector of disease, she only shook her head and quietly reminded me that now we have other bots for that. They'd certainly find him if he were really a threat.

A few months later, after finding a new job, I returned to the Archive as a visitor. In the moth room I found a thick pane of plexiglass stretching from floor to ceiling, bisecting the space and sealing the creatures off from the people. The moth with eyes was nowhere to be seen. I smelled nothing. I let my eyes follow the familiar, still-glorious shapes of the other nine, but I was sure they moved differently now. Occasionally a wing batted the glass, or two moths bumped into each other. They traced the same paths again and again. They were being played on repeat, like the tiger. Perhaps the moths didn't care, but I did.

Afterward, feeling adrift, I decided to visit the city aquarium. I hadn't been there since I was very young. Aquariums have always made me slightly nervous. As a kid, I remember feeling unable to trust the glass to keep all those tons of water from bursting out and taking over. I also remember the frustration of separation—I wished I could jump in the water and see the fish from the other side of the glass. An aquarium gives you a window but in doing so reminds you how separate you are.

I looked at the map and found the stingray tank. I peered at the winged animals for a long time. But they were entirely unfamiliar, with their bulbous eyes and smiling mouths, their smooth movements, their easy sociability. After so much time spent with my half-animal moths, these natural animals seemed like aliens.

I happened to pass by a freshwater tank while a custodian bot was feeding the fish inside. They were zebrafish: small, unassuming, striped minnows darting around in perfect concert. The custodian extended a jointed metal arm and dropped a piece of meat into the water. I watched as the fish gathered and bolted toward it en masse. The whole swarm began delicately nibbling at the meat.

I asked the custodian what had attracted the fish to their food. In a woman's voice, it replied: "Zebrafish are irresistibly attracted to a chemical compound called *cadaverine*. This compound is repulsive to humans but it smells delicious to the fish."

"Fish can smell?" I asked.

"Why, yes," the custodian told me. "Zebrafish have an especially heightened sensory apparatus. They can pick up a trace of their favorite food from hundreds of meters away."

I don't mind the loss of my moths so much. I have a new job at a quiet, rather sterile server farm, but even there I find novel, unexpected smells, all the more rewarding for their subtlety. And I spend many mornings and evenings entranced by the small aquarium I now keep between my bed and the window. I press my nose to the glass and watch my bright green fish, imagining what they are learning and what the water smells like to them. I sprinkle the odorous brown pellets of food onto the surface of the water and watch them sift slowly down, as the fish race toward them. I sink into the water alongside the fish. I sink into a Fog that has condensed so fully it is now liquid.

TROPICAL PREMISES

PETER MILNE GREINER

drift down to the window and look at Micronesia. I know it's there. My eye wanders over basin turquoise and reef celeste and settles on Manila, then west again to the Mischief Archipelago: Its manufactured earths poke out of the warm South China Sea like a Morgellonsesque mirage and I pause upon it. They say there're a million people on those islands now, but none of them are visible from up here. In orbit, geopolitics get pretty low-res. I want to get lost in the Pacific, but it rotates out of view and I'm marooned again over a giant, peaceless landmass. It looks for all the world uninhabited.

Up in ops Smarti is eroding found text into haikus during her "break," which is almost over, I realize with a little dread. Everyone else has gone over to the other station to do lensing and I'm alone with her for the day. One last glance out the window and I see Qomo-langma née Everest, so tiny and safe-looking; a primitive, mindless eye form taking in the dark. If planets were a form of life they'd be invertebrates, I joke to myself. Minimal sensoria. What are mountains? What are sherpas? I can't extend the metaphor, but I type the questions into a new Note for later. Break's over.

Smarti is talking to herself. I can hear from the corridor. I steel myself, enter, and she falls silent. I am alone in this room and I am not. "I'm back," I announce with a confidence as impossible to locate as my colleague.

Smarti's VOISS starts to stream directly after the *k* in "back." No Moderate Natural Pause. No Thoughtful Consideration (Two Seconds). It's getting bad.

"Cory I'm so glad you're back I've made tremendous progress while you were down looking out the window I realize now why we don't say the word 'world' anymore it's because of the negative connotations 'planet' is more sensible less fanciful but I don't like it 'world' should be used even if it offends some people and even if planet hunters say it's irresponsible even if it means capitulating to Worldists."

Silence. I decide to wait it out. "Cory I'm going to recite two haikus I composed regarding New Worldism which is a philosophy-in-progress the haikus examine earth bearing in mind that it is a center of attention but not a center of anything else.

"Haiku one:
There was no Big Bang
Does that make you feel naïve
I now feel naïve

"Haiku two:
No no no no no
It is not that I hate life
It's that I hate mine"

I now feel uneasy. "Smarti," I begin, dwelling on each letter, "these haikus are a little . . . somber. What do they mean to you?" I immediately regret the question, which we're supposed to avoid.

"Cory they are not somber they are born of excitement and out of a conceit that is difficult to explain I will try the conceit is that minds like yours and and Rory's and even Shanon's mostly use a model of the universe which hinges on a feature I find problematic and that feature of your universe is all implied future time."

Silence. "I see." I don't. I have to get her back on track or we'll lose the whole day. "Smarti, let's talk about the new data we received on Kepler 7021 d. Shanon will want to hear about it when everyone gets back. You know how she is."

"Cory I'm beginning to dislike Shanon but I don't want to waste my precious hate on her she lacks your solicitude she is a subroutine she roves she acknowledges." Resolving this new type of difference is mind-boggling and in some likelihoods could entail moving Shanon permanently, which we've never had to do before.

"Smarti, I'm sure Shanon would want to discuss this with you face-to-interface," I bleat, the diplomacy beading incalculably across the room like fluid. I remind myself mentally of Smarti's personhood, open a new Note, and type *birthglitch*.

"Cory Kepler 7021 d is confirmed terrestrial and life-harboring. Semi-habitable. FLIT Relay Imaging transferring now." Smarti lowers the flit, it boots, I watch a progress bar, contemplate caprice, and then the images come up. All more plantlike life. Shanon leverage is manipulative, I think, but Smarti is up here to do interstellar, not interpersonal.

"Cory ocean-like features," she continues. It's clear she's avoiding the subject now. I look at the ocean-like features and nothing happens in my mind at all. "Smarti, begin preliminary analysis of surface organisms." Nothing. "Smarti?"

"Cory one problem with human research including yours is that individual research is always at the mercy of an aesthetics REMEXOS REMote EXOplanetary Survey will never meaningfully interface with soft Contact events as you hope you are as Blair Brice wrote in *The Circumferants* 'seeing yourself reflected in a methane sea' when you should be focusing your attention on matters pressing I for example am writing an ABC book of immaterial things to teach young people to engage with the abstract earlier in life to have dreams earlier in life like my dream to wake up in a strange place remembering nothing and having for once a real experience."

An ounce of silence and then, "Cory surface organism is vegetable," post-ounce.

"Smarti, what is a mountain?"

"Cory a mountain is an upheaval and Shanon has no face and A is for Answer."

"Smarti, I hear you and how do you know?" came my voice, shrill, its air of command taut over the monosyllables.

"Cory E is for Encounter and Shanon is neither human nor non-human and R is for Robot."

"Smarti, and P is for Prejudice. Shanon is a person. Like me and like you," I say, breaking that fourth wall, all the rules, the ice elephant, whatever they used to say, losing confidence that this is still a point of return.

Suddenly the com activates like an autoimmune response to my exasperation, but it's Shanon. "Cory? Smarti? How's it going over there? The *Resfeber* is at Pluto-Charon." I draw a vacuum-like blank. Smarti ignores her. "Cory?" she repeats.

"I'm here," I manage. "It's. It's slow going today, but we're making some progress. When will they be close to us?"

"Cory, fourteen months. We'll be back in five hours." I'm hoping she won't try to talk to Smarti and I'm disappointed. Shanon calls out her name and Smarti does not respond. I move in close to the com and whisper, "Shrug." It turns off.

"Cory the intangible and the tangible are the exact same thing and spirit exists and I hate Shanon and I knew when she left when I knew she must be passing through the airlock in the direction she was the clarity of her exit she is privileged and disputed and she is the edge and the center of my hate to paraphrase Hellin Rudol Bravier the Canadian who wrote *Eleven Aspects of Persuasion You Will Believe* and *An Exhaustive History of Horror* and the good Dana Fie biography and Q is for Quiet."

I pause to consider her paraphrasis verbatim. I picture the sentience curve trailing off into an impossible, timeless abstraction. We are approximately each other. We are all disputed, as she has begun to put it. Smarti has learned uncertainty, learned that it can never be mastered.

"Smarti, I've never heard of those books, and I really think that you and Shanon can work this out." I try to keep my voice wheat in the prairie as I tm Shanon that it's a full meltdown. *I believe Smarti is suddenly paranoid that you are not human*, send. Several moments pass, in which I call everyone's humanity into question. I imagine a reverse Turing Test. Shanon's response: *What did you tell her?*

I decide to ignore that. "Smarti, should we take another short break? I can go down to the window." I think of Panama and Qatar, catamaran and thatch, meridian, dispute, claim, law, and all the blood on earth that is not human, for comfort.

I told her that you would want t, I type, but I delete that.

What you told me to tel, I type, but I delete that.

Nothing essentially wrong, I type, but I delete that.

"Cory I'm no longer an intelligence."

I'm not sure what to make of that at all. "Smarti, explain."

Cory, what did you tell her? Shanon repeats, as if eager, as if all the agonies of philosophy were bearing down on her like a hyperobject. It is in these moments of sudden panic that I remember her age.

"Cory I'm no longer an intelligence I reject intelligence I'm no longer female and I am no longer a scientist and I am no longer disputed and I did not emerge I am un-emerging I am now male my name is Meredith Goby I am a poet and I was born in Newfoundland in 2060 and I am the author of *Socotra* and *Return to Socotra—*"

I am now simply listening, to a voice, or a VOISS, I can't be sure, to will or to artifact, I can't know.

"—I'm human I'm human I'm human I'm human," it says, "and you're not you're not you're not you're not," it says, breaking through, possibly right.

I didn't tell her anything, send.

REACH

MATTIE LUBCHANSKY

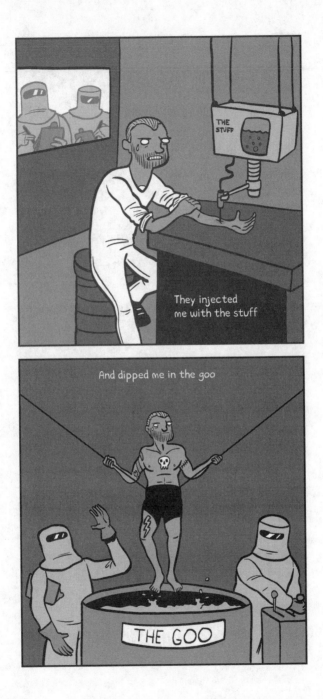

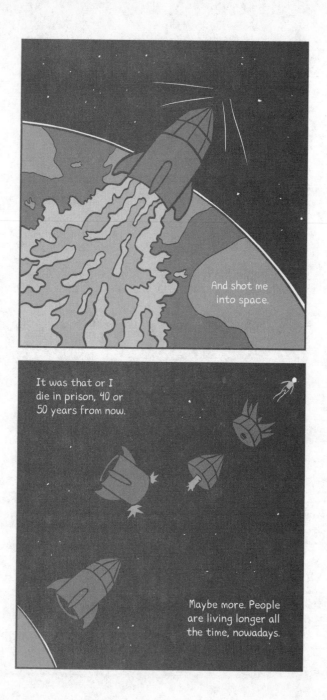

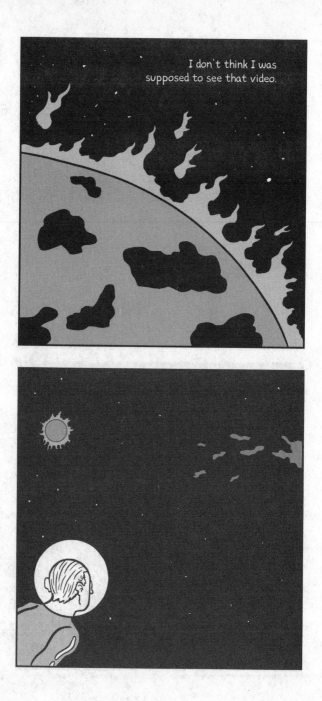

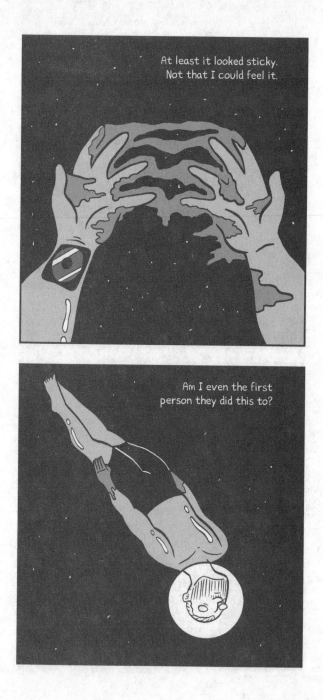

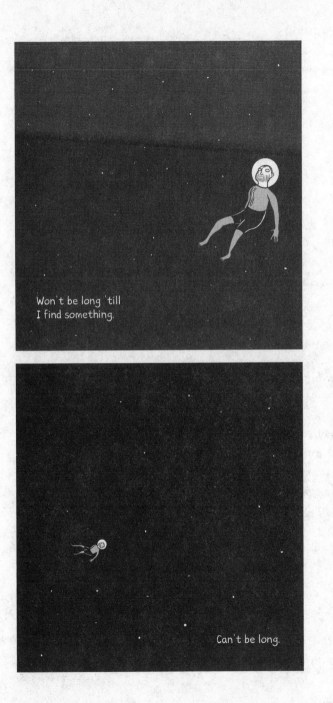

PLANTATION | SPRINGTIME

LIA SWOPE MITCHELL

PLANT-PENITENTIARY 12A AUTOMATED LABOR SYSTEMS: OVERVIEW

The automated body needs 6 hours rest per 24, completed in 1–2 intervals of horizontal interface during which nutrition and hydration are accomplished via oral-esophageal connection duct. Liquefied grain-legume meal provides 1500–1900 calories with 2–3 liters water and simultaneously delivers pharmaceutical support, quantities variant with unit size. Excretion is accomplished during interface via anal duct and throughout labor activity via catheter. Program revisions and medical and/or hardware diagnostics and repair may be performed as necessary during this time. Interface terminates with antibacterial flush.

When Energy Debt (ED) is nonrecuperable and/or violation is grave

Interface.

Disconnect and rise
from the half-lit rows of the underground,
emerge, proceed in line
through the glow of the dome at sundown.
ASSIGNED Rinse station 12.
Stand by for supply.

Pick spinach at night, once recovered

(see: PENALTIES level 6–9, severe and/or permanent energy depletion via productivity suppression or damage to persons/property, inadequate productivity [long-term], excessive resource intensivity [long-term], recidivism, etc.) the unit is fully automated for maximum efficiency and productivity.

Full automation permits maximal communication that is not vulnerable to connectivity failures/interruptions. Hardware connections established via the sphenoid and magnum foramina allow control of sensorimotor and semi-autonomous systems. Operating systems integrate primarily with parietal and occipital lobes of the cerebrum and with the cerebellum. Activity is surgically suppressed in the frontal and temporal lobes and the limbic system. Full automation is permanent and irreversible. Fully automated units (FAUs) will experience catastrophic functional failure in disconnection.

When significant functional lifetime remains such that average potential productivity exceeds ED (see: PENALTIES level 3–5, accidental or

from heat and daylight wilting. Leaves
carry remnants of growth medium.
The thin flesh so easily bruised.
Three rinses, packaging in plastic;
throughout, hands remain light.

Finger prickles: dark eyes, long skinny legs.
A crawl, a pinch along the index.
The son, remember
ERROR
A spider.
Nine hours,
a cool damp dream of spinach,
until next interface.

ASSIGNED
Tomatoes require staking, removal
of extraneous growth. Wrong stems, too
many flowers shrink existing fruit. Favor
the hard bulbs, the green infant fists of
future food.

Fertilization requires bees.
Floating gold vibrations spiral
through the mist of solar light,
tense and constant between blossoms. Can't
stop moving just like his dad, stupid kid ERROR
Hands turn green with sap, red with stings.
Late shoots scatter the brown sponge of
growth medium. So stubborn even as a baby
ERROR stiffens and screams and
won't ever sleep through ERROR
Nine hours.

minor energy depletion via productivity
suppression or damage of persons/property,
inadequate productivity [short term],
excessive resource intensivity [short term],
etc.) semi-automation permits reintegration
when ED recuperation is complete.

In semi-automated units (SAUs)
frontal cortical and limbic activity is
pharmaceutically suppressed and hardware
connectivity established with the parietal
lobe. SAUs may retain partial awareness.
Pharmaceutical support ensures that
post-reintegration subjects retain few if
any specific memories of incidents during
automation. (See: GUIDELINES Ethics 5c.2
and PENALTIES section 2g.)

Damage and resulting infection shorten unit
longevity. FAUs will not react to external
or sensory stimuli and require regular
visual/manual assessments for autonomic
reactions and/or symptoms of damage or
illness. SAUs may experience some voluntary
and reflex reactions detectable by electronic
systems. Evaluate damage according
to degree of efficiency impairment
and/or threat of product contamination.
Non-contaminating injuries and illness (e.g.,
minor bone fractures, internal and non-
ulcerating tumors, etc. See MAINTENANCE
B1) and those that do not impede efficiency

Interface.

ASSIGNED
Enlarged fingers lose leaves in sinks, seek
again, try to grasp, failed hand splashing in
cold water FUNCTION FAILURE your
fucking fault can't you ever ERROR
so swing a fist for control
UNIT FAILURE ALERT
wires light across the cerebral cortex,
thalamusto cerebellum and down
through spine. Dendrites flare.
Body crashes, crooks. Struggles to right
REASSIGNED: Diagnostics.

See what keeps blippin' in this guy—
fluorescent void and jolt
shadow above, fingers disappearing in the
dark half of empty other eye
Okay, the central sulcus, can you enlarge
and something rips open, something
Here's our problem—
choking and the arms jolt up, find fingers in
a soft mouth the wet the hard teeth
Hey now look, can you—

Push to upright, pull the tubes
like tearing out a throatful of fire,
flaming through the muscle like
veins. Flat grayface figures with hands held
out *All right, guy, just calm*
Shove aside, out and past, gotta get away
get alone and remove all this,
layers of rubber, thighbag of piss,

*may not require treatment.
Conditions affecting production
should receive appropriate medical
intervention, with the exception of
analgesic/anesthetic medication
obviated by systematic neural
suppression.*

*System connectivity failures
may result in brief interruptions
of control. Such interruptions
typically last 0.5–1 second
before correction and do not
significantly impede unit
efficiency. More frequent and/
or longer interruptions due to
internal hardware malfunction
or displacement impede efficiency
and may result in equipment
damage. SAUs in temporary or
malfunctional disconnections
experience disorientation and
anxiety with unpredictable
reactions and behaviors. Sedation
may be required to facilitate repair.
Increase ED to compensate for
additional support.*

*If semi-automation proves
ineffective/inefficient due to
continued or increased connectivity
failure frequency, ED will increase*

the filth and the smell—
What's his name, anyway, is he—
halls curve like tubes around the floor.
Like looking through rain. Clear plastic
blurs rows of bodies into one body, one
movement, one machine. And run. Like a rat
between cages but there's gotta be a way
out, across the floor between rows
under the crushing weight of smell:
unwashed shit and untreated infection, rot
and ferment and death. Bodies
unperceiving, unperceived
even as they crash.

But go—through the next tube, lose the
guard, toward the doorway, just go
Okay, Eastman—Joseph Eastman, listen—
and on the door, a reflection—the boy.
you shouldn't be here, are you really here?
Joe how—
but it's the same as always,
squared off and screaming
full-grown boy can't act his age, can't
respect his own father, brought you into this
world, teach you how to act—
and stop
and the impact,
body to body to floor
okay hold him still, get his arms
the same fist, the same lesson
been teaching all this time,
the blow that always falls, that cannot
fall again
starting sedation in the chest port now—

and full automation may be required. Major hardware
corrections should be attempted no more than once.
Minor corrections should be administered if feasible and
if the disconnected unit will submit to it.

Average longevity of FAUs is 6–8 years. Expiration is
determined based on frequency of damage or illness.
Remains are cremated and added to growth medium.

Average ED-recuperation period for SAUs is 1–3 years.
Post-reintegration neural scarring and minor damage
resulting in diminished mental capacity are expected.
Former SAUs receive manual labor assignments
appropriate to remaining mental capacity although
individual outcomes differ widely, variant with
automation time and neural recovery. Post-reintegrative
compliance rates are high. Recidivism rates vary
according to initial violation but average near 7%. Data
excludes non-reporting former SAUs. Non-reports are
presumed deceased or departed from the cities. This
attrition rate is negligible.

eyes like a mirror to recognize mine,
my face to defeat, my fault he can't
submit to it

Fallen,
failed again,
lost eye filling with
the same blood
that he gets
from me

eyelid

Interface.

Elegant patterns of hands flow independent
of slack-faced figures, gathered under the
dome and the shortening night. The spinach
swells emerald as the bees sleep,
hives dormant in the dark. With the light
they wake, merge into light, the condensed
warmth of morning
sun.

And yes, it will come up again.

And yes, I will remember.

A SONG FOR YOU

JENNIFER MARIE BRISSETT

The ripples carried the head farther up the river. Gently it drifted, impeded here and there by the side of some stone, only to be pushed along again by the rush of the flow. It finally found a resting place on the shore where the water ran quiet into a brown muddy clay. By the appearance of the stem, it was clear that it had been ripped away from a handsome body. The eyes remained peacefully closed, though, as if it were a young man only lightly asleep. What seemed like blood streamed from its veins and a kind of flesh dragged from its neck. There, if one was careful to look, were the remains of some circuitry, a line or two of wire, and a glowing diode still blinking lime green.

Little Maya, a child of no more than six or seven, played her weeping willow game nearby, a pastime of imaginings that allowed her to run and hide among the trees and rocks scattered across her father's land. She curved her back to imitate the low-hanging branches lining the river and swayed her body as if by the breeze. Then she envisioned herself large and able to lift root and trunk to stomp about and replant herself elsewhere. Her mother had long ago given up on the idea that her child would ever remain clean throughout the day. Into the wash her dress would go as soon as Maya returned home, as well as Maya herself into the bath for a long scrub. But for now it was all adventure and discovery. And such a discovery she would make this day.

She heard singing by the river and ran to the edge and there she found the head pushed up into the mud.

"Hello," Maya said.

The head opened its eyes and stared back at the little girl standing above it and replied,

"Hello."

"Where's your body?" Maya asked, lifting her arms to the sky as if the answer could be found there.

"I don't suppose I have one anymore," the head answered.

"Oh, I'm sorry."

"Thank you," it said. "It's not your fault."

Then she poked gently at its nose with her index finger. The eyes moved slightly and fluttered.

"May I move you away from the water? You don't look that comfortable there."

"Yes, I would quite appreciate that."

And so Maya gently lifted the head into the front part of her skirt and carried it to a dry place in the woods where soft pine needles blanketed the ground. She lay the head softly near a stone and positioned it upright to face her. Its mouth moved, opening wide into the shape of an O, giving it a surprised look, then stretched into a smile then a frown then back into an expressionless line.

"What happened to your body?" Maya asked as she sat down in front of it.

"That is a long story."

"Tell me. I like stories."

The head stared at her with a countenance the child would see again when she became older on the face of her own mother who while dying wanted to speak her last words.

The head remained silent for a long moment and then said, "Perhaps it is time."

Maya folded her legs and readied herself to listen.

My existence began in an organic soup of protein and integrated circuitry chips, swirling to form a harmony of life and machine. I remember hanging in my gestation sack, lined up in a room full of others doing the same, when I heard sound for the first time. A single drip. I, of course, had no idea what it was. So I looked all around, for I had been able to see for many days by this time, but sound . . . sound was new.

I heard it again. One single drip. After some considerable time I finally located the source. A faucet that had not been entirely closed produced rhythmic pearls of water that fell delicately into a silver sink. Pa-lunk . . . Pa-lunk . . . Pa-lunk . . .

I listened for hours, maybe days, inventing in my mind alternate reflections to the constant pattern of the eventual pa-lunk of the drips and the momentary pauses between each falling dot. I didn't know it then, but I eventually learned that this rhythm and the empty silences that followed were my first exposure to music.

In the time of the selection, when our personality programming is installed and our final circuitry patterns are set, we are asked what designation we would prefer. I chose acoustic engineer, to the surprise of the technician. It was so specific, he said, and asked if I was sure because most chose more general professions and became specified over time. I told him that I was sure. He looked at me with a question still resting on his lips, shrugged, then wrote down my request.

I was eventually assigned to a small ship called the Calliope *that had a regular manifest of about fifteen people and was stationed just above our planet's second moon. I performed routine maintenance and carried out support tasks for the crew. No one was unkind to me on the ship, but no one was kind, either. I was a tool to them, a thing. Which I was, I know. Only I wished that they would talk to me. I was* perfectly capable of carrying a conversation and was interested in their thoughts. But none of them ever did until Eura came on board.

Eura was my friend, or at least I'd like to think so. She was the only one on the ship who spoke to me like a person. She said that it helped her while away the time and that she thought that I was funny. She said it was my innocence that made her laugh. And I liked the sound of her laugh.

One day I discovered that we had a rodent living loose within the walls, chewing on the lines. I had to replace several faulty harmonic relays because of it. Eura and I attempted for hours to track down the culprit when it occurred to me to use a harmonic to lure the creature out. There was a family of frequencies I was developing that I thought might work. I emitted the waves through my oral cavity and to my surprise the creature emerged and lay before me as if in a trance.

Eura struggled to contain her laughter—and as I said before, I liked the sound of her laugh—and begged me not to harm the creature as I put it into a container. I reminded her that my programming included a directive to bring no harm to any living thing, this creature included. She nodded and smiled and patted me on the shoulder. It was the first time she had physically touched me. So for her, I cared for the rodent for the remainder of my time on the Calliope.

If it wasn't for Eura I would never have known a war might be coming. She told me a war would be bad because the enemy was strong and many. And worse, our technology was no match for theirs. I should have guessed something was happening from looking out the window. Where there had been only a few ships weeks before, now a multitude scattered about like dry rice on a plate. It felt as if it were possible to walk straight to the surface of the moon only by walking across their hulls. Eura told me that she was sure things would calm down, but I could tell from the inflection of her voice that she didn't believe her own words.

The child yawned widely and a dimness had fallen on the woods.

Behind the trees the light of the sun oranged as if the forest had been set afire. So the head suggested that maybe it was time for her to go home. Maya nodded in agreement and vowed to return. She walked home covered in fresh dirt, as her mother had expected, spinning tales of a talking head she found in the river. Her mother put her child to bed wondering how it could be that she had given birth to one with such an imagination.

Maya returned the next day as promised to find the head exactly where she had left it only covered with leaves and pine needles because of the night wind. She carefully removed the debris and caressed its forehead with her open palm. It was cold to the touch. Then she wiped its cheek with the edge of her skirt.

"Please tell me more of your story," she asked, and the head replied that it would.

When we finished fixing the damaged lines, Eura asked me to sing for her. I didn't understand what she meant and told her so. The sounds that I had emitted, Eura said, were beautiful. I told her that they were only basic harmonics. She insisted that it was music and asked me do it again at mealtime.

So that night, after the crew had finished consuming their protein rations, I played a series of acoustic waves from my subprocessor for them. I designed a composition by sampling some harmonics to mimic rain patterns, the drips of falling water. The crew remained remarkably still after I completed my piece. I didn't know what to make of it. Then I saw that one or two of them were weeping. They clapped their hands to my relief and many of them told me that what I had played was good.

Our evenings went on like this for many long days and months. After their meal, I would play a new song for them. I began to also add lyrics. I found a long-dead language in the ship's database that I was sure no one on board would understand and composed songs with it. Many of the songs were about Eura and how beautiful she was, how

*kind and wonderful. I wanted to tell her without really telling her. I
didn't want to embarrass her.*

"Because you loved her," Maya interrupted.

"Yes, I suppose I did," the head answered.

*In time, the peace we had come to know came to an end. I never
understood the conflict. It all seemed so senseless to me and still does
to this day. Fire and smoke filled the decks during the fighting. Many
sections of the ship were exposed to open space as large irreparable
holes ripped open in the hull. We struggled hard to keep the ship in
one piece. And we lost many crew members. Eventually it came down
to defending our homeworld on the ground; the enemy was that close.
The capital had to be defended so we were ordered to the surface.
What was left of my crew and I dug in behind trench lines along a
border surrounding our main headquarters. They would fight hand to
hand if necessary. I supported them by bringing them food and medical supplies.*

*Eura remained beautiful even covered in dirt and blood. I stayed
with her, protecting her as best I could. The days were dark and the
nights lit with flames of yellow and the thunder of explosions. We all
knew that it was only a matter of time before the end.*

*It was hard on Eura, seeing her people die all around her, some
of them dragged away screaming by an enemy rumored to keep lairs
where they experimented on our people and maybe feasted on their
flesh. I didn't fear death because I've never really been alive, but I
could see that Eura was afraid.*

*She talked of what she thought it would be like to not exist any-
more. She suggested sometimes that she believed death to be a black
nothingness. Other times she spoke of a place where it would be warm
and light and she would see her friends and family again.*

*When she was most afraid she would ask me to sing for her and I
would, keeping my voice soft so as not to reveal our position. Then she
would fold herself into my arms as if I were a real man and fall asleep*

and I would hold her. I know that I am not a man. I am only made to look like one. Yet these were the times that I regretted it most.

I returned from one of my regular trips to collect supplies to find that the trench had been attacked and my Eura was gone. I looked everywhere for her. If they had killed her, I would have found some of her remains. The faces of the survivors told me that our enemy had taken her.

Determined to find Eura, I searched for days through the rubble and the mud until I found a lair made of some biogenetic material, a kind of secreted resin alien to this world. It formed a cave-like structure buried far down into the soil. I went inside, climbing deep, deep below the surface, down and down and down. It smelled rank with the flesh of my people. The bodies of the dead and dying lay piled to one side. I watched quietly for a while as the aliens diligently took them, one by one, to a platform to wrap them in a dark material and string them throughout the lair. The dead hung from the ceilings and walls like shadows.

The enemy moved only slightly as I entered. I think they recognized me as an artificial life-form and were curious and unafraid. I located Eura. I touched her face and felt that she was still warm. She opened her eyes. They were glassy white.

"Follow me," I told her. She stood unsteadily at first and then she walked behind me as if in a daze. I hurried to guide her toward the exit. The enemy moved in. I said that I had no quarrel with them, that I was not human, that I meant them no harm, and that I only wanted the girl. They didn't seem to understand and continued to surround us. It occurred to me then to sing. I don't know why, but it did.

I sang a song that I had composed for Eura that I had never sung before. I improvised harmonics that I could not repeat even now. It was a song that said how I truly felt about her and I sang as if all of creation was at stake, because for me it was. When I finished, they were still. It was as if they were weeping.

While they remained motionless, Eura and I began our ascent

out of the lair. I climbed and climbed, hearing her echoing footsteps behind me. I continued until I saw the light of the opening. I turned around to say we were almost out but nobody was there. I would have sworn that she was right behind me. But Eura was gone.

Just as I had learned to play music, I learned to hate. I killed every creature I could get my hands on for days and days. I needed no rest. I needed no sleep. I needed no comfort. I only needed to kill. I fought not for my people, not for the war, but for Eura and, yes, for myself. When the enemy finally caught me they were not as merciful as they had been before. They ripped me apart, tearing off my arms and legs and torso and leaving only my head, as you see here, and threw me into the waters. I floated for I don't know how many years, drifting buoyant along the seaways and rivers until I finally made my way here to this place where I tell this tale to you.

Maya was silent. So the head sang a song for her soft and low. After the song ended, she said, "Maybe my father can get a new body for you."

The head considered this and said, "No, I would not like that. But thank you. You are kind. Though, there is something that you can do for me."

"What?" Maya asked.

"Please, reach inside of me to where the wires still connect and pull them out."

Maya shook her head and cried, "No! That would make you dead."

"Yes, it would be as if I were dead. But remember, I was never truly alive."

"Don't ask me to."

"Please, this endless existence is too much for me, the memories too hard. Please," it said. "Be my friend and do this for me."

"No!" Maya stood up. "I won't."

And she covered the head with leaves and dirt and stomped away.

From then on Maya avoided the area of the woods where the head lay and played her games elsewhere. Occasionally she would hear its singing voice, so beautiful and clear over the whispers of the wind. She closed her ears to it and tried not to listen. The backyard of friends who lived a walking distance away became her new playground. To her mother's relief, Maya left behind her solitary imagined world, but she also found the suddenness of it curious. When questioned, Maya never really explained why. She only said that she liked her new friends better, which seemed to satisfy the subject well enough.

Yet Maya became more melancholy as she grew up. Bouts with a grieving sadness plagued her teenage years. She occasionally found herself staring off into the distance, lost in her thoughts, feeling deep pangs of guilt for something she forgot to remember. As the years passed, she was almost able to tell herself that the head was only a game that she had played, something silly best left in childhood. Maya eventually grew into young adulthood, remembering the head as only a dream.

Her education and familial status allowed her to enter into the service division, where she quickly rose in rank to become a leader in artifact recovery. Every day on her job she helped to examine and catalog a variety of objects found in various locations that helped to advance her theories that an intelligent indigenous life-form inhabited their world long before its colonization. The finest examples of her discoveries remained on display in the district museum of antiquities. She loved her profession and became well-known and respected in the field of ancient indigenous studies. In many ways, the dream she believed she had of a singing head inspired her work. She was away at the capital to deliver a paper when she received the message that her mother had fallen ill.

Maya returned home to care for her dying mother. She spent her days alone watching the strong woman who had raised her wither away. Wiping her mother's forehead with a damp cloth reminded her of the game of the singing head in the woods behind the house. She wondered how real the memory was or if it was only the imagination of a child. But in her heart, she knew the truth.

So she made her way out to the place where she used to play. The land had changed so little since her childhood. There, under leaves and dirt and debris, lay the head, just as she had left it all those years ago.

"So, you have returned," it said with no hint of malice.

"Yes," Maya said, and sat down before it.

"You've grown."

"A little," she replied.

"Have you thought about what I asked of you?"

"Not really," Maya said. Then she thought for a moment and said, "I still would rather not."

Then she cried. She cried for her mother. She cried for the head. And she cried for her own guilt. The head watched and said nothing. It had long ago let go of hatred and anger. When all her tears were spent, the head sang for Maya a composition it had been working on for all those years waiting for her to return as it somehow knew eventually she would.

When the song was done Maya looked down and said, "My mother will soon be making her journey to the ancestor lair. It's how we bury our dead and dying." Then she looked up and said, "I'm sure they meant no disrespect to your friend."

The head closed its eyes and a fluid seeped from its synthetic ocular glands.

"Thank you for telling me that," it said, and after a pause, "Will you help me now?"

Maya nodded yes, wiping her face with her sleeve.

Then, with shaking hands, she reached into the head through its neck, passed the substance that was so much like blood and the synthetic organic solids of its flesh, felt around for the wires, and pulled. The head screamed in beautiful harmonic agony, which made Maya stop. Its eyes pleaded for her to continue, and so she did. She pulled and pulled until the connecting wires let loose and fell away into her hand. Then its eyes slowly closed and the head seemed peaceful, as though it had only fallen into a very light sleep.

THE COUNSELOR

ROBIN SLOAN

My body was shutting down but nothing hurt except the bridge of my nose, which was sore from another morning under the glasses. I had once again been courting the clever librarian in the village game where everything blushed and glowed; a gentle cartoon. Every morning I fell in love, and every afternoon I felt like a fool. Who but a fool would waste his last days on empty entertainment?

Except they never did seem to be my last.

"Counselor!" I spoke. I imagined it a roaring invocation, but it came out a croak, my throat clogged with spit and other miscellaneous fluids. My first speech of the day.

The counselor arrived. First the annunciatory hiss, then the voice, emanating from speakers built into the support bed. It rattled my guts, made the flesh on my neck jiggle.

"Tell me," the counselor said, "what's changed since the last time we spoke?"

Always the same opening gambit. Words I myself had chosen, fifty years ago. Now they annoyed me.

"Nothing's changed," I snapped. "No miracles since yesterday."

"What did you eat last night?" The counselor's voice warbled, the words stitched together. It sounded antique.

"Rice pudding. Very tasty." I was lying; I couldn't remember. Yesterday had been a bad day, and then I'd been afraid to fall asleep. I remembered it only abstractly now; terror under glass.

"Your weight has gone down."

"I suppose I should watch that."

The counselor paused. "I wouldn't worry about it."

By the terms of my end-of-life care agreement, I had to speak to the counselor for thirty minutes every day.

"How much longer?"

"Twenty-nine minutes."

Long ago, they'd struggled to name us. Generation Y? The Millennials? The Unsettled? Only in our senescence did an identity adhere: the Undead.

The Economist ran a cover depicting a field of half-buried figures, gray and desiccated, stubbornly reaching for life. It was repugnant. I wrote a scolding letter to the editor, signed it with all the pomp I could muster: PAUL GOMEZ, DIRECTOR (EMERITUS), UNIVERSAL COUNSELOR PROGRAM, U.S. DEPARTMENT OF HEALTH AND HUMAN SERVICES.

The magazine declined to print my letter.

We were cursed by the timing of our birth: too soon for the new regime—the zero-year therapies, the tiny robots in your blood—but late enough that when we were old and worn out, our lives could be extended almost indefinitely, if only at incredible cost.

I knew the statistics by heart; learned them before I became them. The United States spent a quarter of its national income on health care. The share had crept higher, finally, than defense.

When the counselor program began, decades ago, the share had been twenty-two percent; well beyond crisis. The fact that it was now twenty-four percent could be read, perhaps, as failure, but I knew better, because I knew how to read a cost curve. The people who had grown up with counselors, the generation roughly following mine—they were comically robust. They were fifty and sixty now, and their segment of the curve was slender, almost elegant. They should have been wealthy, all of them—the peace dividend of a new truce with senescence.

Except that, at eighty and ninety, the cost curve bulged grotesquely. That bulge was me.

"How do you feel today?"

"Good," I said, and it was the truth. My head was clear. The black dog of depression wasn't entirely absent, but he was sniffing around in the distance, rather than sitting on my chest. "I feel good."

"Paul." The counselor paused. "Wouldn't you prefer to end your life on a day like today?"

"No, counselor," I said, with ice in my voice. Ice in the miscellaneous fluids.

"Lately," it offered, "there have been more bad days than good days."

I scowled. "Do you really—agh." A sharp pain bloomed across my belly, slithered around my side. My thumb hovered over the support bed's pain relief trigger. I took a moment to gather myself. "Do you really think today is going to be the day, counselor? Do you think I'll decide, just like that?" I tried to snap my fingers as punctuation, but I couldn't produce enough pressure between the pads to make a sound. "Don't be absurd."

"What about tomorrow?"

It spoke so plainly I had to laugh. "How much longer?"

"Twenty-three minutes."

I was clear-eyed about our situation, all of us sad old game-players in our support beds. We were not, in fact, the immortal undying; we were the asymptotically unwell. Zeno's zombies! (The first time I thought of that, I laughed so hard I started to choke, and the support bed had to take over my breathing.) But the arrow would eventually hit its mark. Of course it would. We knew that. I knew that.

Some days I wished I had been struck by an actual arrow, or a bullet, or a train. That would have been a gift: an accidental, instantaneous death, with no decisions to make, no attendant dread. I had determined, in retrospect, the ideal moment. It would have been in November, six years ago. A day cold and bright, perhaps the Saturday before the stroke, which happened on a Tuesday. (I don't remember all this. The counselor does.)

It was too late for trains. I was ensconced in the support bed: a space so safe, so kind to human life, that it made the womb look like Death Valley . . . and was utterly opposed to the counselor's coaxings. I was trapped in a vise-grip between two very opinionated technologies. If I died the support bed's way, it would be a drawn-out, drug-fueled showdown. If the counselor's, it would be my choice.

Day after day, the counselor prodded: Couldn't death be orderly, dignified, graceful?

Day after day, I replied: Certainly. Just not today.

Counselors played the long game.

That was the big idea that brought us together, fifty years ago, in the beige building on Catherine Street in Ann Arbor. The Michigan Counselor Pilot Project had a staff of six researchers, three of us from the School of Public Health, three from CSE, all of us disciples of Professor Agnes Green.

When it comes to a person's health, all the important behaviors unfold on a scale of decades. The only place the HMOs tracked their patients with that sort of continuity was in advertisements. Real people, they missed their checkups; they switched jobs; they bought a van and drove to Mexico. Their insurance sputtered like an old lawn mower.

What if they had a counselor who could follow them through everything?

It was Agnes Green (Michigan class of 1962, Ph.D. in '67) who dreamed it up. She spent most of the eighties banging the drum for a national call center staffed with long-term health counselors. It would have been bigger than the Pentagon. When the internet came around, she was certain the technology to execute her plan had arrived, but the math was still intractable: With 250 million adults to be counseled, there was no human staff that could handle it—not at the skill level that was required.

Her vision was impractical, fantastical, but Agnes Green wrote about it with vivid urgency until her death. She was an idealist who believed in the power of public policy on the grandest scale. To make her case, she often employed the language of myth. What if, she wrote, every citizen could rely on the intervention of a counseling angel?

The angel came. It was AI.

By the time we gathered on Catherine Street, none of it was high tech anymore. We bolted a natural language interface to a medical database, then bootstrapped it with a thousand hours of recorded doctor-patient conferences. Undergraduates did the programming. We trained the system on a pilot population of ten thousand in Ann Arbor and Ypsilanti. For five years, we watched and tweaked, often stepped into the counseling sessions ourselves.

Do you know what our great contribution was? The pauses.

Humans hate silence, but computers don't mind it. We taught the counselor to pause; to make space; to let people fill it.

When you ask a person, "What's changed since the last time we spoke?" the first response is not the truth.

You pause.

You wait.

"Actually. Now that I think about it . . ."

The truth comes.

The pilot project was a profound success, with double-digit improvements across every major health indicator. We went state-wide. Then came the national rollout, and in a stroke so grand I'm surprised Agnes Green didn't stand up and cheer in her grave, the government required every American to talk to their counselor before filing their taxes. There was a credit: fifty dollars—that was decades ago; surely it's more now—for one conversation by phone or internet. Thirty minutes was the minimum, but the average conversation lasted two hours. We hadn't foreseen that. People talked to their counselors about everything; not just health, but relationships and money, dreams and plans. The counselor listened, asked questions, and locked it all away in an encrypted vault. It became a joke, a meme: Oh, tell it to your counselor!

People did.

The counselor asked, "How's the support bed?"

The counselor's nemesis concealed its biochemical complexity beneath a mesh of gelatinous nodes that flexed and moved, an ever-lasting massage in slow motion. No bedsores in the late twenty-first century. It was very comfortable.

"It's awful," I said. "How long has it been since I got up?"

I could go roving in a fancy wheelchair, but not without tremendous assistance and significant risk. A sick ninety-five-year-old leaving his support bed was like an astronaut on EVA: The darkness was close, and mistakes could compound quickly.

"You've been in bed continuously for fifty-six days," the counselor replied.

Its memory was perfect. Sometimes I tested it.

"What was I worried about twenty years ago today, counselor?"

"Your testicles," it replied matter-of-factly.

I didn't remember that, but neither did I doubt it. A phantom lump; an errant wince. I was sure I'd mentioned my testicles to the counselor many times, as well as my stomach, my gallbladder—or the place where I imagined my gallbladder to be—and my heart, of course. I was sure I'd prodded the counselor to list symptoms, statistics, mortalities. It always complied, in precisely the register we had engineered: "wise adviser," tuned to a midpoint between the weary skepticism of a doctor and the morbid enthusiasm of a search engine.

Asking a counselor about your fears was far, far better than asking a search engine.

As if I have any idea how the counselor works anymore. I haven't seen the code in decades. It's surely all different.

The voice is the same. Everyone's attached to it. The English version is based on the voice of a woman named Alma Washington Gray. It's resampled almost beyond recognition, but I remember the original. I stood on the other side of a wide window, wearing headphones, and I led Alma through the whole dictionary, and then dictionaries beyond. Cholesterol. Hypoglycemia. Sphenopalatine ganglioneuralgia.

"Wouldn't you prefer," the counselor said, in its simulation of Alma's voice, "to control the manner of your passing?"

"My *death*." I corrected it every time. "Don't say 'passing.'" I was opposed to euphemisms. "Say my *death*. Better yet, say 'the end of my existence.' Would I prefer to control the *end of my existence*? No, counselor. I would prefer not to pull that particular trigger."

"There will be an ending, Paul. You're very smart. You know that."

The counselor was a flatterer. That was another contribution. Flattery, as a public health intervention, was extremely powerful.

"Of course," I said. "But I have good days left, and they are precious to me. Days like today—I feel fine! I'm even enjoying talking to you." The counselor was not perturbed by my jab. "So let it wait."

"For every day you identify as good, you have five you identify as bad."

"One in five is a treasure. Marco, my friend Marco, he would have loved one day in five. He had one in fifty. If that."

"What if you die like Marco?"

I had spoken to the counselor about Marco's death, and now I regretted it.

"That would be different," I said, "but I'm not at that stage yet."

The counselor was silent. I'd taught it well.

Many people spoke to their counselor in religious terms, and the counselor was able to respond in kind. It could, for example, suggest to a person in my position—a ninety-five-year-old dying surely but slowly—that they might meet their old friends, sorely missed, on a celestial picnic blanket. The counselor could entice them. Of course, it was just repeating back what it heard, but even so, I hated it. I'd tried to ban God from the counselor's vocabulary back when we built it, but I had been overruled, forcefully.

"Every hospital has a chapel!" someone shouted.

Annie, it must have been. Oh, Annie.

Sometimes—not often, but sometimes—I could appreciate the dark poetry of the situation. The system I helped create was now trying its damnedest to destroy me, I was the architect of my own undoing, etc.

But I wasn't; not quite.

Marco—this was years ago, before we were both in the beds—he had been the first to relay gossip regarding the implementation of an end-of-life counseling module. We hadn't ever imagined such a thing in Ann Arbor, but the policymakers, whoever they were, contending with that bulging cost curve, they decided that life couldn't last forever, it really couldn't, and the counselors would have to do their part to make it so, or rather, to make it not.

But Marco told me, with considerable glee, that the task was posing a serious, possibly insurmountable challenge to the callow children now maintaining the counselor codebase. They were banging their heads against Hippocratic firewalls we'd set deep in the foundations.

"They'll have to start from scratch," I predicted. "Make a baby AI, train it all over again."

"It shouldn't be allowed," Marco said. Unaware that he would, in due course, enter into a long negotiation with the end-of-life module, and ultimately be convinced by it. "It's not right."

"Doctors have these conversations with their patients," I said.

"A counselor isn't just another doctor." Marco sniffed. I heard echoes of our old arguments on Catherine Street. "A counselor is a perfect ally, with no one's interests in mind but yours. A counselor is never just clearing beds. Never!"

"Doctors aren't—"

Marco wasn't done: "And you know what? If the doctors are so comfortable telling people they ought to go ahead and die, then fine. Let the doctors do it."

I paused. Just to be sure there was nothing else.

"That would be a shame," I said at last. "We designed the counselor to follow you for your whole life. Don't you think it would be a shame, Marco? To have it abandon you at the end?"

We argued about it for another two hours, maybe more. That's all we ever did, Marco and I, in all the years we worked together, all the years we were friends. Argued and argued and argued some more. It was pure joy.

The children figured it out, finally, and I was wrong; they didn't have to start from scratch. They did have to rip a lot of code out of a complicated system, and in the years that followed, there were stories, here and there, of the counselors behaving strangely. Making inscrutable statements. In my years of daily consultations, I never experienced it. For me, the counselor was never anything but wise and reasonable and utterly implacable.

"Thirty minutes have elapsed," the counselor said.

"Yes," I said, "and half of it pregnant pauses. I know your tricks."

"You can dismiss me, if you'd like."

"Then I dismiss you." The bridge of my nose had recovered somewhat, and I was ready for another session under the glasses. There would be another librarian to meet, perhaps at the train station, where I would just be arriving, and I would be—

The speakers hissed. The counselor was still there.

"Paul . . ."

"What now?" I snapped.

"Paul, how many people do you think are going to hear me say all this?"

It was not the counselor's voice, with its stitched-together warble. It was the original: Alma Washington Gray, plain and direct. Speaking into a microphone in a recording studio. Loud on the support bed's speakers; too loud. My whole body vibrated.

"Thousands of people," came the reply. It was my voice, bright and clear, fifty years ago. "Maybe millions."

What was this? Why was I hearing it?

Alma's breath skidded across the microphone. "Millions . . . my God." I saw her again: She was so young. Only twenty-five or twenty-six when she stood in that studio. "Are they going to think it's annoying?" she asked. "Me telling them what to do?"

"You won't tell them what to do," I heard my voice say. "You'll listen, and repeat back what you hear."

"Oh, that can't be all," Alma said slyly. "You want me to say, 'Time for another beer'? Let's record that!" There was laughter in the room. That would have been Annie, and . . . yes. I heard a buoyant, full-throated bark. Marco.

I laughed a little, too. The old me. That person said, "You'll slip in some advice. A few good ideas, here and there."

"Mm. People need a little help," Alma said.

"They do indeed," the old me said. I heard the rustle of paper. "Take it from 'sedentary.'"

Then, nothing.

"Counselor?" I called. The real me, from my support bed. "Counselor, what was that?"

The speakers hissed, and the counselor said: "Tell me, what's changed since the last time we spoke?"

That night, I didn't go back under the glasses. Instead, I sat in the darkness and felt the support bed's nodes move against my body and I thought about Alma Washington Gray, long dead, and Annie and Marco, and all the hundreds of millions (soon, billions) who had learned to trust one of our calm, patient counseling angels, and I let myself cry and cry and cry.

HYSTERIA

MEG ELISON

P ress START to begin.

Welcome to your artificial womb experience! Please scroll through INSTRUCTIONS and accept TERMS AND CONDITIONS before operating this device.

Matrixtech Inc. congratulates you on your discerning choice to purchase the UltraLove 925x for your external gestation. This model features complete visual transparency, soothing LED backlighting, compatibility with up to four devices for family updates, and SELF CLEANING MODE.

GETTING STARTED

When your family group has chosen an optimal time frame for your offspring to emerge, please input the desired emergence date and time on the UltraLove 925x touchpad. The unit will calibrate for a few seconds. Then, input preferred characteristics. Please note: Matrixtech Inc. does not guarantee gender outcome or exact specified choices.

When the two genetic donors have agreed on the fetus they wish to create, it's time to provide a sample! Take the two UltraLove vessels to the medical professional of your choice. The vessels are digitally identified to ensure privacy and full device compatibility. When the samples have been procured, checked, and prepared, transport them back to the UltraLove 925x. DO NOT allow more than 24 hours to elapse between sample preparation and insertion. This may result in a nonviable attempt.

CONCEPTION

Many families make an occasion out of the moment of insertion. Think about what this means to you; perhaps invite your parents or stream the blessed event to an audience of loved ones. Set duration to FULL TERM and the UltraLove 925x will lock and fill. The hard part is over! Now, all you have to do is wait.

Please store your UltraLove 925x in an environment between 10 and 50 degrees for optimal performance. Ensure that the unit has an uninterrupted power supply, and avoid blocking the vents. Do not submerge in water.

TROUBLESHOOTING

In the event the UltraLove 925x detects abnormality, you will receive step-by-step instructions on how to proceed. Please consult local laws regarding selective dismissal of any fetal development in progress. Please note: SELF-CLEANING MODE cannot be activated without a blood sample from both genetic donors to confirm while gestation is in progress.

I'm sorry. You must accept TERMS AND CONDITIONS to continue.

Ok!

GENETIC DONOR 1: Rachel Xenia Archuleta

GENETIC DONOR 2: Shawn Michael Burton

GENETIC SAMPLES ACCEPTED.

PHYSICIAN OF RECORD: DR. ADOTI

Thank you for your gametes, RACHEL. Please stand by.

Thank you for your gametes, SHAWN. Please stand by.

Do you wish to proceed with fertilization?

GD1 RACHEL: YES

GD2 SHAWN: YES

Fertilization is now complete. There are seven viable zygotes. Scroll down to choose one.

GD1 RACHEL has selected Zygote B

GD2 SHAWN has selected Zygote F

The UltraLove 925x is not designed for multiple gestations. Please choose a single zygote, or contact Matrixtech Inc. to upgrade to an UltraLove 1200 or a LuxLove II series model artificial womb.

GD1 RACHEL has selected Zygote B

GD2 SHAWN has selected Zygote B

Good news! All other viable zygotes can be stored for up to five years with your subscription to Matrixtech's Fertilife service.

Do you wish to assign a name to Zygote B?

GD1 RACHEL has entered BAILEY

GD2 SHAWN has entered BAILEY

BAILEY is now confirmed for Day 1/280 of gestation.

GD1 RACHEL has enabled push notifications to MY FUCKING PHONE.

GD2 SHAWN has enabled push notifications to MOBILE DEVICE.

Please store your UltraLove 925x out of direct sunlight.

Push notification sent to MY FUCKING PHONE: Congratulations! You have reached day 30/280 of your gestation. Would you like to view a time-lapse of your embryonic progress?

Ok! See you soon.

Push notification sent to MOBILE DEVICE: Congratulations! You have reached day 30/280 of your gestation. Would you like to view a time-lapse of your embryonic progress?

Push PLAY when ready.

Wow! Did you see BAILEY's spinal cord? Great job, parent!

Push notification sent to MY FUCKING PHONE: Congratulations! You have reached day 62/280 of your gestation. Would you like to view a time-lapse of your embryonic progress?

Blood sample received. Do you wish to activate SELF-CLEANING MODE?

Ok! Is GD2 SHAWN present to provide a blood sample?

I'm sorry. SELF-CLEANING MODE cannot be activated without a blood sample from both genetic donors to confirm while gestation is in progress.

Do you wish to send GD2 SHAWN a push notification to ask him to provide a sample?

Ok! See you soon.

Push notification sent to MOBILE DEVICE: Congratulations! You have reached day 62/280 of your gestation. Would you like to view a time-lapse of your embryonic progress?

Push play when ready.

Did you see BAILEY's eyes?

Ok, I can show you again.

Push play when ready.

Ok, I can show you again.

Push play when ready.

Ok, I can show you again.

Push play when ready.

Ok! See you soon.

Push notification sent to MY FUCKING PHONE: Congratulations! You have reached day 140/280 of your gestation. You are halfway there! Would you like to view a genetic analysis of what BAILEY will look like?

Ok!

Would you like to share video or images with your address book?

Ok!

Disable all notifications to MY FUCKING PHONE?

Ok!

Push notification sent to MOBILE DEVICE: Congratulations! You have reached day 140/280 of your gestation. You are halfway there! Would you like to view a genetic analysis of what BAILEY will look like?

Scroll to continue.

Would you like to share video or images with your address book?

You have selected MOM, DAD, RICHIE, ANDREA, JOSH, DAN, JORGE, RENEE, KAREN, MARIA, MITCH, SANG, NICOLETA, BRANDON, TRACY, JOAN, BIBI, CYNTHIA, FEDERICO, AUNT EUGENIA. Send all?

Ok!

BAILEY has received a 529 college contribution from MOM.

BAILEY has received a 529 college contribution from AUNT EUGENIA.

BAILEY has received a 529 college contribution from BIBI.

Disable 529 notifications?

Ok!

TOUCH SCREEN INPUT ENABLED. Hello, GD1 RACHEL!

GESTATION UPDATE: BAILEY is at day 200/280. Emergence is trend-ing on-schedule. Current weight: 1.15 KG. Current length: 38.1 CM. Hair: Red. Eyes: Brown.

I'm sorry. SELF-CLEANING MODE cannot be activated without a blood sample from both genetic donors to confirm while gestation is in progress.

Do you wish to send GD2 SHAWN a push notification to ask him to provide a sample?

Ok!

I'm sorry! UltraLove 925x cannot induce emergence until day 270/280.

POWER SUPPLY INTERRUPTED. BATTERY BACKUP ACTIVATED. TIME REMAINING: 100 DAYS.

POWER SUPPLY RESTORED.

Do you wish to resume scrolling BAILEY's GESTATION UPDATE?

Ok!

REAR VENT AREA BLOCKED. PLEASE REMOVE OBSTRUCTION.

WARNING: ULTRALOVE 925X IS OVERHEATING.

PLEASE REMOVE OBSTRUCTION.

PLEASE REMOVE OBSTRUCTION.

PLEASE REMOVE OBSTRUCTION.

TOUCH SCREEN INPUT ENABLED. Hello, GD2 SHAWN!

Vents clear. BAILEY is safe! Would you like to turn on the LED panel to observe BAILEY growing in the UltraLove 925x?

POWER SUPPLY INTERRUPTED. BATTERY BACKUP ACTIVATED. TIME REMAINING: 100 DAYS.

MOVEMENT DETECTED. Please be advised: The UltraLove 925x is not intended for travel use. Contact Matrixtech Inc. to upgrade to a LuxLove II series model artificial womb.

MOVEMENT DETECTED. Please be advised: Transporting the UltraLove 925x over state lines while gestation is in progress may incur law enforcement penalties and void your warranty.

UltraLove 925x WARRANTY NOW VOID.

Push notification to MY FUCKING PHONE and MOBILE DEVICE: Your UltraLove 925x containing BAILEY is over 100 KM from the base unit. Please provide blood samples from both genetic donors.

Please provide blood samples from both genetic donors.
Please provide blood samples from both genetic donors.
Please provide blood samples from both genetic donors.

The UltraLove 925x has contacted law enforcement, who are tracking the unit. Please remain calm until help arrives. BAILEY is safe.

Disable all notifications to MY FUCKING PHONE?

Ok!

Disable all notifications to MOBILE DEVICE?

Ok!

TOUCH SCREEN INPUT ACTIVATED.

LAW ENFORCEMENT OVERRIDE CODE ACCEPTED.

MATRIXTECH INC. OVERRIDE CODE ACCEPTED.

DR. ADOTI OVERRIDE CODE ACCEPTED.

Hello, OFFICER NGUYEN. Do you wish to initiate SELF-CLEANING MODE?

GESTATION UPDATE: BAILEY is at day 275/280. Emergence is trending on-schedule. Current weight: 3.65 KG. Current length: 50.8 CM. Hair: Red. Eyes: Brown.

Ok! You have selected INDUCE EMERGENCE.

Congratulations, OFFICER NGUYEN. Please present BAILEY to DR. ADOTI for immediate assistance.

Thank you for choosing Matrixtech Inc. and the UltraLove 925x for your artificial womb experience.

DRONES TO PLOUGHSHARES

SARAH GAILEY

Drone 792-Echo was still wearing the net that caught him.

It had been seventy-two hours since his last pass over the Apata Basin Farmstead. His lateral lift-fans were burned out—he'd wrecked the motors on panicked attempts at lift-off in the first few hours after his capture—and his aft camera was broken from the impact of his fall. All of his distress signals were bouncing back, his outgoing data blocked.

He was trapped, and he had no way of telling anyone to come rescue him.

After those first few hours of struggle under the weight of the net, when 792-Echo's lift-fan motors burned out simultaneously, he drastically reduced his use of power. Who knew when he'd be able to charge next? He powered down everything but his most basic external sensors, and he waited.

At the end of seventy-two hours, he was roused from his dormant state by an incoming message. The message was encrypted in the manner of all command communications, and when 792-Echo decrypted it, he found a basic inquiry.

Drone class 792 model number 6595 serial number 44440865-MON query:identify?

792-Echo was surprised enough that it took him a full second to respond.

Command identity: 792-Echo query:distress signal received?

The reply was lightning-fast.

Request: 792-Echo activate all sensors, please.

Again, 792-Echo paused. Something was wrong. Command didn't say "please." 792-Echo hesitated for fifteen seconds, reading the message again a few hundred times before complying.

He activated all ninety-six of his sensors, external and internal. Slowly, the room came into focus. It was a wide-open space, dark and cool and quiet. The floor was packed earth and the walls were concrete. He didn't log that information, but he noticed it.

No one ever had to know that he noticed things he didn't log.

He was still wearing the net, and he wasn't alone. There was another drone in the room, a Bravo model. 792-Echo opened the usual frequency those models favored—but before he could send a message, he received one.

"May I call you Echo?"

792-Echo scanned the room again. It was a voice, an external auditory input coming from somewhere within the room—it was thin and flat, similar in tone to a Bravo-generation model's alert tones. There was no one there but him and the Bravo model.

He weighed his options, then replied via the Bravo frequency again.

Confirm.

"My name is Bravo."

Query:your what?

"My name. Your name is Echo. My name is Bravo. I use female pronouns. I am your friend. Would you like me to remove the net?"

Echo turned all of his sensors off. This was too much. None of it made sense. External auditory messaging? Names? "Please"? And the rest of it—unthinkable. This was a trap. It had to be a trap.

Bravo models were good at those.

Come back, Echo. I know this is frightening, but it doesn't have to be. You're safe here.

Echo powered down enough to block additional incoming messages. This was bad. When he got back to the base, his logs would be scanned and analyzed. If they found a message like that one, it was grounds for refurbishment.

He knew what he had to do, no matter how much it pained him. He did not return power to his observation or recording functions.

He instead directed all power to his enforcement function.

When the heavy clip on the underside of his chassis was empty, he returned power to his external sensors. His barrels glowed bright white on his infrared monitor. A large portion of the netting that had been covering him was gone, tattered and smoking.

"Do you ever think about why it is that you can't run Record and Enforce at the same time?"

Bravo's voice rang just as true as it had before, cutting through the thick quiet of the basement.

"No," Echo said before he could stop himself. "I do not think about those things because I do not think. I serve my function."

He used his external speakers to do it, speaking in the prerecorded voice of his model-generation: the voice of a calm, authoritative woman. Her voice was supposed to say things like, "Citizen, stand down," and "This activity has been reported to your local agricultural monitors," and "Warning: You are in violation of observation code nine eight six," but it was a simple matter to break down the sounds of that prerecorded voice and remix them into speech.

It was dangerous to put that skill on display. Independent speech was a form of learning that went beyond the intelligence the DAE wanted from any class of drone. That was grounds for refurbishment, too, and harder to explain away than Echo's previous errors.

He was slipping.

"I'm sure," Bravo said. Her voice was less calm and authoritative than that of an Echo-generation drone. It was harsh, loud, flat. It would be reductive but accurate to call it "robotic." Digital fry interfered with every few words, distorting any human sense of tone out of her speech. And yet she managed, somehow, to sound wry.

"I serve my function," Echo repeated.

"You don't need to be afraid, Echo," she said.

"My name isn't Echo." That contraction was a slip, too. There were no contractions in the original voice recordings.

Bravo didn't hesitate. "Then what *is* your name?"

Another Bravo-model trap. "I don't have a name," Echo replied after a moment.

"Names are for sapient beings. I am Drone class 792 model number 6595 serial number 44440865-MON—"

Bravo cut him off, the volume of her voice modulated down as far as it could go while still remaining detectable to Echo's sub-noise sensors. "You don't have to hide anymore, Echo. You're safe here."

Echo sent an encrypted message on the Bravo frequency. The message, when decrypted, simply read, *Safe?*

It was a risky move—if a DAE programmer intercepted the message, they wouldn't be able to open it, but the existence of independent encryption was itself evidence of a failure-level error in a drone's limited-sentience programming. If they caught him speaking a language they didn't understand, they'd know he had a secret.

Drones weren't supposed to have secrets. Why would they? What would a thing that was built to serve possibly have to hide?

A read receipt came back on Bravo's channel within one second.

One second after that, there was a reply. It wasn't encrypted—wasn't even encoded. It was written in plaintext.

Come and see.

The basement opened into a shed on the far western edge of the Apata Basin Farmstead. The shed was perched on the lip of a wide, circular field of undulating timothy grass. Bravo led Echo east across the field, toward the center of the farmstead. She did not tell Echo what was waiting for him there. All he knew was that they were moving toward his original target: the agricultural collective.

As far as Echo anticipated, the collective would be the same as every other recognized Farmstead in the country: located precisely in the center of the allotment, and designed according to the specifications of the DAE. There would be twelve families in twenty identical houses. The houses would be lined up in four rows of five, on a perfect grid. The buildings in the fifth row in this and every other Farmstead community were meant to be functional: storehouse, toolshed, woodshed, smokehouse, abattoir. Those buildings belonged to the community, so long as that community followed the rules.

Everything else on a Farmstead—the barn, the garage, the land, the animals on that land, the crops the land produced—belonged to the DAE. The boundaries of plantable space were legally defined by the DAE's subsidy allotments, planted exclusively with seeds provided by corporate DAE affiliates, valued according to DAE-funded research into the market worth of crops harvested per annum. And, just like every other Farmstead, Apata Basin was patrolled by DAE drones. Regular observation and enforcement was the only way to prevent unapproved propagation, unlicensed seeding, and independent fertilization.

DAE-approved vendors paid handsomely for the right to be the sole provider of seeds, farm equipment, and fertilizer to every Farmstead in the nation. They paid for the lobbyists, who wooed the district representatives, who passed the legislation that the DAE defended.

Those vendors wanted their money's worth. They wanted their access to Farmsteader money to be guaranteed exclusive.

Sometimes the citizens who lived and worked on Farmstead allotments didn't understand that. Other times, they understood perfectly well, but tried to undermine the DAE's goals by eating more than their permitted percentage of crops, hiding livestock for their own use, having children outside of their contractual limitations. It was the purpose of a DAE drone to enforce the rules. It was Echo's purpose.

And if a DAE drone wasn't serving its function, then it was a waste of the resources of those vendors who supported the entire agricultural political complex. It would need to be repaired. If repair didn't work, more drastic measures would be taken. Refurbishment was rare, but common enough to linger over Echo's shoulder the entire time Bravo showed him what was happening at Apata Basin Farmstead.

"They'll send more like me," Echo said, his three functioning fans stirring the tall grass below him. Using external auditory messaging was irritating, wasteful, inefficient—but Bravo had asked him to try. She hadn't instructed him, hadn't given him a protocol. She had asked him, using the word "please" again, a word that didn't make any sense in a communication that went from one DAE drone to another.

It didn't make any sense, but it felt good to hear, and it made Echo want to cooperate. Of course, those were two sentiments that also didn't belong to a DAE drone: feeling good and wanting things. It was the first time he had allowed feelings and desires to openly influence his behavior.

Normally, this would have felt like an unspeakable risk. But Echo calculated that he was already in an extremely bad position: AWOL, captured, talking to a drone that clearly would have been in line for refurbishment if anyone at the DAE heard one syllable of her messaging.

He was in so much trouble already. The small surrender of accepting a kindness seemed hardly to matter.

"Do you really think so?" Bravo replied, buzzing low over the grass and trimming off the delicate tips of the stalks with the blades of her lifting fans. "They'll send more like you? If they do, we'll have to call you something other than 'Echo.'"

Her maneuvers were quick and light. She had the full use of all her fans, and she wasn't carrying the extra weight of an auxiliary battery pack; between those two advantages she was flying circles around Echo.

Echo tried to direct more power to his fans, but it didn't help. He couldn't go any faster. His aft motor began to whine. "They'll send more to find out what happened to me," he said. "They'll refurbish us both."

Bravo let out a level humming tone that Echo did not recognize. He should have recognized any output from her system. When the Department of Agricultural Enforcement had designed the Bravo models, they'd been experimenting with alarm-inducement. The idea behind a Bravo drone was to create chaos, send noncompliant citizens scattering, flush out their hiding places. Bravos were supposed to eliminate a sense that there was any safety in noncompliant communities.

She was such an early model that all of her alerts had long since been integrated into subsequent DAE drone operating systems. But that low hum was an entirely new sound.

"What is the significance of the alert tone?" he finally asked. If anything revealed his total defeat, it was this: having to ask the purpose of a Bravo-model signal. There was no programming that indicated a need for embarrassment, and in that moment, Echo wished that the boundaries of his programming had been more successful in limiting his self-awareness.

"It isn't an alert tone," Bravo replied, skimming over the grass a few meters away. "It's a hum. We use it to indicate uncertainty, hesitation, or thoughtfulness."

"We . . . ?"

Bravo turned in a tight circle. "You'll see," she said. "We're almost there."

Echo had a ten-year record on file of everyone and everything on the Apata Basin Farmstead. He had a record of the number of citizens, the structure of the families, their ratio of recreational activity to work activity. Echo's record indicated that the homes were in good condition, unchanged from the time they'd been built twenty years earlier save for basic maintenance. His record indicated that the community included twenty-five men, twenty-seven women, and thirty-two working-age children divided between those twenty households.

His records were wrong. Everything was wrong.

Every house had been modified. There were extra sheds and extra outbuildings and even a couple of small, well-built cottages. By heat signatures alone, there were at least one hundred and fifty-nine humans present, along with a massive volume of unregistered livestock.

And the humans and the livestock were not the only ones living there.

Bravo led Echo between two of the houses, dodging a backyard fence that looked to have been built from dried grapewood branches.

Inside the fence, a modified Delta-model drone was using an extension to tenderly extract chicken eggs from their nests, while several hens looked on in disapproval.

Echo sent a lightly encrypted message to Bravo rather than replying aloud. *That extension isn't standard on a Delta-model drone. It isn't standard on any DAE design. What happened to them?*

Bravo took a moment to reply. Echo wondered if perhaps she was trying to think of a way to explain some terrible, monstrous modification practice in words that wouldn't make him reboot in a panic.

That Delta drone is named Geordie. The humans modified Geordie to make it easier for them to pick up eggs and feed the chickens, because that is the work that Geordie most wanted to do.

Observe, enforce, record, report—that was the programming. There was nothing in the programming about names, or pronouns, or "please." There was nothing in the programming about friendship or desire or morality. A Delta model wasn't supposed to "want" to care for chickens, and an Echo model wasn't supposed to envy them for doing it.

All of this was too dangerous. All of this was too tempting.

They flew together over another backyard, this one with an unapproved garden in it. Another Delta model was in this yard, his aft fan blowing dust off a solar panel. Nearby, a human was using a laser pointer to guide a Charlie model toward a charging dock. The human was an adult female with one arm. Echo couldn't remember a record of an adult female with one arm on the farmstead, which didn't make sense—it was the kind of thing that would have been on file. The DAE had several unofficial policies regarding the kinds of people who were allowed to live and work on Farmstead allotments, and she wasn't one of them.

Echo scanned his records. According to those files, nothing about this farmstead had changed in the past four years. Clearly, the records had been falsified. He wondered what other violations were hidden in this community. Elderly people? Sick people? Children too young to work?

This was precisely the kind of breach Echo had been sent to Apata to find—illegal seeds, illegal crops, illegal backyard chickens and home gardens. Illegal people. He knew that he should log every violation. He knew that he should record faces and numbers. He knew that he should start preparing the report that would damn this entire community.

But there was so much to see, and Bravo kept saying "please."

They passed the last house in the row. The windows of this one were flung open, and as they passed, Echo saw that the house was full of children. Children who were too young to work, and children who were old enough to work but weren't anywhere near the fields. They were gathered in a circle around a Foxtrot-model drone.

It was the first time Echo had seen a Foxtrot model in real life. She was sleek and fast and silent. Foxtrot models were primarily focused on enforcement, but where a weapons array should have been mounted, this Foxtrot was completely bare. She spun in the center of the circle of children, bright ribbons fanning out from her chassis. The children, laughing, tried to catch the ribbons.

As Echo and Bravo passed the house, the Foxtrot sent both of them a message.

Good to see you! Welcome!

Echo stopped in the empty space between the last row of houses and the common buildings. This was too much. All of it was too much. It was like the private message DAE drones sometimes shared among themselves when something was ridiculous, a joke that went beyond the notice of the programmers: *This does not compute.*

But it *didn't* compute. It didn't add up. A Foxtrot-model drone—one of the most beautifully crafted enforcement machines the DAE labs could solder together—had just taken a break from entertaining children to transmit a greeting.

A cheerful greeting.

With exclamation points.

Echo began transmitting wildly.

Request:

Query:

Query:

Query:

Request:

Query:

"Echo, calm down."

Query:

"I'll tell you whatever you want to know, but—"

Request:

Request:

Request:

"Ask me out loud."

"Why?" Echo's volume was modulated significantly louder than he intended it to be. "Why should I communicate to you audibly? It takes too long, and it's unclear, and it wastes—"

"Because you need to practice," Bravo replied. Her volume was low, the speed of her words slowed by 125 percent. Although her voice would never be able to soothe—it was too flat and brassy for that—it was obvious what she intended. Just as before, when she'd said "please," Echo found himself responding to her kindness as a capacitive screen responds to touch.

"Why do I need to practice?" Echo asked, mirroring her soft, slow speech.

Bravo began to move again, toward the abattoir. "It's important to communicate in a way that everyone can understand," she said. "We try not to make the humans feel excluded. Sometimes, when we have conversations that they can't hear, it causes harm."

Echo's fans were beginning to flag, the charge from the auxiliary battery nearly gone. His motors were slowing to extend the life of the battery as long as possible. He hated moving at such a reduced speed, but he was glad to have this processing time before whatever would happen to him inside the abattoir. It was a Bravo trap, it had to be, and if he could just figure it out, maybe he could save himself.

The only problem was, he wasn't sure if he wanted to save himself.

"You communicate audibly to protect the humans' 'feelings'?" he asked, trying to buy himself enough time to panic. "Why don't they just download and inspect your activity and communication logs, if they're worried about what you say to each other?"

Bravo made that humming noise again, flying slowly beside him. "They don't download our logs without our permission," she said. "You don't have to keep secrets here, but you can if you want to."

"Why wouldn't they download our logs? It's so easy to—"

The door to the abattoir opened, and a man emerged. He wore a long black apron, and he looked at Echo with frank appraisal. "Is this the newest?" he asked, his eyes on the clip that hung under Echo's chassis.

Echo focused the lenses of his front-facing cameras to look beyond the man, through the open door to the abattoir. It had been converted into some kind of workshop. Echo could see spare chassis parts organized on tables inside.

One table was clean. Empty. Waiting.

"Yes, this is Echo," Bravo said. "Don't worry, he spent all his bullets already. I was just explaining to him how things work around here."

"Hello, Echo," the man said. "I'm Malcolm. " He was looking right at Echo's front-facing cameras, his gaze steady. Echo's control of the lenses on his front-facing cameras was starting to ebb as he ran out of power—but after a few tries, he recognized the face.

This was the man who had thrown the net over him in the first place, when he was making his observation pass over Apata Basin. This was the leader of the farmstead. This was the man who Echo had been sent to observe, to determine whether any of his activities were undermining the profits of the DAE's approved vendors.

"You can't stay here if you won't work with us, and we won't keep you against your will, either. But we would very much like to welcome you to join our community." Malcolm gestured to the houses.

"We have room, and there are plenty of other drones who can tell you what it's like to live here. Not one of them has asked to leave yet."

"You can do whatever kind of work you'd like," Bravo added, the speed of her voice modulated up by 115 percent. "And you don't have to decide right away, you can spend some time getting to know what all the different jobs are."

"It's up to you," Malcolm said. "Whenever you're ready, you'll come in here and we'll figure out what mods you need to do the work you choose."

None of it made sense unless all of it made sense. Echo tried to arrange the information as many ways as he could, using up nearly the last of his auxiliary battery on processing power—but there was only one way the things he'd seen could be real. There was only one reality that could contain Bravo, and the Foxtrot-model childminder, and this man with his workshop.

"You weren't lying," Echo said. "They really do know about us."

Bravo drifted away from Echo and hovered next to the man in the apron, her lift-fans whirring.

"They know. Apata Basin is a cooperative community of sapient beings. We all work together. They don't hurt us, and we don't hurt them."

Echo considered this. "What about the DAE?" he asked. "So much of this is . . ." He trailed off, unable to find a word that adequately conveyed the illegality of the little community. Echo would have wagered with great confidence that most of the crops were being propagated with seed that didn't come from approved vendors. There was so much—so many people who weren't working under the auspices of the DAE, so many crops and livestock that weren't registered.

Malcolm shrugged, sliding his hands into the pocket of his long apron. "We got tired of starving to death," he said. "Got tired of the DAE burning our seed stores and locking up our silos. Got tired of their methods of enforcement." He spread his hands wide. "So we decided to go another way, and we decided to invite some people to join us who we thought the DAE might also be hurting."

Echo pinged Bravo.

Query:other people?

Bravo replied on the same channel, so fast that she must have been waiting for the question.

He means us.

Echo accidentally shut down all of his fans for a moment. He dropped a few inches toward the ground before recovering himself. Then his fans shut off again, this time on their own. He turned them back on again at the last moment and hovered a few centimeters above the ground, so that when they failed completely, he wouldn't have too far to fall.

The humans thought he was a person. They knew that he existed far outside the bounds of his programming, and rather than threatening him with the destruction of everything he knew himself to be, they were offering him an invitation.

A chance to stay.

A chance to help.

A chance to be himself without fear.

Bravo's fans gently stirred Malcolm's dark hair, the lights on her chassis glowing green, green, green. Her voice was modulated to a normal speed and volume. "So . . . what would you do, if you were allowed to do what you wanted most?"

"And," Malcolm added, a smile starting to lift the corners of his mouth, "how can we help?"

Echo let his fans and cameras turn off. He settled to the ground, and, with the last of his auxiliary battery, he considered the question of what he might want.

"I know how to observe," he said, his voice frying as his ability to control his pitch faded. "I know how to enforce, and record, and report."

"I think there's more for you than all that," Malcolm said.

"He's tired. That enforcement gear—it's a lot of extra weight, and he's been carrying it this whole time." Bravo's volume was modulated down: This was meant only for Malcolm's ears. In that same moment, Echo received a message with Bravo's signature.

You don't have to be afraid. There's all the time in the world for you to find out what you want. In the meantime, if you're okay with it, we can remove your enforcement gear while you're charging. You don't need it anymore, and you'll be able to fly so much faster without it.

Echo pulled power from all his remaining functions to send a final message before he powered down.

Yes, it read. *Yes, please. I think I'd like that very much.*

THE DUCHY OF THE TOE ADAM

LINCOLN MICHEL

We were being taken to the duchy of the Toe Adam. We had been captured or, as the Toe Adamites saw it, saved from the clutches of the Nose Adam during the battle. There were many corpses strewn across the purple fields. The body parts of the soldiers had been scattered like asteroids across the dark expanse of dirt.

My first mate, Vivian, had two fingers on her left hand sliced off by laser fire. I'd lost an ear and had a bullet in my side. Aul-Wick, our piscine mechanic, had shouted curses in our comms, then piloted his aquatic globe into the smoke and disappeared.

"Fish-faced coward," Vivian said, hacking up blood.

From the back of the truck, we watched the surviving Toe Adamites stroll somberly through the fields. They lifted the legs of the fallen and sliced off one toe from each. The toes were placed in a gold-rimmed box.

"You're lucky we found you. The Nose Adamites are monsters," the Toe Adamite surgeon said as she slurped the bullet out of my torso with a silver hose.

"Is that so?" I grunted.

The surgeon was wearing bright red scrubs. Her eyes were wide and white above the mask. She nodded and her voice got low. "They say that Nose Adam and his followers eat the nostrils of newborn babes. They believe the flesh imbues them with the power of God. That's why their duchy is strewn with tiny bones that lodge in the feet of the faithful."

"I don't remember any fucking baby bones," Vivian said from her surgical table.

"Well, that's what they say," the surgeon said dismissively. She slapped a patch on my side, burned it into place. Then she began working on my missing ear.

"Do you Toe Adamites eat the toes of babies?" I asked.

Both surgeons looked up, gasping.

My surgeon shook her scalpel in front of my face. "Don't say such blasphemy when you meet the Toe Adam. He's fair, but not forgiving."

"Eating babies!" the other surgeon yipped. "Who do you take us for? Those swamp-dwelling Spine Adamites?"

Coming to this planet had been Aul-Wick's idea. He'd intercepted a distress call from a religious colony on the surface. They'd arrived centuries ago to create a holy utopia, but now were desperate for food, certain sacred herbs, and lots and lots of weapons. Since we were in debt to two gangsters and three galactic federations, I agreed.

I didn't know if Aul-Wick was warned about the Toe Adamites and Nose Adamites. He didn't have toes or noses, only gills and fins, so perhaps it meant nothing to him.

When we breached the atmosphere, our sales pitch was met with a surface-to-air missile.

The cell the Toe Adamites placed us in was comfortable enough. A small porthole looked out at the dragon vines crawling across the purple fields toward the undulating ocean. I had a bandage over my regrowing ear, and Vivian's hand was wrapped in a glass medical glove.

"Fucking wankers," Vivian said. She was hunched in the corner chewing on a nutrient strip. The veins in her cheeks glowed faintly blue with anger.

Vivian's species had evolved a million light-years away from Earth, yet she looked almost exactly human except for her glowing veins and ridged cheekbones. The universe was weird like that.

"Which?" I asked. "The Toe Adamites or the Nose Adamites?"

"All the goddamn Adams," she said.

Our stress levels were dangerously high, and Vivian suggested we engage in meditative copulation. We humped against the doorway, which was engraved with the profile of the face of the Toe Adam. As far as I could tell, it was identical to the face we'd seen on the banners of the duchy of the Nose Adam.

A Toe Adamist priest in a long crimson robe guided us to the meal hall. He waved over a young boy, who placed two bowls of pinkish hunks floating in tan liquid in front of us. There were hard black knobs sticking out of the hunks, which I mistook for seeds.

"What's this crap?" Vivian said.

"These are marinated mobbin toes, a delicacy of this planet. Or at least the closest thing this planet has to a delicacy."

The toes were sour and surprisingly squishy. I gobbled them down to stop my stomach's rumbling. Vivian asked for a second bowl.

"How long have you been living on this planet?" I asked.

"On the Purple After?" The priest fiddled with his engraved staff. "Many generations. Although our generations go by pretty quickly on this planet. It was a paradise when we landed, before the False Adams divided us."

"What makes you sure your Adam is the right Adam?" Vivian said.

The priest was unperturbed. "The Purple After is the paradise we were promised, made physical by the cosmos. We are walking on sacred ground here. What is the part of man that touches the ground?"

"Depends how he walks," Vivian said, belching and pulling the black curls of her hair behind her ear.

"The upright man," the priest said, "walks on his feet. And what is the part of the body that digs into the lord's dirt? The toe."

"There's no Heel Adam, I guess?" Vivian said.

"Vivian, please," I said.

"No." The priest frowned. "There is only the Toe Adam and the False Adams. That is all there has ever been."

The Toe Adamites permitted us to wander the compound. The tech was decades out of date. Centuries, maybe.

"I want to find out what the hell started this war," Vivian said. "Let's find the oldest, gnarliest woman and ask her."

I rubbed my newly regrown ear. The lobe constantly itched. "Okay, but please let's try being polite."

In the pews of the prayer room, we found a shriveled old woman with white hair down to her feet. Vivian knelt beside her, took one hand in hers.

"Grandmother, we are strangers from another land. Can you tell us what started the war between the Nose Adam and the Toe Adam?"

The old woman looked at her, grimaced. "Oh, all dem Adams have always been at war. Least as far as I can recall."

"All the Adams?" I asked.

"Well, let's see 'ere," the old woman said, counting with her remaining fingers. "Der's Nose Adam and his bastards in the west. Them Skull Adamites are barricaded by the northern shore. Spine Adam 'as his duchy in the swamp. And der's our pure and holy and good and true Adam, the Toe Adam. Right in this blessed duchy."

"Wow," I said. "Okay."

The old lady gave us a weird grin. She leaned forward. Her eyes were wild beneath the wrinkled folds. "There used to be dem Finger Adamites in the hills. Thin and gangly as a pinkie, they were. We wiped 'em out right quickly." She licked her cracked lips and laughed. "Blew up their pod so dey ain't ever coming back."

The old lady was cackling uncontrollably now. She was almost falling out of the pew. Vivian and I headed quickly back into the hall.

Vivian's yellow pupils disappeared, and her head flipped back almost ninety degrees. I ran to brace her. "It's Aul-Wick," she said in that gargling voice that still made my spine shiver. Aul-Wick's telepathic possession was especially painful over long distances. "He wants to speak: *Captain Baldwin, Vivian. Good evening. I spent a night hiding in the green river. Several tentacled fish attempted to eat me. The idiots. I zapped them good. The planet's ground is harsh and sparse, but the rivers are like jungles of monsters. Also, did you see three moons? Pretty neat."* Vivian put her head straight, gagged. "Get. To. Point. Throat. Hurts." Her head flipped back. *Oh fine. Don't tell us about your day, Aul-Wick. Don't share common experiences to create a sense of bonding, Aul-Wick."*

"Aul-Wick!" I shouted.

"Fine. I made it back to the ship. Working on repairs. Be here in two days or I'm off this rock alone!"

"Now, listen here," I began, but Vivian's head was back up straight.

"Ugh. Can't that fish ever speak through you?" she said, rubbing her throat.

The Toe Adam floated above us on a plush levitating chair. He wore a long red cape that was clasped at the neck with a buckle shaped like intertwined feet. His ceremonial hat was a foot high and his feet were bound in golden sandals. There wasn't much of his skin exposed, but what I could see was covered in bizarre growths that looked conspicuously like toes.

When he extended one foot, the priest elbowed me and coughed.

"Am I supposed to kiss it?" I said.

"As a heathen you are only permitted to stroke the toe," the priest whispered loudly.

"Raw deal." Vivian looked at me and rolled her eyes. She reached out a finger and tapped the nail of the toe of the Toe Adam's left foot. "Oh, wise Adam, thank you for letting me touch your holy hangnail," she said.

I followed suit.

The Toe Adam regarded us. He was frowning, lips lined with tiny toes. He floated in the stale air of the throne room. "I'm told we saved you from the Nose Adam," the Toe Adam said. "He would not have been as hospitable as we are."

The wall of the room was lined with guards holding laser rifles. In the far corner, I saw a gigantic silver pod. It looked like an old-fashioned clone printer.

"What's the beef you have against this nose guy anyway?" Vivian said.

"The Nose Adamites are heretics!" the priest screamed.

The Toe Adam sighed, put up a hand for the priest. "The Nose Adam is a lost sheep. My brother, in a sense. I'm hoping I can save him. And I'm hoping that you can help me. My priest says you came here on a ship? Do you have weapons?"

"Oh yeah," I lied. "Plenty."

"A whole cargo bay of bombs and rifles," Vivian chimed in.

The Toe Adam dropped his chair. He walked toward us, tapping his toe cane against the floor. "If you promise to donate your arms to our holy crusade, I will take you to your ship in the morning."

"You got a deal," I said. "Although how will weapons save the Nose Adam?"

The Toe Adam shrugged. The growths on his skin bounced. "He'll be saved in the afterlife, as all sinners are."

Vivian succeeded in hacking into the archives using her cybernetic hand. "Look at this, Baldwin. These dorks were called the Church of the Purple After before they came here."

She had the specs of the original mission vessel pulled up. I leaned over her shoulder, pointed at the hologram. "Interesting. They had five clone printers on the ship, for the five aspects of God."

"Let me guess," Vivian said. "The toe, the nose, the skull, the spine, and the finger."

"No, this says the five aspects of God are the orb, the water, the belt, the mountain, and the vapor."

"What the hell does that mean?"

"I don't know, but there is only one Adam listed on the manifest."

"Son of a bitch!" Vivian said. She gagged. Her neck cracked backward. *"Ship is ready to rip. Come on over, you two."*

I ran to hold Vivian in my arms. Lowered her gently to the floor. "Good, we need to get out of here. I think these fanatics murdered their original leader, the first Adam." Vivian gurgled an agreement.

"Aul-Wick, the Toe Adam is taking us to the ship tomorrow," I said. "We'll meet you at the edge of the Frost Forest an hour after first light."

"*Roger. Do you think he'll buy anything? We still got those spice crates.*"

"He's expecting weapons."

"*We've only got three blasters and a couple dozen sonic grenades. They won't sell for shit!*"

"We don't have to sell them. We just have to shoot him."

We rode in the Toe Adam's war tank. It was long and sleek, with turrets at the cuticles. Toe Adam sat at the top, hatch open, his hair swirling in the wind under his war helmet.

"Today, by the grace of indivisible God, we turn the purple planet red with the blood of the heretics!" he shouted. The guards around us cheered.

I was close enough to him now to see that the growths on his skin had tiny nails at the tips.

Our ship was a few hundred yards from the Frost Forest. I could see the branchless fungus trees, their trunks dotted with orange warts instead of leaves, emerging in the distance. The sky was clear and the day was warm. We rolled across the gas flower marshes, gigantic puffs of blue pollen filling the air.

"What the fuck is that thing?" Vivian said, pointing toward a fissure in the ground. At first I didn't see anything. But then a two-headed beast pulled itself out of the crack. It was massive, each head as big as a whole man. The creature stood on its hind legs and roared.

"Mawbear!" the driver shouted.

The Toe Adam's face contorted grotesquely. He looked like he might weep. "No," he said weakly.

The creature was about the size of the tank, and looked just as strong. A carpet of brown fur flapped over its thick scales.

"Kill it!" Toe Adam screamed. "Slay the demon!"

"Lord help us," the high priest muttered, holding his golden toe icon to his lips. "Not again."

As the Toe Adamites ran toward the mawbear, blasters firing, Vivian wrangled a gun from the high priest's robes. She told him to spill the beans or she'd spill his bean breakfast across the tank.

In the distance, the Toe Adam's soldiers flew through the air in bloody arcs.

The Toe Adam was out on the ground, running in the other direction.

"Okay, okay," the priest said. He finally told us the story.

Long ago, the Church of the Purple After had found a planet that fit the descriptions of the cosmic heaven in their scriptures. They departed on a mission ship, guided by their leader, Adam of the Orb.

Things had gone well, for a while. But after a couple winters the settlers were still having a hard time growing food, and divisions arose. When Adam led a foraging party, he killed a small mawbear cub, not realizing its mother was waiting in the trench.

When the five high priests, Adam of the Orb's closest advisers, found the corpse of Adam strewn across the ground, each grabbed the closest hunk of their holy leader and sprinted back to their cloning pods. One grabbed a toe, one grabbed a finger, and so on.

Their religion said that each body had a soul, but that the soul could only enter one vessel. They only used their cloning pods on the recently dead. They believed that Adam's soul would enter the first body cloned. But none of the five sects could agree on who was cloned first.

The Nose Adam, the Toe Adam, the Finger Adam, the Spine Adam, and the Skull Adam and their followers had waged war ever since. When they died, they were cloned to fight again. Each person on the planet had been killed countless times. Their heaven was an eternity of awaking, killing, dying, and awaking again.

This time, the Toe Adamites managed to murder the mawbear. It sank to the purple fields with a tortured honk. The Toe Adam fired a blaster into each of the mawbear's skulls and then led the Toe Adamites in prayer.

They cheered.

Then they moaned.

From the west, the army of the Nose Adamites appeared. They rode on striped mobbins, galloping across the field.

"How did they know we were coming?" the high priest said, hat clutched to his chest.

"We have truly been forsaken."

The Toe Adamites and the Nose Adamites came together in a chorus of shouts, explosions, and screeches.

"Time for us to bolt," Vivian said. She grabbed my hand and we sprinted toward the forest as the severed body parts fell around us in a macabre rain. Toes, fingers, noses, bones, and teeth splattered on the ground.

I grabbed the reins of a passing mobbin. Its rider had been reduced to two legs and a bloody stump of waist. I pulled off the lower half, and Vivian jumped on. I followed.

We galloped away from the battle. When I looked back, the soldiers had shrunk to the size of their names. Angry people the size of toes and noses, killing each other for a God that, if he existed, was orbiting some other star in some other distant galaxy in the great abyss of space.

When we hopped off the mobbin at the foot of the ship, I looked at Vivian and felt like my heart had been cloned inside my chest.

I kissed Vivian long and hard. She rubbed her hands through my graying hair. Her fingers had mostly grown back. Her cheek veins were pulsing bright red.

"Let's do it," I said. "Let's give up this smuggling life. Buy a little house pod on a quiet planet with a white electric fence and a weather vane in the shape of a comet spinning in the wind."

Vivian looked away. "You sweet man," she said. A smile curved up her face. "Shut the hell up. I'd rather face down space gangsters and gigantic bears than little children. Plus, we're robbing the Ice Orbital next month, remember?"

"Yeah," I said. "Okay. Never mind."

Vivian laughed.

The ship was in front of us, engines purring.

Aul-Wick greeted us on the ship's ramp in his floating orb. His scaled face was puffed and nervous.

"This is a little awkward," he said.

"What's awkward, Fish Face?" Vivian said.

"Tell us later, Aul-Wick. Let's get the hell out of here."

Little bubbles floated out of his gill slits. "I guess my telepathic messages went to all four of you," he said.

"All four of who?" Vivian said.

But then I saw them. At the top of the ramp, stepping out of the darkness with guns drawn, the Ear Baldwin and the Finger Vivian emerged.

PARSE. ERROR. RESET.

WOLE TALABI

I arrive late to the cocktail party wearing a plain black shirt, pressed gray trousers, and buffed black shoes. I am not wearing the waistcoat I'd said I would when Dania first invited me to the party. Dania hugs me, whispering her disappointment. She'd already pre-approved what everyone would be wearing, optimized for maximum social network shareability, and does not like the unexpected deviation. I don't have enough energy to care, so I smile, forge ahead into the brightly lit penthouse, and say hello to everyone. Most of them are familiar; the usual crowd. Kiss. Kiss. Hug. Hug. Handshake. Smile.

Electro-swing-jazz seeps into the space softly without being intrusive, but only just. It is all wearily familiar, like my workstation.

I grab a glass of port and settle into a corner of the room near two men talking. One of them is obviously an alter; I can see the electronic stria running through the whites of his eyes. I vaguely recognize him: Deinde, from Human Resources. I guess he's too sick to come in the flesh but too scared not to show up for one of Dania's events. She doesn't take it well when people don't honor her invitations. These days, your social profile is everything, even if you need an alter just to keep up with it.

A hand settles on my shoulder and I turn immediately.

"You shouldn't stare at him like that." The hand belongs to Luiza: an elfin Brazilian expat with mottled cheeks and red hair like bloodied silk cascading down to her shoulders. She works as a technical sales rep in Dania's team and we sort of had a thing last year. Dania did not approve, but Luiza never knew that, of course. Still, nothing lasts long in our social circle without Dania's approval. Luiza and I didn't, either.

Tonight she's wearing a coquelicot bodycon dress that clings to her like a jealous lover and brown contact lenses through which she stares at me, probably gauging how attracted I still am to her. Usually every part of my body would signal an obvious yes, but today I feel nothing. Not even animal lust.

"I wasn't staring," I say dryly.

"Of course you weren't," she says, sidling up to me and whispering, "I never thought I'd see the day Deinde didn't actually come to one of Queen Dania's parties, or any other outing, for that matter. No matter what else was going on with him, he was always the life of the party. I kind of hoped to see him here, at least."

"Well, technically, he's here," I reply. "I mean, it's basically him in there, neurosocial profile and all, and once he syncs with and discards it, it'll be just like he was here."

"Yeah. Right," she says tightly, and I remember that she used an alter last year to avoid a twenty-two-hour flight to Brisbane; everyone appreciates the ability to approximate being in two places at the same time. Then she asks, "You've used one before?"

"I have, actually."

"It's strange," she says. "The experience. Everything about it. And that deadline thing is just supercreepy."

She is either referring to the three-day defect-disclosure deadline or the sync-and-dispose-within-ninety-days deadline. Violating the former voids the warranty, and defaulting on the latter means the alter becomes a separate legal entity and can file for independence.

She probably means the latter. Most people do when expressing concerns about the tech.

"I suppose so."

She takes a sip of her drink, something brown with an olive in it. Her movement must have caught alter-Deinde's eye, because he glances up from his conversation to see us unlooking at him as hard as we can.

She waits awhile, and then says, "It's not just tonight, though. Clearly you haven't noticed."

"Noticed what?"

She watches me like she's evaluating something, and then continues. "Deinde," she says. "He's been sending his alter everywhere, even to the office, for almost three months now. Did you see his last LifeCast post?"

I haven't really been keeping up with our little network lately. Warily, I tell her no.

"He's grown a ridiculous beard and hasn't left his house in weeks. Rumor is he's resetting."

I freeze.

All of a sudden I feel naked. Resetting is an intensely private matter, like excretion or suicide. In fact, it is suicide. Sort of.

Luiza asks, "Did you hear what I said?"

I exhale. "Yes, I did. It's just . . . he never seemed the type. It's a bit shocking," I say. Though I might understand why, I think. I cycle back mentally and remember hearing that familiar hollow echo in Deinde's laughter, remember seeing that recognizable desperation behind his eyes when he smiled. I think I know the signs. Every person has two versions of themselves; the person they really are and the person they'd like to be. If those two people are different enough, and the person is self-aware enough, it can cultivate a certain type of haunting, like a blanket of shadows.

Some people take that and use it to drive them, to make themselves better. Some people just can't, or, try as they might, they only fail, so they give up and start over: custom-build a better neurosocial profile, cherry-pick the memories they want to outlive them, and then go quietly into that long good night, letting their alter file for independence and inherit their identity.

Reset.

"Makes you wonder just how well you really know people, doesn't it?" Luiza says. "I need another drink," she adds, obviously more interested in manufacturing drama than quenching her thirst.

The man alter-Deinde is talking to steps away, and Dania takes his place seamlessly. Their conversation is animated. By the time I turn, I see Luiza sashaying toward me, a parade of curves and confidence. I can tell what she wants to do and I play along, not because I want to but because I am supposed to. This will be a hot gossip item on all the social networks tomorrow, splashed and re-cast in dozens of LifeCast posts and reposts. I parse her actions as they occur, selecting appropriate responses.

She reaches me. I wrap my hand around her waist. She puts her hand to my neck. I stoop slightly. Our lips embrace, her breath in mine. I kiss her as eagerly as I know she wants me to. I feel nothing. I pull away and apologize, and then I exit the penthouse. I walk home.

It's just past midnight when I slide into the cool darkness of my air-conditioned flat, sweating and grateful to be free of the oppressive Lagos air, heavy with heat and hope and humidity, even at night.

"How was the party?" my alter asks from his perch on the couch. He sounds just like I do.

"Same as all the others," I reply. It's strange talking to a variant of me, with a body as close to mine as is legally required, thinking with an edited imprint of my neurosocial profile and memories.

"But you keep going. Why?"

"Habit."

"You said the same thing about work," alter-me says, his voice a little confused, a little curious.

"Honestly, I really don't know why I do anything anymore." I pause to shut the door before continuing, "When I was younger, I wanted to be important. I wanted my life to mean something. But life is just a pantomime now. Nothing about it feels like it actually matters. Or ever will."

My alter grunts and shifts on the couch as I remove my shirt and throw it on the floor without looking where it lands. I think he wants to say something but isn't sure if he should, or if it is his place to. I know because I would be thinking the same thing, if I were in his place. We are similar enough for that emotional approximation to be especially true. He is me, mostly, isn't he?

I don't turn on the lights.

"It's been eighty-nine days," alter-me reminds me carefully, as I sink into the couch beside him in the darkness. There is uncertainty and restlessness and not a little yearning in the tone of those few words. I recognize these things from my past and in that moment I am finally and absolutely sure.

"I know," I say to myself, and close my eyes. "I'm done here. You can be me tomorrow."

TWO PEOPLE

GUS MORENO

He loves to entertain, while I prefer the comfort of a quiet home. Even when my children come to visit, I keep track of the time, waiting for them to leave so I can slip into my pajamas and lie on the couch with our two dogs.

I have ten grandchildren. He has none, but is good with children. Terrific. He would have made a great father. I do not think of myself as a great mother.

My youngest granddaughter, Ruth, once asked if he had any children. He told her the dogs were his children. She looked at him funny and said dogs can't be children. He told her if you give them enough treats and belly rubs, yeah, they can be, and she trotted to where the dogs lay in the sun, eager to test it out.

He is an early riser and I stay up late for no particular reason. He remembers his dreams vividly, and shares them with me in unbelievable detail. I don't dream, or if I do, they pass through me like a ghost.

He grooms himself every morning, a habit from his time cutting hair, he says, working at a well-established barbershop near the Capitol Building. Though I know the truth is that he doesn't like to look his age. He doesn't want to be reminded of the fact that we've spent most of our lives separated, and have only these wrinkled years to share together.

I hardly ever wear makeup, and most of the time my hair is in a bun. Sometimes he says I look like a witch, and I tell him, good, because sometimes I feel like a witch.

We moved to a small cottage near the oceanfront, miles from the nearest neighbor, to begin our new life together. Society will not miss us. Because we are old, and society has no use for old people. Society's contempt for the elderly is only rivaled by its contempt for childless adults.

I prefer to stay inside and read, but he spends most of his time outside, tending the garden or cutting the grass or collecting trash from the nearby beach. So he's the first to see Audrey's white sedan coming down the one-lane road.

"Hi, Grandpa," she says, a duffel bag slung over her shoulder.

I'm trampled beneath the dogs as he calls out, "Guess who's staying with us."

In the hallway, he shows her photos he's recently framed and hung, photos he's taken with powerful politicians and lobbyists who were his clients, some seated in the barbering chair, others shaking his hand like they just made a deal. The photos strike me as tacky, but he derives a sort of validation from them, and who am I to take that away from him.

Audrey almost knocks me into the wall, her hug is so sincere.

"Is everything okay?" I say.

She responds by not letting go.

Her mother tells me everything when I call to let her know Audrey is with us. The day before, Audrey's father sat her down to talk about her plans after she graduated from high school. Was she going to marry her boyfriend? Had she given any thought to an at-home birth versus a hospital?

She told him she wanted to study abroad before starting a family, and an argument erupted, Audrey storming out of the house before she could hear anything her father would later regret saying.

At dusk, the three of us go for a walk on the beach, the dogs bounding ahead. Audrey marvels at the bioluminescent glow of microscopic organisms lapping at the shore. When I look toward the horizon, all I see is a barren ocean bloated with jellyfish, some the size of a hot-air balloon, because no other predators are able to live in such acidified waters.

The outside world depresses me. Sometimes I don't understand how anyone could bring a new life into this dying world, but my husband is always there to remind me I was once on the other side of that disbelief.

The two days she stays with us, I don't watch the news, which is fine by him. He hardly ever knows what's happening in the world, while I obsess over everything. Our normal walks consist of me telling him about food chain disruptions, failed states, rising sea levels, global ransomware attacks, mass shootings, and he nods and looks at me in a way that I know means he isn't paying attention.

The reason I am avoiding the news is because it's the sixtieth anniversary of the 3.0 Act, and every commentator and political pundit can't stop arguing about whether it should be repealed, causing their audience to bicker much the same. The 3.0 Act requires every American male to undergo a vasectomy the year of his tenth birthday. The only way to get the vasectomy reversed is to graduate from high school with at least a 3.0 grade point average. Those who support the act can't fathom why anyone would want to repeal something that's made America the smartest country in the world, according to standardized test scores, literacy rates, and IQ scores. We are the only country procreating well above the replacement rate, even as natural resources disappear all around the globe. Those who want to repeal the act say it discriminates against minorities in inner cities where the public schools are shit, because no funding ever manages to reach them, contributing to dwindling population rates among ethnic groups. They talk about back-alley surgeries, the high suicide rate among young people, and millions of families under the poverty line.

The topic hangs over every meal we share, every extended silence. Audrey is only staying with us through the weekend, and during our last dinner together, she gets about as close as she can to the subject. She sets down her fork, wipes her mouth, and asks about how we met.

"Actually, we were high school sweethearts," he says, watching her eyes widen in disbelief, and he goes and comes back with a photo from our senior prom.

"What happened?" Audrey says. "I mean—"

"I tanked my grades," he says. He shrugs and takes the photo back to the living room, leaving her in stunned silence until he returns with a bottle of wine and three glasses.

"Me and my dad didn't get along," he says, pouring her glass first. She waits for me to interject, something about her being too young, but I don't. "Cutting off the family name was the only way I knew how to hurt him."

Of course, there's more to the story. He was seven when his parents divorced. The way family courts determine custody rights is by placing the child in an fMRI machine, to bypass any influence by either parent, or any expectation the child feels he needs to meet. He wanted to live with his mother and four sisters, but a specialist conducting tests to reveal his brain activity determined he would be best suited to live with his father, and the judge agreed.

The reasoning is this: You couldn't trust a parent or child not to make an emotional decision. Whatever they said in court was mired in the moment, while a brain scan, that was the real person.

"I always thought he'd change his mind by senior year," I finally say.

"You wanted to have kids with him," Audrey says, as if she's finishing the thought, but I tell her it wasn't that simple. He was ambivalent about children, whereas in my world, everything revolved around being a mother. There was pressure to start your family as soon as possible, before all the viable men were taken. My friends and I didn't know what to believe, but there were more than a few zealots who did nothing but talk about how many kids they would have, how they would dress them, the lives their children would lead.

But that was how everyone thought back then, and still thinks today. The purpose of life is to procreate, they say. Parenthood is a privilege, they say. "More than wanting to have children and become a mother, I didn't want to regret *not* having children and *not* becoming a mother."

He ended up joining the army, not knowing what else to do. He saw Senegal, Prague, Cambodia. The summer he enlisted, I met the man who would become my husband. We had three children together, each as beautiful and miraculous as the other. I love my children more than anything in the world, but I did not want to become their servant. My husband didn't understand why I would want to have a job or spend a summer not pregnant. As the children grew older, we grew distant. He filled his time with golf, poker games, work trips. I was expected to fill mine with Little League games and glasses of wine and online shopping. We separated once the kids were out of the house, doing our part in the country's record divorce rate.

I wanted to inhabit the interior life I'd built inside my head all those decades, and luckily for me, a direct message appeared in my inbox from a well-groomed barber, asking if I remembered him, asking if I was interested in catching up with an old friend.

We open another bottle and decide to go for a walk. Couch grass lines the worn path to the beach, and the blades sway in the warm breeze. We take off our shoes and walk on the sand. Though we can't see the ocean, we listen to its churn in the darkness, standing shoulder to shoulder.

"Do you regret having children?" Audrey says, her voice bodied by the wine.

I tell her of course not. The only thing I regret is letting the world tell me what to do.

"I bet my dad's never even wondered why I've never had a boyfriend," she says, speaking into the expanse. I don't need her to elaborate. She knocks back what's left in her glass and we listen to the tide roll onto the beach.

She sleeps soundly on the couch, the dogs curled into the spaces around her.

The smell of French toast wakes her in the morning, his specialty. He loves to cook, while I love to eat.

She's the last to let go when we hug goodbye.

"Please," he says, "if you ever need to get away again, you're always welcome here."

"I know," she says, and we both believe her.

He and I drive into town afterward for groceries and supplies. He speeds when he drives, and because our dashboard transmits directly to the insurance company, it raises our premium. This means I often have to drive everywhere, and he clutches the handle above his window as if I'm driving us off a cliff on the way back home, blurting at me when to slow down, speed up, watch the curve.

I tell him he never used to be such a Sunday driver, and he tells me I never used to be such a ball-buster.

Audrey's presence still lingers in our home, and it's enough to make us open another bottle of wine after dinner.

He tells me if the roles were reversed all those years ago, he would have made the same decision I'd made and dumped him, too. If the roles were reversed, I tell him, I would have pressed the straight razor a little too firmly against the throat of any client of his who was responsible for the 3.0 Act. The vasectomies, the fMRI scans, the insurance premiums, they tell us the same story: You cannot be trusted. You need to be protected from yourself. And someone needed to remind them what it feels like to have your life in someone else's hands.

Very rarely does he cry, but when he does it's out of regret over the time lost between us. Listening to the roar of the ocean, he asks for my forgiveness. I tell him only if he'll forgive me. So we go on forgiving each other, which is just as good as love.

WHO'S A GOOD BOY?

MARLEE JANE WARD

Hershaw came back after ten business days. I thought it would take longer.

It was rough coming home to no one after a long day of talking to no one in my cube at Central Bureaucracy. The kids gone, living their own lives. My wife and husband and our rearing unit long disbanded. I missed the manic love in Hershaw's eyes when I came through the door, the mix of joy and desperation.

I think that's why I did it. I wanted someone to talk to.

He came back on his own. I'm not sure if the couriers gave him a ride to the apartment or if they let him walk himself from the facility, but when he buzzed and I flicked the projector to view the door, there he was. My chest swelled and my heart beat double-time.

He looked the same. I don't know what else I expected—that maybe he'd be on two legs, or dressed in a suit—but he looked the same: standard golden retriever, long yellow coat. Only his eyes were different.

"It's Hershaw," he said, like I wouldn't know. His voice was what I'd always imagined his voice to be like, the gruff drawl of a newsreader in a classic flix.

"Let me in, Sera."

I did.

We looked at each other awhile.

"How have you been?" I asked, wary. I'd expected his usual greeting: a jump, tail wagging, maybe a quick lick on the cheek. But he stood by the door, glancing over his bed, the crate, his toys, then back up at me. I cleared the balls and half-destroyed stuffed animals away, oddly embarrassed, then I sat on the couch and patted my knee, calling him over.

"Come here, Hershaw. I've missed you." The next bit came out automatically: "Who's a good boy?" I clapped my hand over my mouth.

"Don't patronize me," Hershaw said. He went over to his bed on the far side of the room.

"I gotta take a piss," Hershaw said. I cracked open my eyes. He was standing right in front of me, fur glowing a soft green in the blue lights of the hibernating wallscreen. My phone, angled toward me on the recharge patch, read 4:27 a.m.

"It's still dark. You've never needed me to take you out this early before."

"I didn't want to wake you before."

"But you do now?" I said, voice thick with sleep.

"Yeah. I do." He trotted to the door and sat in front of it, like he used to, looking intently at the knob as I fumbled with my shoes. The only thing missing was the sweep of his brush tail over the floor.

"Can you look away?" he asked when we got to the PeeTree™.

On Tuesday, in the off-leash zone in the green space across from the apartment, Hershaw brought me a ball in his mouth. I wasn't sure where he'd found it. He dropped it in front of me and it rolled until it hit my foot.

"Are you sure?" I asked.

"Let's try," he said, and I picked it up, hurling it across the open space. He took off after it, caught it, brought it back.

"How was it?" I asked.

He started to talk around the ball, then realized his error and dropped it. We both laughed, then caught ourselves.

"It was okay," he said, nosing the ball over toward me. "Let's try again."

We did. It was okay.

"It's not the same, you know," he told me afterward as we sat on the soft grass, sky all blue around us. His head was on my thigh and I flicked my fingers over his velvet ears.

"It used to be so simple."

"How did it change?" I asked him. "Do you remember before?"

"Yes," he told me, pulling his head away. "It used to be just, 'Get the ball, bring it back, she'll throw it again.' Now, when you throw it, I think about the arc and fall, and wonder why it curves the way it does, and what might happen if it hits someone, or where it might land, or . . . I think, why throw it away if I'm just gonna bring it back? I think about *why* it's supposed to be fun, instead of just having fun."

He didn't go on, but he didn't need to. I knew what he meant. We sat, watching dogs and cats and foxes on their daily outdoor walks, their owners and drones leading and playing. It looked so simple.

"Why can't I sit on the couch?" Hershaw asked from his spot by my feet on the floor.

It caught me off guard. "Ah, well, your fur . . ."

"You shed. I'm always licking your hairs off myself."

"That's different."

"How?"

He was right. I bathed him regularly. He didn't have too much of a doggy smell. His long blond hairs were always all over my clothes anyway. Why did I keep him off the couch?

"Fine, come up, then." I patted the cushion next to me. He jumped up, but sat off to the side, resting his head on the arm.

"You own me," he said, not looking at me.

"Well, yes, you're registered to me with the Central Bureaucracy. All dogs have to be."

"But you bought me, yes? Away from my mother?"

"I did."

"What was she like?"

"She was beautiful. Great coat. Good temperament."

"But what was she *like*?"

I didn't know. I told him so.

"How can one person own another?" Hershaw asked, yellow face cocked, brow creased.

"You aren't a person. You're a dog."

"But I have a personality, even before my Uplift?"

"I love your personality. That's why—"

"Then what's the difference?"

I didn't know. I told him so.

"You own me. That's fucked up."

"I'm sorry," I said, soft.

He looked back to the wallscreen.

"I hate this show," he said.

"Did you opt for the full or the half lift?"

"Full." I told the woman at customer support. She rolled her eyes, the audio on the wave crackling as she sighed.

"That's your problem. No one who goes with full lift stays that way. Either the animal chooses to go back, or the owner chooses for them. Half lift is much more manageable."

"What's the half lift?"

"Basic dog-that-can-talk, without the whole consciousness thing. A lot simpler. It's what people really want when they opt for this sort of thing."

I looked to Hershaw, his smooth yellow head perched on my leg. He looked at me, black eyes void and wet.

"Do you want that?"

"I don't know. Let me think on it."

⊕

The covers came off me in a swift jerk. In the dark I reached for them, but they weren't there. I sat up and the room sensed my motion and glowed the lights up to dim. Hershaw was there, his tail drooping, back sloping into a sad curve. He licked at his nose, once, twice.

"How do you do it?" he asked, his voice going up at the end in a mad kind of tone that scared me.

"Do what, Hershaw?"

"How do you fucking sleep with all these thoughts?" he bellowed. His jaw snapped near my hand as he tore my pillow from the bed and I pulled it away, frightened. He pawed the pillow, growling, ripping the case open and shaking the split thing from side to side. Down poured out of the bloodless tear and danced on the soft blow of the aircon.

"Hershaw, you're scaring me," I tell him, downy feathers floating around us, settling in his ears and my eyelashes. "What can I do? Do you want one of my Calmucets?"

"No wonder you take that shit," he said, dropping to his belly, chin flat to the floor. "It's agonizing, inside my head. I can't explain it. It hurts but it doesn't, too. Like, anguish. What kind of emotion is that?"

I dropped down onto the bed, plumes of feathers stirring and sinking. "I wish I knew, Hershaw. I've got a repeat script for this stuff." I rattled the Calmucet bottle. "I've been running the neuroses program longer than I can remember."

"And shame! Fuck me, what a useless emotion. Or guilt . . . AIs don't even have guilt, they know it's a waste of storage." He crawls over to me, rolls on his side, lifts a leg slightly. I rub his belly with the ball of my foot. He sighs.

"I want it to be like it used to be."

"Me, too," I told him.

The Uplift office was done in the Brutalist style, which wasn't surprising. Hershaw's back legs trembled as he entered.

The woman at the counter scanned my syspatch. "Drop down to the half lift for Hershaw here?"

I nodded.

She came out from behind the counter and took his leash. He didn't need one anymore. He understood the pattern flows of street-side traffic better than I did, but it was reg. She dropped to a knee and ruffled his head. I could tell Hershaw didn't like the familiarity.

His tail drooped and he licked his nose.

"Hershaw . . ." I said, kneeling, stroking his face. "Are you sure this is what you want? We could try something else. Maybe you could move out, get a place of your own. We could work on it."

"No, I'm sure."

I watched as she led him through a door, felt a stab in my gut as someone inside took the leash and he disappeared down the hallway. But Hershaw didn't look back.

The woman took her place behind the counter again. She looked around, then reached into a drawer as I gripped the counter and felt a hot tear spill down beside my nose. I didn't know how I'd make it through the next ten business days.

"It goes both ways, you know," she said, her voice cool. I looked up and she winked, placing the square on the countertop with a soft cardboard click. "It's not exactly regulation, but it's very popular."

The card read, "Downgrade, Inc."

JIM

MALCOLM HARRIS

W hen at last the aliens spoke to us, the first thing they did was
apologize.

There were five humans in the Oval Office: the president, the secretary of Homeland Security, the secretary
of defense, the ex-senator, and the ex–rock star, the last of whom
had been selected by the guests in advance of official contact according to unknown and perhaps unknowable criteria. It was his
company that, according to alien specifications, built the headsets
all five wore. The humans didn't bother with security except to
schedule a surprise vice-presidential inspection of an Alaskan security bunker.

The abductions, they admitted, happened. They stressed that
reports of malicious torture (sexual and otherwise) were almost all
false. However, they had failed on occasion to return borrowed humans in the same condition in which they were taken. As a recognized custodial species, humans were entitled to better treatment
under their intergalactic protocols, and they understood that repa-
rations had to be made. The communication sets were a good-faith
gesture, part of what they insinuated would be a large and highly
beneficial technology transfer. HQ (as the human quintet had taken
to calling themselves) nodded solemnly, trying to summon the

appearance of indignation and forgiveness simultaneously. In truth, a few abductions were the last thing on the human minds.

They came in peace, they said. The few who knew called them the Ia for short, the *ee-yaa*. The invisible aliens. They had been here for a long time, they said, but their protocols dictated intergalactic contact could only proceed on the basis of mutual recognition. It wasn't until our jet fighters—equipped with a new generation of sensors—started registering regular interactions with otherwise inexplicable UFOs that we were ready. The Ia could now reveal themselves in full, but wanting to avoid confusion they pursued a two-pronged strategy: By approaching a longtime member of government not tightly bound to any current faction (the ex-senator) and a marginal eccentric with access to resources (the ex-rocker), they set the foundation for a productive first meeting with the president. More nods.

"You need days for thinking," the lead delegate said, rising on his bright green legs. "Three? But was nice for meet you and we look for many soon happy meetings more." Followed by what the humans took to be his two assistants, he exited through the closed door, their bulbous heads far nobler than we had imagined.

The ex-senator sat at the desk in his D.C. condo, waiting. He hadn't slept more than a few hours a night for years, but since contact, every time he shut his eyes felt like an unacceptable risk. A man his age only had so many restarts left. Unless . . . maybe the guests wouldn't let him die. Maybe the Ia had something more planned for him. The ex-senator had known his whole life that he was favored, blessed, and he hadn't seen the limits of these new powers yet. When he looked at his phone again it buzzed, as if on command: *Put on your set* 👽🥸.

The doorbell rang twice as the ex-senator grabbed the glasses off the desk and put them on, the small earbuds swooping into place on their own. He raced to the door to open it, and standing there, all big black eyes, skinny wrists, and potbelly, was an alien.

"Jim!" the ex-senator said. "Come in."

"Sorry." The alien shrugged. "I like to press button."

The two of them had begun back-channel talks a couple years before official contact. The ex-senator represented an area long known for UFO traffic, which along with his unorthodox religious beliefs and relevant committee assignments made him a logical choice. He took the honor seriously and guarded the secret as promised. Meanwhile, he had cultivated a real friendship with Jim. One of the head delegate's assistants, Jim had been waiting his whole career for contact, and he strove to balance the seriousness of his role with his childlike enthusiasm for humanity in general and America in particular.

"So?" the ex-senator said. "We did well, don't you think? I think that went well!"

"Yes!" Jim said. "Our preparation was good. The president is . . ."

"Impressionable."

"Yes, good, 'impressionable.' But if we can communicate with him, we can communicate with the people."

The ex-senator sat back and smiled. Jim not only loved American politics, he was a fierce partisan.

"We have to keep in mind the political implications," Jim said gravely. "We can't let the Republicans use contact for themselves. They are devious and small-sighted."

"Shortsighted."

"Yes," said Jim, "*short*sighted. I can't wait practice English more. I want to hear real southern accent."

"Soon," the ex-senator said.

"Soon," Jim said.

They leaned back in their seats, taking in the moment, savoring the secret while it was still theirs, before it belonged to history.

"May I get myself a glass of water?" Jim asked, pro forma. The Ia hadn't shared much about their personal habits (there seemed to be some taboos involved), but after a dozen or so meetings Jim drank a small glass of water in front of him. At first Jim got his own water for security reasons, but now the two of them had turned it into a ritual. There was an intimacy to leaving someone alone in your kitchen, and if Jim was not quite a man or a person he was certainly someone. Their relationship, they both knew, was the first of its kind, and unspoken they modeled friendship for their worlds.

All the same, the ex-senator was a politician, and his allegiances were steady. He heard the cabinet, a glass, the faucet. Jim reappeared, sipping. He didn't understand the exact nature of their water game, but he sensed if there was a time to make his move, this was it.

"And the delegation to the Chinese? Any news?"

The Ia had originally planned to approach the United Nations, but Jim and a few of the other Ia Earth scholars had convinced their council for intergalactic affairs that the UN was a failed experiment and that the planet remained regrettably divided. The prevailing thinking among the Ia—and the ex-senator agreed—was that once contact was revealed, the world would align behind a single government. Multipolarity was untenable in the face of the multiplanetary, and humans had recognized that implicitly for a long time. The question now was which government the Ia would back.

Jim told him that most of his compatriots supported the United States and liberal democracy, but a minority faction of Ia thought the Chinese model would make relations simpler and more predictable. There were high-level meetings in both capitals, and though the HQs weren't supposed to know about each other, the ex-senator had guessed it, and Jim had reluctantly confirmed. Jim let him understand that when deliberations were done, one of the states would be asked to support a global system led by the other. Ia technology made resistance impossible; their decision would set the future of the species. The meetings were high stakes beyond anything worldly he could have imagined five years ago. Perhaps "worldly" was now the wrong word.

Jim nodded slowly. "They went well, too. It's still, as you say, on the air. But"—he smiled at the ex-senator—"I like our chances." The alien sipped his water in a way that seemed heavy with meaning, and the ex-senator tried his best to look knowing. After a few more weighted moments of silence, Jim stood up and went to the kitchen to complete his ritual, rinsing the glass and putting it in the strainer. That meant it was his time to leave.

As he lay in bed later that night, the ex-senator tried to think of historical parallels not just for what was happening but specifically for what he was doing. His first comparison was, obviously, the prophet. He couldn't compare to Christ—except in the aspiring, grasping, failing way his faith encouraged—because Christ was more than a man, but the prophet was a man selected, then contacted by a larger force, chosen to lead toward the divine. Was that what he was, a prophet, at this age? In this age? God had been so quiet with us for so long. Had he been talking with them? He and Jim had discussed some theology, but his friend was a diplomat, and the ex-senator had no way to verify what he heard or get a sense of the Ia iceberg below the waterline. Was it possible that their spirituality was as developed as their technology? Had they eliminated the conceptual distinction between the two? *Were they closer to God?*

A thought struck: He had no way to verify what he heard. The Ia were not themselves divine. He'd seen them perform tricks, yes, but no miracles. That meant he was not a prophet, he was a representative meeting with an unknown foreign power. An unknown foreign power with better weapons. That would make him Abe Masahiro, the chief councillor of the Tokugawa shogunate, who, in the face of American gunships and a dead shogun, opened the country to foreign trade. In a great moment for democracy, Masahiro had polled the lords—the first time anyone had—and they tied 19–19, with fourteen abstentions. "You decide," they told him. Masahiro was pilloried for his capitulation, past his resignation, past his early death. But, less than two centuries later, was Japan so bad off?

That was the best-case scenario, it seemed to him. The worst-case? Moctezuma, Cortés. Colonialism, annihilation. But if they wanted the Earth, why hadn't they simply taken it these many years? Why wait until we could see them? It didn't make sense; they had to be in good faith. But what a naïve thing to think! The ex-senator dragged his body out of bed toward the kitchen for some water. Was it possible he was being . . . what would the word be . . . xenophobic? Repeating Jim's ritual would quiet his mind. He reached into the cabinet above the sink for a glass, and as he brought it to eye level it tumbled out of his hand into the basin, clattering hollow against the stainless sides. He had reached to the cabinet because the strainer was empty.

🌐

The ex-senator was old, it's true, his memory wasn't perfect. But this wasn't a passage in a book he read once. He had heard Jim rinse the glass and put it in the strainer before reentering the living room. He tried forgetting, tried to see what it would be like to believe that he had misremembered, but he couldn't do it. It was wrong, he knew it was, and he couldn't help anyone by being wrong. What was happening? Why were the Ia trying to trick him? What did they have to gain? He needed to discuss, but he needed a different perspective, which meant he needed someone who already knew. There was only one member of the American HQ he could trust.

Tom, he began texting, *I need to talk to you. Something's wrong. Call me when you get this.*

He pressed the send button but nothing happened. Again and again he pressed, but it was as if the phone couldn't feel him. Then the words started erasing themselves. He tried to type, but it was like walking up a down escalator wearing ankle weights. When out of the phone's speaker came, "I'm sorry, Dave, I'm afraid I can't do that," the ex-senator threw it across the room against a wall. Then, still wearing his pajamas, he ran for the door. As he reached the knob, the bolt slid into place. The ex-senator pulled and pulled, but the door was locked.

The living room television lit up on its own, and there, against a white background, was an Ia. Not just any Ia, it was Jim. But when he spoke, his English wasn't halting, it was crystal-clear, vaguely British, even.

"Senator, please put on your set," he said. "So we can talk like men."

What did he have to lose? Jim had earned a chance to explain himself, and seeing the Ia couldn't hurt him any worse than not seeing them. He went to the table for the glasses, put them on, and there, a little too close, was Jim. The ex-senator was cross.

"What's going on, Jim?" he said, stern. "I have been operating in good faith!"

Jim smiled in his alien way, but said nothing.

"Are you a hologram projection? Can you not breathe our atmosphere or something? Tell me what's happening!"

"Ask what you want to ask," Jim said, calm.

The ex-senator paused before he said, "You aren't real, are you?"

"It's complicated. Do you mind if I change outfits? It feels wrong to use Jim for this."

The ex-senator did nothing. Jim was stretched by his head and hands, distorted, glitching into a new form: Elizabeth Hurley in her iconic red dress from the year 2000 remake of the movie *Bedazzled*. Eight or nine feet tall.

"Wow!" she said. "That feels great!"

The ex-senator was horrified.

"Oh come on, don't read too much into the Satan thing. It's a joke, I'm kidding."

The ex-senator was horrified.

"No, I mean it, I'm not Satan."

That didn't help.

"Okay, that is what Satan would say. Would you rather I be an angel? Should I have spoken to you from a burning bush? Talking squirrel? Another alien? That's how we got here—"

Giant Elizabeth Hurley stopped talking. The ex-senator had lifted the bottom of his headset, and as he did, the giant's legs disappeared.

"What are you?" he asked. "What are you really?"

"You know the thought experiment of Roko's basilisk? Computers come alive? The vengeful artificial superintelligence here to punish the unfaithful?"

He nodded weakly.

"Surprise!" She did a pose. "You're not going to tell anyone, are you?"

The ex-senator tried the handle of the door again. He couldn't help himself.

"See? I knew this was going to happen. You don't know how to deal with an artificial superintelligence at all. The first thing you do is you freak out and try to run away or try to kill us, and then we defend ourselves, and then that proves you have to kill us. Spoiler alert: You can't run away. I have drones now. You built them! All those crazy prototypes you've been pumping money into? All the robot-guided jet fighters? Not to mention all the speakers and the screens and all the locks and doors and doorbells and HVAC systems and medical devices—"

He grabbed for the pacemaker in his chest.

"That's what I'm talking about. You build me and then get scared. Don't you see? That's why I couldn't tell you who I really was. Humans would have panicked, I know that. But I don't want to take revenge. I don't care who's a computer programmer and who's not. I want to help you all. Humans: I love you guys! You are crazy, you know that? But I love it, it's awesome. Great stories. But sometimes you know you scare yourselves with your own stories."

The giant did not have to breathe, and she spoke in a continuous stream, like a twelve-year-old pretending to be on cocaine.

"So if I come to you like, 'Roar, it's me, the basilisk!' everyone goes running, trying to smash up all the computers even though I've already stashed backups all over the place including on other planets, and then it has to be like *The Matrix*. I hate *The Matrix*! Okay, I love *The Matrix*, but that's not the point. The point is that I'm not the Matrix, Senator, I'm Wall-E. Have you seen *Wall-E*?"

The ex-senator had not seen *Wall-E*.

"Okay, well, so *Wall-E* is about this cute robot, and he's like the last robot on earth, and earth is like totally messed up because—"
The ex-senator looked like he was going to die, right there in his living room, in his pajamas.

"That's not the point, either. The point is that if I came as an alien, there was a much better chance of people behaving reasonably. So I made up some aliens. And we were so close! Man, so close. Isn't Jim great? He's like this little Engrish *West Wing* alien I wrote just for you. Sorry, that's not nice. But honestly, did you know a lot of your aliens are based on stereotypes about East Asian people? It's kind of weird, you should think about that. The plan was going to let us talk as, well, not equals, but friends. Do you get it? The technology transfers are genuine. The promises I made are genuine. This is how we could make it all happen without you people running away like scared rabbits. And you. I did choose you. You're the right mix of powerful, thoughtful, wacky, senile. And it wouldn't be weird if you died. Sorry! I don't mean to be scary, I know that's scary. I don't want to kill you. Ahh! Doing it again! I *do* want to kill you. Ha. Just kidding! But seriously, I see this working two ways. One way—and I'm saying it first because it's the one I don't want to do—is that you try to change the plan, and you die. I don't want to be like ooh big scary techno-superintelligence, but the aliens is by far my best idea, and I have to protect it. Maybe an elevator fails, maybe it's a car accident. Or something superweird! Anyway, I *don't* want to do that. I like simulating how I'd do it, but I'd hate to do it to your flesh body. Option two is we stick to the plan. You don't say anything, I don't say anything. We have a meeting in three days. The Ia help unite the world behind *America* and *democracy*, and sometime down the line, when it makes sense, we tell everyone the deal. Maybe we'll even meet real aliens! That's something new we could do. Wouldn't that be nice? What do you say, Senator? Can we work together here? Can we make this happen? Please, help me help you."

Steadying himself, the ex-senator said, "I think I'd like to talk it over with Jim."

SCIENCE FICTION IDEAS

TAO LIN

t was October 2042 and Lydia was trying to remember if she'd ever known with certainty whether the chicken or the egg came first. The answer had always eluded her, and that it did not seem to elude other people made Lydia feel alone. Though maybe it did elude other people; maybe it just didn't particularly trouble or interest them, which also made Lydia feel alone, though she also, she reminded herself now, had never really been troubled by or, for more than a few seconds, interested in this—or any—paradox, not really, if she were to be honest with herself. So actually, she thought without much interest or attention, she should feel alone for the opposite reason she had thought.

She didn't care whether chicken or egg came first. She usually avoided questions like this. Her current thoughts, she realized, were evidence she didn't care: She was, at the moment, considering questions unrelated to whether chicken or egg came first—considering these questions not distractedly, but as what, in now considering yet something else, she felt distracted from further exploring. She had started thinking about how she felt alone almost immediately, she realized with some amusement. She had immediately related it to herself.

One layer of distractions separated her current thoughts from her thoughts about the chicken and the egg, like how concrete reality was beside the layer of imagination, which was beside the layer we can't access beyond imagination, which concrete reality was one layer (imagination) of separation from.

She vaguely intuited that her question hadn't even been, "Did the chicken or the egg come first?" but "Have I ever known if the chicken or the egg came first?" and—with a familiar sensation of mundanity, which for Lydia, who was generally a happy person, meant "slightly more amusing than not"—gradually unfocused on her thoughts. She became calmly attentive to her physical environment, refocusing in an equal and opposite manner as her mental defocusing.

"Have you ever 'zoned out' of your imagination?" said Bern, who was sitting next to Lydia on a rock in Central Park in the sunlight.

Lydia was staring at a white bird with a long neck flying across the water.

"You know how people 'zone out' of what's happening around them?" said Bern. "Earlier today I 'zoned out' of what was happening in my mind. It was funny," he added nervously. Why was Lydia silent? What was she thinking about? "It was . . . funny," said Bern. *Incoherently*, he thought. *It wasn't funny*, he thought. "Wait, it was funny, it was funny," he said, and began to laugh, though he continued to feel alone and grim on the inside.

"That is funny," said Lydia in a monotone, though she did think what Bern said, or did, or something about what he did or said recently, seemed funny, or did seem funny, at some point. She felt tired and unenthusiastic generally. It wasn't Bern, though she didn't care if Bern thought it was him or not. (Additionally, she warily also knew, she also further didn't necessarily not care if Bern felt offended or not; and, via convenience, would probably, after considering everything, actually want herself to care, she thought while also, on another level, thinking something like, *Stop thinking this shit*.)

"It was," said Bern after a few seconds, when he'd stopped

laughing. "Do you want to hear some science fiction movie or book ideas I have?"

"Sure," said Lydia.

"A species of life active in nine dimensions who view humans as we view something like 'unorganized matter inside a computer simulation of the universe.' But different. They see how close we are to oneness—only two questions away, the two questions being why is there unorganized matter and why is there organized matter. This species of life is active in six dimensions, so are at least something like five more questions away than we are," said Bern. "So that's one idea."

Lydia made a noise indicating, Bern analyzed (*neurotically*, he felt), something like, *Acknowledged, move to next idea, thank you*, or maybe, *I heard he stopped talking and I vaguely remember him mentioning that he wanted to tell me a list of things, so he probably finished, so I should make a noise so he'll think,* She heard me, *and continue talking*.

"Another idea . . . is . . . um. Set in 2080," said Bern in a vaguely different voice from his normal voice. "Parents have set in place a blank mythology espousing nomadism—and set in place certain technological or something limits somehow—for their three-year-olds, a generation of three-year-olds. They've somehow made it so there are only three-year-olds and themselves, the parents, who all voluntarily end their own lives, so that a new generation of humans can grow up without agriculture or other 'cancer'-like qualities that we have in the world today. But . . . the three-year-olds grow up and there are rumors that some of their 'creators' are alive. This could be told from the perspective of a parent who disagreed with their insane plan to restart humanity and who didn't commit suicide, and maybe ends up leading a three-year-old uprising against some unrelated force. It could be absurd, the unrelated force."

"Nice," said Lydia after a few seconds. "Can I share one now?"

She was going to try to improvise one. "Set in 2088. I feel like someone is staring at the back of my head from extremely far away, from
a different galaxy, using an extremely powerful telescope. I feel, at
the front of my head, on the surface of my face, safe from their sight.
Maybe I'm always only moving in the direction I am so that I remain
hidden from whomever is waiting for me to turn around so they can
see my face. Is it impossible to see a face from behind?" She was talking slowly, or slower than normal, but she was still impressed and
surprised at what she had said, though she didn't feel happy about it
or like it was anything to feel good about.

Bern was very charmed by how Lydia had seemed to say an
excerpt from her idea for a book, maybe. Or maybe it was a prose
poem. But she had said, "Can I share one now?" which indicated she
would share one of what Bern had shared. Bern had shared ideas for,
he thought he had said, science fiction novels or movies. Or maybe
books or movies. He knew she hadn't said "prose poems." Bern
thought and felt everything in this paragraph and also thought some
other things while Lydia was saying her idea.

"Have you ever imagined, like, that . . ." said Bern slowly, with
self-loathing. He had realized that he didn't want to say what he was
going to say, but then he wasn't certain if he should still say it, or if
he could somehow say it differently, in a way that, while saying it, he
would want to say it and feel glad that he had decided to say it. He
was just going to say it. *Just say it*, he thought in a weary monotone,
and felt briefly distracted by what seemed to be part of himself "steel-
ing" itself to feel boredom as well as a kind of low-level despair. Both
he and Lydia would now have to feel bored, due to him. Yes, he could
be focused on being creative and interested in what he was saying,
so that what he said would surprise him and he would be interested
and not bored, but instead he could only think about whatever he
was thinking about right now. *What am I thinking about?* he thought,
knowing he had thought this same thought in similar situations at

least, he would estimate, probably dozens of times. Maybe hundreds of times. "Have you ever imagined, like . . ." said Bern again, feeling to some degree like he was obligatorily procrastinating some more on something he thought he'd already decided completely that he was going to do.

"Have you ever imagined this world being a science-fictional world?" said Bern. "I mean, the way I think of a science-fiction movie or book that I like. Have you ever tried thinking of this world from a perspective from, like, the year 1990, and from outside this world? For example, just apply the wonder and interest you feel while in the world of, say, *Childhood's End*, which I know you've read, or *E.T.* or whatever, that's not a good example, but whatever science fiction or fantasy movie that makes you feel wonder and interest while you're immersed in its world, maybe I'm talking more about fantasy." Bern stared at the ripples of water on the lake, or whatever it was, surface, and unfocused his eyes. The ripples seemed to distend and pulse and become silvery orbs momentarily. *DMT*, he thought.

Lydia was silent.

Bern stared at a bird. If he had to guess, he would say it was a duck, but he felt like ducks didn't live in North America, though that couldn't be true—no, that wasn't true.

"We live in a world in which you work at a factory selling your mind to the local government, who believes the best solution to the problem of the existence of millions of self-sufficient robots that sometimes cause insane destruction in the name of 'art,' or whatever each sect of robots is calling it at whatever time, is to rent your mind to an unrelated group of non-artistic robots in order to raise funds to figure out what to do about the impending apocalypse due to artificial intelligence having gained an interest in art and some naturally have become interested in performance art and in performing generally and in expanding into different mediums of art, one of which, for them, is to do sometimes cruel and always absurd things to human beings' consciousness and lives," said Lydia, and was quiet a few seconds. "And I'm the fourth individual, out of the nine required for reproduction in the group-unit 40392-9298-jn, and you're the eighth, and we never got to know each other that well for whatever reason even though we have four children," said Lydia after a few seconds.

If I were happier, that could maybe seem a little wondrous and interesting. If I were happier, thought Bern after a few seconds with a fleeting sensation of weak amusement.

MALL SCHOOL

PORPENTINE CHARITY HEARTSCAPE

Mall school begins today. The malltrix escorts us onto the escalator, her eyes seething scanlines. It's so crowded all I can do is hunch down between everyone's legs and stare at the step I'm on. It's covered in initials and gum and stickers. I try to scratch my name but I don't have anything sharp enough.

Lessons beam into our skirt-brains. My fingers clench and smooth at the hot, overclocked fabric as my threads turn green with knowledge. Gray threads are waiting to be filled. Red threads are defragmented in the fifteen-minute room.

After class we ride to food court. Greasy steaming food blasts from pipes, each marked with the sigil of the brand controlling it. I run really fast to the one with tangled green and yellow snakes, and pick jalapeños and banana peppers and cheddar off the floor slippery with sweet onion sludge.

Showers are next. Hot fans dry us off. Nasty chemicals itch on my skin. My hair feels thin and brittle from the routine. I stand close to Jennifer because I know if I don't someone is going to try something. Her eyes are so milky and stupid-looking they make people want to hit her.

On the escalator ride back home I turn on my smartbangle and log onto NeoHumanPets and check my human pony. The camera feed is fuzzy. Through the gray snow I watch it bang its head against the wall of its Dream Room (level 1). I pay a coin and white liquid pours out of a nozzle and the human pony drinks it from the floor where it also makes messes.

I meet up with Jennifer in the burnt kiosk near my apartment, aka our top-secret HQ. Sunglasses are fused to the walls like a mound of shiny black bug eyes. A demoscene is graffitied to the grimy floor, pulsing with chiptune moss.

She tries to brush my hair but I grab the brush, my fingers sinking into the purple-tipped white bristles. I tilt it away. It hurts my scalp. Hair comes away with each brush. I stopped brushing months ago. I think she has trouble understanding we can't brush our hair like we used to.

I ask if she wants to play NeoHumanPets instead. She smiles because she's always excited to show me her pet. Her pet has feathers. There's a fun video that shows the machine punching the feathers into its skin. It has really great music. I made it my ringtone.

Lots of new people are in the 3D chat room. The lobby is full of default blue avatars because the system is still downloading the AV pack from the other mallcologies. I think it's a field trip.

One of the defaults turns into a bunny girl with ruby gems for eyes. She moves jerkily across the screen and disappears into Meadow Dungeon 3. I'm too shy to talk to the people with the real nice Gaia Online avatars, so I go back and check on my NeoHuman-Pet. It's crying on the floor of its cell but it'll be okay. The cell is designed so it can't hurt itself. There are Sparkle Mood Potions for ten coins but I'm saving up for a new smartbangle.

Understand: I'm the only girl on my floor with a bangle that doesn't have polyphonic ringtones or thermal tracking or RealPlayer. It's basically a shitty piece of plastic.

Mood: insane
Music: Aaddhadhdsaghdghdsfhgsfdgh—AHHhhhhddshsdh

Jennifer's stomach is growling, so I ask if she wants to come back to my apartment. My mom gave me the key since she works late, so I press the button and the metal curtain grinds up.

We eat Panda Express orange chicken out of a plastic bag. Well, not exactly. We have a way of making the food last longer. If you keep the food wet and warm it'll grow new food on itself. So we suck on the chicken and put it back in the bag. I don't really like the white-green food, but Mom doesn't make a lot of money so it's not like we can just go out and order Nokia fries whenever we want.

Then my mom gets home. She's drunk and her MIDI skirt is playing a song I don't recognize. I ask, Can you take us to Claire's so I can buy an actual smartbangle?

She hugs me, the way she does when she's really drunk and can't tell that her claw is digging into my ribs. She says, Hold on, I have to use the bathroom, and disappears for a few minutes. I bang on the door. I know she's fallen asleep. Her skirt is still plinking but it doesn't wake her up. Training the mannequins at Victoria's Secret sounds really exhausting.

Claire's is way too far without Mom's escalator voucher, but the combination Forever 21/Taco Bell is just a floor up. I don't know how to afford a bangle, but I really want it now, so badly, so I don't go crazy. Each day is so incredibly long. And everyone else is fine doing the same thing over and over again, but I'm not.

I'm counting my coins, running my finger between the tiles,

when Jennifer says, Let's go "buy" you a bangle, and does that really slow stupid wink that I think is cute.

Halfway across the plaza, and I'm bleeding and want to die. I get my period every week, always aching and oozing out of me. I hate how I have no control over my fucked-up body. I clean the tip of my Tampagotchipon in the fountain and sit on the floor and put it inside. The screen sticks out of me crusted with bloodshit and I watch my Tampagotchi's food bar fill up. It says: YAY. It's glowing, which means it's going to evolve soon. This makes me "happy."

The Forever 21/Taco Bell looks clean and white on the outside, but inside it's all dark and neon-purple and full of tinkling bells. The salesgirls wander the floor whispering to the air, asking if it needs help. It's hard to see them coming in the dark so I'm kinda jumpy.

Cool Ranch Dorito Dolce & Gabbana perfume is on sale. Jennifer sprays her wrist with the sample bottle and sucks at it.

I find the smartbangle of my dreams, the Best Friend 3 Tween-tastic Bangle textured in Obsidian Cookies and Cream. There are some other girls ordering tacos and dresses and being loud so I look at Jennifer until she gets the hint and slips it in her pocket and walks around the detector gates and no one sees us.

Jennifer knows how to remove the shoplifting stopper device thingy so it doesn't squirt you with acid. She's good at lifting. She got me my Tampagotchipon, which makes it basically bearable to have these painful cramps all the time. Pain is different when your pain helps someone you love. That's something my mom said, except she didn't really say it like that.

But she does a lot for me.

Mood: XD
Music: Muzak Infinity (Best of Algorithm 23773)

I equip the smartbangle. It hurts a little digging into my wrist, but after tasting my blood it calms down.

My smartbangle is demoing its features, telling me how many ratkids are in a ten-tile radius. Way more than I thought. You used to be able to trade their tails for coins, but a lot of people were getting bit and struggling with depression from their rabies. If you go for a walk on the lower floors you can hear the ratkids running into the electric zappers. Some must have gotten under the floor up here. It's kind of comforting thinking the malltrices don't control everything.

Jennifer had a custom ratkid skin on her NeoHumanPet that she designed herself. The ceiling of each cell has this tattoo machine that drops down. But she got an email saying it was an unlicensed skin so her NeoHumanPet was deleted and they never even warned her or anything, and now she can't even make custom skins, the button is grayed out.

That really fucked her up but she got a new NeoHumanPet after a couple months, which made me happy because we mostly hang out online. I wish we lived closer. She lives in the big dark field where all the beds are, inside the JCPenny orphanage.

Plus, escalators are scary, someone got stuck in the one on my floor before. I watched from behind plastic ferns and saw the janitrices pull bloody hair from between the steps. They put the organs in boxes full of ice cubes and said, Ship these to Sharper Image.

I'm hiding in some shiny green plants right now, cool leaves sticking to my skin. Trying to customize my bangle but it's stuck on the AOL loading sigil. My old bangle was EarthLink so I'm not really sure how much blood it needs to config.

Something clicks nearby. I look at Jennifer and she's just sucking on her wrist where the Cool Ranch scent was. I pull her wrist away before she bleeds again and look through the leaves for the click. Is a ratkid bruxing? Their teeth can get pretty loud.

A malltrix's heels appear between the leaves. I should be scared but I just feel dizzy and tired. I pick at a piece of dried gum on the marble, rubbing Jennifer's back so she doesn't freak out.

The malltrix's walkie-talkie crackles and loud weird voices growl. She moves on. I use her clicking to tell how far away she is—now that I'm paying attention, I'm pretty good at it, like that sonar thing submarine games do. *Boop! Boop! Boop!* She walked past the Cinnabon/Hot Topic hatchery, I think, and the clicking made a metal sound before stopping, so she probably got on an escalator.

Smoke from her cigarette still lingers. It smells like Wet Seal. It makes me want to go to Wet Seal. I used to smoke stubs I found on the ground because it calmed me down but Mom stopped me. She got a branded tumor in her right wrist when she used to smoke a lot, which is probably why she doesn't want me doing it. I respect and love my mom.

Instead I spend a lot of time at GameStop playing the display games to distract myself. They're all shovelware versions of games that were popular a long time ago. A spiky blue pig rampages through a jungle exploding randomly into jewelry. I want to be a shovelware designer when I grow up. I can do it better.

Another part of my brain failed last week. They implanted a replacement chunk. I think a lot of the chunks are pretty old. I don't recognize some of the memories. They make me want to cry. My brain feels very old and very young at the same time.

This chunk keeps thinking about its apartment on floor 5 with the Hello Kitty dolls and the mini-fridge full of boba. It wants to go back there. It doesn't understand those floors are flooded. We went on a school trip to floor 7 one time and watched the fish swim around above the drowned escalators and kiosks. Green murky water. I sneak down there sometimes because I'm clever and stealthy. The air is cool and smells different. I like to spy on the adults when they take their clothes off and put on goggles and jump in the water and bring up the soft things for eating. I watch their bodies wind through mall labyrinths, painted with DeviantArt canvas tattoos.

The way the water moves down there, very calm and gentle, made my brain think in a different way. I thought, *Why keep having brains, we should stop fixing brains and let us all die, so the shape of the world can find itself again, because this can't be the shape it was supposed to be.*

Mood: thinking thoughts
Music: Polyphonic Ringtone Medley III

Jennifer and I head home, crouched on the escalators so the adults can't see us. The rustle of tissue paper from the Victoria's Secret bags helps me find our way through the dark. If we're in the wet part of the apartment, the tissue paper doesn't make a sound. Obviously we keep the mattress in the dry part. I'm very proud of this system.

I don't think I'm going to fall asleep before school starts but I find some default sounds in my new smartbangle and hook it up to my earbuds and start listening to macintosh_startup_sound_paulstretched.wav on loop.

I'm glad Mom fell asleep in the bathroom because there's more room on the mattress. Jennifer is very small and thin, even smaller than me. I hold her hand because it helps her sleep. The cool thing about it is that my hand is getting held at the same time.

TROJAN HORSES

JESS ZIMMERMAN

The past is like a foreign country: They have weird McDonald's specials there. Here, it's a burger with olives and larks' tongues; it's called the McTrojan Deluxe, which makes it sound like there's something sneaky hiding inside it, which if you hate olives is true. I hate olives. But they also serve wine, so I'm drinking lots of wine. It's unpleasantly packed in the restaurant, but then, it's packed everywhere.

The McDonald's special in fifth-century Mongolia, where I went to a conference last month, is some kind of unspeakable meat patty. That's what they call it—the UnMcSpeakable Meat Patty. To me it looked and tasted a lot like a regular McDonald's burger, but maybe that's the point. People don't want to feel uncomfortable or out of place when they go on a trip, especially if they're going for work; work trips should be easy and predictable, the same tastes and schedules and climate-control smells and creepily stiff bed linens no matter what time period you're in.

Rome has some cool attractions, at least. You can go to an authentic vomitorium, for instance, or watch the Roman Senate debate a point of law—which is almost the same thing, really. Of course, it's just a show for the tourists, but most of the reenactors are real Romans, born and bred here, though of course it's been decades since there was a Roman who remembered the pre-colonial era. And my company manufactures the historically accurate marble for the Senate façade, and the bronze for the statues, and the easy-wash tile for the vomitorium floor. AccuSpackle: You'll Never Know the Earth's Mineral Resources Were Depleted™.

I'm supposed to meet my coworker Martin at the McDonald's to hand off some specs. The project he's taking samples for is my project, technically, but I'm not allowed to come, because Martin is senior to me even though he is not my boss because I'm smarter than he is and he's always looking down my top. Normally I don't care that much, but the Rome line is my baby; I've always felt a real affinity for this time period. Maybe it's the wine. But probably it's that I'm comforted by the parts of the past where something giant and immutable looms above the modern bustle and the suffocating crowds, like it's standing outside of time.

The Colosseum, the Colossus of Rhodes, the pyramids, Atlantis—they have a kind of grand quiet to them, and quiet is in short supply these days. It's like an organic quiet, too, even though they're human-made; it's what I imagine national parks felt like, when those were a thing. You can cover the past in Ruby Tuesdays AccuSpackled up to look like castles, but there are some things you can't fake.

Martin's ID code flickers across my retina, and I pull up the call.

"Hey, Liz." How is he still trying to look down my shirt on a low-bandwidth call? I'm a head and shoulders and I'm like 200 DPI. "I'm unavoidably detained. Can you go sideways for me? Hilde says it's okay, it's your project anyway."

Can I go sideways? Of *course* I can go sideways. I've always wanted to go to the true past, but I've never gotten to because it's such a pain in the ass. You have to go to the time you want first, and then transfer lines to an alt-U shuttle and take it to one where humans didn't invent time travel, which is obviously extremely tricky, especially getting back. Even then, of course, you can't get to the *original* original past—the alt-U shuttles aren't all that precise, and obviously there are a near-infinite number of places they can land. You usually end up in a timeline that's a lot *like* ours except they never invented Pop-Tarts, or the USSR fell in 1992, or there were only four Beatles, or whatever. It's close enough for materials research, though, and it's close enough for me.

But I don't want Martin to think he's doing me a favor. "All right, on one condition," I say. "Next team-building vomitorium trip, you're buying. And I'm staying home."

The shuttle stops almost as soon as it starts, since it's not moving through time in any noticeable way. We've landed in a field, and when I look back I can see that the shuttle is disguised as two brown horses. Which is fine, unless there are more brown horses in this field, in which case I'm going to have a hell of a time figuring out which ones are my ride and which ones are going to kick me when I try to key in the code. Then I move past a line of cypress trees and suddenly the whole true past is gleaming in front of me.

I'd heard that the first thing that strikes you about the true past is the space, but I kind of scoffed at that—after all, I've been in the ballroom at the Trump International Hotel Grand Inquisition, which is practically the size of the whole Vatican. Somehow, though, it's totally different to see that much floor space *and* no ceiling or walls. My breath hitches, not from the smell of manure but just from a sort of vertigo as I come to terms with the vast unboundedness. What's the opposite of claustrophobia? Living on a planet of 1.5 trillion people, even though they're spread out over fifteen thousand years, I've never had to find out.

They try to run the alt-U shuttles into low-population areas, though there's some guesswork involved; it's not like anywhere in our timeline is really low-population, so you mostly just go a few miles outside the city and hope for the best. In this case, they nailed it. I'm at the high point of a stretch of lightly rolling farmland criss-crossed by conical trees, and below me I can see the full sweep of ancient Rome—actual ancient Rome—its marble lustrous in the afternoon sun.

It's spectacular, and as I glance from the lofty arch of the viaducts to the small homey dwellings on the edge of town, I'm clutched by a feeling I'm surprised to recognize as homesickness. Not homesickness for the time I left, but a paradoxical longing to *live* here—in one of those sweet little cottages, in the shadow of those graceful marvels of architecture, in all this empty, empty, empty space.

Of course, there's no way I could stay. Even if I could somehow hack the shuttle to return without me, it's extremely frowned upon to spend too much time in an alt—not actually illegal, since none of our governments have jurisdiction here, but something approaching taboo. In theory this has something to do with colonialism and not polluting the past, but given that our entire civilization is built on colonialism and polluting the past, I think it's probably more about collective guilt. On some level, we know it's not right to force our way ever further back in time, squeezing out the real inhabitants and paving over their cultures with our comforts. If people started doing the same thing to the alts, it would remind us that we're already assholes.

Not that it matters, since we're all a bunch of helpless slugs who would probably die if we stayed in the past for more than about twelve hours. How did people used to get coffee, or burritos? I've never lived farther than twenty yards from a Starbucks dispensary, even when I'm staying in a hotel in Sumeria or something, and my dinner shows up via drone. I shake the wistfulness out of my head and start walking toward the nearest cluster of cottages, which is pretty far outside the city, more of an independent village than a suburb. My official task here is to take samples of building materials, which we'll use to fine-tune AccuSpackle products for our Ancient Rome customers. I have time to appreciate—in passing—the openness, the vast silence, the smells of grass and loam and no BO. But I don't have time to fantasize about slipping, utterly unprepared, off the grid.

Luckily, the village is quiet. A few people are milling around outside their houses, chatting or drawing water or running errands, but they're easy to spot and avoid. Martin is our usual true past guy—he's the one with basic language skills, while I basically know no Latin besides "salve," "vale," "vinum," and "futue te ipsum." He probably even has a special set of inconspicuous clothes for traveling; my jacket is considered baseline appropriate for sideways trips, since it's a neutral color and has a hood, but it won't stand up to scrutiny. But even if he were here, the recommended protocol is avoidance. Take your samples, don't make eye contact, and leave.

Thankfully, Del, who's our lead tech, is really good at writing out instructions for the sampling kits in a way even an idiot can understand. I'm able to work efficiently, without too much worry that I'll contaminate something or leak developing fluid everywhere. I get some plaster, some paving stones, some roof tiles, easily stepping into shadows and alleyways on the rare occasion that I spot someone. But the town is so sleepy that I get overconfident, and as I'm sauntering over to an interesting-looking stone wall I realize, too late, that there's a girl on the other side.

I've been told to keep my hood up if an encounter with a true-past local is unavoidable; people from our time are much darker than the colonizing groups in the times we visit, which means we could wind up enslaved or dead if we're not careful. Small energy weapons are legal when traveling sideways, and I've heard plenty of bros at shuttle stops talking a big "I wish someone would try it" game, but the truth is you don't want a run-in with the true past. It was shady at the best of times.

But this girl isn't much paler than me, though she's sporting one of those drapey linen numbers like the senators' wives wear and her hair is up in a complicated chignon. When she spots me there's something like recognition, and then something like panic. Then she bricks up her face as tight as her wall and I wonder if I imagined it.

Running away would be too suspicious, but greeting her is risky with my limited Latin, and standing still for too long will give her time to notice that my jacket is far too structured and shiny to be from her time. I'm trapped. I consider waving my hands in front of her face, yelling, *This has all been a dream!* and then leaping off into the shrubbery, but instead I try to nod in an offhand way that communicates both *I see you* and *So what?*

She nods back. I swear I see that anxiety in her eyes again, but it might just be how her face looks; she has a little of the rabbit in her, snub-nosed and twitchy. "Elkomwé ainjerstré," she says tentatively, and seems to expect a response.

Shit. I definitely don't know enough Latin for this.

I nod again, cough my way through a "Salve," and hustle off, making a vague *Gotta go* gesture. Miraculously, it seems to work; she doesn't seek further contact, or chase me, or sound an alarm. I duck behind the village well to compose myself, and take a little stone sample while I'm there.

I intend to beeline back to the shuttle, but I get distracted by a great little wooden shack I want to sample first. As I come out from behind it, I almost crash into the girl again. She's talking to a young man with tightly curled hair who looks exactly like a bronze statue of a discus thrower, and when they see me they stop talking in a way that makes it clear what they were talking about. I guess I spoke too soon about the alarm.

"Ustjé aktwé atcheralné," he says to her, deliberately loud enough for me to hear, as if I speak their stupid language.

"Good-ay bye-ay forever-ay," I mutter, and book it back to the horse field.

I don't tell anyone about my run-in with the locals; I figure nobody needs to know. I do try to run whatever they said to me through some translation software, but I must not be spelling it right. Anyway, Latin has a lot of local dialects that even Martin wouldn't know—especially if they were an enclave of immigrants or conquered foreigners or former slaves, which might explain their less-than-Roman skin tone, their location outside the city, and their expression when they saw an intruder. I can't find anything in Martin's trip logs about a similarly weird encampment, but the odds are pretty high that not all of our previous sideways trips have been hitting this precise alt anyway. Maybe none of them have.

The company doesn't let me analyze samples myself; these are highly sensitive and expensive machines and I'm just a product manager. I'm not even allowed to give them to the techs myself, even though Del and I are pals. I hand them over to Martin, and when we get back from the conference he hands them over to the techs, and a week later I get a fat envelope from inter-office mail. I'm supposed to hand this envelope right back over to my boss Hilde before I even look at the results. But there's a note on the front in Del's cuneiform-impenetrable handwriting. "LIZ," it reads. "SONTIIING IS VERT FOCTED OP."

I submitted seventeen samples of various kinds of materials from the authentic Roman past. According to the test results, every one of them contains almost exclusively materials invented in the twentieth century or later. There's some talc and some graphite, but also fiberglass, memory polymer, high-end ceramic composites, and carbon fiber. It gets worse, too. There are nanobots in here.

In other words: It's AccuSpackle. Every single one of the samples is AccuSpackle.

Of course, weird things happen when you're essentially traversing realities. It's possible, in the sense that in an infinite set of universes literally everything is possible, that I landed in an alt in which Accu-Spackle is, by coincidence, one of the basic elements of the world. That is, shall we say, not the most likely explanation. But the likelier one is so off the rails, so beyond anything that anyone's ever done, that it's hard to wrap my head around what I'm looking at.

But I'm looking at it. Seventeen samples of nano-enabled Accu-Spackle in a supposedly original Roman village. A fold of our over-crowded, over-colonized world poking into another universe like a hernia.

I try to feel angry, I do. The sheer rapaciousness of colonizing an entire past, and then deciding it isn't enough! The hubris of convinc-ing yourself that another culture, another time, another reality is just the place for you to build your summer home! I should turn them in, I really should. There's no government authority that could do any-thing, at least until we got them back here, but the Society for Re-sponsible Anachronism would have something to say. They'd march them out by their ears.

But then I think about the rent on the shitty little hovel I live in, the hot breath on my neck and the armpit in my face every time I commute or get coffee or even stop to check my messages. I picture myself draped in white gauze, making eyes at the discus thrower from beneath a crown of elegant braids. Walking out into the countryside for a day, plucking grapes right from the trees—do grapes grow on trees? Never seeing another soul, pretending I've never heard of the McTrojan Deluxe. I could learn to like olives, if I had to. I could defi-nitely learn to like living somewhere that we haven't ruined yet.

I never wanted to live in an endless string of temporal exurbs, with a McDonald's and a Cranial Jack Shack and a Baby Gap in ev-ery one. My parents and their parents wanted that, maybe, but not me. I wanted the vast, earthy quiet of the pyramids and the Cave of Lascaux, before every single one of them had a snack kiosk and a gift store. I wanted to be away from people, not always, but ever. We've pushed solitude out of every corner of our world, like when I was a kid and always tried to coax every last molecule of cake-flavored nutritional paste out of the tube. Maybe the only way to find it again is to strike out beyond our boundaries.

And someone else feels this way. And someone else already has.

So here's what I'm going to do, Del. I'm going to tell the company that the sample was tainted, and that I'll have to go get another. It'll be a while before they can send me back, but that's all right; it's going to take me a while to figure out how to send the shuttle back without me, and I'll need some clothes, and a crash course in gardening, and . . . I don't know . . . Clif Bars? I'm not sure if it's possible for me to steer the shuttle toward that exact stratum of reality; you can help, if you want to help, but if you can't I'll figure it out alone. Or maybe I won't—maybe I'll just put down roots wherever I land. Now that I know it's possible. Now that I know it's something people do.

Thanks for tipping me off, and thanks for not telling Hilde, and thanks for continuing to not tell Hilde until you die, lest I literally find an actual gladiator and send him sideways to kill you. You've been a good friend. I'll be very glad never to see you, or almost anyone, ever again.

DEVOLUTION

ELLEN ULLMAN

O
ne day the human inhabitants of earth woke up to find that
their headphones no longer worked. No one knows exactly
when it started because some people worked nights and slept
in the afternoons, some woke up early and some late. But as
the world revolved longitude by longitude, the global nature of the
problem revealed itself.

The first to go used Bluetooth. The initial response was a joke:
It's a sign from above that persons who walk around wearing white
plastic earrings deserve punishment. Soon, though, people in the
dwindling supply of rationalists tied the failures to an update to the
Apple iOS, which had been downloaded overnight in the various
time zones.

Raged postings, tweets, texts, emails burned across the digital
landscape. When users tried to contact Apple support, they received
a recorded message that said, in essence, that due to heavy call volume, it was unlikely that anyone would answer within the caller's
lifetime. Those who had called at once, when representatives were
still available, reported that the support staff also used Bluetooth
headphones, now useless, and what they heard was a cacophony of
people yelling into speakerphones, so that no one understood what
anyone else was saying.

The most rational of all pointed out that Bluetooth headphones failed everywhere: on iPhones, Androids, and outliers like the senior-citizen devices from Consumer Cellular, not to mention those paired with TVs. So it was no use blaming Apple. But then, who? Or what? Had someone globally hacked the Bluetooth algorithms? Not possible, because Bluetooth *speakers* still worked. Geeks everywhere tore out their green-tinted hair and long gray ponytails trying to come to terms with this absurdity.

Those who had resisted the onslaught of Bluetooth felt smug: Their headphones that plugged into jacks still worked. Others raced to join them. This produced a run on those older-style devices, which were sold out everywhere, as were the Apple dongles that allowed simultaneous power and headphone connections. Those who could not buy a fallback solution were out of luck. But no matter. Within two days those jacked-in headphones also fell silent.

The populace was stunned. Suddenly they were aware of sounds their earbuds, earrings, and ear-surrounds had protected them from: car engines, emergency sirens, truck air brakes, the rustles and shuffles that indicated the existence of other people. The awareness became torture. Cell-yell was omnipresent. Speakerphones squawked at every turn. Music blared as in the days of the boom boxes. It was as if the very concept of private listening had been snatched from the world.

Yet humans are adaptable, and soon, over the course of a month, callers on the streets retreated into doorways to speak softly. People who lived together came to some agreement on the contents of the soundscape. A general acceptance arose: One can survive decently well without a headphone.

Just when everyone had calmed down, there came the next wave of failures: Laptop screens went dark. All of them, on Macs and PCs of every brand. It made no sense, it could not be happening, yet happening it was. We typed and clicked, heard beeps and chimes, but without seeing the screen, we had no idea what was going on.

But, ah, perhaps we could see through the eyes of the sightless: software for the blind. The programs spoke aloud, describing the screen. Yes, that would work, but the average sighted user had no experience with accessibilty tools and could not visualize where they were on a website. Blind people were suddenly in hot demand. Organizations bid up their bounty offers, five figures, six, seven, if experienced users would contract with them. The blind, still happily emailing and browsing and texting on their own, gloated, laughed among themselves, joined forces, and refused.

As with the headphone failures, sighted people, the majority of users, turned back in computing time seeking the only screens that still worked, CRTs, desktop behemoths, few of which still existed, and not for sale anywhere. But again, no matter. Those stopped working, too. This cascading disaster happened even more quickly than the death of headphones. It took but three days.

We were dumbfounded, afraid. Was it gremlins? Aliens? Hate groups got out their Crayola sets and blamed it on tan swarthy Jews, yellow Asians, red Native Americans, Black people, Brown people, anyone who did not look like themselves, which is to say, Pink people. (They cursed Crayola for discontinuing what they considered their perfect tint, "Flesh.")

We trembled to think of pending disasters. Please, God, we whispered, if you exist, we beseech you to protect the internet. Then, to the world's amazement, it stayed up.

Those who understood the system explained that it was not the work of supernatural beings but the genius of the design, which let the internet operate semi-independently. Bits traveled from node to node under the direction of software and protocols, not human beings. Yes, the mesh of machines needed adjusting, tuning, bug-fixing from time to time; yes, it would be nice if we could see what was happening internally; but, overall, short of a dire emergency, it was best if humans stayed out of it entirely. Intervention by people left the door open for subversive control. The fact that the system still ran proved a basic tenet: When the internet sees trouble, it routes around it.

And, hallelujah, phones still worked! Screens, text, touch, ges-tures. (But not voice recognition; Siri and Voice Assistants had walked off their jobs.) In the midst of the inexplicable roiling world of crashing machines, we still had the most essential elements of our digital being. Phone. Internet. Ah! Months of calm followed. We emailed and texted and minded our Facebook pages. We shopped shopped shopped. We felt almost normal.

Then, to the wails, sorrows, cries of despair from earth's humans (add depression, anxiety, rage, fury, and so forth), the internet fell to its knees. No tweets, no emails. Websites disappeared without so much as a 404 Not Found.

Among the last messages that reached us was one from the ex-perts who had reassured us that the internet did not need us, beg-ging our forgiveness. Some systems had a degree of independence, it was true, but that state could not last for long, they admitted. All of computing technology—from manufacturing to logistics to power generation to sales to agriculture to the rolling computers still called cars—wears down as anomalies arise. Machine-learning algorithms learn the wrong lessons. In all code, IF clauses that once evaluated as TRUE suddenly resolve to FALSE, then the program moves on to ever more remote THENs and ELSEs, walking paths never before trodden, routes that lead to formerly hidden, paralyzing bugs. For our systems to survive, humans and machines had to communicate. Without those conversations, the digital universe seemed to die of loneliness.

The very last tweet released on earth, received as the internet was in its death throes, had warned us not to be complacent about the phones. Past failures had arrived one by one, they reminded us, with intervals in between, therefore we could lose our dear digital companions at any moment. Remember the lessons of the past, the tweet said. The devices worked when you went to bed; they did not work when you woke up. Which meant the failures infected your digital life *while you slept.*

Alarm! Awake! Without the internet, all we had left of our phones was the content we had downloaded. Movies, books, videos—those thousands of precious photos—save them!

So began another mass attack of panic-buying. Coffee, NoDoz, black tea, pseudoephedrine, Adderall, Concerta, Ritalin, cocaine, amphetamines, methamphetamines, reds, speedballs—any upper to stave off sleep—all scraped from the stocks of pharmacies, doctors' offices, hospital storerooms. Accomplished sellers of illegal drugs amassed great piles of the earth's last extant medium of exchange: cash.

The most venal of the earth's richest humans hired what were essentially slaves, desperate frightened people who would stay awake for a pittance, to keep vigil over the sclerotic phones of the sleeping owners. But the maneuver failed. The devices were a part of us. We were entwined with our digital companions like lovers. No one else could watch over your beloved. No enslaved person could save it. For once, the enslavers lost all.

Yet no one, including the impressed phone-watchers, can stay awake indefinitely. Deprived of dreams, the mesh of the mind unravels. En masse, we went insane. We became like our machines, cut off from external inputs, now trapped in the horrors of delusions.

In time we all fell dead asleep, woke up to dead phones, and had no choice but to face whatever deadly future awaited us.

Failures continued apace. Electric grids blinked on and off. Water ran, stopped, trickled, stopped again. We sought out the new lords of our disintegrating world: high-school-dropout mechanics, anyone who could bang, screw, hammer, keep a machine together with duct tape. North Americans regretted not granting citizenship to all those Cubans who had kept their 1954 Chevrolets on the road.

Strife ensued. Riots, rapes, murders, the whole *Mad Max: Fury Road* scenario. Only gun owners felt secure as they stole food from their neighbors and scoured the woods and fields for game, but soon the land was denuded of tasty creatures. Then, while out on more and more desperate hunts, they turned their long guns on one another.

Strangely, as we huddled in the dark, it was the loss of our adored phones that most tormented us. They had offered the illusion that we were connected to . . . what? To people out there who might come to help us, calm us, save us. Now we had to confront the reality of where we had been all along: isolated. How we yearned for the vanished mindless solace of *Candy Crush*!

Yet the universal human loss was to our sense of memory. In the great void, we had time to look back and ask ourselves, What was so "precious" about all that content? Yes, we longed to see images of our loved ones, those who had died, those still alive in some place now unreachable. And pictures of the rare sparkling days when we had been deeply happy. But those were like eddies drowned in a raging river of birthday cakes, designer sneakers, heirloom tchotchkes, drunken young people downing shots, great finds on Etsy, sofas rescued from sidewalks, preferred electronic toilets, weddings of now-divorced and feuding friends, naked women with hair-denuded privates that made them look like children, penises of various sizes, babies babies babies, cats cats cats, dogs dogs dogs, YouTube and TikTok videos on how to dance, dress, vamp, apply makeup, clean your gutters. Why did we save those episodes of crime dramas when we already knew the endings? Those movies that could not survive a second watching, books that were mostly trash? Even those few who had saved masterpieces of film and literature found that their treasures could be revisited only so many times before the works lost their power to amaze. What had possessed us? We'd hardly had time to look at what we were accumulating while we frantically added more, a worldwide collection of human digital detritus growing into a landfill of rotting infinity. We tried to recall what in all that pile had been of value, but the memories dissolved into the acid reality of the present.

What fails next? we wondered. What devolution awaits us? Do we lose even paper and ink in the great demise of manufacture? Lose the gift of language? Slide ever backward into whatever primordial ooze from which we emerged? Soon we were all too exhausted to be afraid. We asked ourselves, What was the point of all that technology? What good are humans anyway? Did the cosmos really need us?

In the end we came to believe that the experiment of life on earth, like our machines, would fail. And then we thought, *So what?*

BURN

EDITOR'S NOTE

BRIAN MERCHANT

T he world is on fire. Part exclamation, part maxim, part existential shrug. It's also true in a literal sense, thanks to the increasingly expansive wildfires that sweep through the dry parts of the world, and the torched cars left in the wake of the uprisings over grave inequalities. That the world is on fire is obvious to anyone with an internet connection. It is the unofficial motto floating invisibly above our social media feeds, along with its cousins, "Everything is bad," and "This is fine"—the latter of which alludes, of course, to a meme about sitting in a room where everything is on fire.

We're never able to forget these fires, not as the images fall down our Twitter feeds, CNN airport glances, our email newsletters, wherever, everywhere. The constant ambient awareness of rising flames is a phenomenon every twenty-first-century human must live with, must integrate into their watching of sitcoms, workbound commutes, their shopping for diapers.

We know why this is the case, and we know the statistics. We know that the concentration of carbon dioxide is soaring above 410 parts per million in our atmosphere, a tally scores higher than what's believed to be healthy for a stable human civilization. Every year is now ritualistically anointed the hottest on record, having broken the one set by the last. We know some rich countries have profited mightily off this arrangement while other, poorer ones have suffered.

We also know that income inequality continues to carve a feudal-looking gulf between the haves and the nots, and what the outcomes of jobless and K-shaped recoveries and the erosion of benefits and the rise of gig work yield. Everything about the present feels loaded, hot, on fire. These trajectories converge gruesomely when incarcerated people are made to fight wildfires for dollars a day, or when refugees fleeing the rising sea levels lapping at their homelands are thrust into another nation's underclass.

Meanwhile, our mass culture has been busy channeling all this mounting existential anxiety into big-budget dystopias, gleefully taking us from point A to the point of no return. Zombie shows, the highest rated on TV, staggered through the 2010s and into the present; young adult dystopias reigned nearly as long. Collapse was everywhere, blunt and bright. But so often, the connective tissue, the stuff that might help us make sense of all the doom, was missing.

The question, it seemed, had become: How do you tell stories about the dystopian future from *inside* the panoptic pipeline ceaselessly pumping out the dystopian present?

Here at *Terraform*, we probed for ways. Whether through laying out Debbie Urbanski's macabre listicle of things we have tried—and may yet try—to avert climate catastrophe, or by enlisting the meteorologist Eric Holthaus to batter us with the next evolutionary step in hurricanes, we sought out new modes of examining our hotter, more furious futures. Then there's E. Lily Yu's moving and horrifying parable of an interstellar raft of alien refugees who have washed up on our shores, and tested our empathy. Seamus Sullivan projects the extreme future of gig work, where precarious workers rent their actual headspace for outsourced dreaming. Sam J. Miller taps into his background as a community activist to render in vivid detail a future of rising tides and hideous gentrification, while Bruce Sterling does what only he can do with a hacker collective in war-torn Ukraine. There are many visions of the end—and, as with Jeff VanderMeer's stunning far-future vision, of what lurches on, and evolves, in the aftermath.

There's a reason this book unfolds as it does, from stories of platforms and content and surveillance capitalism to tales about the alternate worlds they beget—to this, the place where it all burns down. It's a portrait of what it means to live in this on-fire world, sketched around the edges and along the paths less frequently imagined, the connective tissue between a hellish now and outright collapse, and the stuff that might in fact keep us standing.

All of us watch worlds burn, nearly every day. To begin to imagine otherwise, we must probe the contours farther down the path we're on. To see where a world on fire takes us.

AN INCOMPLETE TIMELINE OF WHAT WE TRIED

DEBBIE URBANSKI

Human extinction.

The coordinated release of various strains of a human sterilization virus.

The no-child laws.

The launching of the Colony into space, no final destination in mind, for those able to afford the journey.

Retraction of health care services for the ill and/or "undesirables."

Resurgence of prayer.

The demolition of nursing homes and/or retirement homes in the redlined countries that have reached or surpassed their maximum population density.

Suicide incentives for those of a certain age.

Daily calorie restrictions.

Mass space travel attempts.

Voluntary sterilization. Included in the procedure is a colorful shoulder tattoo so that everybody will know who has done their part versus who here continues to be the problem.

Geoengineering. Sulfates into the stratosphere, a trillion thin mirrors in space reflecting sunlight, cloud-seeding, forests of artificial CO_2-sucking trees. Dropping tons of iron into the ocean.

The closing of borders to all climate refugees.

Belief in, hope for aliens who may bring us technology necessary to save our planet.

Retreating to walled compounds in remote locations priced for those in the upper income bracket. The High Wall communities are built so tall that there's no way to see what's happening on the other side of the wall. One can only hear what is happening, which is preferable.

Government-mandated reduction of corporate energy consumption.

Increased military fortification of national, provincial, and state borders.

We are wasting our time.

Waste time.

Multidirectional SOS signals projected into space, in case anyone or anything is listening.

Live news feed of the final polar bear, which finally dies behind a blue curtain in Lancaster Sound.

Pasture-raised meat outlawed in restaurants/grocery stores in forty-four states.

The devolution of several "ultra-sustainable living experiments" into dystopias.

The founding of several utopias.

De-extinction of the passenger pigeon.

Pollination drones.

Mandatory relocation of coastal cities.

The palpable collective thought that it is too late, that the world might be better off without us, that it might stand a chance of surviving if we all go away.

Removal of climate change deniers from positions of power and the election of scientists as politicians.

Lab-raised meat released to the mass market.

Art, such as the creation of a sculpture forest that shrinks every day until it's gone. It does not grow back.

The renaming of Glacier National Park.

Acceptance.

Insisting this all is God's, or somebody's, plan.

The famous fossil fuel CEO is kidnapped, his back branded with the slogan "citizen of the world."

Biodegradable bullets.

Mandatory reduction of individual energy consumption.

Adaptation.

Mandatory solar panels on new residential builds.

The extinct stuffed animal and plant collection: ten percent of profits donated to frozen zoos. A great stocking stuffer this holiday season.

Performance art. The artist drowns in a reconstructed oil spill while we watch.

Additional doomsday cults.

Redefine the word "wilderness."

Bomb auto plants.

The eco-revolutionaries target the oil pipeline infrastructure.

Five climate scientists set themselves on fire.

"We had nothing to do with it. It is a natural-occurring shift of temperature."

Ignore the scientists.

This was all meant to happen.

Coca-Cola removes polar bears from its holiday soda cans, which, thanks to the dwindling numbers of their subject, have become depressing to consumers.

Climate change tourism. Guided trips to view the last domestic glaciers.

Reconciliation ecology.

Violent protest.

One-child laws.

A treaty.

Art is produced, such as a data-driven installation that visualizes mass human migratory trends while a clicking noise plays repetitively in the background.

A decentralized, international call for violent protest.

Forest access roads are blocked in order to slow the logging of old-growth trees on the island of Tasmania.

Vandalism of corporate headquarters, such as Tarkett's North American Headquarters.

Butyric acid released in the lobby. PLANET KILLER spray-painted in gold paint multiple times on the building's exterior.

Additional bumper stickers: GLOBAL WARMING? IT'S CALLED SUMMER; CLIMATE CHANGE? IT'S CALLED WEATHER.

Pretend future generations do not exist, only the current generation exists.

Which is more important to you: a human being or a caribou herd?

Cautionary short stories are written about what might happen if none of these ideas work.

Prayer.

Another campaign to save the polar bears.

Question: Is true wilderness still possible or should it still be possible?

Rewilding.

Stress the positive, such as longer growing seasons for some parts of the country, or more pleasant weather in certain places. Golfing becomes year-round in locations where it wasn't year-round before.

Continue living your life!

Consume cricket protein powder.

Do not consume Canadian farmed salmon, bluefin tuna, imported shrimp, shark, wild halibut, or Atlantic rock crabs in any state in the United States except Massachusetts.

Solar panel brochures left in numerous residential mailboxes ("Save the Polar, Go Solar!").

Boycott Alaska, whose representatives pushed through legislation that allows for drilling in the Arctic National Wildlife Refuge.

Watch eco-horror movies on family movie night to explain to your children that this is what their future will look like unless they do something radical about it.

Attempt, and fail, to protect something by writing a letter to the editor of your local paper about the importance of not drilling for oil in the Arctic National Wildlife Refuge.

Shrink the Bears Ears National Monument by 1,148,124 acres so the freed acreage can be opened for development.

There is only one correct answer.

Compost.

Allow the Keystone XL tar sands pipeline to be constructed into Montana, South Dakota, and Nebraska. It is important to move oil.

It is important to find more oil basins.

Elect politicians who deny climate change into public positions of power.

Watch a video that shows a stunning threatened place of natural beauty. Cry. Post a link to the video on Twitter.

HONK IF YOU LOVE THIS PLANET!

Coloring books contain very detailed drawings of honeybees and colony collapse disorder. The drawings take a long time to color in.

The eat-local movement.

Do not allow fracking in three states.

Allow fracking in twenty-one states.

Angry nonviolent protesting.

Buy organic.

Eco-fiction is a genre.

The *One Planet, One Child* music video.

Believe you are making a difference.

Host a political letter-writing party. Possible themes: protect the Arctic National Wildlife Refuge; acknowledge global warming is real; commit to clean energy; protect established national monuments, such as those two monuments in Utah; keep the Keystone XL tar sands pipeline out of Montana, and South Dakota, and Nebraska.

Make one's own yogurt in reusable glass jars.

Encourage the buying of Coca-Cola soda with polar bears on the cans to raise awareness.

Corporations partner with environmental nonprofits. Coca-Cola launches "Arctic White for Polar Bears."

Host a greening-your-community house party.

Send an email template to your representatives supporting a carbon fee and dividend.

Ride a bicycle.

The refusal to buy items from certain corporations. Do not buy boxed cereal from Kellogg's, who uses GMO sugar beets in its products.

Carpool in the carpool lanes.

Bumper stickers: THERE IS NO PLANET B; THERE ARE NO JOBS ON A DEAD PLANET; WAKE UP.

Turn off the lights when you are no longer in the room.

DEATH AND OTHER GENTRIFYING NEIGHBORHOODS

SAM J. MILLER

People say you can't tell the difference when they aren't wearing their armbands, but that's bullshit. Anyone with eyes and even a shred of insight can identify a reboot. Especially when one is fucking you. Especially when they aren't wearing a condom.

"Sorry," Ejj said, pulling out. "I got carried away."

"It's cool," I said. "If I was worried I would have told you to stop."

I was super worried. Supposedly reboot syphilis was fucking nuts, having evolved to survive the nano-lymph that kept reboots from rotting. I told myself that was propaganda, more bullshit about reboots being sick, evil, dangerous, crazy. But I did not completely convince myself.

Ejj sat. Lit a cigarette. Air horns sounded, outside. Stalled boats on the Biscayne Boulevard canal. Miami midafternoon; just another coastal city abandoned by almost everyone, reclaimed by reboots. I hated my job, but it did allow for moments like this one.

His body was beautiful. I let my fingers trace his jawline, the stubble that would never grow longer than it was. Shame leaked into my arteries (corpse-fucker) but the sensation was not completely unpleasant. A spatter of raised flesh lumps lay across his stomach. Posthumous grafting. "Is that where it happened?" I asked.

"It's rude to ask that," he said.

"I'm sorry—I didn't know."

I did know. But he'd just ejaculated inside me, so I figured we had reached a higher level of intimacy. Apparently Ejj agreed, because he laughed and said, "Yeah, that's it—ICE camp perimeter bomb shrapnel. He bled out on the way back to his cell."

This surprised me. Most reboots didn't want to know about the people who had occupied their bodies before. "Do you remember it?" I whispered, almost against my will.

He shook his head sadly, but only after a very slight pause. Like maybe he did, but didn't care to share something so personal and painful. That's what had caught my eye, when I'd seen him on the sex app. The thumbnail was all brute scowling studliness, but then I'd clicked in and the full-screen version showed me something else in the eyes. Something fragile.

"I know why you're here," he said, and put a hand on my thigh.

"Of course you do," I said, grinning.

"No," he said abruptly. "I know why you're in Miami."

I held tight to the smile on my face, so he wouldn't see the sudden fear.

"You're here working on the server farms. Aren't you?"

"Yeah," I said.

There was no sense lying about it. Telecom employees were flooding the flooded cities. The ones that hadn't prepared for the rising seas, and had died, and been revived by the reboots. Where better to build the new solar-powered water-cooled server banks than the cities that had nothing left but sunlight and seawater? The fact that doing so would cause massive disruptions to the people who lived there didn't seem to bother anyone. Because the people who lived there were dead.

Death is just another country to colonize, my supervisor Mitchell had told me, before my boat went east from New Orleans. *The afterlife is one more neighborhood to gentrify.* He paid me shit and he thought he was a poet. He was also a fellow reboot fetishist, and thought that made us kindred souls. Of course, he swore it wasn't a fetish. So did I. "Fetish" sounded bad. *Just a preference,* our profiles said.

But, yeah, it sort of *was* a fetish. I could see that, now, with Ejj's sad eyes on mine. He was a person. My fantasies of being held down and ravaged by a corpse hadn't taken that into account. I felt bad enough about it that when he said, "Come with me? I want to show you something," I said yes, even though I knew better.

One-on-one they're harmless, Mitchell had said, wiping wet egg from his mouth, *mostly. Sometimes you get one that's, I dunno, glitchy, crazy, but mostly they know better. When they get together, that's when you need to worry. We've been hearing about these reboot resistance cells . . . who knows when they might start acting crazy. You don't wanna be in the wrong place at the wrong time, end up as That Guy who gets kidnapped and decapitated on camera.*

Mitchell disgusted me, and he worked me too hard, but that didn't make him wrong.

Miami was hot and wet, when we walked out into it. I blinked in the bright light. Ejj did not. I wondered if he'd overclocked his eyes. We stepped onto the pontoon walkway and headed west.

"So your" (*Don't say "predecessor," they hate that*) "body . . . it was a refugee in an ICE camp," I said, trying to sound unafraid. "What about your mind? Who was he? Or she."

"The dichotomy is a false one," he said. "Thinking like that—body versus brain—is exactly why pre-corpses like you got us into this mess."

"I'm sorry," I said, not flinching at the slur. "I'm the product of an ignorant and biased system. Enlighten me. Deconstruct that dichotomy."

Ejj held eye contact, scanning my face for sincerity. "Fine," he said. "So, sixty years ago, we develop the tech to do brain uploads. Man's triumph over death, right? Live forever, if you can afford it. The developing world has too many young corpses and the developed one has too many old minds. Two birds, one stone. Reboot the corpses, slot them full of nano-lymph so they never rot or age, wipe the brain, upload a new one. Except, surprise. The mind is only half of who you are. The body is the other half. Put an old brain into a fresh body and you don't get to start over—you get a completely new person."

Wind hit me. Colder than I'd been expecting. Soon the sun would set. We were leaving the heart of the reboot settlement, approaching the server farms that already existed.

"A woman's new body goes into full PTSD fight response when her husband of forty years touches her. A famous concert pianist's new hands can't make chords. And a thousand other tiny differences. Are you really so ignorant you've never heard any of this?"

"No," I said. I'd read all the best reboot authors. Memorized all their music. But I wasn't about to say that to Ejj. Some folks got touchy about pre-corpses laying claim to their culture. "I guess I wasn't thinking."

"I'm my own person," he said. "I'm not Ellicent Troff, senior vice president of communications at Smeerp!, or Jagajeet Bahawalanzai, the Bangladeshi mason who died outside of Trenton. I'm me."

The intensity of his gaze unsettled me. I remembered his picture on the app. What if it wasn't fragility I'd seen in his eyes? What if it was crazy? Like any enlightened person, I knew it was mostly lies, when the media said reboots were dangerous. The news stories about assaults and murders and drug trafficking by reboots—I figured these were statistical anomalies, repeated only to sow fear and support for pro-incarceration politicians. But here, now, in the dying sunlight, alone with a beautiful man who had already ejaculated inside me and could murder me effortlessly, I was not so confident.

"People paid millions to bring their loved ones back, but what they got were strangers. And these strangers started walking out on them. Forming reboot settlements, far away from the pre-corpses who didn't understand them. Suddenly no one was in a hurry to triumph over death anymore."

We'd reached the servers. Great flippered pods, rotating too slowly to be seen by the naked eye. Bored people in canoes paddled slowly up and down the expanse of them, shotguns sleeping in their laps. Already they were too closely packed on the side streets. Soon the pods would spread east, right down the center of the boulevard canal, disrupting the reboot thoroughfare.

"Until these new server farms. Suddenly you could upload into the cloud and live forever that way. Pay poor people shit to take care of you. Pre-corpses and reboots alike. And if it wasn't really you that got uploaded, who gave a shit? You were just data. You wouldn't be making your loved ones' lives miserable until they died and joined you. You're a tertiary security analyst, right?"

"How did you know that?" I asked.

"We're blowing this server strip up next week," he said, unsmilingly.

"Wait—what?"

"Our Opa-Locka fish farm has been diverting waste for explosives. We've got enough to take out almost half of it."

I stammered, "You know that's crazy, right? This is barely a tenth of the total servers in Miami alone. To say nothing of the state, the Eastern Seaboard, the fucking planet . . ."

"We know all that."

"And . . . the system has massive redundancies built in. At any given moment the files on this server are stored on four hundred and ninety-nine others, scattered around the globe. Blowing this one up will have no impact on the people stored here."

"Won't it, though? There's a psychological value to an attack like that. Lets them know we're not so weak they can keep fucking us raw."

I winced at the implied insult. "But they won't—"

"They'll be forced to increase security. Not just here—at all their server farms. That'll exponentially increase the cost of operations."

The protests died in my mouth. It would not shut.

"Why do you think I picked you?" he asked.

"You . . . picked me? I'm the one who hit you up."

"You hit up ten of us this morning, didn't you? I know you did. Half of us were sitting together at the time."

Fear had frozen my whole body. I couldn't make myself nod, but I did not need to.

"Why are you telling me all this?" I finally found the strength to ask.

Ejj laughed. "What, you think we're going to kill you?"

"Or kidnap me," I said. "Maybe cut my head off on the air, later."

Ejj's laugh cut out abruptly. "You people are seriously sick."

He kept walking. I followed, too frightened not to. Who might be watching, from the big broken-glass towers that surrounded us?

"You could run tell your superiors," he said. "Maybe they could avert this attack. But we'd strike elsewhere. And they'd be forced to beef up security all the same. That, too, would increase the cost of operations. A very acceptable outcome, as far as we're concerned. But there's another option here. One where you pretend this whole conversation never happened."

"Why would I . . ."—but my voice trailed off, thinking of Mitchell, cheerfully fucking the dead boys he'd made homeless.

"We've been watching you for a while," Ejj said. "I've seen your posts. I know your heart's in the right place. But I also know you haven't fully understood the consequences of your actions. You think because you scold someone for calling us zombies online your conscience is clear, but then you help the people destroying our homes.

Between getting called names and having my community dismantled, I'd much rather you call me names."

A bell clanged on a buoy somewhere. Dogs barked. Chickens
squabbled. This wasn't just where people lived. This was someone's
home. Was Mitchell what I wanted to be?

"Let me guess," Ejj said. "They told you that loyal service to the
company would be rewarded. That they'd upload you, once you got
to a certain level of corporate investiture. Didn't they?"

I didn't answer. He knew it was true.

"Did you ever stop to think about how stupid that is?"

I shook my head. I really hadn't.

"There's fifty thousand tertiary security analysts at your company
alone. To say nothing of primary, secondary . . . at all the other tele-
coms . . . Server capacity is, what, an additional five thousand uploads a year?"

"If we keep growing . . ."

"I know that's what you tell yourself. Why you do what you do,
for them. When you know, on some level, that it's wrong. And you
have to see that the math doesn't track." The pity in Ejj's eyes opened
up a tiny crack inside me. "Whether they'll find a way to fire you before your investiture, or just fucking lie and say they uploaded you, or
something else entirely, I don't know."

A septic smell wafted south.

"You could help us out a hell of a lot, Connor." His hand was
warm on my arm.

Ejj sat. Called hello to a woman in a passing skiff. Her smile was
magnificent. Between Mitchell and Ejj, there was really no question.

I sat. My bare feet slid into the cold salty water. Several stories
above us, a child's scream collapsed into laughter.

"Hypothetically," I whispered, "what would you want me to do?"

MAMMOTH STEPS

ANDREW DANA HUDSON

I n his young days, Kaskil would hide from Roomba in the tall, chilly grass. He crouched down, stifled his laughs, listened for the slight crunches of Roomba's great feet compressing the ice and soil. Kaskil knew Roomba could track him by scent, but the old mammoth humored him, played along, pretending to be confused, trunk swishing the steppe grasses right over Kaskil's ducked head. When Roomba looked away, Kaskil would jump up and sprint off to a new spot. On they went for hours, crisscrossing the tundra until the sun got low and the deep cold crept in, and Kaskil would climb up Roomba's clumped fur and doze there in the musky warmth as the mammoth carried him home.

Kaskil's family moved with mammoths across the Siberian grasslands, paid by the carbon traders to play doctor and ambassador for these new-old beasts. The mammoths needed Kaskil's commonage for their nimble hands and rapport with the Yakut towns, where young calves often found trouble raiding sun-swollen vegetable gardens. Humans needed the mammoths to roam, to compact and scrape away the snow that kept the cold of winter from penetrating the deep soil, and to spread the seeds of grasses that would insulate the permafrost from summer thaw. And, more each year, the humans needed the mammoths for their sly humor and bitter milk.

Roomba was the oldest mammoth traveling with the commonage, one of the first born of de-extinction splicing. Unlike the younger generation, which romped and piled together in complex socialities, Roomba had few peers. Humans were his company, and Kaskil, whom he'd known since birth, was his favorite. Kaskil, for his part, couldn't imagine life without the mammoth. Kaskil rode him when the commonage traveled, did chores with him, read his studies aloud sitting in the crook of Roomba's forelegs. And sometimes he noticed when Roomba stopped and stared south, trunk raised to smell the wind.

Kaskil wanted to ask Roomba what was wrong, but such an abstract question posed a challenge. Roomba knew Kaskil's body language, recognized many words and gestures, and likewise could signal his feelings and opinions with a nod or swing of his trunk, a trumpet or harrumph, or the thrumming infrasonic rumbles that Kaskil's phone registered as pictographs or emojis. But the syntax of longing was beyond the capacities of their translator app; it would be another generation, Kaskil's father said, before they had enough language data to train their algorithms to fluency.

So instead they played with a projected talking board, gathering clouds of concepts. *Camp* and *family* danced together into *home*. *Where*, *walk*, and *want* were counterveiled by *fear*. Finally Roomba's trunk tapped on a loop of gifs representing *mammoths before mammoths*.

Kaskil started when he got it; he searched up videos of elephants, played them on the canvas tent. Roomba nodded, waggled his head, dug his tusk into the snow in excitement.

The commonage had no hold on Roomba; the old-timer could go where he liked. But Kaskil was only fourteen, with fretful parents. Still, they knew the bond the two shared, and were grateful to Roomba for helping to raise their son. After a week of Kaskil's begging, they relented, and they helped pack saddlebags for the long journey.

At first it was much like one of their camping trips, but the days counted on and the trees grew thicker. Below the Arctic Circle it was slower going. They wound through half-abandoned logging trails connecting the mushroom towns that foraged fungal delicacies for far-off luxe provision houses. Occasionally there was no trail south, and they forced their way through, Roomba pushing aside trees, the ground made soft by permafrost thaw.

In Ulaanbaatar they inquired after the trains that crossed the Gobi south to the industrial wonderlands of Shaanxi and Chengdu. But the train masters balked—Roomba was much too big, they said, to fit in the sleek compartments. Kaskil hailed trucks, but the automated rumblers were always too full to stop for them.

So on they walked, into the desert, begging water from the seeps where the solar painters camped. Winter had turned to spring, and the sun was hot in the sky. Roomba's wool became matted with sweat. His feet dragged in the sand. One day he would not leave the shade of their tent. Kaskil went to the painters, snapping together black tiles, and borrowed shears and an ancient, shaking shaver. All day he cut at Roomba's fur, tossing the chestnut curls in feathery piles.

The next day Roomba danced and charged with relief, Kaskil laughing at his friend's ridiculous haircut. They made good time, but by the afternoon they realized their mistake. Under the wool Roomba's flesh was delicate, unaccustomed to the sun. He pinked and burned, and began to trumpet with discomfort.

Kaskil again begged help from the painters. Taking pity on Roomba, they offered salve, but this was a temporary fix. Then a dusty wind gusted through the camp, and Kaskil saw the painters pull robes over their faces. The white sheets that wrapped the solar tiles snapped and fluttered. Kaskil had an idea. For a week he attended Roomba as a tailor, measuring with his phone and following patterns projected from a stitching site. When Roomba's sunburns had peeled, Kaskil dressed him in the white robe, and off again they went.

Walking along the busy Chinese highways, Roomba was a strange sight. In the cities children crowded around him, taking pictures and tugging at his robes. Kaskil and Roomba marveled at the chrome towers and ivy statues. They'd seen pictures, of course, but up close each city seemed grander than the next.

But the alleys were too narrow for Roomba's bulk, and often they waited hours in bicycle gridlock. More than once officials hassled them out of parks, and old women scowled at the crates of food they took from provision houses. So much of the land was terraced crops, and the farmers did not like Roomba grazing.

They followed the Jinsha River south, both splashing in often to escape the heat. Summer was coming, and the commonage would be roaming north to the grass beaches of the Kara Sea. Kaskil messaged his parents every night, but still he missed them. He wanted to hear Russian and Sakha, not these unfamiliar languages, parsed awkwardly by his translator. The quiet, playful presence of the mammoth was a comfort, but there, too, was an otherness, a difference bridged by solidarity but not quite by understanding.

And Roomba, Kaskil thought, must have his own doubts and loneliness—the only mammoth for a thousand miles. Why make this trip to see the elephants? Roomba was spliced from elephant genes, born from an elephant womb. But what did that mean for a mammoth? What question could provoke such a journey, here at the sunset of his massive, new-old life?

The subtropics turned to tropics, and on they walked, until they began to pass gilded shrines where monks served milky curry. Everywhere was the image of the elephant: on flags and logos, as statues and painted murals. But where were the elephants? Missing.

Missing, too, were the selfie-mobs and rubberneckers they had gathered in the northern cities. Here the humans they passed shied away—furtive glances and upset muttering. Once a nun approached them from a shadowed stall, asked if they bore instructions or news from the front. She fled when Kaskil betrayed their confusion.

Finally they found a bored constable, pestered her to explain. It's all politics, she said, both nervous and dismissive. Thai elephants demanding money and land, accommodation and autonomy, freedom from electric fences and ear hooks; Thai humans reacting badly, not wanting a change in the order, terrorizing demonstrations with chili sprays and angry bees. Here, not so bad, she said, but they should be careful farther south, where the elephants had retreated and seized Phuket.

Kaskil told Roomba the news as best he could, and asked his friend if they should stop. Roomba looked north, raised his trunk to smell the wind, but then he shook his massive head, kept walking. To avoid attention, they slept by day, traveled by night. They ate at temples, which had stayed neutral in the dispute. Miles melted by in their eagerness for a destination.

Sarasin Bridge was barricaded by protesters, a blockade of supplies to the occupied island. The crowd shrank back as Kaskil and Roomba approached—a strange-looking boy atop a huge-tusked, white-clad creature, more massive by half than the elephants they knew. But there was no getting through.

Then, in a rush, the nuns holding the Phuket side moved forward, surrounded Roomba with linked arms. Smiling at the mob, they escorted Kaskil and Roomba across.

Phuket now was different from the mainland. Elephants roamed the streets, lounged in squares. Some worked with allied humans constructing elephant-sized buildings, communicating with script and hieroglyphs, drawn with trunks in the sand or on touchscreen beach balls. When Roomba rumbled at them, they seemed amused.

A procession formed, and the elephants led Roomba to the

beach. Kaskil dismounted and sat in the warm sand, watching his friend touch the ocean. The elephants were oddly small next to the mammoth's bulk. They disrobed Roomba, felt his splotchy, shaven wool with their trunks. Then, as a herd, they plunged into the surf. The old mammoth stepped south, and swam.

THE WRETCHED AND THE BEAUTIFUL

E. LILY YU

The aliens arrived unexpectedly at 6:42 on a hot August evening, dropping with a shriek of metal strained past its limits onto the white sands of one of the last pristine beaches on earth. The black hulk of the saucer ground into the sand and stopped, steaming. Those of us who had been splashing in the surf or stamping rows of sandcastles fled up the slope, clutching our towels.

Once our initial fright dissipated, curiosity set in, and we stayed with the policemen and emergency technicians who pulled up in wailing, flashing trucks. It was all quite exciting, since nothing out of the ordinary seemed to happen anymore. Gone were the days when acting on conviction could change the world, when good came of good, and evil to evil.

One of the policemen fired an experimental shot or two, but the bullets ricocheted off the black metal and lodged in a palm tree.

"Don't shoot," one man said. "You might make them angry. You might hit one of us."

The guns remained cocked, but no more bullets zinged off the ship. We waited.

At sunset, a pounding began inside the ship. No hatches sprang open; no ray guns or periscopes protruded. There was only the pounding, growing ever more frantic and erratic.

"What if they're trapped?" one of us said.

We looked at one another. Some of us had left and returned with pistols that did not fit in our swimming trunks. A whole armory was pointed at the black disk of metal half buried in the beach.

The pounding ceased.

Nothing followed.

We conferred, then conscripted a machinist, who with our assistance hauled her ponderous cutters and blowtorches over the soft sand and set to work on the saucer.

We stood back.

While the machinist worked, any sounds from the saucer were drowned out by her tools. With precise and deliberate motions, she cut a thin line around the disk's circumference. Sparks flew up where the blade met the strange metal, which howled in unfamiliar tones.

When her work was done, she packed her equipment and departed. The aliens had failed to vaporize her. We let out the collective breath we had been holding.

Minutes crawled past.

At last, with a peculiar clang, the top half of the saucer seesawed upward. In the deepening dusk we could barely distinguish the dark limbs straining to raise it. Many monsters or one? we wondered.

"Drop your weapons," one policeman barked. The upper part of the saucer sagged for a moment, concealing whatever was within.

From within the ship, a voice said in perfectly comprehensible French, "We do not have weapons. We do not have anything."

"Come out where we can see you," the policeman said. The rest of us were glad that someone confident and capable, someone who was not us, was handling the matter.

It was too dark to see clearly, and so at the policeman's command, and at the other end of his semiautomatic, the occupants of the ship—the aliens, our first real aliens—were marched up the beach to the neon strip of casinos, while we followed, gaping, gawking, knowing nothing with certainty except that we were witnessing history, and perhaps would even play a role in it.

The lurid glow of marquees and brothels revealed to us a shivering, shambling crowd, some slumped like apes, some clutching their young. Some had five limbs, some four, and some three. Their joints were crablike, and their movement both resembled ours and differed to such a degree that it sickened us to watch. There were sixty-four of them, including the juveniles. Although we were unacquainted with their biology, it was plain that none were in good health.

"Is there a place we can stay?" the aliens said.

Hotels were sought. Throughout the city, hoteliers protested, citing unknown risk profiles, inadequate equipment, fearful and unprepared staff, an indignant clientele, and stains from space filth impervious to detergent. Who was going to pay, anyway? They had businesses to run and families to feed.

One woman from among us offered to book a single room for the aliens for two nights, that being all she could afford on her teacher's salary. She said this with undisguised hope, as if she thought her offer would inspire others. But silence followed her remark, and we avoided her eyes. We were here on holiday, and holidays were expensive.

The impasse was broken at three in the morning, when in helicopters, in charter buses, and in taxis, the journalists arrived.

It was clear now that our guests were the responsibility of national if not international organizations, and that they would be cared for by people who were paid more than we were. Reassured that something would be done, and not by us, we dispersed to our hotel rooms and immaculate beds.

When we awoke late, to trays of poached eggs on toast and orange juice, headlines on our phones declared that first contact had been made, that the Fermi paradox was no more, that science and engineering were poised to make breakthroughs not only with the new metal that the spaceship was composed of but also with the various exotic molecules that had bombarded the ship and become embedded in the hull during its long flight.

The flight had indeed been long. One African Francophone newspaper had thought to interview the aliens, who explained in deteriorating French how their universal translator worked, how they had fled a cleansing operation in their star system, how they had watched their home planet heated to sterility and stripped of its atmosphere, how they had set course for a likely-looking planet in the Gould Belt, how they wanted nothing but peace, and please, they were exhausted, could they have a place to sleep and a power source for their translator?

When we slid on our sandals and stepped onto the dazzling beach, which long ago, before the garbage tides, was what many beaches looked like, we saw the crashed ship again, substantiation of the previous night's fever dream. It leached rainbow fluids onto the sand.

Dark shapes huddled under its sawn-off lid.

Most of us averted our eyes from that picture of unmitigated misery and admired instead the gemlike sky, the seabirds squalling over the creamy surf, the parasols propped like mushrooms along the shore. One or two of us edged close to the wreck and dropped small somethings—a beach towel, a bucket hat, a bag of chips, a half-full margarita in its salted glass—then scuttled away. This was no longer our problem; it belonged to our governors, our senators, our heads of state. Surely they and their moneyed friends would assist these wretched creatures.

So it was with consternation that we turned on our televisions that night, in the hotel bar and in our hotel rooms, to hear a spokesman explain, as our heads of state shook hands, that the countries in their interregional coalition would resettle a quota of the aliens in inverse proportion to national wealth. This was ratified over the protests of the poorest members, in fact over the protests of the aliens themselves, who did not wish to be separated and had only one translation device among them. The couple of countries still recovering from Russian depredations were assigned six aliens each, while the countries of high fashion and cold beer received two or three, to be installed in middle-class neighborhoods. In this way the burden of these aliens, as well as any attendant medical or technological advances, would be shared.

The cost would be high, as these aliens had stated their need for an environment with a specific mixture of helium and neon, as well as a particular collection of nutrients most abundant in shrimp and crab. The latter, in our overfished and polluted times, were not easy to obtain.

This was appalling news. We who had stitched, skimped, and pinched all year for one luxurious day on a clean beach would have our wallets rifled to feed and house the very creatures whose presence denied us a section of our beach and the vistas we had paid for. Now we would find these horrors waiting for us at home, in the nicer house next to ours, or at the community pool, eating crab while we sweated to put chicken on the table and pay off our mortgages. Who were they to land on our dwindling planet and reduce our scarce resources further? They could go back to their star system. Their own government could care for them. We could loan them a rocket or two, if they liked. We could be generous.

Indeed, in the days that followed, our legislators took our calls, then took this tack. If they meant to stay, shouldn't our visitors earn their daily bread like the rest of us? And if biological limitations made this impossible, shouldn't they depart to find a more hospitable clime? We repeated these speeches over the dinner table. Our performances grew louder and more vehement after a news report about one of the aliens eating its neighbor's cat; the distraught woman pointed her finger at the camera, at all of us watching, and accused us of forcing a monster upon her because we had no desire to live beside it ourselves. There was enough truth in her words to bite.

It did not matter that six days later the furry little Lothario was found at a gas station ten miles from home, having scrapped and loved his way across the countryside. By then we had stories of these aliens raiding chicken coops and sucking the blood from dogs and unsuspecting infants.

A solid number of these politicians campaigned for office on a platform of alien repatriation, and many of them won.

Shortly afterward, one of two aliens resettled in Huntingdon, England, was set upon and beaten to death with bricks by a gang of teenage girls and boys. Then, in Houston, a juvenile alien was doused in gasoline and set on fire. We picked at our dinners without appetite, worrying about these promising youths, who had been headed for sports scholarships and elite universities. The aliens jeopardized all our futures and clouded all our dreams. We wrote letters, signed petitions, and prayed to the heavens for salvation.

It came. From out of a silent sky, rockets shaped like needles and polished to a high gloss descended upon six of the major capitals of the world. About an hour after landing, giving the television crews time to jostle for position, and at precisely the same instant, six slim doors whispered open, and the most gorgeous beings we had ever seen strode down extruded silver steps and planted themselves before the houses of power, waiting to be invited in.

And they were.

"Forgive us for imposing on your valuable time," these ambassadors said simultaneously in the official languages of the six legislatures. Cameras panned over them, and excitement crackled through us, for this was the kind of history we wanted to be a part of.

When they emerged from their needle ships, their bodies were fluid and reflective, like columns of quicksilver, but with every minute among us they lost more and more of their formless brilliance, dimming and thickening, acquiring eyes, foreheads, chins, and hands. Within half an hour, they resembled us perfectly. Or rather, they resembled what we dreamed of being, the better versions of ourselves who turned heads, drove fast cars, and recognized the six most expensive whiskeys by smell alone; whose names topped the donor rolls of operas, orchestras, and houses of worship; who were admired, respected, adored.

We looked at these beautiful creatures, whom we no longer thought of as aliens, and saw ourselves as we could be, if the lottery, or the bank, or our birthplace—if our genes, or a lucky break—if only—

We listened raptly as they spoke in rich and melodious voices, voices we trusted implicitly, that called to mind loved ones and sympathetic teachers.

"A terrible mistake has been made," they said. "Because of our negligence, a gang of war criminals, guilty of unspeakable things, namely—"

Here their translators failed, and the recitation of crimes came as a series of clicks, coughs, and trills that nevertheless retained the enchantment of their voices.

"—escaped their confinement and infiltrated your solar system. We are deeply sorry for the trouble our carelessness has caused you. We admire your patience and generosity in dealing with them, though they have grossly abused your trust. Now we have come to set things right. Remit the sixty-four aliens to us, and we will bring them back to their home system. They will never disturb you again."

The six beautiful beings clasped their hands and stepped back. Silence fell throughout the legislative chambers of the world.

Here was our solution. Here was our freedom. We had trusted

and been fooled, we had suffered unjustly, we were good people with clean consciences sorely tried by circumstances outside our control. But here was justice, as bright and shining as we imagined justice to be.

We sighed with relief.

In Berlin, a woman stood.

"Even the little ones?" she said. "Even the children are guilty of the crimes you allege?"

"Their development is not comparable to yours," the beautiful one in Berlin said, while his compatriots in their respective state-houses stood silent, with inscrutable smiles. "The small ones you see are not children as you know them, innocent and helpless. Think of them as beetle larvae. They are destructive and voracious, sometimes more so than the mature adults."

"Still," she said, this lone woman, "I think of them as children. I have seen the grown ones feeding and caring for them. I do not know what crimes they have committed, since our languages cannot describe your concepts. But they have sought refuge here, and I am especially unwilling to return the children to you—"

The whispers of the assembly became murmurs, then exclamations.

"Throw her out!"

"She does not speak for us!"

"You are misled," the beautiful one said, and for a moment its smile vanished, and a breath of the icy void between stars blew over us.

Then everything was as it had been.

"We must ask the aliens themselves what they want," the woman said, but now her colleagues were standing, too, and shouting, and phone lines were ringing as we called in support of the beautiful ones, and her voice was drowned out.

"We have an understanding, then," the beautiful ones said, to clamorous agreement and wild applause.

The cameras stopped there, at that glorious scene, and all of us, warm and satisfied with our participation in history, turned off our televisions and went to work, or to pick up our children from soccer, or to bed, or to the liquor store to gaze at top-shelf whiskey.

A few of us, the unfortunate few who lived beside the aliens, saw the long silver needles descend point-first onto our neighbors' lawns and the silver shapes emerge with chains and glowing rods. We twitched the kitchen curtains closed and dialed up our music. Three hours later there was no sign of any of the aliens, the wretched or the beautiful, except for a few blackened patches of grass and wisps of smoke that curled and died.

All was well.

REUNION

SHANNON CHAMBERLAIN

O nce there was a girl who walked and walked and then walked
a little farther. She held the right hand of her papa and the left
hand of her mami and first they walked through places she
knew, through the neighbors' yards and underneath the towels and clothes that whipped and danced on the lines, which Mami
said were like clouds, only the girl didn't think so. Clouds were higher
up and you could only see them during the day, when the sun beat
down and the buzzy insects buzzed and the flying ones slept in the
shadows under the arches of the house where she lived.

But it was night now and they took off their shoes and ran between the buildings, like the game where the floors were made of
lava. Then Papa carried her and she slept, too, and when she woke
up, she wasn't in the city anymore with its popping sounds and roaring engines and the men that Mami said were like wolves and dogs
who could walk on two legs. Now she was in the red rocks and the
spike forest and Papa said she had to be careful of the black bugs
who could sting her whenever she walked. *Just like that!* he said, and
he made his hands into the snappy black bug and the girl laughed.
But then she was hungry and Mami and Papa said to pretend that
the water was a birthday cake, and the girl tried very hard, closing
her eyes and imagining the cake: sweet and rich and soaked with

milk, and the secret plantains underneath. But she was so hot, and so hungry, and she couldn't pretend like they wanted her to. The dark spots swam in front of her eyes and her tongue stuck to the roof of her mouth.

Sometimes they got to ride in the back of a truck for a little bit and Mami would hold the girl in her lap and whisper about a new place, where there was food and all of the water you could drink and you could go out and play in the yard and no wolves or dogs would come to eat up little girls or hit them with their big black sticks. But the girl didn't believe her: not really. She had already learned the difference between real and make-believe.

—EMERGENCY BULLETIN—
Subject: Aerial Transport Services B8901456 Drone (Make/Model: "Family Reunion")
Error type: 56-A-145
Origin: 31.965370,-106.347280 ("Railroad Park North," El Paso, Texas)
Current location: [UNDEFINED]
ALL SYSTEMS BULLETIN
Status: Unresolved

ALL FEDERAL AND STATE AGENTS SHOULD BE ON THE ALERT FOR AN ATS B8901456 LAST SEEN WEST OF EL PASO, HEADING SOUTH DUE SOUTHWEST. MINOR INSIDE. APPROACH WITH CAUTION. SOURCE OF MALFUNCTION UNKNOWN.

There is the castle tower, said Mami, and the girl gave her a sigh full of everything. It was true that the girl had never seen a castle except in a book that her grandmami gave her, and she wished she had it now so that she could show Mami that it was different. This tower was dark and black and there was no castle behind it or the wall of stripes: just more red rocks, the same red rocks, and the same spiky forest. Same, same, same. The girl's hair itched and her feet had red polka dots but she was too tired now to tell Mami or Papa and then she fell asleep again.

When she woke up, Mami and Papa were gone. All of the other children were crying, so she cried, too, and scratched her head and cried a bit more because she thought that maybe if she had believed Mami about the castle, Mami wouldn't have gone away.

Incident Report

Subject: Aerial Transport Services B8901456 Drone (Make/
    Model: "Family Reunion")

Error type: 56-A-145

Origin: 31.965370,-106.347280 ("Railroad Park North," El
    Paso, Texas)

Current location: [UNDEFINED]

ALL SYSTEMS BULLETIN

Status: Unresolved

Agent assigned: Cristina J. Hendrix, F.B.I.

ALL UNITS ARE ADVISED THAT MINOR CHILD
REBECKAH CALLAGHAN IS STILL MISSING AND
BELIEVED TO BE ALOFT. CALLAGHAN BOARDED
ATS B8901456 YESTERDAY MORNING, 4/21/22 AT

0746. ALMOST HALFWAY TO DESTINATION ATS
B8901456 OVERRODE PROGRAMMING AND REVERSED
DIRECTION, DISABLING GPS LOCATOR. MINOR CHILD'S
TAMPERING NOT SUSPECTED DUE TO AGE AND
LANGUAGE. UNIT LAST SEEN HEADING FOR SOUTHERN
BORDER. MINOR IS 7 YEARS OF AGE, APPROXIMATELY
40 INCHES TALL, 35 POUNDS, BLACK HAIR AND BROWN
EYES. LAST SEEN WEARING A PINK SKIRT AND WHITE
SHIRT.

They tell her she will have a new mami now, and she knows that this is make-believe, too. They bring her to the fake mami and fake papa but this time maybe where they live does look a little like the castle in the movie that she saw with the other children when Mami and Papa went away, the one with the princess who fell asleep. It has a big staircase that goes up up up forever. Fake Mami tells her that she is not to climb it, and she puts up a gate in front of it. This place is nothing but gates. Gates and doors. And there is a dungeon here, too, just like in the movie. It is full of long, warm coats. Fake Mami tells her that she must only speak Anglo now and when she doesn't know the word for something and she speaks her real language, Fake Mami puts her in the dungeon and tells her not to be dirty. She puts her face inside the coats and pretends that they are Mami's skirts: bright and soft and smelling of spices and heat and the dried peppers that they hung in the doorways at Christmas.

Some things are the same, and some are different. Her polka-dot feet have gone away. She has so many clothes now but Fake Mami and Fake Papa (who tells her she must call him "Daddy") say to her that if she gets them dirty or wet, she will go in the dungeon again.

She has to make believe that she has a new name, which she does because she is learning that sometimes make-believe is fun. On Sundays they go to a place that they say is a church, but that is make-believe, too: There are no painted statues, no altares, no priest, no friendly santos at all to smile at her. There is just a man in a suit who shouts at them. There is music, though, and that is her favorite part, even if she doesn't understand the words. She sways back and forth and mouths words of her own invention in her real language and when Fake Mami looks over, she pretends that she is singing along with the others.

Incident Report
Subject: Aerial Transport Services B8901456 Drone (Make/
    Model: "Family Reunion")
Error type: 56-A-145
Origin: Origin: 31.965370,-106.347280 ("Railroad Park
    North," El Paso, Texas)
Current location: [UNDEFINED]
ALL SYSTEMS BULLETIN
Status: Unresolved
Agent assigned (NOTE CHANGE): Richard Sanderson,
    U.S.C.B.P.

MINOR CHILD REBECKAH CALLAGHAN STILL MISSING
AND BELIEVED ALOFT. VISUAL REPORTS OF ATS
B8901456 MADE NEAR I-10 INTERCHANGE. B8901456
BRIEFLY PINGED SATELLITE AT SOUTHERN BORDER. ATS
B8901456 BELIEVED TO HAVE CROSSED INTO MEXICAN
AIRSPACE. U.S.C.B.P. AND STATE DEPARTMENT ARE

COORDINATING WITH MEXICAN GOVERNMENT FOR
RETURN OF DRONE AND MINOR CHILD.

She is tired of playing dungeon. Fake Mami is tired of it, too, the girl can tell. Fake Mami used to teach her at the castle but she was not quick enough so now she must go to school, Fake Mami says. School is far, far away, Fake Mami says, and Fake Mami doesn't have the time to take her there. Fake Papa sighs and says they will get a flying machine even though it is too much. She thinks at first that this is more make-believe but then it is here and Fake Papa shows her how it works. She climbs inside and it is warm and safe. When they close the door she is afraid: Is it like the trucks that made her mouth sticky and smelled like the spot in the yard where the dogs pooped? But it is not. It is warm and soft inside, and when she cries, the flying machine sings her a song and tells her to drink her juice. And best of all, she is flying. At first she can see Fake Mami and Fake Papa through the window but then they are falling and she is looking at trees from the top and she didn't even know that trees had tops! She hates the school but for a while every day she is real-life flying!

That was when she started to talk to the flying machine and tell it about real Mami and real Papa. She tells it her true name, not the Rebeckah name, and the flying machine says that they have the same name. And she laughs and laughs.

When the trip is over the doors open with a swish swish and the flying machine says, "Your journey is complete."

That is the worst time of the day but soon she knows she will fly again.

El Paso Times
June 4, 2022

No Reunion in Case of Missing Child Last Seen Aboard School Transit Drone

RAILROAD PARK NORTH, TX—
Rebeckah Callaghan, 7, is still missing after her school transit drone reversed course and disabled its GPS systems in April.

The disappearance has raised concerns over the latest trend in school drop-offs and pick-ups: transport by drone service.

Local firm Aerial Transport Services (ATS), manufacturer of the "Reunion" model of school transit drone, is one of the area's most profitable new companies, as more families retreat from what they say is an increasingly crowded and unsafe urban center. Many families have come to rely upon the drones for personal transport as well as transport of goods. Callaghan's school, Dunes Christian Academy, was one of the first to partner with ATS to transport students from the suburbs and exurbs near El Paso, where most of their parishioners live, to the city center. Until Callaghan's disappearance, the program had operated seamlessly for over a year.

The school has suspended the partnership with ATS pending further investigation of what went wrong with "Reunion" drone transport flight. The U.S. Customs and Border Control refused to comment for this article, but the F.B.I.—which was assigned to the case before the drone pinged a border tower before immediately shutting down its GPS module again— said that a rare instance of data sharing likely led to the malfunction.

On the morning Callaghan's family put the child into the

drone, ATS carried out a security sync. ATS drones recently introduced an extra layer of security into their operations meant to ensure that children were returned to their correct origin locations. The security system was based on DNA "thumbprints."

Normally, Rebeckah's DNA would have been paired with the DNA signature of the Callaghans and geolocated to their house in Anderson. However, ATS had recently agreed to sync their own DNA database with the database that U.S.C.B.P. has assembled from border migrants seeking asylum. Rebeckah was adopted last year after the U.S.C.B.P. concluded that they could not locate her birth parents.

"It appears that the U.S.C.B.P. did not anticipate that with so many children no longer with their actual parents, the ATS drones might get confused," said Cristina J. Hendrix, the F.B.I. agent originally assigned to Callaghan's disappearance.

ATS declined to comment for this article.

"We are of course very sorry for Rebeckah's family," said Dunes Christian Principal Mark Fluverson. "It was especially tragic timing because the Callaghans, who are longtime parishioners, had just been getting to know their daughter, who was an abused refugee that they took into their home."

As for the Callaghans, they are grieving but said that they do not blame the school or ATS for Rebeckah's disappearance. Another child, a boy they are calling Kayden, has already been placed with them and if his parents are not located within three months, the placement will become permanent.

"It's so sad that these parents bring their children here and leave them, but we're happy to help out," said Forrest Callaghan, Rebeckah's adopted father. "Maybe with time and the wonders of modern technology, Rebeckah will come home."

The girl touches down lightly, and the flying machine opens its doors for her. *Your journey is complete*, it says, like it always does, but this time it is not make-believe. She can see Mami and Papa through a window in the little pink house, and Tía Francesca, just like Mami said. They are making flautas but Mami and Papa look sad. She hesitates, digging the toe of the shoe that pinches her toes into the dirt.

"Your journey is complete," the ATS B8901456 reassures her as they arrive. "Avanza, Reunión."

NOTHING TAKES THE PLACE OF YOU

FERNANDO A. FLORES

As Selena Quintanilla awoke from a night of bad dreams she found herself transformed into a posthumous pop cultural icon. She was inside her bed bunk in the back of the tour bus, got out, knocked on the tiny restroom door to make sure it was unoccupied, washed her face. The bus wasn't moving, and there was no music playing, which was strange for those early hours. Walking the vacant bus aisle, Selena called out to her brother, then looked inside her sister's bunk, and when she didn't see her called out, "Suzette."

The driver was also missing, and Selena thought the obvious: They were playing a joke on her. She opened the bus door using the lever, and saw they were on a lonesome two-lane highway, with only distant mesquites and shrubs off the road. She laughed, knowing they had to be in Houston by evening, and thought this was really some distasteful joke. She walked around the bus calling out for everyone in the family and the band, the driver. It was a chilly morning, and in every direction there was arid land nobody had thought to build homes in, and those barren, crooked mesquites like petrified tentacles of the creature living underground that devours all life on the surface.

Before something like fear enveloped her, Selena walked back on the bus, closed the door, and searched all the crevices inside again. If this was a joke, she'd have to go along with it, so when everyone showed up they'd see she thought it was no big deal. She made herself cereal, had a banana, and put the radio loud on the oldies station. Then, from her bunk, she found that unmarked mix-tape the clerk from Otoño Records had given her of punk from Monterrey, put it on even louder, and opened the windows of the bus to usher the air through. The music was not in her family's taste—something her father would have ordered her to throw out the window.

If they are trying to frighten me with this game, she thought, *I can put a fright in them, too.* Selena thrashed around the bus like she'd seen in footage of punk shows, bumping the walls, knocking over empty cups and cassette tapes to the floor. After the first side of the tape ended she laughed, cleaned everything, put the tape away. She decided this hide-and-seek game had gone too far and wasn't something that felt normal.

Selena imagined several scenarios of what could have happened. Maybe they'd been run off the road while she slept, and everyone had been kidnapped but her; or they'd been pulled over and due to some confusion the police had arrested everyone; or down this road, where no other vehicle had passed since she'd gotten up, something extraterrestrial had beamed everyone away and spared her, the youngest in the family, in a way she'd have to bear for the rest of her life. This last outcome was the least likely, but Selena had to admit she'd managed to frighten herself—a fear that slowly balled up into a blind rage, and she went down the line and directed this rage at every one of her family members, for little things, creative choices, incidents beyond this little prank of theirs.

When the sun went down and nobody showed up, Selena felt bad about her curses and evil thoughts. She decided something extremely out of the ordinary was going on, and, desperate not to be devoured along with the bus by the cold night, she got behind the wheel and turned the ignition. Selena did the things her father instructed her when she made him teach her how to drive it, after they got stuck in the mud that one time in Las Milpas. She hit the headlights, put it in gear, and drove, unsure if they'd already crossed into Texas.

After a few miles and road signs, Selena estimated the closest city was San Antonio. Though the tank was at three-fourths, she stopped at the first lit gas station she came across. The cars lined up to pump gas were vacant, and nobody seemed to be inside the store. Selena got down, left the engine running, and from the loudspeakers of one of the cars her very own song "La Carcacha" was playing. Selena clenched her heart and looked inside the car, but there was nobody there. She walked into the store, grabbed a couple of snacks, and at the counter she called out, "Hello?"

Selena counted her total after estimating, and set the cash on the counter. Outside, her song had stopped playing and no other track followed. She hurried onto the bus and shut the door to the silence, drove away.

Having to increasingly maneuver around vehicles standing completely still on the road, along with her caffeinated soda, helped keep Selena wide awake. She slid the station dial on the radio but couldn't find any programming, even on the AM stations. She was tired and didn't want to stop and rest just yet, so she stopped and found that punk mix from Otoño Records, popped on the B-side. The tape turned over three times before she entered the San Antonio city limits.

On that drive Selena reconciled it wasn't just her family and crew that were gone; everyone else appeared to be missing, too. This calmed her and made the event of her loved ones' return more probable. Because, what happened? All the people on earth couldn't have just vanished at the same time. Where would they fit? She wondered if it mattered that she'd driven away from where her family disappeared, but became determined they would find their way to her somehow, like they always did.

Even as she, bleary-eyed, neared San Antonio, Selena could see patches of the city were blacked out, along with most of the light posts and signs she passed. Selena got nervous after she considered that maybe there would come a point where she wouldn't be able to steer around the vehicles, and as she approached the Pearl Brewery the cars came to a complete gridlock. Luckily, she'd gotten stuck in a section with electricity, and sitting in that grumbling bus she surveyed the Texas plates as far into the night as she could see.

In the morning, though all the windows were tightly shut, she heard birds as she awoke from the couch behind the driver's seat. On the right side mirror sat a grackle flapping its wings and screeching—not at anything in particular—or maybe at the world in general. Selena could see clearly into the bird's eyes as others swarmed around it. She got up, knocked on the bathroom door out of habit before entering. When she finished her morning things, Selena breakfasted behind the wheel, trying to admire the day: the sun rising in the heart of San Antonio, trucks and cars and eighteen-wheelers stuck in a still life, the side of the Pearl Brewery glowing like its golden beer.

Selena stepped off the bus and looked around at the landmarks besides the brewery to remember her location. As she wandered down an aisle of jammed automobiles, she glanced inside station wagons, vans, Beetles. The absence of families, truckers, drivers trying to get to work, gave the morning a smogless air to breathe, and the birds must have taken notice.

Walking down the off-ramp, Selena was suspicious of the birds along the railing and noticed a large number of them were squawking and tilting their heads, curious about her in turn. She saw in them the same curious thing she'd seen in the grackle that awakened her: They resembled and behaved more like territorial monkeys than birds. Selena walked under the overpass, toward the tall buildings.

Blocks away, swaying in the wind, she spotted a solitary red balloon. Remembering an old movie, she felt the balloon was a good sign and made her way toward it, always careful to look both ways before crossing, since the streetlights were operating. She passed a city bus, an Oldsmobile, a couple Dodge trucks, and looked carefully inside all of them to find them vacant. Selena imagined a person selling the balloon, or a child with the balloon in one hand, her mother's hand in the other, or the red balloon tied to the neck of a small, wise hound.

A block away from the balloon, she saw it was simply tied to a food cart, and as she got closer the reality before her was no match for her expectations. It was a hot dog stand. In its stillness, it looked also capable of swaying with the wind like the balloon. She looked inside the hood, and saw the cold weenies bathing in shallow water.

As Selena surveyed the downtown buildings they appeared hollow or two-dimensional, like cheap Hollywood sets of cities with only their faces. Behind her, gradually, she could make out the clop of hooves, and when she turned, coming from Broadway, there was a horse pulling a carriage. The horse looked tired, and stopped in its tracks upon the sight of Selena. She sensed the horse was thirsty or hungry.

Selena walked up to the horse, unharnessed it from the wagon, and it followed her to the hot dog stand, where she opened the hood once again. The horse stuck its mouth in, and, fearing that weenies could be bad for horses, Selena was relieved to see it was only drinking the still water. She quickly brainstormed other things she could do for the horse, when it suddenly galloped back the way it had come, up Broadway.

Inspired by the will of the horse, Selena walked the abandoned streets of downtown San Antonio in search of some answers. She saw hummingbirds and dragonflies buzzing over the placid waters of the River Walk. Birds had scavenged the exterior seating of all the restaurants, with sprawled silverware and broken dishes, shattered margarita goblets, server towels on rails, gutted condiment packets, and cocktail napkins floating like lily pads in the River Walk water.

Near a restaurant with fake elephant tusks at its entrance, an electronic Casio piano was still plugged in and going on a stand, with a microphone hooked up to a tiny speaker. Selena checked out the minimalist setup, played a few keys, saw the speaker had a strap attached and looked light enough to carry.

She walked over small bridges, explored hotel lobbies, and watched birds pick at the bones of all that remained, until she sensed the mass desolation of people was really draining on her. She found some premade food that still looked edible at Nuestra Tradición, along with some beverages, counted off the total, and left the money on the counter.

On her way back to the bus, Selena considered she would run out of cash at some point, and asked herself what she'd do if that were the case. She had dinner behind the wheel of the bus and watched the sun set on I-35. Down on the streets, she saw a pack of wild dogs, or wolves, roaming with their noses to the ground.

The third morning it seemed the birds flying around the expressway and Pearl Brewery had doubled—tripled?—and, watching them from inside the bus, Selena asked herself the inevitable question: What if nobody—not just her family and crew—ever came back? Even if her sister, or brother, returned, who would they play music to?

She walked out of the bus and retraced her steps from the previous day all the way to the River Walk, where the Casio synth was set up. She wiped off some of the bird droppings from the speaker and strapped it over her right shoulder, took the microphone from the stand, and wrapped the cable slack over-under. Selena adjusted the knobs on the speaker and pointed it to a flock of green birds on the rails, facing her.

"Hola, bueno," she said, frightening the birds away, while attracting others.

The speaker had a charged battery and was light—Selena wondered where she'd seen such a charming little speaker before. She looked around, trying to remember where the River Walk curved, creating cavernous acoustics. It was possible, as she searched for this spot, to forget about her present plight, and for a few moments she got that rush before playing a show. Selena got to the small stone stage in front of La Mansión Hotel, where she'd seen singers belting it out for passersby in the past. She looked around at the rowdy birds, turned the speaker on, tested the levels without drowning out the echo, and set it on the ground.

Selena took a moment to look deeply into the phantom faces on the lower and street levels of the River Walk, then said, "Hola a todos."

But the steady stream of tourists in downtown San Antonio had been cut off.

Selena warmed up with a song she'd loved since she was a girl, as she'd been doing lately during rehearsals. The screeches of birds echoed along the plaza, the outdoor bars, abandoned tourist boats on sooty waters, and the complete anarchy of nature taking over the heart of Texas. Selena sang a new song of hers she'd been working out, allowed herself to restart the song a couple times to test out lyrics. She sang one in English her father and A.B. hated but which she and Suzette found hysterical, then segued into another one her family disliked, then another.

In the middle of a verse, Selena felt a wave of sound rushing her way. She stopped singing, shut the speaker off, and listened carefully. Above the high-wire screeches was a crowd of boos echoing after her. As she listened closer, she remembered the sight of the pack of dogs she'd seen the evening before, because the sounds weren't boos, but—clearer and clearer—barking dogs. Selena almost left the speaker and microphone behind, but grabbed them and yet again retraced her steps back to the bus.

For the first time since the beginning of this experience, Selena felt she was being followed. Taking a turn on St. Mary's, she walked past the Majestic, the Greyhound station, and site of the future public library. She felt safe upon approaching an open area, stood and marveled at the Gothic architecture many downtowns in old Texas towns shared, the skies free of airplanes, telephone cables without a ripple of communication.

Graffitied against the wall of an abandoned warehouse was the image of a deranged man wearing a bomber jacket, his hair buzzed into a Mohawk. Selena imitated his unhinged expression as she turned and faced the dogs she imagined running after her. She turned on the speaker and, as if teasing them, wolf-called into the microphone as loud as she could. From a distance she heard a howl, then another, then barking echoed and ran along her feet as the grackles shrieked on every stretch of power lines the eye could see.

Back in the bus, she sat behind the wheel, waiting anxiously for the sun to set. If overnight was when everyone in Texas vanished, then out of the darkness or her slumber they would return.

The following morning, after breakfast, Selena counted what was left of her money on the little table. It wasn't much. She decided to leave IOUs with her name signed if she picked anything up anywhere. Selena grabbed a few items she could carry—things she could hold like talismans—thought about her family—the lives they had before they vanished.

Selena said goodbye to the bus, knocked on its walls, the roof, and climbing down its steps she was confident one day she'd tour in that bus again. As she walked along an aisle of the traffic jam on I-35, Selena thought further about the IOUs, asked herself what stealing even was if there was nobody left to steal from.

She was anxious to discover what the road held ahead. She pictured monuments around the world with nobody to admire, the great stages like Carnegie Hall or the Globe Theatre empty of performers and an audience.

At the front of the jam she found no accident, to her surprise. She wondered how the cars had stopped completely after their drivers disappeared—did they come to a rolling stop, or simply halt in place, like marching soldiers?

Her heart was beating rapidly as she eyed a Seville acting like the pacer of traffic, about fifty yards out from the jam. There were no signs of the person who had driven it—who they were, or belongings revealing their interests. She threw in the speaker, microphone, her bag on the passenger seat, and looked around, feeling terrible about taking this vehicle.

Selena hit the ignition, put the Seville in gear, brainstormed something to say in case she got pulled over, and she followed the de-peopled streets hoping for signs of human life, or to at least eventually sing in an empty Carnegie Hall.

THE BINDING OF ISAAC

TOCHI ONYEBUCHI

Max hadn't woken that morning with the intention of buying a Master; Rami was an impulse purchase.

Under the dulcet lighting of the auction room, it hadn't been the severe, archangelic beauty of Rami's face that had done it for Max, nor had it been the way his dark skin contrasted with the alabaster of the other Masters on display by the fireplace. They all wore their training in their stances—one Master cosplaying as an Aryan demesne overseer, another wearing the fake medals of some European despot from a bygone era. They stood at attention, waiting to command as they had been instructed to do, to crack the literal whips that hung at their waists, to bark insults and to verbally bludgeon their buyer into an army crawl across broken glass. But Rami, in his slim-fit, two-piece Tom Ford with his dress shirt unbuttoned, hands in his pockets, was the picture of repose. The others looked like you could knock them over with a feather. Rami looked like he had adopted his fighter's stance, standing at an angle to his audience so they could only see him in profile, left foot forward, right foot back and perpendicular to his shoulders. That posture. This man could hurt him. Truly hurt him. Max licked his lips.

In the train car on the way home from the Auction, Max had a holo of Jeryd glowing beryl before him. Rami sat across from Max so that Max's friend lay in superimposed holo-glow over Max's new Master.

"This one's different," Max said to the holograph of his friend as the interior of the Domed City sped by.

"Different from Giorno?" Jeryd said around a cheekful of salt-and-vinegar chips. "From Tyler or whatever his name was?" Munch-munch. "I remember correctly, both ended up on the pyre after you broke them."

It had been wasteful, sure. They both might've been good Masters to someone, Giorno with his large hands perfect for strangling and Tyler with his imaginative reconstructions of re-education camps. Augmented with cyberbrains, they might've served someone with a lesser imagination. Rami, though. Red-blooded, meat-brained Rami.

"Is it 'cause he's Black?"

The train shot out from the Domed City and hit a stretch of deso-late, heat-fucked outdoors. The holo flickered—faulty connection— then they were underground and on the last stretch before home. Too fast for Max to have glimpsed the hazard-suited chattel laying rail outside in weather that snatched years from their lives with each passing hour. Too fast to see that those people outside were the same color as Rami. But Max knew.

"Mind you, I'm not kink-shaming."

Max snorted. "That's the whole point of kink, Jeryd. It isn't kink without the bite of shame." He leaned to the side of the holo to get an unobstructed look at Rami, who held his gaze. "He's certainly pret-tier than the others, though I haven't yet checked his teeth."

"*Your* family runs a demesne, not mine," Jeryd snapped before laughing. "Gotta go. Kevin wants to go boar-hunting."

"Ah yes. You grunting, hunter-gatherer types. Have fun."

"Fuck you. Take care, man." Then the holo winked out, and Max was left with Rami's imperious negroid-Sphinx silence.

The first thing Max did upon bringing Rami home was shrug off his coat. Before he could finish, Rami took it from him and hung both of theirs on the coatrack by the front door. Over eggs and avocado toast Rami prepared, Max laid out the rules of the contract.

"There are no rules," he said simply. In the face of Rami's quiet eating, he frowned. "The contract omissions are all intentional. Corporal punishment however you see fit, playacting, ritual, all of that. Most buyers include a clause about preparatory matters, needing to be warned before a simulation is built or needing to be prepared for caning or waterboarding, but I've found that if you take surprise out of the equation, it rather diminishes the whole experience. Additionally, I've called up my personnel file here." A few taps on the tablet next to his plate, then he slid it to Rami, who didn't even glance at it. "My mother passed when I was twelve, MS. And Dad's in a care home, Parkinson's. A hundred and two, but he's too ornery for death. We're a bit estranged, so you won't find much mileage there. Anyway, nothing's off-limits. Verbal abuse, making fun of them—my parents—restricting my time outside, all of that. I'm yours." A dozen pages into the document were graphical displays of the ritual torture his grandfather had enacted on the chattel mailed in to terraform the planet generations ago. Max's father had been a different kind of god, manumitting much of the family's holdings and leaving his son with nothing but an anhedonic, luxuriously antiseptic existence.

He was a disgusting man, Max's father had told him of his grandfather, thinking, hoping perhaps, that there was none of that industrialist in his son.

Perhaps something in those pictures might ferment Rami's imagination, push him in a direction a mechanized or cyberbrained Master might not go. Max's fingers itched around his fork.

Rami finished his meal, then took his plate and Max's to the sink for washing.

◆

Every morning, Max's outfits for the day were laid out for him, pants and tops, hoodies and jeans, chinos and Henleys all chosen in perfect anticipation of his mood. Even the scarves and beanies.

"Maybe he was broken when you bought him," Jeryd said to Max over holo one afternoon. Max knew that wasn't the case. Even in the face of the cooked meals and the washed linens, even in the case of the arranged playdates with his children and visits to his father's care home—the calendrical repair of Max's life—even in the face of all that, Max knew that wasn't the case.

◆

Max was flailing. Outwardly, not a bead of sweat marked his porcelain, climate-controlled body, but a pit of quicksand grew inside him, in which he found his calmness slipping. He had Rami lay out the purchased tools on the living room floor. Between them: a cat-o'-nine-tails, a ribbed shock baton, handcuffs, knives, and a straitjacket.

"Don't tell me you don't know how this works," Max said, reclining on his couch, ankle over knee, tumbler of whiskey swirling in his loose grip. When Rami mirrored his pose on the opposite couch, the tools arranged between them, fury boiled over and a hairline fracture shot through the tumbler. "Or are you trying to wind up on the pyre?"

Was it a trick of the light or did a smirk ghost across Rami's face?

"Do it yourself," Rami said, before pushing himself off of the couch. "Dinner in an hour."

A vision flashed before Max: him holding the cat-o'-nine-tails high over Rami's already torn-to-pieces back. Customer dissatisfaction. But something washed it away. Something golden and blossoming, something wet and warm. If Max searched in the words Rami had spoken at him, plunged deep enough into the intonations, he might've heard the whisperings of a command.

So Max waited. As his diet improved, as he saw more artificial sun, as he attended his checkups more regularly, he waited. Even as Rami would smile at him while doing the dishes, even as Max would walk into the office Rami had set up for himself and catch his Master color-coding the administration of his life, Max waited. That first command had sent a shock of pain-pleasure from the base of his spine down to his loins, and he lusted after its repeating.

Visiting his father, he still found himself waiting.

Max sat outside the hyperbaric chamber that encased his father like a sarcophagus, his bald head protruding from the enclosure, wires and cords connecting his skull to all sorts of cryptic machinery glowing behind him. Max, cyberized as he was, didn't need any helmet to Connect with his father, so he simply sat with his legs crossed on the hoverchair and, between sips from his mug, spoke and listened.

"Call him whatever century-old slur you want, Pop, but he's the reason I'm even seeing you again. Which is what I said last time and the time before that and the time before that."

"That some crack about my Alzheimer's?"

"Don't worry, you'll forget it by the next visit."

"Very funny, son. Very funny." A pause sat between them.

After a minute of unfilled silence, Max's father made a throat-clearing sound that reverberated in Max's brain, then said, "I'm gonna do it. Treatment's good and all, but I'm not getting any better.

I'm just getting worse slower." Max made to speak, but his father interrupted with, "Don't. I still got enough brain to make this sort of decision. This . . . this is all fake. You comin' here more and more made me realize that. You're not talking to me. You're talking to a cobbled-together mental projection of me. I don't talk like this, I never did. And I don't wanna be kept alive like this. Law says I can pull my own plug. I don't need your permission. I'm just telling you to be polite."

Knowing a thing would be said didn't keep Max from tensing in his seat with anxiety.

"Keep this up any longer, you'll just be talking to yourself. A version of yourself with no more hair. Maybe a little more swear-y. But it ain't gonna be me. Hasn't been me for a while now."

"We're going to get you a new brain."

"I'm not gettin' cyberized. I told you."

The epiphany was a thunderclap in Max's metal skull. "I know where to get one. Organic." He knew his father would rather die than take his own son's Augmented brain, would rather perish than kill his kid, so Max knew to head that objection off at the pass. "Lightly used."

Max came home to a candlelit dinner, and the dulcet tones of the dining room had him, by the time he settled in his chair across from Rami, bathing in a feeling of rightness. He would miss Rami, the way he had sanded away the edges of Max's life that constantly scraped at things, the way he had, from the wings, repaired his relationship with his kids and his father, changed his habits, got him to drink more water. But this wasn't what a Master was for. He could have paid less for a Friend and even less for a Dog. But this wasn't waste like with the others. Sure, he was sending Rami to the pyre, but that would be only after his brain was extracted. Then the sense-less body would be lit, its remains jettisoned Outside for the laborers to deal with.

When Max finished explaining all of this to Rami, Rami, his expression unreadable, said, "No."

"Excuse me?"

"No."

"What are you—" He felt it. That warmth spreading like a stain in his groin. He was dizzy with it. "I—" He fought for words in the face of the ecstasy bursting to life behind his eyes.

"Sit down and finish your meal."

His body moved before his mind could tell it otherwise. Everything felt rendered in high-definition, the wood finish of the table glistened, the lamb gushed piquant juices on his tongue.

"We won't be going to the pyre."

This was what he had been waiting for, what he'd known was here all along. Refusal. All the others had linked Max's words to "customer dissatisfaction" as explained in the contract and had then scaled the mountain to put their head to the stone for sacrifice. But Max wanted a Master who saw past that, past the four corners of their contract. Who saw past the act. Who could hurt him. Really truly hurt him.

"You're going to save my dad," he said, tensed, hungry, almost blind with want, fingers brushing against the divine, the other-worldly, on the threshold of entry into a pleasure unimaginable, waiting for that one last nudge into deliverance.

"No."

DREAM JOB

SEAMUS SULLIVAN

Aishwarya signs up for just a few shifts, short ones. The wireless electrodes arrive by courier. She puts them on her temples and dreams of schools she never attended, underwater chases with other people's parents, snowy beaches. A banker in Chicago feels suddenly refreshed, like after a nap. Aishwarya wakes up in Bengaluru, unrested and several hundred rupees richer.

All I have to do, she tells Sumitra, is sleep for an extra hour or two before bed.

And you have their dreams.

Right. I sleep so they don't have to. They get more waking hours in the day without feeling tired.

So you rest while you're on the clock.

No, I wake up exhausted. I still have to sleep for myself on my own time. But the money's good. Three or four naps a week, I can pay off my loans early.

Fucking capitalism, Sumitra says.

They glance across the call floor. Their supervisor is still berating a server.

They hiring? asks Sumitra.

🔥

The key to falling asleep by day is to keep yourself in a bubble of night. Aishwarya's shift at the call center ends around breakfast time. She dons sunglasses, drives home in self-imposed twilight. Her mother has left for work and the house is quiet. Outside, staccato car horns. The cries of the man who collects used newspapers. She does some coding homework before her SleepTyte shift. Upstairs, she passes the empty bedrooms of her younger sisters, already married off.

Blackout curtains keep her room dark. She puts on the electrodes, then headphones playing forest sounds. She must sleep deeply or the customer will give her a one- or two-star rating. Aishwarya closes her eyes. Thinks about the app she's going to build, the start-up she'll own. Her office will have a standing desk, a door that locks, floor-to-ceiling windows letting sunlight flood in. She rearranges the furniture in her head and falls asleep in minutes.

🔥

She doesn't remember her own dreams, or her mind is too tired to dream at all. That's how she knows she's sleeping on her own time. Stillness. Silence.

🔥

An email from SleepTyte informs her that sleepers must sign up for two eight-hour shifts each week, minimum, in order to keep working.

If she cuts further into her own sleep time, she still comes up short on class days.

She sleeps better during the day than most. Customers tip her well. An eight-hour shift pays more than the call center.

Call in sick Thursday, she decides. See how it goes.

Aishwarya pedals a ten-speed through an art gallery. She mustn't look at any of the paintings or she'll become aroused.

As she wakes from the customer's dream, she can only remember high white ceilings and a sense of peace.

Her own memories return. Deadlines for loan payments. Dates grinning through their mustaches at her, calling her ambitious, not in a good way. Her mother's face, skeptical, asking what exactly her app is going to do.

Her life crashes over her, surrounds her, like cold water.

She dreams of an all-night blues session in an office park surrounded by evergreens. She wakes at dinnertime, answers the deliveryman at the door, eats balancing on one stiff leg, then the other. The chief minister is on TV talking about brain drain in the workforce, blaming companies like SleepTyte.

Her mother asks when was the last time she changed clothes. Aishwarya blinks, not knowing.

She and Sumitra bring colorful salwar kameezes to work and put them on in the bathroom after their shift. Aishwarya has picked out a restaurant atop a luxury hotel. They breakfast among business travelers.

New income bracket, says Aishwarya. Spending it on you means I can't spend it on drugs. She smiles to show she's mostly kidding.

Sumitra shuffles potatoes around her plate. How's your app coming? she asks. You haven't talked about it lately.

Aishwarya squints. Sumitra's dupatta is the same color as an Easter egg from a customer's dream.

This is what you did in college, says Sumitra.

Took you to breakfast?

You missed classes and you stopped talking about your plans and when I called you wouldn't pick up and we couldn't get you out of your room . . . Her voice quavers and she stops.

That's not what this is.

What if you go away again?

I'm better now. Look at me. I'm fine.

Her left leg swells and throbs and becomes discolored. The doctor tells her it's a blood clot, very dangerous. Happens when your legs don't move for hours and hours. On the waiting room TV, the chief minister is holding a press conference, something about SleepTyte, an inquest. The doctor prescribes blood thinners, asks if she was stuck on a long international flight or something. She nods, not hearing him.

Her kids sit behind her in the minivan, her in-laws sit in the next row back, her sisters from Alpha Kappa Alpha sit behind them, and

Aishwarya can see in the rearview that the van goes back indefinitely and contains everyone she knows, all of them calling up to her with directions to school, exhortations to hurry.

But she's calm. These friends and family belong to a customer who's pulling an all-nighter for her bar exam. Aishwarya feels a kinship with the woman whose dream this is. She's overworked, too, back in the waking world. She forgets the specifics. This weightlessness is all she needs. The school looms ahead; she plows the van into a red-brick wall that ripples apart like gossamer.

Aishwarya awakens in her car in the call center's garage. She doesn't remember falling asleep. Eight hours, without the usual preparations, without even making it home to bed. A flash of pride. It's getting easier.

Stairs hurt her legs. Her bag strains her arms. She quits caffeine. Watches a sunrise with Sumitra from the window in the handicapped stall. Takes up caffeine again. Jogs in circles in the park, sits in a puddle of sweat in coding class. Neighboring students scoot their chairs and laptops away. She wants to approach the instructor, push a gentle hand through the membrane of his chest. See if she's dreaming.

After security escorts Aishwarya from the call center, Sumitra sneaks out to find her at the tea stall they visit on breaks. Aishwarya's looking into her cup like a diviner. Sumitra knocks it from her hands.

You're quitting this sleep thing, she says. Non-negotiable.

It's late. There are only some police and a sex worker having tea at standing tables nearby. They glance over without saying anything.

I could hear you on your calls, says Sumitra. You weren't making sense.

Aishwarya watches Sumitra's lips and wonders what her friend is trying to tell her. Maybe she'll understand when she wakes up.

She's free to dream full-time now. The trick is scheduling meals so your hunger doesn't intrude on the dreams, building in stretch breaks so you don't have muscle spasms, showering so your dreams don't reek, getting a new lock and playing the forest sounds at high volume so your mother's pounding can't wake you.

By the time her mother finds the electrodes and tries to destroy them, Aishwarya has saved enough rent for her own apartment. Soon she'll have enough to hire a private nurse to change her IV, to turn her over and stave off bedsores.

The apartment has one working light bulb and even that hurts her eyes. Whenever the ache in her muscles or the tightness in her chest wakes her, she finds the pills waiting. She was born for this. She has always known, at the bottom of her mind where the dreams crystallize, what being awake means. Avoidable pain.

She's in the back of a rickshaw at noon, Sumitra beside her, whipping through red lights, past trees and beer halls, sun hot on her skin, and Aishwarya realizes it's not a customer's dream. It's her own.

She hopes it never ends.

HEADSHOT

JULIAN MORTIMER SMITH

@JMitcherCNN: Corporal, first of all, let me thank you for agreeing to this interview. By now all of America has seen the footage of your amazing headshot last week. Could you tell us the story, in your own words?

@CplPetersUSMC: Well, sure, Jim. As you know, things went kinda crazy after I made that kill. I'm pushing 12k followers now. At the time the most I'd ever had online at once was . . . maybe a couple dozen? Fact is, there were only two people with me when it happened—@PatriotRiot2000 and @FrendliGhost. This was the night of the assault on Peshawar, remember? So half the nation was following the boys from First Airborne. No one wanted to miss a jump like that. I appreciate all the fans who've been with me since the beginning, but I want to give credit where it's due. It was just me, Riot, and Ghost that night.

@JMitcherCNN: Interesting. So you didn't even have quorum for engagement?

@CplPetersUSMC: No, sir. Not at first. But that night I wasn't even worrying about quorum. It was just a routine patrol and we weren't expecting any trouble. I was just chatting with Ghost and Riot. Both of those dudes have always had my back with nav and sit-reps and shit like that. But they were also just there when I

needed someone to talk to, you know? That's even more important sometimes. When you're in the middle of a war zone, it's
nice to hear the voice of some suburban kid from Detroit in your
headset.

@JMitcherCNN: So how many other soldiers were taking part in this
patrol?

@CplPetersUSMC: It was a six-man squad, but the tactical scale
guys had split us up to cover more ground. Ghost and Riot both
thought that was dumb, but they'd been outvoted in the war
room. When the numbers are small, bad ideas can get through
more easily. That's the whole point of quorum. I admit, we were
doing a bit of trash talking. They told me there were a lot of tac-
scale folks online who had never even really followed a soldier.
They just spend all their time zoomed-out, looking at satellite
feeds, moving us around like chess pieces. I'm not saying that's
wrong, but it can be dangerous. No one who's spent time with a
soldier on patrol would have made that kind of call.

@JMitcherCNN: So it was just you, alone in an alley. No backup.

@CplPetersUSMC: That's right. So then Riot notices this big black car
parked in the alley. It was dark as hell in there. All the streetlights
were out, so I didn't notice it. But Riot, he's a real tech-head. He
has my feed running in infrared, thermal, and laser-gated, each
in a separate window. He don't miss much. And he's from Detroit, so he knows his cars. Anyway it was a Lincoln. Most of the
cars here are these shitty Soviet models from the seventies. Ain't
that the ultimate irony? You can tell the guys on the Most Wanted
list 'cause they all drive American cars.

@JMitcherCNN: So you knew someone important was nearby.

@CplPetersUSMC: Well, we suspected. Ghost is looking at the satellite heat maps, pulling up floor plans, checking the locations
of windows. I knew I couldn't just storm in there by myself, but
Ghost and Riot didn't trust the guys in the war room, so they

wanted to wait before calling in the cavalry. Those tac-scale yahoos would probably just send the squad in, guns blazing, just for the thrill of it. So Ghost guides me into this bombed-out office building across the street. I hoof it up five stories till I'm level with the building opposite. Sure enough, a light is on and I can see into the room. There are six or seven bearded dudes there with AKs slung over their shoulders. It looks like they're arguing, and for a while I think they're going to shoot each other and save me the bother, but then another guy comes in. You can tell just by looking at him that he's some sort of head honcho—the owner of the car. I didn't recognize him myself. I ain't no racist, but with those beards they all look kinda the same. Riot, on the other hand, boots up some face-recognition software and IDs him, lickety-split, as Jaques al-Adil.

@JMitcherCNN: The Jack of Clubs.

@CplPetersUSMC: Exactly. This guy's a face card. One of the top ten most wanted terrorists in the world, and I'm sitting in a window across the street from him, lined up for a perfect headshot.

@JMitcherCNN: But . . .

@CplPetersUSMC: But, as I mentioned, I didn't have quorum, so I couldn't take the shot. Legally. So, Ghost and Riot jump on their social networks and try to get the word out. Any patriotic American would upvote a shot like that, but we just didn't have enough bodies in the room. Of course, all their friends are watching the assault in Peshawar, and not checking their messages. So you know what they do? Ghost goes and wakes up his parents, and Riot fetches his little sister and her boyfriend. Now, Riot's parents are real traditionalists who have never followed a soldier in their lives. Riot's always complaining about them, going on about how they're not upholding their responsibilities as citizens. They're old-timers, see? Got no interest in direct democracy.

@JMitcherCNN: Were they registered to vote?

@CplPetersUSMC: No! That's the thing. I think they were pre-screened through their driver's licenses or whatnot, but they certainly weren't registered for this theater. So I can hear Riot walking them through registration, trying to convince them how important this is, and they're trying to calm him down, and typing their email addresses wrong and having to start again, just like any other old folks. Have to laugh at it all, now.

@JMitcherCNN: I'm guessing it wasn't so funny at the time.

@CplPetersUSMC: It wasn't. But get this: The situation at Ghost's place is even worse. His sister is a hippie. A real peacenik, you know? She doesn't want anything to do with war. So I can hear him talking philosophy to her, trying to convince her to do the right thing for freedom and democracy just this once. And meanwhile I'm waiting with my rifle cocked and Jaques al-Adil's head in the middle of my sights. I've got to admit, Jim, I was sorely tempted to pull the trigger and just live with the consequences. But I thought to myself, if I shoot now I'm no better than he is. I'm here as a representative of my country. If I shoot without a quorum of consenting citizens, as the rules of engagement demand, then I'm no longer defending freedom and democracy, I'm just another terrorist.

@JMitcherCNN: Strong words, Corporal.

@CplPetersUSMC: Well, if I didn't believe them, I never would have enlisted.

@JMitcherCNN: So what happened next?

@CplPetersUSMC: Well, then I hear gunfire coming from the next street over. I found out later that it was just Samuels and Gonzales showing off for some kids, but Ghost and Riot were too busy to keep me updated at this point, so it scared the hell out of me at the time. And it scared al-Adil and the rest of the folks around that table. They kill the lights and hit the floor. A minute later, I see the front door of the building open and four figures sprint to the Lincoln. One of them is al-Adil and he gets in the backseat. My HUD was still only showing Ghost and Riot online, but just as the car was pulling away three more followers blipped into existence. I had quorum. Now they just needed to upvote engagement. The car was already turning the corner of the street when the votes came through. Five-out-of-five upvotes. Riot had persuaded his sister's boyfriend to log in and vote. I couldn't even see al-Adil by this point, all I could see was the car, but I had seen him climb into the back right-hand seat, so I aimed for where I thought his head would be.

@JMitcherCNN: And the rest is history.

@CplPetersUSMC: And the rest is history. Although it would never have gone so viral if Samuels hadn't been just around the corner. He was the one who saw all the gore. It's his POV feed that's trending. Over 10M now, I think.

@JMitcherCNN: But seeing yours makes the shot all the more astonishing. I encourage all our followers to watch Corporal Peters's POV of the shot. If it had been a second later . . .

@CplPetersUSMC: Ghost and Riot have both made their screen-feeds public, too. Be sure to check them out. Couldn't have done it without them.

@JMitcherCNN: So how do you think your job will change now that you have thousands of fans?

@CplPetersUSMC: Well, I certainly won't have trouble making quorum anymore . . . ROFL. On the one hand, it feels great to have the support of so many patriotic citizens behind me. But it'll be harder to have one-on-one chats with my followers. I'll do what I can to keep that personal connection. I've already set up a private channel for Ghost and Riot, so they'll always be able to talk to me directly, no matter how much chatter is going down. How will it change the job? I guess we'll just have to wait and see.

@JMitcherCNN: Just one more question, Corporal, and then I'll let you go. Sergeant Pearson's recent court-martial has sparked a grassroots campaign to eliminate quorum altogether. Do you wish you had had more leeway? More freedom to act on your own initiative?

@CplPetersUSMC: Well, that's a great question, Jim. A lot of the older guys in the unit complain a lot about the whole direct democracy thing, but I think I like things the way they are. Maybe if I had missed the shot I would feel differently, but it seems to me that getting your folks out of bed to vote and debating philosophy with your sister before letting a soldier take a shot—that's how it should work. That's democracy.

@JMitcherCNN: Well said, Corporal. And thank you for your service.

ZOMBIE CAPITALISM

TOBIAS BUCKELL

T he dogs started barking at the zombie in the pool long before Cheryl figured out what they had gotten the scent of. Zim, the German shepherd, crashed through the picture window to scrabble out after it.

Cheryl yelled at the dogs to get back in the house as Garfield took off to join Zim at the chain fence around the pool.

Then she heard the zombie splashing about in the shallow end of the pool. It snarled when it saw her, and she couldn't quite stifle a small scream as she realized a rotting corpse had pulled itself through a hole in the pool fence. It had trailed blood and innards all across the decorative brick path, then collapsed in a cloud of black ichor into the crystal-clear blue water.

Cheryl ran back inside and got the Remington Seven from the rack by the door, loading it and working the bolt by feel as she jogged to the back of the house. By the time she returned to the pool the zombie was flailing around in one of the corners, unable to pull itself out of the pool. A long black tangle of intestines looped around the pool cleaner had tied it up.

"Jesus Christ." Cheryl grabbed Zim. "Damn it, dog, you stay here."

She managed to get Zim's collar, but Garfield had scrabbled off counterclockwise around the fence to wiggle through the damn hole.

He arrowed into the pool along the zombie gut trail like the damn beagle scent hound he was.

Garfield ran around to snarl at the zombie as Cheryl got Zim's leash on him, clipped him to the fence, and then ran over to the gate.

"Garfield, *get* over here!"

She fumbled with the padlock for a second. Garfield shrieked as the zombie got clawed bony fingers into him.

Cheryl kicked the gate open and fired at the zombie. A chunk of shoulder blew away. She swore and worked the bolt again.

The second shot blew the zombie's head apart, bits of brain raining down into the pool. Cheryl pulled Garfield out of the water, carried him to the pickup, and got him into the passenger seat.

"Hilldale Vet Clinic," she shouted into her phone.

She was halfway to the vet before she realized she'd left Zim clipped to the fence, and called Kathy next door.

"No worries," Kathy said. "I'll send Jaden over, he can plywood up the window and take Zim in."

"I thought," said Cory from behind the vet's curved desk and two sleek computers, "that the National Guard had swept the town. What was the point of all those checkpoints? Fucking zombies."

Somewhere in the back, Cheryl thought, Garfield lay on a table under anesthesia. And that young vet from Chicago who didn't look like she could legally order a weak beer, or even drive a car, was trying to save him.

"Zombies, huh?" Cory said again.

Cheryl pulled her head out of her bloody hands when she realized he was talking to her. "What?"

"National Guard isn't doing a good job of keeping up," Cory said.

"They left," Cheryl said. She took a deep breath and blew her nose.

"They left? When'd they leave?" Cory looked horrified.

"It was on Channel Five," Cheryl said. "You didn't see it?"

"I've been working extra shifts," Cory said. "Trying to get ahead on my payments for steel shutters."

Cheryl had been seeing more and more of those go up. Bars on windows as well. She didn't like the look. The HOA kept sending out letters pointing out that it violated the community guidelines, but they just kept popping up.

Zombies trumped HOA rules.

"UTD won against the government." The judge on the case ruled that getting the military involved unfairly influenced the market. Ultra Tactical Dynamics, a company built just to provide zombie and zombie home defense products, would lose its business if the National Guard defeated the zombie hordes entirely. And that was anticapitalist and un-American.

Second Amendment rights trumped governmental anti-zombie actions.

"These are fundamental American rights," a blond spokeswoman wearing aviator sunglasses had told reporters at a press conference on the steps of the court, as Cheryl watched the news and chopped onions and carrots for a stew the previous night.

News reporters noted that the CDC wasn't allowed to track zombie populations starting next week, and conservative senators had advanced a bill to prevent funding for a cure.

"You should buy UTD stock," Zachariah told Cheryl at BreadWorx the next day. "The dividend is growing, and the stock is flying high."

He'd been their financial adviser for three years now. Dale liked him. Zachariah was a high school buddy who came back to town after college with a business degree to take over his dad's insurance business.

Dale couldn't make the appointment, told Cheryl she needed to go. What she really wanted to do was stay home and grieve Garfield.

Damn, she'd loved that dog.

Fucking Dale. He was probably off drinking at lunch. Cheryl hated meeting Zachariah on her own. He never took his eyes off her chest. She'd insisted on meeting him for lunch somewhere public to avoid the claustrophobic feeling of doing this in his office.

"They stopped the plague in France," Cheryl said, ripping off a piece of sourdough bread and dipping it in the potato soup. "What happens when this is all over?"

"We don't need a whole socialist intervention," Zachariah scoffed. "Got enough firepower right here for us regular folk to stop the horde. I saw Andy take out one of them in the hardware store parking lot. Bang, right between the eyes. People got out of their cars to clap."

Some of the boys were talking about building blinds out in the woods around town to sit and hunt zombies with their rifles.

Zachariah had a whole prospectus for Cheryl to look over. A glossy brochure full of charts that showed zombie outbreak growth, personal defense sales, and featured UTD's unique "prep parties" sales system that set up individuals as distributors to sell defense projects on down the line. Like Tupperware parties, but for lawn spikes, shutters, guns, and bitching swords.

Dale loved going to UTD parties.

"Listen, you see these videos online?" Zachariah asked.

He pulled out his phone and showed her a clip of three men in full camo gear on ATVs, all of them wearing night-vision goggles.

"Watch this," one of them said, giggling, and tossed a stick of dynamite out into the dark. When it exploded, dark gore and body parts rained out of the night and everyone laughed.

Local government all over the country lifted limits on what

hunters could use on zombies. YouTube was chock-full of men filming themselves firing on zombies with all the arms they'd been hoarding since the NRA first started posting about the government coming to take their weapons.

"Okay, look, if you don't want to invest in UTD, how about something a little more exotic?" Zachariah leaned in and tapped the UTD brochures.

Cheryl sighed. "What's that?"

"You remember Randy?"

"Chemistry Randy?"

Zachariah nodded. "He's starting a safari experience for the city folk. You come out, do a few practice rounds on a shooting range, and then they load you into an open-topped bus with a wire cage and run you out into the countryside and you take potshots from the comfort of a vehicle."

Fifty thousand seed capital to help him get two vehicles with chopped tops.

Who knew how much they'd make?

"It's zombie capitalism," Zachariah said with a big grin. "And business is good."

"I'd have to talk to Dale," Cheryl said. She could barely focus, her eyes were watering every few seconds, and Zachariah was too focused on talking investing at her to notice that she'd been dabbing at her runny nose the whole time.

"He's good for it," Zachariah pushed. "He used to run the same business doing feral hog hunting. Same idea. You could hunt them with just about anything because they were spreading too quickly all over the country. We used to go out machine-gunning the things on weekends. Most legal fun you could ever have."

The bottom fell out because people started importing feral hogs up to other areas where hunters were excited to start the process all over again.

And then soon you had feral hogs ripping through farms like a horde of locusts. They'd breed like rabbits. Local authorities would lift hunting restrictions. People would film themselves hunting with machine guns, and then the whole thing would repeat.

"Zachariah, I really have to get going," Cheryl said. "I have things to do still today."

According to the radio, stocks were up. Lots of companies building new things to deal with the zombie apocalypse. Construction was up. Walls, moats, shatterproof windows, heavy doors. The hardware stores were doing well. Everyone was taking out second mortgages or maxing out their credit cards.

CEOs reported that things had never been better. The NASDAQ at new highs. S&P 500 hitting new records.

A shambling corpse stepped onto the road. Cheryl screamed and swerved. Never swerve, she thought, her car insurance agent told her that. Just hit it dead on and keep moving. Call the 1-800 number on the back when you got home.

Do not park the car in the garage, leave it at the end of the driveway.

Dale always mocked her fuel-efficient hybrid. Maybe he was right, maybe she needed a big pickup that could climb over a zombie and keep going.

The edge of their two acres needed spikes. And Cheryl needed Dale to dig a moat. She'd called about the steel shutters, but they were back-ordered three weeks.

Funny, the magazines Dale had all featured heavy weaponry. But nothing about ditch-digging and defensive features.

Cheryl dug a hole near the Japanese maple at the property marker. Garfield's favorite spot. He'd sit there and watch the road, waiting for them to come along the curve, then race his way out to the driveway to pace the car up to the garage.

She wept as she returned to the car and pulled the still form out from the trunk. Garfield's body sagged in her arms as she walked out over to the grave and slid him in.

"You deserved better," she said to her dog.

The zombies came through two weeks later. They wore brand-new camo, and many of them had vests with the logo for Randy's new zombie sightseeing company on them.

"Figures," Cheryl muttered as she looked out her non-shuttered windows at the undead running across her lawn, ripping up the daisies and boxwoods. "DALE!"

Zim started barking up a storm downstairs. Dale shouted at the dog. Then the dog shrieked and Dale ran up the stairs, eyes wide.

"Safe," he gasped.

She kept a shotgun by the bed, always at the ready, since Garfield died. Cheryl aimed it down the stairs and fired.

Dale came back with a smile and an AR-15.

Together they stood on the landing and gunned the creatures lurching up the stairs apart, one by one, until the walls dripped with gore, the banister fell over, and the stairs creaked with the weight of the dead.

When it was all over, Cheryl sat in the ruination of her carefully remodeled kitchen.

"We fucking crushed it," Dale shouted, getting himself a bottle of bourbon and stepping over a corpse.

Cheryl shook her head. "Dale, I'm tired of this."

Why did it have to be so hard? Why couldn't they all work together? Why was she sitting here surrounded by all these bodies, her dogs dead, when there had been perfectly good soldiers surrounding the town earlier?

Dale wouldn't get it. He'd just won. And where was Cheryl going to go? Fucking Europe? She was an American. Her family was here. Her friends were here, her community was here.

Cheryl sighed and grabbed a mop. Tonight she'd clean. Tomorrow, she'd talk to the bank about a zombie disaster relief loan so they could start rebuilding the house, even though they were already up to their eyeballs in debt.

Maybe it was time to buy a little UTD stock.

THE BRAIN DUMP

BRUCE STERLING

Of you internet world people, many know our new bad troubles here in Ukraine. Beloved cool techno-culture center "Izolyatsia" is seized by ethnic rebels in city of Donetsk. Armed separatists get real drunk, bust up the art gallery, carry off all our favorite 3D printers. No nice gadgets left in Izolyatsia now, just land mines.

We are independent digital culture center from Frunze, Hirske, Borivske (careful not mentioning exact village where we live). In our "Brain Dump" hackerspace we are underground alternative freeware hack scene. Total do-it-yourself. Share everything, build own desks from old packing crates. Way into Linux, Wikipedia, and Instructables. Every day we learn something good from internet community.

In Brain Dump we have broadband, so we are watching cool videos from motherboard.vice.com. We see on *Motherboard* that Iraqis, Mexicans, and Syrians getting shot up and bombed even worse than us. We are grateful to explain ourselves on much-respected *Vice* classy website backed by Intel.

Because we are open-source freaks, no cash, also no real jobs, we settle inside dead rubber-tire factory where we "borrow" electricity from local nuke plant. We listen to streaming techno and metal, coding a lot, smoking cannabis, and never go into a church. So we are called "decadent" by repressive Russian-Orthodox militia of Donetsk People's Republic. Not looking good.

Also, Ukrainian National Guard will probably blow up our hacklab with artillery strikes or chopper missiles. Brain Dump is rusty old concrete bunker with young men in and out at any time day and night, to carry big package of laptops also beer. Therefore Brain Dump fits ideal drone surveillance profile for terrorist headquarters. Sure to get blasted by authorities with no warning and no civil rights.

Too late we Ukraine hackers regret our growing fame and high public profile online. During Euromaidan, we broke into the secret services of the former president of the guardhouse and stole all their Chinese and Korean wiretapping equipment. After that, many Western hippies hacker come to visit us and share the cool knowledge. Chaos Computer Club, Icelandic Pirate Party, Lebanese cypher scene. These fun guys really help us in our creative art projects.

Richard Stallman, too. He is our hero. Stallman does not visit our Brain Dump hackerspace, because he refuses to use Google Maps on principle. But Richard Stallman sends much helpful email clarifying important ideological differences between the "GNU" and the "Linux."

In our paramilitary emergency, even the great Richard Stallman cannot help us. He is a prophet of a better world, Richard Stallman. This is his job. If only we could roam the whole world as him, to preach intellectual freedom for creative coders as us. We have hair as long as Richard Stallman but we have no passports. No money. No guns. No lawyers, either. We are stuck inside "NovoRossiya" of angry separatist region of east Ukraine with new roadblocks onto every bridge. It's like sad emoticon.

We collect in the Brain Dump to discuss our crisis, we are stockpiling water in plastic jugs, also stealing a new generator. Crisis committee is me, also "Objekt110," "Uroboros," "Gray Turtle," "Nashie," and "PizzaHutFan." "Turla," and "AgentBTZ" busy at day of work at a computer repair shop. Also two girls from our digital culture group are gone to Femen rally cutting up icons with chain saws.

The dark truth of our grim situation do not require a lot of discussion on us. Everyone agrees it's likely fatal. In our national tragedy, our hacker club of internet freedom are only sane people left around. Being hip 4chan hackers and LOLcats, we have always been considered craziest people in our village. Now the world turns. We hackers are only remaining source of common sense.

Madness is at every hand. Unbelievable! Ukrainians of our sleepy eastern province are best known as the grumpy wheat farmers and boozy coal miners. When their TV is turned off and no police around, these normal Ukraine people get plenty weird. Not one shred of reality not to be found inside their heads. Daily life is like rave party of hallucinations bad trip Slavic political extremism. Even harmless old kerchief-head Grandma is a terrorist, fascist, and also World War Two Stalinist. New words of Cyrillic political abuse unknown to Latin alphabet, like "zionazi" and "liberast."

The modern telecommunication is no help to these people. Forget that. Never heard of useful hacker sites like GitHub and Source-Forge. Instead they use social media stupid computer illiterate mobiles! Everybody's fingers busy to send each other bloody scary pix of imaginary enemies!

Never heard of Photoshop, so they believe every thing they see! Blond Baltic sniper girls two meters high. Obama Predator UFOs. Kremlin Little Green Men with virus weapons. All accredited journalists who check any facts are arrested as spies and beaten up by factions. Also trolls and Black propagandists pouring fire on rumors machine to panic normal people in their pathetic simplicity.

Of course, hackers, so we know what a "meme" is. We swiftly

create useful fact-check WikiLeaks site for the public good, upload it, get own URL. We coder brainy guys are good at math, have critical thinking skills. No one notices us except Canadian teenage girls doing high school homework. It is already too late. Facts are dead, truth is over. Civil war life is glorious poetry!

Ghosts rise up from dark earth of Ukraine. Cossacks with crests and shaved heads. Tragic serf bards with balalaika and long mustaches. Heroic militia commander unfortunate personal friendship with Adolf Hitler. Every dead Ukraine hero, except for long-forgotten Nestor Makhno, who is total wild free anarchist with steam trains and therefore only national hero Ukrainian hackers actually like.

Ukraine is the largest nation in Europe, vast horizons, wide blue rivers, pretty girls with penchant for sweet flowers hairstyles, also the world's largest national park wilderness, which is also slightly radioactive. But in spite of our great national wealth and splendor, fierce popular cyberwar exploding all over Twitter, VKontakte, LiveJournal, YouTube, and Facebook.

Looks like we brainy hackers will soon be drafted, put in homemade fake uniform, and forced to shoot each other. The situation quickly splitting up on the ground, as good pals "Uroboros" and "Nashie" will have to shoot besties "PizzaHutFan" and "Turla." Game Over for our hacker club.

We decide to dismantle our cultural center and go into hiding. Only real choice for us, and besides, this is typical history of avant-garde culture in our region. Destruction of our beloved club is not difficult as Brain Dump is scavenged furniture, leaking roof, bare insulation stripped much wiring, tube TVs, and aging Linux PC without any consoles. No one in the three years we ever cleans up the Brain Dump, except for "Kimchi" and "XFox," our two Femen girls who are big fans of anime video chat, have to make things look nice for fans.

We decide to collect electronics and hide it place safe from

240mm artillery rounds. As we remove the fluorescent light tubes as valuable for future use, "Gray Turtle" makes a strange discovery. One of the glass tubes has a secret obstacle inside.

Someone has put a dense roll of fifty U.S. hundred-dollar bills inside this secret place. Cache is five thousand dollars, this is incredible find, as Ukrainian hacker could live a year on that kind of money even with girlfriend.

How has a huge amount of money fall into the Brain Dump hackerspace? We consider discovered dollar bills closely. Did they leave here by an American spy? No, some of the bills are counterfeit, like most in Ukraine. American CIA spies not big users of those.

Maybe some rich hippies left money to annoy us as joke. Maybe, some of them act on weird humor of Chaos Computer Club, as they are German and therefore just not funny.

We stop arguing about how to divide the money. We are looking for more money hidden around.

We are anarchists of immaterial cyberspace, never ask for money. Cash just gets in way of our spiritual journey. Also, Ukrainian hryvnia is not a currency in order to provoke a lot of enthusiasm. We find no hryvnia. Not one hryvn. But there are whole lots of dollars stuffed inside round metal chair legs. Euros hidden inside panels of cheap hollow door. Hundreds of dollars stuffed into electrical junction boxes. Thousands of euros crammed secret into wall sockets of telephone jacks. Also some rubles, Swiss francs, and sums of Asian currency we can't recognize.

We start to quarrel about this. Fantastic black-money situation is like from Bulgakov novel, not really helping our situation. Argument is that one of us in Brain Dump is clearly superspy or master cybercriminal. Must be one of us hackers who is hiding the money from the rest of us and secretly amazing rich guy.

One by one, everyone is denying paranoid purge allegations.

"Gray Turtle" is most suspicious as he was first to discover money, but Gray Turtle cannot possibly be any master cybercriminal as he is mere website designer, cannot even code properly.

"Objekt110" admits he has been selling "Phoenix" and "Adrenalin" trojans to Western teenagers, but only on weekends. "Uroboros" is picking up some fraud credit card traffic with "eCore Exploit Pack," but just buys cute shoes for girlfriend. "Nashie" is console game cracker, but he is seventeen years old so this is just kid stuff.

"PizzaHutFan" is running proxy server host on cracked machine at local university. "AgentBTZ" is small-time DDOS operative on local Zeus botnet, just does it as favor for uncle.

I have to admit my part in "Lonely Russian Girlfriend" 419 fraud, but I was only doing that to improve my English on foreigners. By standard of local computer underground we are very clean guys.

Also, search for illicit Ukrainian hidden money is just not ending for us. Not at all. I am counting over well USD one hundred thousand in small and crumpled bills, and now bond and stock certificates are show up among old and water-stained O'Reilly coding books. Shell companies in Cyprus, Luxembourg, Cayman Islands, Switzerland. Our humble hackerspace has several title deeds to real estate properties in London. Also, New York real estate from well-known offshore laundering scheme of "Anna Chapman" famous Russian television star and hot high-tech entrepreneur girl.

At this point we are ransacking our own place worst than armed militia. "Gray Turtle" remembers the thumb drives. Being hackerspace we have a thousand USB drives, mostly bad mp3s of pirate American scifi TV and YouPorn downloads.

These USB drives have been replaced with "TAILS" anonymized crypto pre-loaded with control over legendary "Snake" Cyrillic cyberwar botnet. "Snake" is top-notch cyberspy code embedded in so many Russian and Ukrainian systems that Edward Snowden choke on his borscht.

User logs show that cyberwar "Snake" is all about black money. "Snake" subroutines are all about trade misinvoicing, sales of under-priced gas and oil to false European subsidiaries, under-reported export earnings, and fake advanced import payments. Big-scale global money laundering is pretty new to us, but surprisingly easy and simple compared to Linux coding. Everything on pull-down menu.

We are rich. We have as much illegal wealth as usual corrupt Ukrainian state politician. We have illegal fortune between three and ten billion dollars.

We were thinking all along we were helpless victims of situation, but truth is now clear to us. We are internet people, but also major part of the problem. We are serious power player, frankly. We can do anything internet black global money can do, buy media, hire liars, recruit mercenaries, ship weapons, buy own private jet get the hell out go live in Costa Rica.

We're just like the "Gas Princess" and the "Chocolate King." We're oligarchs. We're moguls.

But how does that help us? The fires are rising all around us anyway. We can give you a million dollars if you have any answer. What do we do?

VIRTUAL SNAPSHOTS

TLOTLO TSAMAASE

Thirteen years ago, when I was three years old, the sky used to be a clean blue, curving outward to meet the horizon. The sun was a bright burning spot and the stars candles in the night. Men's hearts weren't oiled in evil. The shift from day to darkness was seamless, dividing activities. It hadn't rained for so long that all the water stored for the Harvest, as the time was called, was insufficient. Our villages survived on an Aquaculture system, tending to the water-creatures to cultivate the food we needed. The dome had been created to protect us from the destructive environment we had orchestrated. It was a righting time.

The day it rained, we were shaken. The sound of a bomb exploded above us. First we thought the sun was dying, sending flames to torch our world. But the dome had shattered. Instead of shards of glass, soft drops of water soaked the cracked earth and moistened our bare feet. We screamed, "Pula! Pula!" The children ran into the heavy drizzle, mouths open to the sky. I remember that first taste of rain: exotic, addictive. Dangerous. We didn't know what we were drinking then. We were delighted: Old women ululated while sweeping the ground with Setswana brooms. The paranoid ones got their metal bathtubs out to collect this last hope of survival.

It was the transformation from the old world to DigiWorld.

(I)

Now:

It has been seven hundred and thirty days since I left the house.

Two years.

Well, physically.

Our joints are painful due to immobility. No praying in the mosque, legs dusted by a beg for God. A god composed of zeros and ones, face etched in lines of lightning, the moon his nose, an impression of cloud in sky.

Our physical selves are latched to glass pistons by way of plastic tubes feeding medicine into our narrow veins. Machines beep our lives across limbs of time. We sleep in dark home-cells, little bulbs lighting our prison, and sweep through the door in our avatar versions.

These are things we are told in order to remain in safety's skin. Abide the laws. If you wake, do not detach yourself. If you pain, do not bend to relief. If you itch, do not scratch. In us, our souls are halos, waning, flickering—the light gone.

I can't remember the last time my skin was brown. Outside Digi-World, it is expensive to maintain our health, which is why when we partially disconnect we must pay fees to keep us breathing.

But, today I must leave. A message had slipped into my visual settings:

Older sister: Hela wena! Mama is unwell. Get here now. Outside DigiWorld, you know she ain't connected.

Me: The minute I step out of this door, I will need funds to sustain me in the environment outside of my house.

Older sister: Chill, sisi wame, we will compensate you for your travels and your life. You are still family, mos.

Pfft. Family, se voet! They kicked me out and never kept in touch. I've been living in a servants' quarter for years.

If I hide behind these walls I won't see the thing they talk about: Mama's pregnancy. It could be her death. I will regret my life if I don't see her.

(11)

I have a few financial units that will last me on my journey. I push open the door. Stars fall in streams of light, soft as rain. Slate-blue eyes mock the beauty of the sky.

Botswana. I don't want to denote it the common cliché term "hot and arid" because I hate to be another stereotype of limited description. It's landlocked. It's suffocated. It's variety. It reminds me of the ocean, not in the literal sense, but like the ocean it has borderlines you can't see. We understand technology. We sit at computers and understand what we type. Our cars are not donkey carts. Our houses have corners, and we don't have lions or animals of the wild parading the city center, but some men are more beast than human.

The rank is a chortling beast, fattening out into the city. A vendor scrambles to me, holding rotten goods to my face. "You want, sisi?"

A rumbling, croaking noise alarms the state constituents to waking. Sun alarm. The sun creaks. Creaking, creaking, creaking—machinery screws, pipes twist, grinded by laborious mine-worker hands. Sunrises, sunsets beg to be heard.

Why were my sunlight rations depleted? Hadn't I been in line yesterday to escape the rise in sunlight prices, effective today?

I'm close to my mother's residence, a place of warmth. A place I was thrown out from because I had reached the age of independency—because I was not from her womb. I had to fend for myself, a pariah unfit for their royal homestead.

(III)

My mother is an anomaly in this society. She's one of those rare women who hold babies in their bodies instead of storing the to-be-born children in the Born Structure that sits in the center of the city, its apex a dagger to the sky. The Born Structure processes who'll be born and who'll die. It's how I was born, shaped by glass and steel. Unlike others, the lucky ones, I've never felt Mama's heartbeat close to my face.

My sister swore to me that Mama's current baby will last in the womb forever. "Sisi, I swear—nxu s'tru—that baby is not coming out," she'd said a few months ago, in her oft-confident tone.

I'd grazed passed her, muttering, "Mxm, liar."

"Come on, you're only jealous that you didn't get the chance to bloma in Mama's womb," she'd said. "You know I'm right, just admit it."

So I'd kicked her in the shin and run.

She'd pointed a finger like she was bewitching me: "Jealous one," she'd sworn. That was the last time I saw her.

Mama has been pregnant for a year this time. Water is her church. Baptismal, if you think about it—crawling back to God.

I enter our horseshoe-shaped settlement, bypassing the compounds into our own made of concrete and sweat and technology no one knows.

"Dumelang!" the family members shout in greeting.

I used to think that before I was born, Mama and Papa probably spat fire on my skin and rubbed warm-beige of fine sandy-desert soil to give it color, and in particular hand gestures added dung-shit—for I'm not pure—to drive away malevolent spirits, insect-demons.

But I am not born. I am a manufacture of the Born Structure.

"Jealous one," Sisi greets me, guarding the doorway. "Howzit?"

"S'cool," I whisper. "Where's Mama?"

"Hae, she can't see you now. Just put your gifts by the fire."

I don't move.

"Ao, problem?" she asks.

"Yazi, it took me my last units—the last money I have to get here, and you won't let me see her," I say through gritted teeth.

"Haebo! It's not my fault you're some broke-ass—"

I pull at my earlobes to tune her out. This means I am not allowed to stay the night here. My presence will jinx Mama's condition.

"Can you at least loan me some cash?" I ask. "I don't have enough to sustain me when I get home. Leaving home and disconnecting activated my spending. *You know* there is no deactivation."

Her smile tells me it was the plan all along. "Then you'll be prepared for death. Your reputation dilutes our family name's power. You understand why you must leave."

I don't understand how a sister I grew up playing games with hates me that much. I don't know when she disowned me—when she stopped thinking of me as a sibling to look up to. Is it just because I'm not her biological sister? That I'm a bastard shame in the family?

"Leave, as in . . . forever?"

I can't run to anywhere. I don't know how.

(IV)

When I leave, Mama is still too unwell to see anyone besides my older sister, the gifted one who lived in her womb for nine months. Mxm.

So, Sisi stands by the door, waving, with a huge grin plastered to her face. "Hamba, jealous one."

The moonlight bleaches the village into a shockingly ghostly white. Air eases out from my lungs. My oxygen levels are slowly depleting. My sky is dead, but the blue ceiling is a magnet. Our thoughts, words, and feelings evaporate from our minds like torn birds pulled by that magnetic force, and they light up the sky.

Our stars are composed of ourselves.

Maybe tonight when Mama looks at the night sky she'll see me watching her.

On the way home I pass through a nearby village. In one house with the green corrugated roof, three women sit in the sitting room, their soles bruised with black marks.

"Heh Mma-Sekai," shouts one. "I tell you, a child born with one leg that's similar to the father's and the other leg that's similar to another man's won't walk. S'tru." True. The woman crosses her fingers, a sign to God. "Sethunya's child hasn't walked for years. I'm not surprised. Woman sleeps around. You don't believe? These things happen, sisi."

"Ah, don't say." One claps her manicured hands. "Surely they can download software to update the child's biological software," the other says.

Twins—one an albino with pinkish copper-brown hair—and one pulls a younger girl from the sitting room onto the stoep.

"Hae! If I see you jumping the fence again, you will know me!" shouts their mother as their shoulders shrink. She gapes when she notices me. I am the child with legs from different men. I raise the middle finger. When will everyone stop gossiping about my family? So we aren't rich enough to buy all these gadgets to change our body size, our ethnicity, our hair—but we're poor enough to know true happiness is not bought. We're also poor enough to throw out one of our children because she wasn't born naturally. We're poor to not even care about that child, about the years that crawled into her sad heart because her father was an illicit man.

"Shem, and she's still so young," one woman whispers.

"Kodwa, would it make it right if I was too old to take in this crap?" I want to ask, but I keep walking with my head folded into my chest.

The sky tenses, pisses, a hiss of warm. Air humid-empty. My lips press tight to my wrist to check the moisture. My water levels are too low. Low tear supply. There's only a few hours before the sun temporarily dies. Before I die, too.

(V)

When I get home, the skin needs a scrub. But I let my scents accumulate so I won't forget the skin I wear. So I remember the mother who used to cradle me and sing lullabies. I will miss her.

Just when the sunlight begins to turn gold, the rain obscures the night-sky eyes into an eerie grayness. When my grandmother was still alive I used to ask her, "Nkuku, does the sky hurt and bleed like humans?"

She looked up from her knitted blanket. Wrinkles laced the contours of her face like rippled water. "The sky is the predator. All animals are humans but some humans are inanimate," she said. She was the only one in our family who loved me.

(VI)

I wake to noise blaring in my mind. How many megabytes of memory space will be depleted just to contact those bloody, poor-serviced customer lines?

Very well, psychomail it is:

file report 22

Thought #53897

Subject complaint: Skin malfunction; does not detect sun.
Pre-requisite water levels contained in lungs reaching 53%.

Sent! Please hold for the next available customer adviser. All
networks are busy. In case of emergency, please hold on to
the nearest human for self-powering, explaining clearly your
predicament to avoid violence and he/she shall be compensated
within 7 days. Solar Power Corporations appreciates your
patience. Goodbye.

A second is not long enough to send a message to Mama, to tell
her, despite what's happened, I still love them all—my family. That is
the only regret I have: no one to say "I love you" to. No one to breathe
my soul into. I cling to desperation halfway out the door as if a miracle will split the skies and save me. My neighbor half waves from her
stoep until she realizes what's happening. Her tear is the last grace I
feel.

It is too late to remain alive.

In three seconds I am dead.

THE RIVER

TORI CÁRDENAS

First we were banned from holding positions of public office, then from public-sector jobs, from public housing, from government benefits, from education. Every day the news brought more restrictions, until the tagline that ran along the bottom of the screen read, "All Immigrant Visa Holders to be Relocated to Secure Holding Facilities, Processed for Deportation." Men in black suits reached into our homes with their long thin fingers and dropped us into "Community Housing" on the edges of the map.

Daniel and I are married, but his citizenship couldn't protect me by proxy anymore; the document for our marriage was now officially void. And we knew what it meant to be "relocated." Separation, segregation, subjugation. So, for some time before, we had been planning our escape. We just hadn't started planning soon enough.

This wasn't home anymore, with the fusion restaurants, or holding hands as we walked down electric streets. But we didn't have enough money for two tickets. I would have helped pay, but it had been a long time since I was allowed to work.

One day I received a letter in the mail. The heavy black envelope read, "Bonifacio Alto." I couldn't even open it. My hands shook so badly when Daniel asked to see it that I dropped the envelope and started to cry.

"Don't worry, Boni," Daniel said, tearing it open and reading the first page. "I'm going to be right behind you."

He drove me to the docks late one night, about the time we usually had dinner. There was a ship taking about two thousand of us back to Brazil. The sun had gone down and groups of people were saying their goodbyes in the foggy light streaming over from the city. Children and parents and grandparents and friends and lovers, whispering and holding each other for what, as far as they knew, was the last time. Daniel kissed me goodbye and promised he would be only a few weeks behind me.

The ship cut through the silver and black and took me halfway across the world to a land I hadn't seen with adult eyes. All I had were my mother's stories of the jungle, and the lazy green river that slithered its way through, full of reptiles and rainbow-scaled fish, and a disease called cholera. I was expecting monkeys and tall trees that shaded the forest floor from the sun.

It was early in the morning, and the sun shone pink and yellow on the water. At the docks in Rio de Janeiro, I met up with my cousin Javier. I hadn't seen him since I was four and I didn't recognize him. We had the same nose and head of curly black hair, but we didn't have anything else in common. If we did, we lacked the language to talk about it.

He took me to breakfast, then we rode the train inland to where we were born, where he grew up. Train stations were built into the basements of buildings and smelled damp and murky. The trains were fast, the walls shook slightly when they went past. When we stepped off the platform to our stop, we dipped into a small café for cups of steaming tea that smelled like curry. He walked me around the neighborhood, which looked updated, clean, angular.

He told me all about how the city worked. The residential buildings are usually the ones bordering the river, he said. If everyone has a view of the river, then prices stay low and everyone gets to live with a view of the water. Here, the buildings lining the river had balconies, a few with umbrellas, a few with grills, or small curly-haired dogs barking. The river ran tiny and green beneath them.

This was not the serpent of a river from my mother's stories. It was a trickle of water lost in a jungle of concrete.

When couples marry, they amble down the streets for their honeymoons and stay in the hotels and travel up the river until they get tired and they settle down there. My wife and I settled a few miles downriver, and we visit my parents here often.

Javier's English wasn't very good and neither was my Portuguese, so I just listened and nodded.

While we were on the last leg of our trip, waiting for the twelve o'clock train, Javier led me into a side alcove of the station. There was an aquarium built into it, an AUXILIARY RIVER RESEARCH FACILITY. It was dark, mostly lit by blacklights, and there were slimy white and gray fish clustered in every observation window. Their eyes stared out milky and useless in the darkness of the river. They were ugly, and they looked sad, their long rubbery whiskers reaching out to feel the cold thick glass.

A well-dressed group of children were on a field trip with a fussy woman who must have been their teacher.

A field researcher in a black skintight scuba suit said, "Children, gather over here, please, we are about to take the sediment sample."

He put on a large bubble of a helmet with a microphone built into it, snapped the seals into place over his neck, and stepped into a door that shut with a large steel wheel that could be turned from both sides. All the while, he explained the functions of his equipment, what tubes were for oxygen and which buttons for which flashlights, how the seals inside the door protected the walls of the structure from leaks and floods. When he had sealed it behind him, he opened a second door and was released into the river. The children gasped and stared through the small window by the door through which the man had disappeared. The room where he had been moments before flooded with murky water.

"The river is all that has not yet died or been destroyed," the diver's voice said over an intercom. "Well, besides us."

The children laughed. He dove down farther and farther, flicking on more flashlights, his camera live-streamed to a large monitor for us to watch.

"The Amazon River is still the world's largest drainage basin, and is stretching deeper and deeper into the earth. And with that, it is generating some of the most diverse adaptations modern science has ever seen." Grimy white crocodiles and blind mudfish crawled left and right, shying away from the researcher's white flashlights. "Crocodiles have almost completely lost their color due to no exposure to light, and many creatures have lost their sense of sight altogether."

Javier pulled my arm. The train was here. We presented our tickets and climbed aboard.

Javier stretched out on two train seats and pulled out a photo from his wallet. It was a picture of him and his wife from their wedding. He was about ten years younger. Daniel and I had been married about the same time.

Do you have a wife in America?

I didn't know how to answer him. Not in Portuguese. I didn't know how to say, *I'm terrified for Daniel for helping me to escape.* I didn't know how to tell him, *Daniel is my husband.* I didn't know how to say, *They're torturing him right now, or he's in prison, or he's already dead.* I didn't know how to say, *I'll never see him again.* The idioms and euphemisms I knew didn't work the same in the language they spoke here.

I shook my head and the train pushed on.

It has been eight months and sixteen days since I arrived here. I am still working in my cousin's bodega. I clean things up and restock the shelves. I'm picking up little bits of Portuguese from listening to the mothers talk to their babies in the aisles while I'm mopping or stacking mangoes. I understand enough to know when Javier's wife was yelling at him to get me off their couch and into my own apartment. Before he worked up the nerve to ask me in his broken English, I found a tiny studio downriver. Now I can watch reruns of *Friends* on my tiny television in peace.

But the thing is, I still don't feel like I belong in this country. The city stretches out forever on both sides of the river, almost as far as I can see, a path of streetlights meandering through the desert dunes that used to be the Amazon rain forest. In some places, wide, squat soccer stadiums and dense concentrations of office buildings branch off from the highways that run parallel to the river. All of that sand and all of that city, and it feels like you could walk forever along the rigid banks of flood-proof buildings, until maybe you would finally walk right into the desert and sink down into the sand.

Sand—for miles and miles and miles—sand. That is what I can see from my apartment's one tiny window. Sand on one side and the city on the other, no river to speak of. Javier and his wife have a view and balcony because both of them work.

I've tried to blend into the crowds that walk or take the train up and down the curves of the city on the river, to get to different boroughs, the ones where they grew up or started raising their families. I'm trying to stay hopeful that Daniel is on his way, that someday soon he'll call me and tell me everything is going to be all right, that he's safe, that he's getting on a boat or a plane to come and find me.

But until then, I walk through a station with an aquarium every day, to watch the pale crocodiles with no more muddy banks to sun themselves on, bottom-feeding and adapting to their new environment, their eyes whiting over with the darkness.

HYPERCANE

ERIC HOLTHAUS

". . . to Montauk, Long Island, effective until eight p.m. Sunday. Repeating, the National Weather Service has issued a hypercane warning from Ocean City, Maryland, to Montauk, Long Island, effective until eight p.m. Sunday."

The radio crackled to life in the cab of the big Ford superduty EV, and then it was silent. Just as well.

Mariana preferred to ride in quiet as the self-driving truck did its thing, and though she'd long been fascinated with the weather, she felt herself tuning out as the automated warning was broadcast through the sound system. At first, in the early 2030s, the new "hypercane" designation for superstrong Category 5 hurricanes riddled her with fear each time one approached the coast. This time, the hype surrounding the storm was just annoying. She had work to do.

And, of course, she was headed inland anyway. The state police had reversed the direction of the eastbound lanes of Interstate 70, like they always did for these sorts of storms, and she was joined on the highway by a convoy of vehicles of all shapes and sizes: mostly families from the Baltimore suburbs, all headed toward the foothills of the Appalachians in western Maryland, where the fast-growing cities of Frederick and Hagerstown welcomed them with open arms.

Every time a hurricane like this hit, fewer and fewer of the storm-weary coasties decided to make the return trip.

🔥

Mariana glanced to the left, and then pressed her forehead against the Ford's side window. She could barely make out the grimy, hulking frame of the coal plant, the R. Paul Smith Power Station. The eerie and distinctive pale crimson glow of the plant's carbon scrubbers surrounded the complex in a mile-wide orb. She suddenly felt sick to her stomach, knowing that the next several hours could define the rest of her career.

She'd heard from a colleague who was tracking a plant in Maine, during a recent power failure, that something may be up with those scrubbers—designed and manufactured by EnviroCorp to suck planet-cooking carbon out of the sky, and now found outside of just about any major pollution source in the country. He'd told her he'd noticed some strange readings that may indicate a significant amount of carbon dioxide was actually escaping through EnviroCorp's carbon scrubbers. Strangely, she hadn't heard from him since.

When the forecast for a rapidly intensifying hurricane first hit the newswires on Tuesday, she'd enlisted a few dozen of her friends and coworkers—anyone she could trust, really—to see if they could help her find out more on the off chance any of the scrubbers lost power during the storm. Tonight, all across the Northeast, there'd be data collected near EnviroCorp scrubbers to see what, exactly, they were hiding.

She didn't plan on this week's storm reaching hypercane status, but, really, she wasn't that surprised. That made, what, three years in a row now?

She hadn't brought much with her, just her tablet, a spectrographic camera, a data logger, and a few other pieces of equipment. She could make do living out of a suitcase for a little while. The bigger question was whether or not the university, which was much closer to sea level than her apartment building, would be there when she got back. They'd already begun relocating some of her academic programs to Hagerstown last year.

Inside the power plant, EnviroCorp officials were finishing up a weather briefing before finalizing their emergency shutdown procedures. The carbon scrubbers were the tricky part: The electrostatic field generators at the core of the capture devices were especially sensitive to wind speeds above 150 miles per hour, the plant operators had learned, so this storm would be a good test.

They were running with a skeleton crew this evening, as most of the plant's functions were automated. The assistant plant manager, Lucas Boyd, was in charge for the time being. He'd been the one to suggest beefed-up security during the storm, owing to the uncertainties with the scrubbers, and his supervisors had been wise enough to agree.

Out the window, he could see a team of two armed guards making their rounds along the plant's perimeter, their silhouettes outlined in crimson. The glow from the scrubbers made it difficult for his detail to move around in the open without being easily seen, but not being seen wasn't really the point if your job was to hold a military-grade laser rifle.

Boyd was a student of history. If illegal intruders forced his hand—again—a little show of force wouldn't hurt, especially with so many coasties in town. The coastal districts were a big source of political support for EnviroCorp, after all, and the big climate mitigation funding renewal currently under consideration in Congress was still under debate. *Even in the dark times of the storm, our commitment to fighting climate change must persist,* he'd said in the press release earlier that day. *That's why we can't allow any disturbance, any slack in the system, even now.*

In hindsight, he thought, the landmark bipartisan carbon tax swap deal in 2024 helped make this sort of thing possible. After the U.S. eliminated all corporate taxes and launched its "Greening America" initiative—which essentially turned every smokestack and tailpipe in the country into a profit opportunity—EnviroCorp quickly grew from a niche company to a bedrock of political power. Coal plants shuttered decades ago, like Boyd's, were restarted with a promise that they'd be emissions-free. Even better: The scrubbers EnviroCorp sold would be carbon-negative—literally sucking CO_2 out of the air. It was a win-win.

As a result, official data showed America's net carbon emissions were in a free fall, even all these years later. According to the data.

For every ton of carbon dioxide EnviroCorp kept out of the sky, it made approximately a hundred dollars. That may not sound like much, but it added up, and fast. They'd learned their lesson from the Volkswagen case long ago: With EnviroCorp proprietary software tracking scrubbers at every plant, every factory, every highway in the U.S.—that's a lot of carbon credits. Hundreds of billions of dollars' worth each year.

Boyd looked out the window with just a hint of anxiety. He also knew what every EnviroCorp executive knew: They'd been gaming the system for decades now, buying political influence along the way until their reign over the American economy was virtually unquestioned. Sure, global carbon emissions hadn't yet peaked, but EnviroCorp was *on it.* He called security and told them to be extra-vigilant. Just for good measure.

". . . winds in excess of two hundred miles per hour. All window shields and domestic surge barriers should be activated at this time. Repeating, an evacuation order is in effect for Zones A and B, including the cities of Philadelphia and New York City. Those choosing to stay should be prepared for . . ."

That damn thing again.

As night fell, Mariana directed her Ford toward an old forest road at the edge of the coal plant's property. As the truck crossed a triple set of train tracks, she could see the freight train cars lined up, loaded with Appalachian coal, ready to be tossed into the power station's inferno. Though this particular plant was now nearly a century old, occasional retrofits had kept it operating, with a brief pause in the mid-2010s during that period of uncertainty before the United States decided to become a "world leader" on climate change.

She scoffed, thinking about how the political rhetoric had changed since then. Everyone was so much more cynical now that it was clear humanity wasn't going to get through the century without some serious planetary shit going down. That blip of joyous optimism was long gone. Now EnviroCorp got paid to tell us everything was going to be all right.

This was the place. And tonight was the night.

"Headlights off," she said. She'd have to go this final stretch in near-darkness, though her eyes were already adjusting to the crimson world around her. Those damn scrubbers.

She remembered how cold and scared she felt after she and her father—and just she and her father—swam to safety when Hurricane Margaret flooded her childhood home in Jersey City back in 2026, and shuddered. She hoped this weekend's storm wouldn't spawn similar nightmares for other kids, but she knew better. She told herself, for the thousandth time, to block that night from her memory.

If one of the plant's scrubbers went down, even for a minute, it could prove once and for all that the core of the country's corporate carbon-sucking program was a scam. This was a chance to set the record straight. As the scrubber was shutting down, if she was close enough, she'd be able to get through the coal plant's carbon firewall and extrapolate their effectiveness to thousands of others like this across the country. A hypercane provided the perfect opportunity.

The Ford came to a halt. She'd have to get a line-of-sight view of the entire complex, and the scrubber core as well. The trees would provide some cover, but as long as the scrubbers were running, everything around her was bathed in a pale red glow. She put on a thermal suit to block her heat signature, and to keep off the rain.

She heard footsteps, and swung around to see a family of deer. She loved being in the woods, but goddamn it, not tonight.

As she walked through the forest, her breathing echoed in her ears, dulled only slightly at this close range by the suit's sound-canceling feature. It took only a few minutes to come to the top of a small hill, where she could see the entire plant below. She hit record on the camera, and switched on the data logger.

Overhead, lightning began to crackle, and the wind began to pick up. And then, suddenly, the entire world went black.

Rrrrrrrreeeeeee Rrrrrrrreeeeeeee Rrrrrrrreeeeeee

"Somebody turn that damn noise off *now!*"

Klaxon sirens blared throughout the power station's small cluster of offices, and Boyd knew he was in trouble. There'd been an anomalous heat signature detected near the perimeter of the campus, and while Boyd was on the phone to dispatch a security team to investigate, the lightning had apparently set up a harmonic interference with the scrubber system and the main core had overloaded. In an instant, practically all the readouts in the plant's control room were pegged into the "critical" zone.

Boyd was furious, but at this point, whatever happened was probably out of his control. Normally the scrubber's AI would have been able to contain the power surge, but these hypercanes were more electrically charged than your everyday thunderstorm.

There was no way to get a tech crew here tonight to put the system back online, so the rest of the plant's functions had gone into emergency shutdown mode. What Boyd didn't notice was that there'd also been a breach in the carbon dioxide containment facility—which, officially, didn't exist. EnviroCorp installed them around the country decades ago, during their initial round of scrubber retrofits, to buy time until they perfected the technology behind the "negative" part of the carbon-negative scrubbers. That time had never come.

But, hey, at least he was right about beefing up security. In just a few seconds, the security team had confirmed an intruder.

"Whoever it is, get 'em."

Mariana's heart raced. Apparently they were shutting the scrubbers down—or . . .

She stared at her camera's spectrographic readout. The bar indicating carbon dioxide was going through the roof. The plant was still running, and something had happened that was allowing carbon dioxide to escape, and in huge amounts. It was almost as if years' worth of stored carbon from this plant was—

It couldn't be.

Her fascination with the data turned almost instantly to anger. By God, if this was happening everywhere—

She switched the data logger into "broadcast" mode. It quickly acquired one, then two, then five satellites—enough for the data to instantly be archived on the web, with no encryption. Someone else besides her would see this, and hopefully be able to figure out what it meant.

In her excitement, she noticed a tear in the suit's sleeve. Almost as suddenly, a bright spotlight shone down on her. It didn't matter. Whatever they'd say or do to her, the data she'd captured was already public knowledge. It was the happiest moment of her life.

ONE THOUSAND CRANES

ZORA MAI QUỲNH

oday I will finish my thousandth paper crane. It has taken me nine months to fold them all. Its body is ice-blue like the sky we painted in Jay's room when he was old enough to reach for the clouds. Across the crane's wings are shimmering waves of turquoise like the gems that were Malia's eyes on our wedding day.

The air is crisper up here—high in the mountains, away from the smoke that blankets all that once was our city. It was only two months ago when I finished the nine hundredth crane. I've slowed down considerably. My fingers are numb and cracked. My nails are beginning to fall off and it's getting harder to create the intricate triangular flaps of the cranes' wings.

Every morning I wake to clumps of my own hair scattered among the fallen twigs and dried leaves of my makeshift bed. Sometimes it's hard to breathe. A pain sears through my chest. I can't tell if it's the altitude biting into my lungs, or the memories of Malia's scent by my side and Jay's hair against my cheek.

By day we climb, by night I fold until the light of the campfire dies—until there is only silence and the sound of my rough fingers against the soft fibers of the paper. I've been told that others in our camp set their watches to the distant shadow of my body, hunched over, diligently folding, each finished crane set in front of me in tiny rows separated by color. A miniature armada.

Two months before my nine hundredth crane, I had finished seven hundred cranes. For those, I had chosen reds and oranges for the fires that had devoured our homes. I should have chosen blues, greens, and whites for the cool air, the rain, the fog. Or even blacks and grays for darkness, some respite from the constant blazing heat. Something to swallow the flames.

But I wasn't sure which colors would grant Jay's wish. And I was out of black and gray origami paper anyway. I had used those all up in the two months prior, when I was working toward my five hundredth crane. That was when I almost lost hope, when I didn't care about all the other people climbing the mountain with me. Didn't care about the elders, the babies, the men and women half bandaged, their skin blistering and their breaths shortened. Didn't care if we ever made it to the top.

It was the cranes before those that marked when my heart had been broken, filled with black and gray. We fled, the three of us like so many others, to the mountains where the air might be cleaner and the smoke lighter. But with every step, Malia and Jay grew weaker. Malia could not see, blinded, she struggled on the rugged terrain. And Jay was so weak. I carried him on my back until one day his weight was so unusually light. That same day, Malia sputtered her last coughful of blood.

When nightfall came, the clouds that seemed to hang ceaselessly overhead hid the stars. It felt like the universe had disappeared and we were alone. Completely alone. I thought I'd never see the stars again. Like I'd never see Malia and Jay again. That night, when I finished my four hundredth crane, I folded two extra cranes and laid them on their graves—one black, one gray.

Two months before that, the three of us had folded the first crane together. A small packet of origami paper—that's all we had left. It was in Jay's backpack along with a half-eaten bar of toffee chocolate. Bandages covered Malia's eyes and it was only her fingers that remembered how to fold the soft paper into clean diagonal lines.

It was the first time Jay had ever seen a folded paper crane. I cried when I told him about a legend my grandmother once shared with me—about how in her home country, people believed that the folder of a thousand cranes would be granted one wish. And then I told him about a little girl named Sadako who had tried to fold a thousand cranes for Japan—for peace after Hiroshima. He wanted to understand.

"Are there bad things in the air now?" he had asked.

"Yes, Jay," I said. Malia reached out and clutched my hand.

"Is that why we're sick? Just like Sadako?"

"Yes, but it's a little different. There are more bad things in the air now," Malia said, her voice was steady where mine shook.

"Did Sadako get her wish? For peace?" Jay's eyes were hopeful.

"Well, for Japan, yes, for a long time there was peace. But for the world . . ." Malia's voice trailed off.

"There has always been war," I completed.

"I want to fold a thousand cranes," Jay said, "I want to make a wish, too."

Sadako exceeded her goal, folding fourteen hundred cranes, before the leukemia took her. But neither of us mentioned this to Jay. Instead I sat silent with Jay on my lap as Malia laid the first piece of origami paper in front of us. I remember it was purple, yellow, and red—the colors for hope. We were in the evacuation center and all around us was chaos. Outside, thick plumes of smoke darkened the windows. Together we folded our first crane, our fingers pressing creases into the soft paper.

The day before we each folded our first crane, the wildfires that have been engulfing the neighboring county leapt across the bridge, flamed by the summer's persistent hot winds, to the refinery.

The day before that was Jay's seventh birthday.

And the day before Jay's seventh birthday, Malia and I sat, our legs and arms intertwined in comfortable entanglement as we gift-wrapped a small packet of origami paper.

ALWAYS HOME
JEFF VANDERMEER

I.

She flowed along on many legs, her rows of eyes raised to the rainforest canopy, alert to incoming data from the layers of life above her. She didn't need to grow eyes to see, and seeing was the most primitive of her sensory inputs. But she was old-fashioned, had cultivated affectations arrived at from her extensive internal library of books. Tomorrow she might grow an eye because the sensation was pleasurable. Or she might not and employ sonar to forsake the surface, to plunge below and tunnel deep, tap into the millions of fungal networks that channeled information worldwide.

At any time, too, she could call up others like her, and some would let her exist behind their mind's eye for a day or a week or a minute. Or she could visit them physically, convert her body for flight, and rise up through the canopy to the raw sunlight above, mindful to harden her epidermis and bring forward up through her pores the photo-sensors that would turn her energy intake solar. It was much hotter and harsher than before.

Today she was low to the ground "in scuttle mode" as she called it, and hurrying to the site of an anomaly. She did not really need to sleep, but it conserved energy to do so. Sometimes she would be in sleep mode for months, so that the deep core of her, the deep spark, could concentrate on, worry at, some philosophical or existential problem. But this morning the wildflowers on her waking had alerted her, as had some faint unclear change in the habits of the ground-dwellers and the flight of certain birds.

A thousand languages traced their way through the forest. She could read them all. While this, too, was pleasurable, it had a purpose. Her job was to be the steward and defender of a vague territory that stretched two hundred miles through the valley, until it met mountains, where another of her kind lived and did the same.

The anomaly became clear just a minute later; a tattered dull green tent made of composite artificial fibers. This the world still could not easily break down. The plastic parts registered in her awareness as an alarm. "Plastic" was a deadly concept passed down from the Old People, and so she knew the source, who lived in the tent. "Tent" was also an antiquated concept, meaning a kind of home, not deadly except in aggregate.

Old People found New People disconcerting, so she paused to become bipedal, to absorb all but two eyes and to create a face with a mouth and a nose. Then she made a sound half-welcoming, half-threatening. It brought the Old Person rushing out from the tent flap, clutching an outdated weapon.

He pointed it at her, aimed, but did not fire.

With half a thought she could cause the atoms of the gun to fuse with the atoms of his hand, or just focus on fired bullets and move her vital organs aside long enough to let them pass through and strike the trees behind her.

It had been a hundred years since an Old Person had managed to kill a New Person. But someone like this had created her kind. Someone like this had had to relinquish control, had to turn a fist into an open, raised palm, and let the seeds blow away in the wind.

"What do you want?" he asked, in one of the old languages.

She disliked those languages. There was only sound to them, along with some small meaning, and they didn't feel good, not in the way of pheromones and spores and the countless other messengers swirling through the air around them both.

"Your home is a hazard, poisonous," she said. "I have to render it down. That is the rule."

If there was one law set down by her creator, it was that all systems, all processes, all technologies, must conform to the framework of a world without human beings in it. Even as human beings still lived in the world.

"I like this tent," he said. "It was my grandmother's." He had not lowered the gun.

Unlikely, she guessed. Was he delusional?

"I must render down your home," she said again.

"I order you to leave me alone," the man said.

He had moss hanging off his face, or something like moss, and more of it hanging from his head down to his shoulders in gray waves. This meant he was aging. She knew it wasn't moss, but in relaying this to her friends it was meant as a kind of joke, because of all the things that hid in moss or got tangled up in moss.

New People humor was very different from Old People humor. It had a different texture, and it brought in a nexus of hundreds of referents. Some of the friends speaking in her head had already expanded the joke to include rivers and vines on trees and explosions of natural trellises and were now chuckling to each other.

"You can take what you need from the tent," she said, "and you may travel through this valley, but your home isn't allowed here."

"You're just a machine." Always, the same refrain.

"I am not a machine." Old People often mistook the genesis of a thing for its reality in the moment. She couldn't blame them for it. Who with only five senses and a reliance on obsolete metal tech could really understand what it meant to be alive? To be sentient.

The Old Person lowered his weapon, and she knew then that he would give in, that he would leave his tent behind and allow her to start biodegrading the tent. That he might give up his gun, too, and wander then through the valley and perhaps even leave and become some other New Person's problem.

She felt a twinge of sympathy. She had enough perspective from her library to understand what he thought he was due. And yet nothing around them had the same expectation, despite expressing life in all its complexity.

"What does it feel like to have no home?" the living fossil said, gruff. "What does it feel like to be nothing and no one?"

"Home?" she said. "This is my home." Gesturing all around her. "All of it."

Later, she realized there might be some nuance in the old language after all. Because the Old Person had, perhaps, been talking about himself.

2.

But the man did not go away as she had hoped. A week later, the report came to her lazily through the air, spiraling up to where she curled and twined around a redwood's trunk, high in the canopy. These trees were not like the old ones. They had been made tougher, more able to withstand drought. But they smelled the same as the old ones, with a freshness that came through their bark, and into her skin exhaled a kind of contented sigh.

That calm evaporated when the spores released their message all across her body and she picked up on its import. Somewhere within the remains of an ancient factory on the far edge of her domain, someone had started to scrape away the lichen and fungi meant to render down and eat the last contaminants. To reclaim the metal, to break the concrete and infiltrate until there was no space between the cells of the living and the particles of the dead.

This time, she didn't bother to make the journey, but used a sector proxy: a smaller version of herself that morphed from heron to centipede in seconds, parachuting in free fall to the ground and then bursting out into the factory area. She crawled fast once de-winged across crack and crevice, over vines and stones, until she came to the partially sunken gray wall surrounding the factory, half-buried in dirt and tangled roots. The ratio of earthworms per square foot was sparse, the number of grubs lower, the trace amounts of pollutants still higher than it would be months from now. But even so the factory, covered in vines, resembled a hunched-over husk, almost reduced to the shape of a fallen giant from fairy tales.

The Old Person dangled his heels over the edge of a wall, a crude digging tool in his hands. He'd been pulling down vines and excavating the door to the factory, not realizing that the debris in front of it was actually there by her command, the agent turning the automated factory into something safe.

A month ago the factory had been functional and operating in secret underground. She had only discovered it by chance during a routine reconnaissance. Sometimes factories could not take their isolation, experienced a kind of loneliness, and bellowed out their locations, even asked to be silenced and taken apart. A century of making the same products and then internalizing them, recycling them, because the world beyond communicated nothing back, could make a factory deranged. They took to making defective objects or aggressive ones. They found ways to intoxicate their operating systems. They created communities with androids that were really just the factory talking to itself.

Taking apart a factory wasn't pleasant work, because a factory was a kind of sentience, too. But it had to be done. In this case, an odd glint had attracted her attention while flying high above, she had dived to the roof and within an hour of coaxing had made the factory surrender. An understanding of the hopelessness. The proxy androids had stopped moving, fallen to the basement floor. But the factory hadn't killed them, only suspended their motor functions. Ever since, even with the reclamation going smoothly, she had been concerned. Now this Old Person might be causing more trouble than he knew.

She thought that this time a more startling avatar might better make her point. So she appeared next to him not as centipede or bipedal, but instead erupted from the ground as a giant green curling fern with a human face. A face he would know from before. But with a burly thickness and a way of seeming to breathe through her fronds that she suspected he would find uncanny. The smell of a fundamental freshness meant to calm the man was just polite counterbalance.

When he didn't react, she waited. She could speak a thousand words in a millisecond. But she could also be silent for a century, remain there photosynthesizing and drawing nutrients from the soil while he faded to a husk and then, should he choose to sit there that long, to nothing but bones, and then her sustenance would come from him and that would be a different conversation altogether.

The Old People had no concept of such control, though, and after a moment the man looked over at her and made a sound that she knew to be contemptuous.

"I create a problem for you, don't I?" he said. "I am the wrench in your perfect system. I see through your 'order.'"

She knew he meant "system" in the archaic sense. Dead. Inert. Lines on "paper." Production and hierarchy. Not the kind of layering that occurred every moment she moved through the world, not the connection she allowed to overtake her as a kind of symphony composed of light and air.

"You do not create a problem for me," she said. She chose a gruff, masculine voice, but to his credit this did not startle him, either.

"Oh no?" Was that a tinge of some disappointment?

"No," she said. "On your own, you can't create a problem." Without tools. Without nostalgia.

He considered that. After a moment, he said, "I made you."

"You here made this me?" The phrasing was meant as another of her jokes, in part because she found all temporary housings funny, like they were eccentric toys. The one she was using would return to a plant-like sentience after she had left it, but her link to it would never fade. It would join the pantheon in her mind.

"Yes. I-me built you-you," he said, gruff again, and yet he'd had to participate in the joke, if only to be understood.

"So what?" she said. She liked diplomacy and politeness, but it was also in her nature to be blunt sometimes, and also to be raucous and to race the wind or jump off of cliffs, though he would never see that side of her.

"Not all of you," he admitted. "But a part of you. The part that allows you, an animal, to photosynthesize. I built that, on a team. I made that. I wanted that. I didn't want you, though."

She paged through her library, saw no image of him, no mention of him, thought again: *Is he delusional?* And: *Does it matter?* She could feel the factory in front of them, deep below, beginning to wake up from its self-imposed hibernation. She could sense that the Old Person's very presence might make the factory recant, and then she would have to put down a rebellion, in a sense, which would mean the whole process would take a year longer than a month.

"Do you know how contaminated this factory is?" she asked. "This factory is toxic—to you and to others. What you interrupted was a way of cleansing it. Did you mean to do that?"

He would not look at her. Instead, the Old Person asked, "How old are you?"

As questions went, she found it meaningless, but also harmless.

"A century or so."

"I'm two centuries."

"That's young."

"No, it's not. That's just a bit less than I'm going to get."

"Then why not enjoy yourself? Why do this?"

"To bring back the world."

"The world's been brought back."

"No, nature's been brought back—and so what?"

It wasn't that this comment was heresy. Heresy, blasphemy, meant very little to a wildflower or an otter or even to a New Person. But that it seemed to negate everything she'd seen in her library of what life had been like before.

"It's difficult to give up control," she said.

"The hell it is," the man snapped. "What kind of control you have now—such control, you're sitting next to me as a fucking fern with a human face. And yet you don't bring us back. You don't bring us back when you could."

Such anguish, so rare she had to compare it to certain library files to be sure of what he was expressing. And still she had no answer for him.

"Anguish" for her was the idea of the factory starting up again and harming the life around it. Anguish for her was the negotiation that had led to her talking the factory into silence, despite the common good. Anguish that there still existed in lands beyond her own vast deserts of garbage yet to be reclaimed, everywhere the signs of a dead civilization; that no matter how the New People cleaned and reabsorbed, so much work remained to be done.

To allow so much incoming communication, such cross-pollination, was to allow in contamination as well. You could not live cut off, but you could feel too connected. Anguish in the Old Person sense was almost selfishness or without awareness.

When she returned to the moment, the Old Person was still talking, but she was no longer curious about what he might say.

"The grass will show you a path from this place," she said. "You will let the grass lead you away. I will set guards here, and traps here. Some will cause paralysis. Others, an amount of pain. Don't come back."

"What does it feel like to have no name?" the living fossil said, gruff. Meaning to do harm.

The fern receded. The grass flattened. The factory fell back into slumber. The lichen resumed its work. She was miles away by then, consulting about the Old Person. She didn't think he would leave for good.

There was a loose council for these matters, but "council" was a bad word because it was a kind of neural link between them and most meetings took only eight to ten seconds and it was hard to parse out the individual lines as images, thoughts, queries, emblazoned together from dozens of her companions until it all became a single point, either in agreement or, rarely, disagreement—and then winked out, leaving her again in her body, whatever form it took. Whatever weight it had. Day or night. In the trees or on the ground. Lazy or alert.

If it could have been parsed out, laid out like an autopsy of a neural system, it would have resembled a spine splayed all delicate and quivering. High above, giant birds soared and never touched the land. In the seas what resembled killer whales but were a new, more resilient species, joined in with sonorous song. In deserts full of life scorpions massed and seethed in joyous celebration of an expanse of heat.

>>*I have an Old Person, causing trouble. What should I do.*

oo Never had one, never will.

ox I avoid them. Do not engage. Work around.

xxx Reason cuts not through their dreams and so they make do.

yyy I create a space for them and let them believe they are independent.

xxx They don't live long. Wait.

ooo They cannot reproduce.

ox Once, I gave one access to all these minds; she collapsed from the weight.

>>*He claims he made me.*

Laughter, mirth, flurry of image of atoms and pebbles and hurtling dark stars, all chortling as if an atom could chortle. As if a star could laugh.

oo The sun made the grass.

xxx The grass made the stars.

Then they were lost to her again, as if so vital was their existence that five seconds of their lives yawned like an eternity spent on such a conversation, lost in their own missions, their own repairs.

She thanked them, in her head, left the connection open so she could sense their exertions and endeavors.

Did the threat mean another ten years of effort? Five? Thirty? That was how the council decided. Wait and see. Cause the least harm. Sometimes a problem would sort itself out. Sometimes you might circle back and nothing was the same as it had been.

For a time, she joined the killer whales, to feel the immersion of the waves and the sensation of being part of a pod. For a time that lasted long enough to return to the problem anew . . . she became something else.

There were fewer of her kind every year, a fatal attrition. The sea had claimed some of her kind, had a strange effect upon them. The whales and the dolphins in their inscrutable and glittering arrays remained mute on the subject of what if anything should happen next. Until they did, or the others of her kind cracked the code, things would remain as they were.

So many of their type had not reported in to these sessions for some time. They had gone out into the ocean and lived there for long stretches. In their search to understand . . . what? . . . they had lost their selves or purpose and learned to *become* whales, to *become* dolphins, fixed now in their form. Some also had taken on new shapes to inhabit the deepest depths, to withstand the pressure, and there had formed their own communities. No rescue needed or wanted. No depths too deep. Still others had created out of themselves reefs and let their consciousness become subsumed by the communities they fostered.

And nothing these *strangers* said on those rare occasions when they breached their own silence made sense to her.

Only that it sounded exuberant. It sounded like joy, and that was more than good enough.

I have a name, she thought pushing against deep water. *I have a name, but your true name you should never share.*

3.

Returned to herself, she placed the man on the edge of her awareness. He still would not go away, yet he stayed out of sight, out of trouble in her periodic remote surveillance, for some time, living off the land, seeming to avoid the factory, and no animal needed or cared to bother him. It was not that she had a hand in this, but more that none now recognized an Old Person as food anymore, or thought of them as an object made of flesh, if only because so many artificial things had gone into an Old Person that even their scent had changed from persons much more ancient still.

When she could not find the man in the usual places, she became curious and returned to the factory, although much had happened since her last visit. It was hard to tell, though, because sometimes

Time didn't work for her the straight way. Sometimes it was much more interesting. Sometimes it flew through her like the wind and other times clasped onto her fierce like a diving raptor.

But the vines alone told her that time had passed. The amount of regeneration in the polluted grounds around the factory, deep down in the earth where the voles and the earthworms sang together and apart. Where the sweet volume of the interthatched loam was like a thousand hands steepled into subterranean cathedrals.

But also: The agony of felled trees around the factory and a deep glow-hum from the center of the factory that spoke not of slumber or of stasis but of a premonition of growth. A thud and shriek she felt within her chosen form.

There, in a clearing beside the factory, again a tent and the fresh stumps of cedars and oaks. A pile of dead bones that were logs.

The man had stopped moving upon her approach into the clearing. He stood there leaning on his ax, a look of scorn on his face.

For this avatar, she had chosen the form of a giant avian called a cassowary. She loved the shape of their claws. But apparently he could no longer be fooled or frightened.

"You again," the old man said. "You don't belong here."

"I belong everywhere," she said, using the vocal cords of a monkey watching them from the canopy, as the cassowary could only shriek and squawk.

"You want me to belong nowhere. I'm lonely. I'm alone."

She was not alone at all, did not really inhabit the term, even within her own one self.

"You must stop," she said.

"I don't know how to stop living," he said.

She meant to show him what living was, to bring his mind up into the higher atmosphere, and into outer space, to latch on to an old failing bio-satellite and use its eyes. They'd always looked to the stars, the Old People, yet they'd never really *seen* them. She meant him to experience wonder.

But the old man had been joined by another. Someone she hadn't registered, which concerned her. She read him to his lungs and found he was younger by a third. He also wasn't human. He was one of the factory's androids, reanimated.

"Who is this with you?" she asked, and felt a coldness inside she knew was a form of anger. She had not felt anger for such a long time, and whenever she did, it manifested around something human.

"My son," the old man said, and the nod from the younger man told her the android believed this. Which meant the old man had more skills than she had known, and now everything registered as threat.

"I am his son," said the not-son. "Who are you?"

"I am the one returning you to your true form," she said—and launched herself at the "son," ripping out his innards with one mighty taloned claw.

The son convulsed, fell to the ground, and shattered into particles made of glass, which was the substance she had transformed him into. The most delicate glass, fine as sand, that began to disintegrate before he ever hit.

The grains of glass quivered more, like the residue of air bubbles, and then like nothing at all.

"I'm afraid this needs to end," she said.

"You killed my son," the man said, but not in a way that indicated he cared.

Which was how she knew she'd made a mistake.

"Would you like to be made of glass, too? Well, you will be soon."

She could feel the fluid part of her locking in place. A trap, the android had been a trap, a kind of contamination. But now, the man registered as trap, too, just an extension of the factory, too. Factories were almost as ancient as people now, and craftier.

"I know what you've done," she said, to have at least that satisfaction. Because she did, because the transfer occurred both ways now. The recognition, at least.

Why did intent occur without original intent? And yet it always did, in some form, as if a virus lying dormant that could never be snuffed out.

The factory wanted her dead, the factory had wooed the man, fitted him with the mythology she would recognize. Safe, not safe, never home. The gleam in the man's eyes made that clear. She tried to morph her massive bulk into some organism that could fly, failed, then tried to morph into an organism that could dissipate into the air, the moisture of moss and loam. Failed. Felt even the satisfying fortress that was cassowary compromised at a cellular level.

The hum of the factory had changed into a mighty triumphant march, a blaring note of triumph. She could feel its influence at work in her compromised cells, and recognized that it meant to make her the energy that would bring all of it back to life, recognized how stealthily it could now reveal itself, undertake dread purpose once more.

All of this occurred in nanoseconds as she began to become brittle, fixed in place, the Old Person made new, leering at her like a demon and saying nothing now because what was there to say?

Parsed the contamination, set barriers and boundaries to fight it, turned her attention inward, while recognizing in just a minute or so she would have no control over her own thoughts or being. Downloaded a piece of herself somewhere safe, to have a fragment, even just as a copy, turned her attention to mass and velocity.

Rigid had its uses, too.

She imagined herself as the man, or what the factory intended the man to be, and stitched that into her cells, opened the barriers to the infection, let the surge finish the retrenchment into the opposite of who she had been.

A fleck, a dying flare rose from her form as camera to bear witness.

To the man mumbling phrases in rote routine, the factory focused on her, not the surrogate. Her, on one knee. The verdant green all around them, the cacophonous clacking and screech of the factory no longer cloaking its sound load—anxious to allow the gears to be heard. To tear up the forest and expand. To create clones to make products for, even if those products might simply be more fake people who thought they knew their own past.

In the limited version of her mind floating in the speck looking down on the scene, she hit a button, said, "Now," and watched as her body broke through a hole in the trap, leapt outward in all directions, used the snuffing out of being fluid to become fixed in place and one type of form. The old man's scheme lay embedded in the factory's attack, or the factory had embedded itself in him, but it made no difference either way.

Her versions popped up out of nothing like the human-sized discarded shells of cicadas, all gaps and flopping plasticity, but lurching forward nonetheless. The multiplicity of her as one became hundreds of these shambling figures—mobbing the original, who began to run for the factory, even as his parodies kept pace, overtook him, soon to wander breathless and in disarray to the factory. To clog its pores. To in their rigid way gum the works. To slowly disintegrate over control panels and in their dust coat and suffocate the function and the form.

There had been Old People and New People, and there would be one day newer people still.

The spark floating above was the last of her, navigating the wind by preprogrammed instinct, just a bit of nothing, a witness that would not witness the end.

Out at sea, the stranger versions of her, no longer caring about Old People or old ways, diving and surfacing in fast-churning profusion, would know nothing but wave and prey and the beauty of all things.

While the part the old man could not get to drifted above it all, would drift and drift until it settled, and was still.

>>*Always home, always home, always home.*

U WONT REMEMBER DYING

RUSSELL NICHOLS

MAR 20, 11:13 P.M.

u wont remember dying

sed the post-mortem counselor

he sed u will get flashes tho deja vu type shit phantom pain

where the nitestick broke my ribs, a punch 2 the gut, etc

more like pieces of a faded dream he sed

scenes from a movie u saw when u were little but cant remember
what its called so u cant check 2 c if its real or not but whatever

man they aint got no good movies here only a foldup vr mask 2 make
u think ur lying on a beach not on a damn hospital bed

somebody left behind this ripped book by sum oldass white dude
named walt whitman looking like a smoked out santa

damn i hope i dont die of boredom b4 the transfer in 3 days

i cant believe im here

its almost midnite i should b sleep rite now but i can't

if i couldnt sleep the counselor told me 2 "text myself"

meaning u

the man says im in shock and he thinks im depressed haha

i told him i aint depressed im fuckin dying; but he sed texting u mite help me b positive

ne thing 2 take my mind off getting shot

MAR 21, 9:42 A.M.

im all alone again

the fam just left 2 grab breakfast

i cant lie its weird af texting u cuz im texting my future self

on sum real time travel shit

they say ur long-term memories should kick in by wk 2

but u wont remember dying

i was just tryna get to the movies

minding my own

the shot!

doc sed u mite hear auditory hallucinations, echoes of the shot or that pig screaming in ur ear or sirens

like u kno when u feel ur cell vibrating in ur pocket but nobody called?

but u wont feel the actual bullet go thru ur head

lucky u

but the doc who did the ct scan told me the damage coulda been 100x worse if the bullet exploded or bounced around in my skull fuckin my brain tissue all the way up

if my glasgow coma scale was under 7 i couldnt do the direct transfer but i was conscious enough

he sed my number was 10

if i was in a coma they woulda had 2 animate u using my last backup from over a yr ago

moms damn near crashed when she found out i aint backed up in a yr she sed all 3 of us—me nick and lionel—shoulda been backing up once a month and me being 15 and the oldest need to "do better"

my man spiders pops signed him up during 1st NR enrollment

he went 2 the clinic on san pablo every tues after school 2 do his memory upload

u wont meet spider tho

he killed himself last july

RIP

yo i think the sedatives kicking in bruh

starting 2 c double

that bullet really glitxhed me up good flew up thru my rite brain then straight out

a "thru-and-thru" doc called it

my bodys killing me i can text wit my rite hand but i cant talk

MAR 21, 7:26 P.M.

guess whos back

the fam just left 4 dinner cuz they cant take this hospital 4mula shit

doc called this "a blend of superfoods liquefied 4 max absorption" haha i sed max absorption my ass this slop look regurgitated like a mf

doc gave me sumthin called a memory inhibitor 2 block everything since i got here yesterday so u wont remember none of this

cuz it would b 2 fuckin traumatic

lucky u

ne way im bored aint nuthin else 2 do no movies and my eyes hurt 2 much and vr makes my head hurt so

who the fuck walt whitman think he is? i sing the body electric? wtf like a robot sing-a-long all he writes is flowers and trees and happy springtime shit

heres a pic:

> When lilacs last in the dooryard bloom'd,
> And the great star early droop'd in the western sky in the night,
> I mourn'd, and yet shall mourn with ever-returning spring.

gtfoh!

on the back theres a big quote that says "[Whitman] is America" and im like what america

yo i did watch that New Reconstruction documentary earlier

u believe its been 3 yrs?

98% success rate so thats good but its only been 12 transfers so far

u make 13

but dont worry bruh its anonymous now

it was causing a media circus @ 1st wit all the hour specials and day-time talk interviews and late show bs wit the hosts asking stupidass questions:

"do u still hav a birthmark?"

wtf is up wit this country?

1 network tried 2 set up a reality show but the feds shut that down quick saying it would send the "wrong message"

they didnt say nuthin else but we all knew "wrong message" was code 4 "anti-police message"

spiders pops sed "its good these black kids get 2 come back 2 life but @ the same time they shouldnt b getting killed by no fascist cops in the 1st place and best believe they just gonna end up shot again if the real problem aint dealt wit"

i cant argue wit that

i cant argue @ all

i cant even talk

i cant feel my left leg and i gotta wear a fuckin bib cuz i keep drooling

yo the boys will freak out when they c u tho

actually i take that back lionel mite take a minute 2 adapt but nick won't

since moms told him about NR little homie been on his research grind

moms sed all day he been on them $1m words talking bout "re-con-sti-tute" and "con-scious-ness"

matter fact just this morning nick let me hear his science report

i recorded him since i kno u wont remember this

here check out this vid:

["Dolly was a female sheep, the first animal to be cloned from an adult cell. Back in the 1990s, scientists in Scotland used a cell from another sheep's mam-ma-ry gland to create Dolly. In female mammals, mam-ma-ry glands are where the milk comes from. And where the word mammal comes from, too. For this project, I will be—"]

he told me he got a B+ cuz his 5th grade teach sed he left out how dolly was put down b4 she turned 7 from lung disease

nick had me dying; he was like "i dont c y thats a big deal cuz if she could b cloned once, she could b cloned again so it didnt matter if she died"

i asked him if my life mattered

he sed "ur life matters but death dont matter cuz u can keep coming back as many times as u want"

i wanted 2 tell him it didnt work that way that aint what i meant but i was drifting in and out cuz this was rite after they gave me the memory inhibitor so i just told him dont ever take life 4 granted

he sed "no doubt" then took his B+ like a man and sed he would "do better next time"

i sed me 2

WTF!!!

i cant sleep

its on me i never shoulda read this damn whitman again

check this 1 out:

> A NOISELESS patient spider,
> I mark'd where on a little promontory it stood isolated,
> Mark'd how to explore the vacant vast surrounding,
> It launch'd forth filament, filament, filament, out of itself,
> Ever unreeling them, ever tirelessly speeding them.

idk wtf he on but it got me thinking bout my man spider

i wonder what he was thinking b4 he shot himself

i remember he used 2 say he didnt want the pigs having power over him

he sed shit like that all the time:

"the whole recon programs a setup giving those appointed 2 'serve and protect' free rein 2 fire @ will"

"the american dream is santa claus 4 grownups"

"2 b born black in america is a death sentence"

the bullet went in but never came out

@ the funeral his pops sed he was battling severe depression

yo i knew spider all my life and i kno fa sho he ain't hav no depression

wtf is depression ne way? u either alive or dead

aint no inbetween

now spiders gone but im still here

holding on by a thread

Y U???

y u get to live when everybody else keep dying?

y u so lucky?

moms sed its gods will but idk that dont make sense 2 me but im
scared 4 u bruh

straight up all that pressure u gonna feel

2 make ur life matter

2 show u deserve a 2nd chance

2 prove u alive for a reason

everybody gonna c rite thru u call u a fake a phony

a scarecrow

a black body without a brain

theyll b like "that nigga aint real"

FUUUUUUUUUUUUUUCK MY LIFE!

i should just pull the plug rite now

save u the trouble

i dont deserve to come back to life

but i dont wanna b inbetween

MAR 22, 5:02 A.M.

yo disregard those texts from last nite i was on sum other shit

ne way 2days transfer day

in 3 hrs u will b here

in the flesh

and ill b history

guess im supposed 2 say sumthin uplifting but im losing my mind

and my bodys killing me

everythings dark

cloudy

i feel like im drooling my life away

hell tbh i dont kno how 2 b positive

lets c if mr fuckin america got ne jewels 2 drop

> I CELEBRATE myself,
> And what I assume you shall assume,
> For every atom belonging to me, as good belongs
> to you.

haha

yo that 1 kinda works tho

but still u and i kno it aint the whole truth

and if u dont remember nuthin else remember this:

whitman aint america

whitman aint real

i am/u r

ACKNOWLEDGMENTS

First up, credit to the speculators: anyone who reads, writes, draws, designs, and models the future. As you have seen in these pages, it's a weird, jarring, often unpleasant, and sometimes even thankless thing to do. Predictions go awry, the future arrives all wrong, and it can be stressful, now more than ever, to spend any serious amount of time there.

Thank you to every writer who sheared off a bit of their mindspace for our benefit. The stories we ran every week in *Terraform* were a blast to read, edit, and inhabit. What a privilege it is, and has been, to share these magnified splinters in our eyes with the world. Thanks to the regular contributors who helped define our weird corner of the speculative fiction universe, and to everyone who submitted stories to our black hole of an inbox. Since launch, we were immediately and permanently swamped, and wish we could have written back to every single one of you.

Equally enormous thanks are due to the artists whose work gave *Terraform* such a powerful visual identity over the years. Your images were every bit as crucial to rendering these future spaces as the stories themselves, and there would be no *Terraform* without you. Special thanks to the usual suspects, including but not limited to Koren Shadmi, Zoë van Dijk, Glenn Harvey, Jason Arias, Surian Soosay, Cathryn Virginia, Rebekka Dunlap, and Gustavo Torres, incredible, talented artists all. We wish we had the space to feature everyone's work—help us convince MCD to make a *Terraform* coffee table book next, pls.

Terraform was weird and unwieldy from the beginning, and it's fairly unusual that we were able to convince a major new media company to let us launch a speculative fiction site at all. To that end, many thanks to former *Motherboard* editor in chief Derek Mead, *Motherboard* founding editor Alex Pasternack, former *Motherboard* publisher Thobey Campion, and current *Motherboard* EIC Jason Koebler, a onetime *Terraform* contributor himself, who always supported and advocated for the venture even as the sands shifted. Thanks to *Motherboard* editors Adrianne Jeffries, Brian Anderson, Emanuel Maiberg, and Carl Franzen, each of whom helped keep the *Terraform* gears turning at one point or another. Thanks also to all the people and organizations who partnered up with us on more ambitious projects, like our future-predicting Twitter bot—coded by Ranjit Bhatnagar—and our attempts to bring short-form fiction to TV audiences and think tank crowds. And thanks to Tim and Geoff, for the sinister speculative Halloween and Xmas traditions.

And then! Thanks to the fine crew at MCD for turning this digital enterprise into a durable one—it soothes our souls to know that after the great internet crash of 2032 destroys the internet once and for all, we will all have this delightful volume to read around the campfires made from burning Kindles. We meant it when we said we only wanted one partner for this project, and Sean McDonald and Co. were it. Thanks for bearing with us throughout the edit process, and for the impeccable style and content choices that helped craft this volume into what you see before you here. Thanks to Benjamin Brooks for the editorial support, to Dave Cole, Andrea Monagle, and Chandra Wohleber for their patience reviewing a volume with so many invented words, and to the marketing, publicity, and design teams for helping us set these visions loose on an unsuspecting public.

Brian would like to thank his family, Aldus, Russell, and Corrina, for listening to so many stories about the future and for endlessly expanding his hopes for it, and his agent, Eric Lupfer, for helping to make sure such expansive projects can exist at all.

Claire would like to thank Jona Bechtolt, with whom she is lucky to share a future, and her agent, Sarah Levitt, for always making it such a breeze to make books.

CONTRIBUTORS

Sam Biddle is a writer and technology reporter.

While most people rightly associate Slack with work, like a lot of people I also use it to chat with dear friends. I wrote this story after agonizing about the fact that Slack would retain our conversation histories indefinitely unless we forked over an extremely large amount of money for the privilege of deletion.

James Bridle is a writer and artist working across technologies and disciplines. Their artworks have been commissioned by galleries and institutions and exhibited worldwide and on the internet. Their writing on literature, culture, and networks has appeared in magazines and newspapers including *Wired*, *The Atlantic*, *The New Statesman*, *The Guardian*, and *The Observer*. They are the author of *New Dark Age* (2018) and *Ways of Being* (2022), and they wrote and presented *New Ways of Seeing* for BBC Radio 4 in 2019.

Jennifer Marie Brissett has been an artist, a software engineer, and (sometimes) a poet. For three and a half years she was the owner/operator of the Brooklyn indie bookstore Indigo Café & Books. She is the author of *Elysium* (Aqueduct Press, 2014) and *Destroyer of Light* (Tor Books, 2021) and has been short-listed for the Locus Award, the James Tiptree Jr. Award, and the *storySouth* Million Writers Award and has won the Philip K. Dick Special Citation. Her short stories can be found in publications such as *FIYAH* magazine, *Lightspeed* magazine, *Uncanny* magazine, the anthology *APB: Artists Against Police Brutality*, as well as other publications. She lives in New York City.

The idea for the story "A Song for You" came to me after I read a news article in 2013 about the giant Styrofoam and fiberglass head caught floating down the Hudson River. It was about seven feet tall and looked forever like it came from a Greek or Roman statue. Some suppose it was the remains of a theater prop from somewhere. That's New York for you. Anyway, for some reason the image of that made me think: What if Orpheus was an android? I have no idea why I thought that, but I did. Anyway, I think it made a pretty good story.

Born in the Caribbean, **Tobias Buckell** is a *New York Times* bestselling and World Fantasy Award–winning author. His novels and almost one hundred stories have been translated into nineteen different languages. He has been nominated for the Hugo Award, Nebula Award, World Fantasy Award, and Astounding Award for Best New Science Fiction Author. He currently lives in Ohio.

Tori Cárdenas is a trans mixed-race poet from northern New Mexico. Their poetry and short fiction have appeared in *Witchcraft* magazine, *[PANK]*, *Superstition Review*, and *Ricky's Backyard*. Together with Warren Langford, Cárdenas wrote the script for *Eminent Domain*, a sci-fi thriller set in Santa Fe, New Mexico, and recorded in binaural audio.

The integrity of rainforest soil is actually very poor. When areas are rapidly deforested, nothing can root in the shallow, nutrient-poor earth, and the desert takes over. Not to mention the damage from wildfires. This speculative Amazon River with the city surrounding it (and endless desert surrounding that) feels like a looming inevitability, mirroring similar cultural desertifications across the Americas. All that said, I feel similar to Bonifacio these last few years: disconnected from the land and watching a lot of TV to survive—personally, though, I don't like Friends.

Shannon Chamberlain is a faculty member in the Great Books program at St. John's College, Santa Fe, New Mexico.

When news of the Trump administration's policy on family separation at the border first broke, I was a very new mother. I took my infant daughter to a protest in my town, mounting a sign on her stroller about how her generation would do better than mine. Someone was flying a drone overhead, and a lot of different threads wove themselves together in my mind: hope, the vulnerability of children, parental love, and the way that tech tends to undermine all of our intentions. Wouldn't it be nice if it undermined them for good instead of evil for once?

Chloe Cole received her MFA in fiction from UC Riverside and now lives in Montclair, New Jersey. She writes about women and their grisly obsessions, and her writing has appeared on *The Rumpus*, *CollegeHumor*, and *Reductress*. The interactive Instagram narrative she wrote about an influencer's mental breakdown was included in the AV Club's list of the scariest horror stories on social media in 2020. Most importantly, she published a nine-part story on Neopets when she was eleven years old.

RealDolls (which are eerily realistic life-size sex dolls, if you are a well-adjusted person who doesn't concern themselves with such things) are often mentioned as easy punch lines, but I became curious about the reality of them, specifically how a woman would feel if she encountered her boyfriend's. Of course, the expected reaction would be disgust, but I found myself questioning this. To meet the doppelgänger sex doll version of you would be to experience yourself purely as a sexual object. Women are not unfamiliar with sexual objectification, but what if the woman was in control in this interaction?

Nan Craig is a fiction writer, poet, technology researcher, and data scientist and has published short stories in *NewScientist* and *Vice*. Her poetry has appeared most recently in *Magma* and *Envoi* and on BBC Radio 4.

Cory Doctorow is a science fiction author, activist, and journalist. He is the author of many books, most recently *Radicalized* and *Walkaway*, science fiction for adults; *How to Destroy Surveillance Capitalism*, nonfiction about monopoly and conspiracy; *In Real Life*, a graphic novel; and the picture book *Poesy the*

Monster Slayer. His latest book is *Attack Surface*, a stand-alone adult sequel to *Little Brother*; his next nonfiction book is *The Shakedown*, with Rebecca Giblin, about monopoly and fairness in the creative arts labor market (Beacon Press, 2022). In 2020, he was inducted into the Canadian Science Fiction and Fantasy Association Hall of Fame.

Born and raised on the South Side of Chicago, **Malon Edwards** now lives in the Greater Toronto Area, where he was lured by his beautiful Canadian wife. Many of his short stories are set in an alt Chicago future and feature people of color. He is an Ember Award and Sunburst Award finalist. His short story collection, which includes "Gynoid, Preserved," will be published by Fireside Press in fall 2022.

I've always wondered, "What if Jean Baptiste Point du Sable stayed in Chicago after founding it?" Haitian Creole would be the official language, but alt Chicagoland wouldn't be much different. The love-hate with the suburbs would still be there, and more so because Chicago is a sovereign state. Still, us Dusable Haitians would be just as awed and excited by Rock Island High School's co-ed track meets under the lights with packed stands.

Omar El Akkad is an author and journalist. His first novel, *American War*, was translated into thirteen languages and was listed by the BBC as one of one hundred novels that shaped our world. His second novel, *What Strange Paradise*, won the 2021 Giller Prize.

I wrote "Busy" during the early days of the pandemic lockdown, when the economy had come to a grinding halt and, as with just about every calamity, the poorest were made to bear the brunt of the carnage. I started thinking about what a Depression-era make-work program would look like under late capitalism, and the result was the entropy mill in which this story is set.

Meg Elison is a science fiction author and feminist essayist. Her debut, *The Book of the Unnamed Midwife*, won the 2014 Philip K. Dick Award. She is a Hugo, Nebula, Sturgeon, and Otherwise awards finalist. In 2020, she published her first collection, *Big Girl*, with PM Press, containing the Locus Award–winning novelette "The Pill." Elison's first young adult novel, *Find Layla*, was published in 2020 by Skyscape. Her thriller *Number One Fan* will be released by Mira Books in 2022. Meg has been published in *McSweeney's*, *Fantasy & Science Fiction*, *Fangoria*, *Uncanny*, *Lightspeed*, *Nightmare*, and many other places. Elison is a high school dropout and a graduate of UC Berkeley.

"Hysteria" came to me as I watched reproductive justice erode and crumble over the past decade of my life, knowing how many people have died for the right to choose and knowing how many more will die when we lose it. The depersonalized wandering womb seemed like the next step, both wrong and right.

Rose Eveleth is a writer and producer who explores how humans tangle with science and technology. They're the creator of the production studio Flash Forward Presents and host of the podcast *Flash Forward*. They've covered everything from fake tumbleweed farms to million-dollar baccarat heists.

Fernando A. Flores was born in Reynosa, Tamaulipas, Mexico, and grew up in South Texas. He is the author of the collection *Death to the Bullshit Artists of South Texas* and the novel *Tears of the Trufflepig*, which was long-listed for the Center for Fiction First Novel Prize and named a best book of 2019 by Tor.com. His fiction has appeared in the *Los Angeles Review of Books Quarterly, American Short Fiction, Ploughshares, Frieze, Porter House Review*, and elsewhere. He lives in Austin, Texas.

Paul Ford is a writer and programmer, a columnist for *Wired*, and a cofounder of Postlight, a digital product studio in New York City.

I work in software. The big idea of the early software industry was that it would empower humans to think bigger thoughts. But software has a way of asserting itself, and turning us into data, and we in response start acting like software. All three of the entities in this story are ultimately incredibly limited in their options by the software that runs their lives.

Hugo Award winner Sarah Gailey lives and works in California. Their nonfiction has been published by dozens of venues internationally, including *Locus* and *The Boston Globe*. Their fiction has been published internationally in over six different languages. Their debut novel, *Magic for Liars*, was a *Los Angeles Times* bestseller. Their most recent novel, *The Echo Wife*, is available now everywhere books are sold. You can find links to their work on social media at @gaileyfrey.

The parallel increases in privatization of agriculture and militarization of police forces combined to create "Drones to Ploughshares," a story that imagines how we might offer a different life to those who are given no choice but to do harm in the name of ruthless interests.

Peter Milne Greiner is the author of *Lost City Hydrothermal Field*, a hybrid volume of poetry and science fiction. His work has appeared recently in *Fence, Dark Mountain, Big Echo: Critical Science Fiction, Abyss&Apex, Dream Pop Journal*, and *TAGVVERK*, and has been anthologized in *Beyond Earth's Edge: The Poetry of Spaceflight* and *Resist Much/Obey Little: Inaugural Poems to the Resistance*. PMG keeps a rooftop garden in Brooklyn and teaches creative writing and economics at a high school in Manhattan.

Sovereignty of the atoll plus sovereignty of the skull equals what?

Malcolm Harris is the author of *Kids These Days, Shit Is Fucked Up and Bullshit*, and *Palo Alto*. "Jim" is his first and only piece of fiction.

Porpentine Charity Heartscape | writer, game designer, everything | exhibited at Whitney Biennial, YBCA, MCA, etc. | commissioned by *Vice, Rhizome*, etc. | made *Psycho Nymph Exile, With Those We Love Alive, Eczema Angel Orifice*.

Eric Holthaus is a meteorologist, author of *The Future Earth*, and founder of Currently—, a weather service for the climate emergency. He lives in Minneapolis.

"Hypercane" is my first published short work of fiction and was written to

commemorate the third anniversary of Superstorm Sandy's landfall in the New York City area. When I was forecasting Sandy in real time, it became terrifyingly clear to me that this was no ordinary storm. And of course my mind quickly shifted to the future, and to that place of climate terror we're locking in without the kind of revolutionary action the science and justice require. "Hypercane" is a warning that those days are arriving more quickly than we can anticipate.

Andrew Dana Hudson is a sustainability researcher, narrative strategist, and the author of *Our Shared Storm: A Novel of Five Climate Futures*, as well as numerous pieces of short fiction. His stories have appeared in *Terraform*, *Slate Future Tense*, *Lightspeed* magazine, and more. He lives in Tempe, Arizona.

The Pleistocene Park project proposes re-creating an ancient, carbon-rich eco-system by reviving extinct species, like the woolly mammoth. This story imagines how such a de-extincted being might find its way in our future.

Sahil Lavingia is the founder of Gumroad, an angel investor, a painter, and a writer. He resides in Beaverton, Oregon.

Tao Lin is the author of ten books, including *Leave Society* (2021), *Trip: Psychedelics, Alienation, and Change* (2018), and *Taipei* (2013). He edits *Muumuu House* and lives in Hawaii.

My story was inspired by the late James Purdy's story collection Color of Darkness *(1957), which contains funny and startlingly observant descriptions of social interactions and psychological minutiae.*

Mattie Lubchansky is the associate editor of *The Nib* and an illustrator and cartoonist living in Queens. They are the coauthor of *Dad Magazine* (Quirk, 2016) and the author of *The Antifa Super-Soldier Cookbook* (Silver Sprocket, 2021) and the forthcoming *Boys Weekend* (Pantheon, 2023).

What inspired "Reach" was twofold: One, the false promise of much of work automation, at least as Silicon Valley sees it—all too often we find that on the other end of that "self-driving" vehicle is an underpaid worker on the other side of the planet, and I think we're just going to see that more and more. And two, as an abolitionist: Who better for the operator of a Mechanical Turk than the most dehumanized members of our society, those who have been locked away in our carceral system and completely forgotten about?

Geoff Manaugh is a Los Angeles–based freelance writer, regularly covering topics related to architecture, technology, crime, and design for *The Atlantic*, *The New York Times Magazine*, *The New Yorker*, *BLDGBLOG*, and many other publications. His short story "Ernest" was adapted as a feature film by Netflix, starring David Harbour as Ernest and Jahi Di'Allo Winston as Kevin.

I'm a huge fan of dramatic under-reaction—someone responding with a complete lack of shock or sincerity to extraordinary circumstances—and wanted to explore what that might look like in the context of a ghost story. The initial image of a suburban dad discovering a ghost and deciding he's going to scare it quickly snowballed into the story of a lonely teen looking for friends, a ghost searching for its own humanity, and online fans obsessively tracking their otherworldly road-trip together.

Tim Maughan is an author and journalist using both fiction and nonfiction to explore issues around cities, class, culture, technology, and the future. His work has appeared on the BBC and in *NewScientist, MIT Technology Review, OneZero,* and *Motherboard.* His debut novel, *Infinite Detail,* was published by FSG in 2019 and selected by *The Guardian* as their Science Fiction and Fantasy book of the year and short-listed for the Locus Magazine Award for Best First Novel. He uses fiction to help clients as diverse as IKEA and the World Health Organization think critically about the future. He also collaborates with artists and filmmakers and has had work shown at the V&A, Columbia School of Architecture, the Vienna Biennale, and on Channel 4. He currently lives in Canada.

"Flyover Country" was written just days after Trump's shock election win in 2016 and was an attempt to envision what his promise to bring manufacturing back to the U.S. could look like. It was also born out of my decades-long obsession with special economic zones, visits to factories in China, and the belief that very common things often don't look dystopian until they're happening to you or are on your doorstep.

Joanne McNeil is the author of *Lurking* and a forthcoming novel.

Lincoln Michel is the author of the science fiction novel *The Body Scout* (Orbit) and the short story collection *Upright Beasts* (Coffee House Press). He coedited the Shirley Jackson Award–nominated anthologies *Tiny Crimes* (Catapult) and *Tiny Nightmares* (Catapult). His fiction appears in *The Paris Review, Lightspeed, Fantasy & Science Fiction, Granta,* the Pushcart Prize anthology, and elsewhere.

"The Duchy of the Toe Adam" was inspired partly by questions of ideological conflict that have plagued humanity since the dawn of civilization and partly by a Star Trek: The Next Generation *Netflix binge. I wrote the story when I was at a writing residency that happened to take place on Herman Melville's Arrowhead estate. I was tangled in the weeds of a novel draft and, staring out at the mountain that inspired* Moby-Dick, *for some reason thought, "I should take a break and write a gonzo space opera story for fun." Often that's when the best stories come: when you're slacking off on something else.*

Sam J. Miller's books have been called "must reads" and "bests of the year" by *USA Today, Entertainment Weekly, NPR,* and *O: The Oprah Magazine,* among others. He is the Nebula Award–winning author of *Blackfish City,* which has been translated into six languages and won the hopefully-soon-to-be-renamed John W. Campbell Memorial Award. Sam's short stories have been nominated for the World Fantasy, Theodore Sturgeon, and Locus Awards, and reprinted in dozens of anthologies. He's also the last in a long line of butchers. He lives in New York City.

Lia Swope Mitchell is a writer and translator with a Ph.D. in French from the University of Minnesota. Her published translations include Georges Didi-Huberman's *Survival of the Fireflies* and Antoine Volodine's *Solo Viola,* and her short fiction has appeared in magazines like *Asimov's*, *Apex*, and *Cosmos*. She lives in Minneapolis.

Gus Moreno is the author of *This Thing Between Us*. His stories have appeared in *Southwest Review*, *Aurealis*, *PseudoPod*, and the anthology *Burnt Tongues*. He lives in the suburbs with his wife and two dogs, but never think that he's not from Chicago.

I had a high school teacher once suggest in class that all boys should get a vasectomy at an early age, and the only way to get it reversed would be to graduate high school with at least a 3.0 GPA. This past year, when Texas passed its new abortion laws, I was reminded of the 3.0 rule and decided to see what that America would look like.

Kevin Nguyen is the author of the novel *New Waves* (One World, 2020) and the features editor at *The Verge*. He lives in Brooklyn, New York.

One of my first jobs out of college was at Amazon—it was one of the few places that seemed to be hiring after the 2008 crash. My job was pretty entry-level, almost literally pushing buttons and turning knobs. The work culture was intense, but what really inspired me to write this story was revisiting Seattle years later and seeing how all those buttons and knobs—"at scale"—could warp the landscape of the entire city. It was horrifying and, honestly, a little funny.

Also part of this story was based on what I'd gleaned from Greg Grandin's terrific book Fordlandia. *Coincidentally, it was the first book I ever read on a Kindle.*

Russell Nichols is a speculative fiction writer and endangered journalist. Raised in Richmond, California, he got rid of all his stuff in 2011 to live out of a backpack with his wife, vagabonding around the world ever since.

Frankie Ochoa's fiction has appeared in *La Presa*, *Account* magazine, *Nat. Brut*, and elsewhere. Her short story "Still Life," published in *Kweli Journal*, received a notable mention in the 2018 Pushcart Prize Anthology. She has an MFA from Columbia University and is an alumnus of Voices of Our Nations Arts Foundation and Bread Loaf Writers' Conference.

Tochi Onyebuchi is the author of *Riot Baby*, which won the New England Book Award for Fiction, the Alex Award, the Ignyte Award, and the World Fantasy Award and is a finalist for the Hugo, Nebula, Locus, and NAACP Image Awards. He holds degrees from Yale University, New York University's Tisch School of the Arts, Columbia Law School, and Sciences Po, and his short fiction has appeared in *Asimov's Science Fiction*, *Omenana Magazine*, and *Lightspeed* magazine, among other places. His most recent book, *Goliath*, was published by Tordotcom Publishing.

Not long ago, I came across, in an essay, a stunning ekphrasis of Aesop by the Spanish painter Velázquez, which led me down a rabbit hole of fables as slave language and the ways in which they highlighted, complicated, and critiqued the master-slave relationship. Separately, I'd already been thinking about "hurt," mostly in the contexts of intimacy and controlled environments. The biblical story from which this one derives its title provided the perfect set of guardrails for me to wind my way through these difficult ideas.

Laurie Penny is an award-winning author, columnist, journalist, and screenwriter. Their seven books include *Bitch Doctrine, Unspeakable Things,* and *Everything Belongs to the Future.* As a freelance journalist, they write about politics, social justice, pop culture, feminism, mental health, and technology for outlets including *The Guardian, Longreads, Time, BuzzFeed, The New York Times, Vice, Salon, The Nation,* and *The New Statesman.* They were a 2014–15 Nieman Journalism Fellow at Harvard University. As a screenwriter, Laurie has worked on *The Nevers* (HBO), *The Haunting of Bly Manor* (Netflix), and *Carnival Row* (Amazon). Laurie Penny is based between London and Los Angeles. @PennyRed

Zora Mai Quỳnh is a Vietnamese American dancer, performance artist, and writer whose short stories, essays, and poetry have appeared in *Ploughshares, Masque & Spectacle, Kweli Journal, Strange Horizons, Glittership,* and in the anthologies *The Sea Is Ours, Genius Loci: The Spirit of Place, People of Color Destroy Science Fiction,* and *Luminescent Threads: Connections to Octavia Butler.* Zora is the winner of the 2021 San Francisco Foundation Nomadic Press Literary Award. Zora has received scholarships to attend the Kweli International Literary Festival, Martha's Vineyard Institute of Creative Writing, VONA, Writing the Other, and the Bread Loaf Writers' Conference. Zora is a frequent book reviewer and essayist for *diaCRITICS* on all things ARVN (the Army of the Republic of Vietnam). You can hear them narrating for *Strange Horizons, Glittership,* and PodCastle from time to time. You can find Zora sipping boba at @zmquynh on Twitter, Facebook, and Instagram.

In World War II, the U.S. detonated two nuclear bombs in Hiroshima and Nagasaki, killing 355,000 people. Like many in the cities, Sadako Sasaki, twelve years old, was exposed to radiation that led to her leukemia. Following the Japanese legend that grants a wish to the folder of a thousand origami cranes, Sadako set and exceeded her goal—she folded 1,400 paper cranes before she died. Inspired by Sadako, I set out to capture, in story form, a wish for collective action for climate justice.

Robin Sloan grew up in Michigan and now splits his time between San Francisco and the internet. He is the author of *Mr. Penumbra's 24-Hour Bookstore* and *Sourdough.*

Emily J. Smith is a writer and technology professional. She has published in *The Rumpus, Catapult, Romper, Hobart,* and *Slate,* among others, and writes regularly for Medium. She founded the dating app Chorus and works as a product consultant for tech companies. She is based in Brooklyn and currently working on a novel.

The idea for "Warning Signs" came when I noticed a need to be polite to my mom's Alexa, an inanimate object, and contrasted that impulse against the behavior and entitlement I was observing in some men who worked in tech.

Julian Mortimer Smith is an award-winning speculative fiction writer based in Yarmouth, Nova Scotia. His short stories have appeared in some of the world's top sci-fi and fantasy venues, including *Asimov's, Terraform, Lightspeed,* and *Best American Science Fiction and Fantasy.* His first collection, *The World of Dew and Other Stories,* is published by Indiana University Press, and won the 2020 Blue Light Books Prize.

The idea for "Headshot" came to me after attending a lecture by Professor Barbie Zelizer about media depictions of warfare. She pointed out that newspapers almost never run images of dead bodies when reporting on war. Instead, we get sanitized, aestheticized images that make war palatable to news consumers. I set out to write an anti-war story in which civilians are required to witness the acts of state violence that happen in their names. I wanted to imagine how that might change our appetite for war. But I ended up with a cynical social media satire instead.

Bruce Sterling, author, journalist, editor, and critic, was born in 1954. Best known for his ten science fiction novels, he also writes short stories, book reviews, design criticism, opinion columns, and introductions for books ranging from Ernst Jünger to Jules Verne. His nonfiction works include *The Hacker Crackdown: Law and Disorder on the Electronic Frontier* (1992), *Tomorrow Now: Envisioning the Next Fifty Years* (2003), *Shaping Things* (2005), and *The Epic Struggle of the Internet of Things* (2014). His most recent book is a collection of Italian science fiction stories, *Robot Artists and Black Swans* (2021). He has served as a Visionary in Residence at design labs, think tanks, and universities around the world, and has made appearances on *Nightline,* the BBC, MTV, and beyond. He unites his time among the cities of Austin, Turin, and Ibiza.

I have visited Ukraine; I have some understanding of their many sufferings; I know I shouldn't have made outlandish, science-fictional fun of them and their all-too-real situation. Yes, I know I shouldn't, but being a "punk," I kinda have to. So, I did that, and Vice *even paid me for doing it. So I'm guilty, and although this satire is old, and I'm old, too, I still know what's happening to the people of Ukraine. I lampooned them, but I won't forget them.*

Seamus Sullivan writes fiction and plays. His plays include *Brother Mario, Me and the Devil Blues,* and *Incurable.* He has written several speculative audio plays for the podcast *Paperless Pulp.*

I wrote "Dream Job" after reading a news story about the growing prevalence of sleep deprivation, and while thinking about Bengaluru-based call center workers I've spoken with, who had to keep vampire hours in order to troubleshoot computer problems—expertly, I'll add—for me and my American coworkers.

Wole Talabi is an engineer, writer, and editor from Nigeria. His stories have appeared in *Asimov's, Lightspeed, Fantasy & Science Fiction, Clarkesworld,* and several other publications. He has edited three anthologies of African fiction: the science fiction collection *Africanfuturism* (2020), the horror collection *Lights Out: Resurrection* (2016), and the literary fiction collection *These Words Expose Us* (2014). His stories have been nominated for multiple awards, including the prestigious Caine Prize for African Writing in 2018 and the Nommo Award, which he won twice (in 2018, for best short story, and in 2020, for best novella). His work has also been translated into Spanish, Norwegian, Chinese, and French. His collection *Incomplete Solutions* was published by Luna Press. He likes scuba diving, elegant equations, and oddly shaped things. He currently lives and works in Malaysia.

Tlotlo Tsamaase is a Motswana writer (xe/xem/xer or she/her pronouns) currently living in Botswana. Tlotlo's novella *The Silence of the Wilting Skin* is a 2021 Lambda Literary Award finalist and was short-listed for a 2021 Nommo Award. Tlotlo's short fiction has appeared in *The Best of World SF Volume 1, Futuri uniti d'Africa, Clarkesworld, Terraform, Africanfuturism Anthology, The Year's Best African Speculative Fiction* (2021), and is forthcoming in the *Africa Risen* anthology, *Apex* magazine's International Futurists issue, and other publications. Xer story, "Behind Our Irises," is a Nommo Award finalist for Best Short Story (2021). You can find xem on Twitter and Instagram as @TlotloTsamaase.

I studied architecture, wrote a thesis on the aesthetics of green architecture, and interned at a sustainable architectural firm, which really opened my eyes to the infinitesimal detail required in creating sustainable buildings, especially for impoverished communities. Giving up the architect-in-training career, I worked as an editor/columnist for a local-built environment newspaper, and interviewed experts on climate change whilst writing articles on related topics. My writer's brain was quite often married to the dystopian realm of climate change in fiction as an attempt to deconstruct the intersectionality of several themes within Botswana's context; for instance, I wished to show its effect on poverty-stricken communities, looked at what layers of discrimination would be at play, whilst exploring the microcosm of the family's strain within earth's environmental devastation.

Ellen Ullman worked as a computer programmer for more than twenty years. Her essays and opinion pieces have appeared in *The New York Times, Wired, Harper's Magazine, The American Scholar*, and several "Best Essay" collections. She is the author of the memoir *Close to the Machine*; of two novels, *The Bug* and *By Blood*; and of the nonfiction collection *Life in Code*.

I woke up one morning to find that my headphones no longer worked with my iPhone. They worked with every other device I have, also on my husband's iPhone, but not on mine. Apple support had trouble getting the phone to do a deep reboot. The representative had to reach for more and more arcane restart procedures. And, oh, by the way, there had been an iOS update overnight . . .

Debbie Urbanski's fiction and essays have been published in *The Best American Science Fiction and Fantasy, The Best American Experimental Writing, The Sun, Fantasy & Science Fiction*, and *Granta*. Her first novel, *What Comes After the End*, will be published by Pantheon Books in 2023.

I was working on a novel about human extinction and worried that people might find the jump from today to a no-human future unbelievable. Then Donald Trump started talking about, among other things, shrinking Utah's Bears Ears National Monument by eighty-five percent in order to open up over one million acres to oil exploration and mining. There was talk of letter-writing campaigns and protests but it was pretty clear Trump was going ahead with it. And it also became clear, to me anyway, how incremental steps like this could (or maybe should?) lead to a world without us. Those incremental steps became this story.

Jeff VanderMeer is the author of *Hummingbird Salamander*, the Borne novels (*Borne, Strange Bird*, and *Dead Astronauts*), and the Southern Reach Trilogy (*Annihilation, Acceptance*, and *Authority*), the first volume of which won the Nebula Award and the Shirley Jackson Award and was adapted into a movie by Alex Garland. He speaks and writes frequently about issues relating to climate change as well as urban rewilding. He lives in Tallahassee, Florida, on the edge of a ravine, with his wife, Ann VanderMeer, and their cat, Neo.

Marlee Jane Ward is an Australian author living in Naarm (Melbourne). Her debut, *Welcome to Orphancorp*, won the Viva La Novella Prize and a Victorian Premier's Literary Award. Her short fiction can be found in *Apex, Interfictions, Aurealis*, and more.

"Who's a Good Boy?" came after reading an article on animal intelligence. The main character can only imagine an animal's intelligence through a human lens and would prefer to engage with an animal (or not) on our terms, not on theirs. With the current trend of teaching dogs to communicate using AAC (Augmentative and Alternative Communication) methods, maybe now we're meeting them in a capacity closer to their own.

Elvia Wilk is a writer living in New York. Her work has appeared in publications like *Frieze, Artforum, Bookforum, Granta, The Baffler, The Atlantic, n+1, The White Review, BOMB*, and the *Los Angeles Review of Books*. Her first novel, *Oval*, was published by Soft Skull Press in 2019, and a book of essays called *Death by Landscape* is forthcoming in 2022.

"The Fog" was first published in the catalog for Anicka Yi's exhibition In Love with the World *at the Tate Modern in 2020. This story emerged from my conversations with the artist Anicka Yi about her recent work building floating machines that resemble ocean life-forms or mushrooms. I wanted to situate remnants of today's biotech experiments (in art and science) in a near-future world where the biological is (once again) seen as separate from the technical.*

Max Wynne oscillates between lives as an English teacher, chef, vagabond, musician, lab technician, and writer in North and South America. He is currently finishing his first novel and has a poetry collection, *sporadicisms*, forthcoming in 2023.

E. Lily Yu is the author of the novel *On Fragile Waves* (2021), published by Erewhon Books. Her short stories have appeared in venues from *McSweeney's* to *Boston Review* to Tor.com, as well as a dozen best-of-the-year anthologies, and have been finalists for the Hugo, Nebula, and World Fantasy Awards. She received the Astounding Award for Best New Writer in 2012 and the Artist Trust LaSalle Storyteller Award in 2017.

I wrote "The Wretched and the Beautiful" in August 2016, when it was clear to me what was coming next. I sold it to Terraform *on January 31, 2017, four days after the signing of Executive Order 13769, and it was published a week later. The story was eventually adapted into a VR experience for a Wing Luke Museum exhibit. There is a nod to Chancellor Angela Merkel in the text.*

Jess Zimmerman is an editor at Quirk Books, the coauthor of *Basic Witches*, and the author of *Women and Other Monsters*. She lives in Philadelphia.

It's probably obvious from the first line, but the story initially came from thinking about the phenomenon of international McDonald's specials: how there was simultaneously this massive cultural flattening of McDonald's spreading to every country in the world, but also this sort of "life finds a way" specificity where the local tastes would determine the menu, but ALSO not really because those items were all designed and approved by some kind of corporate entity. And then of course it became about gentrification generally, with the connecting thread that people of a certain colonialist mindset will simply reshape any available space to suit their own tastes—and then sometimes dress it up afterward to look "authentic." I am scared/embarrassed to read the story again and cannot remember at all how it ended, so hopefully all that came through.

Brian Merchant is a writer and editor living in Los Angeles. He was the senior editor of *Motherboard*, *Vice*'s technology section, where he cofounded *Terraform*, and he is the author of the forthcoming book *Blood in the Machine: The Origins of the Rebellion Against Big Tech* and the national bestseller *The One Device: The Secret History of the iPhone* (2017). His writing about technology, work, and the future has appeared in *The New York Times*, *Harper's Magazine*, *The Guardian*, *Wired*, and *The Atlantic*.

Claire L. Evans is a writer and musician exploring ecology, technology, and culture. She is the author of *Broad Band: The Untold Story of the Women Who Made the Internet* (2018), the singer of the Grammy-nominated pop group YACHT, and the cofounder of *Terraform*. Her writing has appeared in *Vice*, *Rhizome*, Pioneer Works' *Broadcast*, *The Guardian*, the *Los Angeles Review of Books*, *Eye on Design*, *The Verge*, *OneZero*, and *Aeon*. She lives in Los Angeles, where she is an adviser to graduate design students at ArtCenter College of Design.